• Praise for *End Game* •

"A fast-paced murder mystery as well
as a spy story."

—Larry Bond,
New York Times bestselling author

"The action is constant, and there are some
head-turning surprises along the way. . . . This
series continues to feel fresh and exciting."

—*Booklist*

"Gripping . . . Each twist in the tale opens
up new possibilities."

—*Publishers Weekly*

• Praise for David Hagberg •

"If you want yesterday's headlines, read
The New York Times. If you want tomorrow's,
read David Hagberg."

—Ward Larsen,
USA Today bestselling author

"David Hagberg consistently delivers thrillers
that truly thrill, with an uncanny ability
to anticipate future headlines. Skill, experience,
knowledge, and a dedication to quality long
have been hallmarks of Hagberg's novels."

—Ralph Peters,
New York Times bestselling author

END GAME

BY DAVID HAGBERG

Twister
The Capsule
Last Come the Children
Heartland
Heroes
Without Honor*
Countdown*
Crossfire*
Critical Mass*
Desert Fire
High Flight*
Assassin*
White House*
Joshua's Hammer*
Eden's Gate

The Kill Zone*
By Dawn's Early Light
Soldier of God*
Allah's Scorpion*
Dance with the Dragon*
The Expediter*
The Cabal*
Abyss*
Castro's Daughter*
Burned
Blood Pact*
Retribution*
The Fourth Horseman*
End Game
Tower Down
The Shadowmen†
24 Hours†

• • •

BY BYRON L. DORGAN
AND DAVID HAGBERG

Blowout
Gridlock

NONFICTION BY DAVID HAGBERG
AND BORIS GINDIN

Mutiny!

*Kirk McGarvey adventures
†Kirk McGarvey novellas

END GAME

DAVID HAGBERG

A TOM DOHERTY ASSOCIATES BOOK
NEW YORK

This is a work of fiction. All of the characters, organizations, and events portrayed in this novel are either products of the author's imagination or are used fictitiously.

END GAME

A Forge Book
Published by Tom Doherty Associates
175 Fifth Avenue
New York, NY 10010

www.tor-forge.com

Forge® is a registered trademark of Macmillan Publishing Group, LLC.

ISBN 978-0-7653-6999-4

Our books may be purchased in bulk for promotional, educational, or business use. Please contact your local bookseller or the Macmillan Corporate and Premium Sales Department at 1-800-221-7945, extension 5442, or by e-mail at MacmillanSpecialMarkets@macmillan.com.

First Edition: September 2016
First Mass Market Edition: August 2017

Printed in the United States of America

0 9 8 7 6 5 4 3 2 1

FOR LORREL, AS ALWAYS

AUTHOR'S NOTE

Kryptos is a series of sculptures, the largest of which is the one in the courtyard of the CIA's New Headquarters Building. Made of four copper plates into which four encrypted messages have been cut, it was conceived by the American artist James Sanborn. The enigmatic piece was dedicated on November 3, 1990, when it was placed in the courtyard in plain sight of anyone visiting the Agency cafeteria.

Three of the messages have been deciphered—the fourth remains unsolved to this day. But the messages are said to be linked. The final solution can only be guessed at from the first line of the first puzzle: *Between subtle shading and the absence of lights lies the nuance of iqlusion.* (The mistaken *q* was deliberate.)

But there are other smaller pieces scattered around the headquarters campus. Some are engraved with messages in Morse code; another has a compass rose and a lodestone.

The men and women who work for the Agency, at headquarters and elsewhere around the world, either in the open, relatively speaking, or in secret as NOCs, agents working under nonofficial cover, are American patriots—but they are also human beings with all their foibles and problems, some of them serious.

This story is dedicated to them—truly our first line of defense!

PART
ONE

Slowly, desperately
slowly . . .

ONE

Walter Wager heaved himself off the floor, using the edge of his desk for leverage, blood running down the collar of his white shirt from a ragged wound in the side of his neck. He was an old man, even older than his fifty-four, because of the life he'd led as a deep-cover agent for the Central Intelligence Agency.

He was no longer a NOC, and he'd struggled for the last year, sitting behind a desk, in a tiny office buried on the third floor of the Original Headquarters Building, trying to lead a normal life, trying to fit in with the normal day-to-day routine without the nearly constant danger he'd faced for thirty-five years.

The beginning of the end for him had come eight years ago when his wife, Sandee, had been shot to death during a situation that had gone terribly bad in Caracas. They were meeting with a cryptanalyst from SEBIN, the Venezuelan intelligence service, who'd promised to hand over the latest data encryption algorithms his science directorate had devised. It was late at night in the warehouse district when the transfer of money for a disk had just taken place, and the headlights of a half dozen police vehicles came on, illuminating the three of them.

Sandee slammed her shoulder into the cryptanalyst's chest, knocking him backward. "Run!" she shouted.

Wager reached for her arm, the same time the police opened fire, hitting her in the back and in her head, and she went down hard.

Something very hot plucked at Wager's left elbow, and on instinct alone he jogged to the left, away from the headlights, and with bullets slamming into the pavement all around him and singing past his head, he managed to make it into one of the abandoned buildings.

Several cars started up, someone shouted something, and police came after him. But he was running for his life, the adrenaline high in his system. And somehow he managed to escape back into the city to the safe house he'd set up in the first days after his arrival. Sandee had called it: refuge.

"Let's hope we never have to use it," she'd said the first time he'd brought her there.

He'd never forgotten her words or the sight of her falling forward, bullets ripping into her body. And no day had gone by since then when her face, the feel of her body, her breath on his cheek, didn't come to him in the middle of the night.

He was dying now, and of all things, what he would miss the most would be his dreams.

Calling for help would do no good. It was well past midnight, and all the offices on this floor were empty. No one would hear him. But security was just a phone call away. And even if they couldn't get here in time to save his life, he would be able to tell them who his killer was.

Though not why.

"Don't touch the phone, Walter," warned the man behind him.

Wager's heart pounded in his ears as he reached for the phone on his desk. He felt no real pain, only weakness from the terrible blood loss, and an absolute incredulity not at what was happening but *how* it was happening.

The face of his attacker was that of a stranger, but the voice was familiar. From years ago, maybe just before the second Iraq war. In the mountains outside of Kirkuk they were looking for WMDs that a lot of people in the Company knew didn't exist. All that was required were a few photographs, something with a serial number or any sort of markings the analysts at Langley could use.

There'd been seven of them spread out over a twenty-five-mile line, and he remembered the guy they called the Cynic, who'd called himself a realist: *the only sane man in a world gone completely batshit.*

The man took Wager by the arm and gently turned him around so they were facing each other. The Cynic, if that was who he was, had a lot of blood around his mouth.

"It's too late to call anyone."

Wager was hearing music from somewhere, very low but very close. Church organ music, complicated.

"You never had culture, Walter. Too bad," the man said. His voice was soft, with maybe a British accent. But high-class.

"Why?"

"Why what? Why am I here? Why have I decided to kill you? Why like this?" The Cynic turned away, his eyes half closed, a dreamy expression on his bloody face.

The music was Bach's Toccata and Fugue in D minor. Wager couldn't say why he'd dredged that up out of some distant memory, but he was sure of it, and it was coming from a small player in the breast pocket of the Cynic's dark blue blazer.

"Yes, why?" Wager asked, his voice ragged and distant even in his own ears. He felt cold and weak, barely able to stay on his feet.

"Sandee was such a lovely girl. Was from the beginning, She never belonged with a bore like you."

The Cynic had a round, perfectly normal face, small ears, thin sand-colored hair, a slight build. Everyman. Someone you would never pick out of a crowd, someone you would never remember. Perfect in the role of a NOC. The accent was a fake, of course, because if he was the man Wager was remembering, he was from somewhere in the Midwest. But how he knew Sandee—who was a big-city San Francisco girl—was beyond comprehension just at this moment.

"I knew her," the Cynic said. "And I was fucking her before Caracas."

A blind rage rose up, blotting out Wager's weakness, and he lurched forward, but the Cynic merely pushed him back against the desk, grabbing his arm so he wouldn't fall down.

"I wanted to get your attention, and I have it now. Maybe briefly, but I have it."

Wager's head was swimming.

"You illuminated the spot with an encrypted GPS marker. I need to know the password."

He was the Cynic from Iraq, but Wager could not dredge up a name—though it would have been a work name, it would have been a start. "It's gone."

"The password or the stash?"

"Is this about money?"

The Cynic laughed softly, the sound from the back of his throat. "Come on, Walter. Is there anything more important?"

Wager could think of a lot of things more important than money in whatever forms it came.

"The password, probably both. The country has been overrun. Holes in the sand dug just about everywhere."

"They didn't find the bioweapons labs. What makes you think they found the cache?"

"Because the weapons never existed. Nor was there any heroin. And you didn't fuck my wife."

"Ah, but I did. She had a small mole on her left thigh, just below her pussy. Remember?"

Wager leaned back against the desk for support, and he tried to hide his effort to reach the phone, but the Cynic pulled him away, a broad smile on his bloody lips. Even his teeth were red, and Wager thought that a bit of flesh was hanging from the side of the man's mouth.

"The password, please."

"I don't have it," Wager said, and it came to him that the Cynic wasn't lying: he had fucked Sandee. But then, in those days, everybody was fucking everybody else. Wives, girlfriends, sisters, even mothers. It didn't matter. What mattered was the moment. It was the game from the get-go, so the stories went. From the beginning of the Agency, and even before that in the WWII OSS. Fucking was not only the ultimate aphrodisiac; it was a powerful tool.

Wager thought that the happiest time of his entire life had been during training at the CIA's base on Camp Peary in Virginia—south of DC. It was called the Farm because when it was a WWII Seabee training base, the commanding officer, Captain S. G. Ware, raised hogs on the base. It became known as Ware's hog farm, later shortened to the Farm. They were young and naive. Anxious for the future, but dedicated. "Truth, justice, and the American way," a former DCI had supposedly once said. They were supermen and women. It was where he had first met Sandee, who was two years older than he was. But they'd been a natural pair from the beginning, though at first he'd thought she'd been working him, been given him as an assignment. But then he fell in love—and he'd always thought she had too—and nothing else mattered.

"Too bad for you," the Cynic said. "But there are others."

Wager started to shake his head, if for nothing else but to ward off what he knew was coming next. But it didn't help.

Grinning like a madman, the Cynic took Wager into his arms and began to eat his face, starting at the nose, powerful teeth shredding flesh and cartilage.

Marty Bambridge, the CIA's deputy director of operations, was awakened by his wife, who kept pushing at his shoulder. He was in a foul mood: too much red wine last night at dinner, from which nothing was left but a son-of-a-bitch headache and a crappy taste in his mouth. Along with that was the rumor floating around campus that the DCI Walt Page was on his way out, and there was talk of a clean sweep. All the old brass was going with him.

Which meant the heads of each directorate—intelligence, science and technology, management and services, and operations, formerly the directorate of national clandestine service.

Bambridge was a spy master, a job he knew he'd been meant for, when as a kid studying law and foreign relations at the University of Minnesota he'd read and reread every espionage novel he could get his hands on—especially the James Bond stories. But never in his dreams in those days did he believe he would actually get to run the CIA's spies.

If it was actually coming to an end for him, he had no earthly idea what he would do with himself. He was helpless and frightened, which made him angry.

He growled at his wife. "What?"

"Phone," she mumbled. She handed it to him, then rolled over and went back to sleep.

"Bambridge," he said, sitting up.

"This is Bob Blankenship, campus security, sir. We have a problem."

"Write me a memo, for Christ's sake. I'll deal with it in the morning."

"No, sir. Mr. Page has been informed, and he specifically wants you involved. There's been a murder here on the third floor of the OHB. One of your people. A former field officer."

Bambridge was suddenly wide-awake. He turned on the nightstand light. It was after 1 A.M. "Who is it?"

"The security pass we found on the body identified him as Walter Wager. He worked as a mid-level operational planner on your staff."

"I know him."

"Yes, sir."

"You said murder? How?"

"I think it would be best if you came in and took a look yourself. Mr. Page did not want the authorities notified before you had a chance to get here. Nor are we moving the body."

"Shit, shit," Bambridge said under his breath. "Any witnesses?"

"He was alone on the floor."

"Surveillance videos? "

"No, sir."

"God damn it. One of the cameras in the corridor must have picked up something."

"They were disabled."

"Who the hell was monitoring?"

"A loop was inserted into the recording unit for the entire floor. Shows the same images over and over."

Bambridge tried to think of some reason he wouldn't have to go out. At forty-three, he had become soft. He'd never actually served as a field officer, though he did two five-year stints as assistant to the chief of station, one in Ottawa and the other in Canberra, neither them hot spots under any stretch of the imagination. He'd never humped his butt in Iraq or Afghanistan like many of the officers who'd worked for him had, so he'd never formed a bond—especially not with the NOCs who he'd always considered to be prima donnas. Just like Wager.

"Turn out the light," his wife said.

"I'll be there in twenty minutes," he told the security officer. "Touch nothing."

He got up and flipped on the lights in the bathroom and the closet. His wife buried her head deeper into the covers. If she had been a thoughtful woman, Marty mused, she would have gotten up and had the coffee on by now.

It was just one more brick in his wall of frustration and anger.

They had a nice two-story colonial on Davis Street NW near the Naval Observatory, and Bambridge had crossed the Key Bridge and was heading north on the GW Parkway to Langley before one thirty. Traffic was very light, the October morning cool, even crisp after a steamy summer, but he felt a heaviness in his chest he'd never felt before. And he was a little worried. His wife sometimes called him a hypochondriac, but over the past few months, and especially this morning, he'd seriously begun to get concerned he was developing heart troubles. It was the stress of the job, he told himself. Lately the stress of losing his job. And just now a murder inside the CIA's campus. It was unbelievable, and the only other word he could think of was *incompetence*. Heads would roll, he would make sure of it.

The security officers at the main gate looked up as Bambridge's BMW breezed through the employee lane; a bar code in the windshield along with a photograph of the driver's face recognized the car and the DDO even before the rear bumper cleared.

Up at the OHB, which was the first of several buildings on campus, Bambridge's bar code allowed him access to the underground VIP parking garage, and three minutes later he was getting off the elevator on the third floor—having passed his badge through the security reader in the basement and submitted to a retinal scan.

Bambridge was a narrow, slope-shouldered man whose acquaintances described him as almost always surprised, but whose friends described him as seriously intent. His features were dark; some French Canadian blood a couple of generations ago, according to his mother, who still lived in northern Minnesota. He harbored the more romantic notion that a Sicilian had gotten in there somewhere, which gave him a penchant for mysteriousness and a touch of violence.

Blankenship, a much taller, broader man in his early fifties, who wore a ridiculous military buzz cut, had been notified of the DDO's arrival and was waiting for him.

"I hope you haven't had breakfast yet, sir," he said.

"No. Let's get this over with so I can."

At least a dozen security officers in short-sleeved

shirts, khaki trousers, badges, and pistols in hip holsters filled the corridor around an open door just three down from the elevator.

"We've taken all the photographs we need, and I've had our techs dust for fingerprints and collect whatever DNA evidence they could find," Blankenship said. "We're also looking at the hard disk on Walt's computer, along with his phone records for the past three months."

"I want his entire contact sheet—computer, phone, and face-to-face—for as far back as you can dig it up," Bambridge replied.

"Yes, sir," the security officer said. "Can you think of any enemies Mr. Wager might have had?"

The guy had to be kidding. Bambridge gave him a look. "North Koreans, Cubans, Iraqis, Iranians, some Russians, Afghanis. Shall I go on?"

"Sorry, sir. I meant here on campus."

"He's only been back less than a year. I don't think Walt even had enough time to make friends let alone enemies."

Another security officer was leaning against the wall just before the open door. He looked a little green. When Bambridge and Blankenship approached, he straightened up.

Around the corner, just inside the tiny office, Bambridge pulled up short. The stench of fecal matter, and of something sweet, hit him all at once, at the same time he caught sight of the blood pooled on the floor. But then he came full face on with the ruined remains of what he could only vaguely describe as a human being. His stomach did a very sharp roll.

Wager, if that was who it was, had been destroyed

from the neck up. Something had bitten or chewed out the entire side of his neck on the left side, blood all down the front and side of his white shirt. His face had been massively damaged as well, as if a pack of wild animals had had at him. His nose was mostly gone, his eyebrows shredded, his lips missing, his teeth obscenely white.

Bambridge stepped back a pace, a sickness rising in his throat. "My God," he whispered.

Wager's body lay on its side in front of a small desk. The chair had been pushed to one side, up against a file cabinet. The back of his trousers was completely covered in fecal matter. He'd lost control of his bowels either at the time of his death or shortly before. If there had been any sign of horror or pain or surprise on his face, it was completely gone. His features had either been eaten away or were covered in blood and tissue—human meat.

It was the most awful thing Bambridge had ever seen or imagined.

"I'm sorry, sir, but I could not have described this to you," Blankenship said.

"Could a guard dog have gotten in here?" Bambridge asked. It was the only thing he could think to ask.

"No, sir. They're all accounted for. Anyway, none of our dogs would have done something like this."

"A wild animal?"

"Maybe, but then someone with the proper badges to get into this building, onto this floor, and into this office would have had to let it in."

"No one saw or heard a thing?"

"No, sir."

A few splotches of blood had stained the desktop inches from the phone.

"Did he manage to call someone?"

"No."

Bambridge tore his eyes away from the horrible thing on the floor, gagging as the smell, associated with what he was seeing, fully hit him. He walked out into the clean air of the corridor, where he leaned his back against the wall.

Blankenship joined him. "What're your orders, sir?"

"Are your people finished?"

"Just about."

"When they are, call the police. I want the body out of here and the mess cleaned up before the morning shift."

"Yes, sir."

Bambridge looked at him. "I'll be back later, but right now I'm going home. I need a shower."

"I understand."

THREE

Istvan Fabry at fifty felt like an old man, though he would never admit it to Fanni, his American-born wife, or his sons, Richard and Mark, but Iraq, and later Afghanistan, had worn him to the bone.

He left the Bubble, which was the CIA's auditorium, and drove his three-year-old Fusion over to the Scattergood-Thorne house just off the GW Parkway, but still on the CIA's campus. It was very late, just a bit before 2 A.M., but he'd always been an extremely light sleeper. Eight hours a night meant a person would be, for all practical purposes, dead for one-third of his life. It wasn't for Istvan.

The DCI was hosting a dozen influential congressmen plus a like number of intelligence and counterterrorism professionals from the FBI, the National Security Agency, and other intel and LE agencies to discuss plans for the top-down reorganization of America's approach to nontraditional warfare. Fabry was front man for the setup, and he wanted to be well ahead of the curve before the 0800 start.

The Bubble's projection equipment was loaded with the proper PowerPoint and video programs, mostly of his own creation, and once the presentation was done, the VIPs would be bused over to the house for the actual conference.

Parking in front of the large colonial that sat partially concealed in the woods just off the GW Parkway, he got out of the car and stopped to listen to the nearly absolute silence. Only a light breeze in the treetops, mournful and a little lonely in a way, and a truck passing on the highway, heading into the city or perhaps to Dulles.

But it was safe here, something his wife, who'd been raised in a reasonably upscale environment as the only daughter of a corporate lawyer in Chicago, could never understand. By instinct, at times like this, alone with just his own thoughts, he would catch himself listening for other sounds. Some distant, some very close. The whine of a drone's engine, or of a Russian Hind helicopter gunship. The clank of metal on metal as a troop of Taliban fighters or Iranian Revolutionary Guard soldiers approached up a mountain pass. The snick of an AK-47 slide being pulled back and released. Footfalls on loose gravel. Someone or something rising up behind him, carrying a knife or a wire garrote.

Suddenly spooked, he turned and looked down the gravel road toward the Bubble, and then did a careful scan of the woods surrounding the house that had been a private residence until the CIA had taken it over in 1987. But nothing moved. He was absolutely alone, and not in a place where harm was likely to come his way. Of any spot in the world, here was the safest place for him to be, and not a day went by that he didn't bless his good fortune for surviving Hungary's turbulence when he was a kid growing up in Rabahidveg, close to the Austrian border.

Two uncles had been shot to death by KGB border patrol pricks, and his father had been taken into custody for reasons they'd never been told. There he'd been tortured day and night for more than a week. Afterward he'd been a broken man, unable even to feed himself or use the toilet without help.

Then Hungary was free, in a large measure because of America's diplomacy and the harsh realities of a Soviet system that simply could not support its own weight. Istvan had specialized in English in school, and when he was nineteen, he went to the U.S. and joined the army, where he was first made a translator—in addition to Hungarian and English, he was also fluent in Russian—and then into INSCOM, which was the army's intelligence and security command, where he became a spy.

The transition to the CIA had been easy at first, until he'd been selected to become a NOC and had been sent first to Afghanistan and later to Iraq. Then the nightmares started, and they'd become so bad that, by the time he'd slipped home on a short leave, Fanni, who he'd known from college at Northwestern while he was in the army, almost left him.

They were sleeping together, and after his second morning back, she'd slipped out of bed to make them coffee. She brought the coffee and a plate of sweet rolls on a tray that she set on her side of the bed, then went around to him and bent down to brush a kiss onto his lips.

He suddenly reared up out of a deep sleep and smashed his fist into her face, breaking several of her teeth, dislocating her jaw, and sending her sprawling onto the floor.

They were both in shock.

After a trip to the emergency room, where her jaw was sent in place and she'd been given pain pills, they went back to the apartment. But she wasn't fearful of him; instead she was puzzled and angry.

"You didn't do it on purpose, Isty; you did it purely on instinct," she told him. "For survival."

They were sitting across from each other at the tiny kitchen table, and he had a hard time looking her in the eye. Her jaw was red and swollen, and she spoke with a lisp because of the missing teeth.

"For survival from what? Have you been on a battlefield somewhere?"

"I can't tell you."

"You can't or you won't?" she demanded, her voice rising.

"Can't."

"Why?"

"Orders—"

"Bullshit. I want the truth!"

"My life and yours could depend on your not knowing what I do."

"Are you a spy, then? Is that what you've become? A traitor, spying for the Russians or maybe the Chinese?"

"I'm not a traitor, Fanni," Istvan said. "You have to believe me." His heart was aching.

She jumped to her feet, the chair falling over. "I won't live with you. Not like this."

"I'm not a traitor."

"Of course you're not. I know it. But if you were a spy, you would never be able to tell me where you were, what you were doing. I'd never know when you would come back to me—*if* you were coming back."

"I'll always come back."

"I can't be sure. Tell me how I can be sure!"

"Because I love you," Istvan said.

In the end it had been enough for her, and they'd both somehow survived his long absences until he had come out of the field to work as an analyst and mission planner in the Directorate of Operations and he'd been able to tell her he had indeed been a spy. But all that was past. He was home for good.

He took a portable handcart from the trunk, and when he had it unfolded, he loaded four cartons of agendas, briefing books, copies of the presentation disks, and lined legal pads and pens, and took them inside, where he laid them out in the large conference room. The fit would be tight, but there was room for everyone. The main topic for review would be the threat the U.S. faced right now from cyberterrorism.

State-sponsored cyberterrorism.

It was something Istvan had become an expert in since he'd come home. He had a knack for it and had been a fast learner—his mentor at the end was Special Projects Director Otto Rencke, the smartest, and oddest, man he'd ever known. But a good man, with an equally odd-duck wife and a lovely child.

He'd come to his office in the OHB's fourth-floor science and technology operations center, where some of the gadgets and ideas that had been created and already evaluated as useful were placed in planning cycles for manufacture and then distribution to stations around the world. After he'd loaded his car, he'd driven over to the Bubble and then here.

Time enough to go home for some breakfast, but he would have to rush to make it back before the guests began to arrive. Anyway, after the field rations he'd eaten over the years, even the cafeteria adjacent to the New Headquarters Building wasn't half bad.

He went outside, where he refolded the handcart and loaded it into the trunk and then got behind the wheel.

Something smelled odd to him, slightly off. At that moment he heard a Bach organ piece and turned around in surprise as the figure of a man who he did not know rose up from the backseat, blood all over his face and lips.

Before Istvan could react, the Cynic yanked Istvan's head backward, breaking his neck. Before he died, he realized that the side of his neck was literally being eaten.

FOUR

Bambridge had spent only a few minutes in his office, making sure everything for the cyberconference was in place for later this morning. He was giving a short presentation at the Bubble once the Power-Point and video had been played, emphasizing the necessity for boots on the ground in the likely spots where such acts of terrorism might originate. Like Beijing. He knew the reaction he would get, but what he had to tell them needed saying. Even Page had agreed.

"You'll be ruffling some feathers, Marty, but maybe someone from the Hill will sit up and take notice, toss us an extra few millions to fight the good fight."

"More like billions," Bambridge had replied glumly. His mood, like everyone else's in the Company, was in the toilet. Change was coming, that much was for sure, but no one was looking forward to what it would bring.

He passed through the main gate, and at the bottom of the slight hill he turned right onto the Parkway, traffic even less at this hour than it had been when he'd come in. By rights he should have stayed till the conference—he still had plenty to do, including rereading the dossiers on all the conferees, to refresh his memory. But he'd told Blankenship the truth: he needed to go home and take a shower to get rid of the stench of death that hung around him like a dark cloud.

Never in his life had he seen or even imagined anything so gruesome as what had been done to Walter Wager. It was beyond his comprehension that one human being could do something like that to another.

Blankenship had called in every available security officer as Bambridge was heading toward town, and dozens of cars were converging on the main gate. If the killer were still on campus, he would not be getting out anytime soon.

Bambridge's phone went off, and for just an instant he debated not answering it, but the caller ID read *Blankenship*.

"Something new?"

"There's been another one," the chief of security said. He sounded seriously pissed off.

Bambridge's heart lurched. "Who?"

"Istvan Fabry. One of my people found his body—what was left of it—in his car, parked in front of the Scattergood-Thorne house."

"What the hell was he doing there at this hour of the morning?" Bambridge shouted, but Fabry was the front man on the PowerPoint and video presentation, and would have gone over to the house to set up for the second part of the conference.

"We're checking. But it was the same MO. Whoever it was waited in the backseat for Mr. Fabry to come out of the house and then attacked him."

"Are the cops at the OHB?"

"They'll be here all morning. The Bureau sent out a CSI unit, and they've taken control. Special Agent Morris Wilkinson is in charge."

"Has he been told about the second . . . incident?"

"I wanted to talk to you first, sir."

Bambridge came to a narrow gravel pass over through the median, and he took it. "I want our people to collect whatever evidence they can first."

"We're already on it."

"Soon as you're ready, turn it over to the Bureau. I want the campus locked down. No one in or out without personal recognition. Get two of your people on both gates to make sure it gets done."

"What about the conference?"

"It's canceled. In the meantime, I want a room-by-room search of every square inch of every building. That includes elevator shafts, air ducts, closets, maintenance spaces, all the subbasements. Every cabinet, under every desk, on top of the roofs, and when your people are finished, I want you to do it again. And again. And again."

"We have a lot of acreage, lots of places to hide."

"Make sure there are no loops or any other glitches with our fence-line video cameras and motion detectors. I want as many helicopters with infrared detectors in the air right now, and I want our K-9 people on it too. This guy has to be covered in blood. Give the dogs the scents of Wager and Fabry."

"It has to be one of us," Blankenship said. "I don't see how anyone else could have gotten in here this morning. It means it has to be someone on the night schedule."

"Plus people like you and me who are bound to

show up at any hour of the day. Narrows field," Bambridge said. "Pull the personnel records of everyone, including mine, see whose psych evals have come up shaky in the past six months. And find out who had connections with Wager and Fabry—not just either of them. I want a common denominator."

"The shift change starts in a few hours. What do you want to do about it?"

Bambridge's knee-jerk reaction was to keep everyone on campus and hold the new shift from coming to work until the buildings and grounds had been sanitized, but he thought better of it. "Let it go on as normal. If we get out of our routine, someone is going to sit up and take notice. Whatever happens, we need to keep the media out of this for as long as possible. We're already in enough trouble as it is."

Two years ago the scandal about the National Security Agency's spying on Americans had bled over to the CIA. The Agency's charter specifically forbade any operations on U.S. soil, but that hadn't been the case since the Cold War days. The CIA went wherever its investigations led, including the continental U.S.

"We'll be letting the suspect walk out the gate."

"What suspect?" Bambridge demanded angrily.

"The killer."

"Give me a name. Everyone on the grounds at this moment is a suspect."

"That's a lot of people."

"Besides anyone with connections to Wager and Fabry, I want the names of anyone who's ever worked as an instructor at the Farm or served time in the field, either working for us or for the military—

special forces. Both of those guys were NOCs, too highly trained to let someone come up on them so easily."

"I've already started on that list. Anyone else?"

"Guys just about set to retire."

"I don't follow you."

"It's about stress. A lot of guys are burned out after twenty—especially Watch officers. And we've made some pay cuts and we've reduced hours. Check those people."

"We don't have the personnel to do this very quickly," Blankenship said. "Could take a month or more of cross-checking."

"Then I suggest you get started right away," Bambridge said, and hung up.

He came to the main gate and stopped directly across from the gatehouse until one of the security guards came out.

"Mr. Bambridge, is there a problem, sir?"

"Yes, why wasn't I stopped for a positive ID?"

"Your tag came up, and you showed positive on the facial recognition program."

"I could have been an imposter in disguise who killed the deputy director and stole his car. I want everyone coming through this gate to be checked."

"Yes, sir," the security officer said. "Is there a problem we should know about?"

"Just a drill. So keep on your toes. There'll be an eval tomorrow."

As he drove the rest of the way through the woods to the OHB, where he parked in his slot in the basement, he could not remember hearing or reading about anything like this ever happening. No business seemed to be immune from the disgruntled employee coming to work with a loaded weapon, or weapons, and opening fire. Or setting off a bomb. Movie theaters, schools, federal building—no place was safe. Except, until now, for the CIA.

Upstairs in his office, he powered up his computer to see what Blankenship was up to, but except for a personnel list with about one hundred names highlighted, there was nothing else. So far the chief of security had not come up with any connections between Wager and Fabry or anyone else except for the people in the sections where they had worked.

He phoned Page at home. "There's been another murder," he told the director.

"My God, who?"

"Istvan Fabry. Looks like the same guy probably did it."

"Has the Bureau been contacted?"

"They're here along with one of their CSI units," Bambridge said. "I'm going to text and e-mail everyone involved that we're postponing the conference this morning."

"Don't do that," Page said. "There'll be too many questions. And make sure the officers on perimeter duty—especially at the Parkway and Georgetown Pike gates—maintain a low key. We don't want to tip off anyone—not the killer, and sure as hell not the media."

"Yes, sir."

"What about everyone else out there at the moment?"

"Sir?"

"Assuming the killer hasn't already left, someone else could be a target. Double up everyone—no one goes anywhere alone. Tell them it's a drill; tell them anything you want to tell them: we're beefing up security because of our VIP guests coming this morning."

"I'll tell them the vice president might drop in unannounced."

"I'll be in my office in one hour. I want you up there, along with Bob Blankenship, and see if you can get Rencke to come in."

"I don't think including him is such a good idea, sir."

"Do it," Page said. "I want answers."

FIVE

Otto Rencke could not remember ever having slept for more than one or two hours at a stretch. Until he'd married Louise, most of his naps were in front of his computer, or listening to music on headphones in a secure spot somewhere. But from the beginning, her primary goals in life had been taking care of their child, now four, and straightening out her husband's act, which included requiring him to come to bed with her every evening for at least six hours.

He'd fought her on that one at first, until she'd told him that sometimes she got frightened in the middle of the night and she needed him to watch over her. And he'd agreed—spending his waking hours listening to classical music and operas in his head, and solving tensor calculus problems, matrices of partial differential equations of the type Einstein had used to develop relativity.

In his early forties, Rencke was of medium height, slender with a head too large for his body, and long frizzy red hair held in place by a ponytail. He almost always wore jeans and sweatshirts—some from Disneyworld and some from the old KGB or CCCP, as a sort of joke inside the CIA campus—and at Louise's prodding, decent boat shoes instead of raggedy sneakers that were always dirty, always unlaced.

Marty wouldn't explain why Page wanted to see him at this hour, but as Otto came up to the main gate, he saw four backed-up cars he had to get through, and while he waited, he pulled up the CIA's mainframe to see what was going on to create a delay here.

Nothing jumped out at him, but when he connected with his search programs in his office, he came up with a series of requests from security to pull the personnel records of everyone working the midnight-to-eight shift. Security's search parameters included psych evals, time to retirement, Agency assignments, previous military experience, and connections with Walter Wager—and with Istvan Fabry, a name he knew.

Fabry had come to him with help on a special cybercrimes project. The guy was bright but something of a milquetoast despite the fact that his rep as a fearless field operative—an NOC—was rock solid. The guy had struck Otto as being the happiest man in the world for finally being in from the cold.

When his turn came, he was passed through security by one of the officers who mentioned something about a drill, which Otto knew was total bullshit, and he drove the rest of the way up to the OHB, where he took his parking spot in the basement.

He went to his third-floor office to make sure nothing had been disturbed since he'd left late yesterday afternoon, then took the elevator to the seventh floor. McGarvey once told him that paranoia was an agent's most powerful tool: *Worry that someone or something might be coming up on your six, and it might save your life one day.*

A security officer was waiting at the DCI's door, which he opened for Otto, who paused just long enough to glance down the long corridor. All doors on this floor were closed this morning. But by tradition over the past fifteen or twenty years, they had been left open. Directors liked to wander out of their offices to visit, especially with the people down the hall on the left in the long narrow room called the Watch. Five officers manned the place 24/7; there they could monitor everything happening in the world on a real-time basis. Connected by satellites and other electronic means, and by constantly updated human intelligence, they were able to keep tabs on developing operations, as well as come up with alerts on hot spots that had the potential to blow up.

All the people working there loved their jobs, because as one of them once said: *we get to know everything.*

"Good morning, sir," the security man said to Otto. He looked a little nervous.

"Too bad about Wager and Fabry."

"Yes, sir, hard to believe."

Page's secretary wasn't here yet, so Otto went straight through to the director's big office. Page was seated in an easy chair across a coffee table from Bambridge and Blankenship, who were sitting on the blue Queen Anne couch. Bambridge looked perplexed, as usual. Blankenship looked angry. But Page seemed worried, which was unusual.

"Thanks for coming at this hour," Page said.

Otto took the chair opposite Page. "Have the families been notified?"

"Families?" Bambridge asked.

"Yeah, Wager's and Fabry's. When officers lose their lives, their families are told straightaway."

Bambridge blustered. But Page held him off. "Not yet," he said. "How did you find out?"

"Lucky guess. So, what happened?"

"We have a serial killer on campus," Blankenship said.

"The extra security won't help."

"Why's that?" the chief of security asked. He wasn't angry, just earnest.

"Whoever's done it is one of us. He knows the system, and since he's killed two people in one night, he thinks he'll get away with it."

"The son of a bitch is nuts," Bambridge said.

"Doesn't mean he's stupid," Otto said. "Someone want to fill me in?"

Page nodded, and Blankenship brought Rencke up to speed with everything they'd learned tonight, everything Bambridge had suggested they do and the results so far.

Otto took out his highly modified iPad and connected with his search programs—his "darlings," as he called them.

"Your machine won't work on this floor," Bambridge said, but Otto ignored him.

In twenty seconds he had the start of what he was looking for, and he was surprised. He looked up. "Besides Wager and Fabry, there are eighteen other NOCs working the night shift. A bigger number than I would have suspected."

"We tend to keep them at the Farm or on this shift," Page said. "Why a NOC?"

"Savagery."

Page cocked a shoulder.

"These folks—three of them on this shift are women, by the way—have been trained to live by their wits in badland. The mission comes first, all other considerations off the table. A lot of them have been alone in places I wouldn't send an armored column to. They've killed to save their own lives— didn't matter who they killed—men or women or children if need be. A lot of the time they've had to improvise, like a lot of our guys in early Vietnam did. Kill to send a message. Kill like an animal, so that the opposition thinks twice about pursuit. No one wants to go into a lion's den."

"We're checking possible connections," Blankenship said.

"That's a start, but there might not be any. This could be something else."

"Like what?"

"Like Marty suggested, someone who's a psycho. And not necessarily someone who works this shift."

"We have the records of everyone coming through security," Blankenship said.

"Yeah," Otto said, nodding. "But you know, every now and then I forget to scan my badge when I walk out the door. The computer thinks I'm still in the building, or somewhere on campus. A flag doesn't go up. Or, just maybe one day I'd scan my badge but then come through another entrance, maybe with someone else's badge I'd lifted. The system isn't perfect. You guys oughta know it. We need entry strictly by personal recognition."

"Impossible," Bambridge said.

"Of course it is, and what's happened tonight— and may still be happening—is a result."

"We've doubled up everyone," Blankenship said. "Told them it was a security drill."

"Come on, Bob. This isn't a box of dummies you're dealing with, ya know. We've got more PhDs per capita here than there are at Harvard. Pretty soon I suspect you're going to have a panic on your hands."

Blankenship's cell phone buzzed, and he answered it. "No reason to hold them," he said, and hung up. "That was the back gate. It's already started. Just a handful so far."

"One of whom could be the killer," Bambridge said.

"I doubt it," Otto said.

"He's not going to break his routine. He'll leave at the end of his shift. He thinks he's smarter than the rest of us," Blankenship said.

"But he isn't," Otto said.

"What do you suggest?"

"I'm going to talk to Mac. He knows more about the NOC mentality than anyone."

"Christ," Bambridge said. "Send a killer to find a killer."

SIX

Over a thirty-plus-year career Kirk McGarvey had developed a sixth sense about his surroundings, and something possibly coming at him out of the blue. And the feeling had been niggling at the back of his head now for the past couple of days.

He was a man in his early fifties, husky, with a square but pleasant face, and gray-green eyes that saw things most other people missed. Running now along a path in the hills above the port city of Livadi on the Greek island of Serifos, he noticed an Aegean Airlines charters helicopter touching down in front of the Serifos Beach Hotel. It was an unscheduled flight from Athens and at the wrong end of the tourist season, so it caught his attention.

The distance was too great for him to make out anything except that only two passengers got out and walked up to the hotel. He couldn't even tell if it was a man and a woman, yet something about them, about the timing, about everything, wasn't right—or a real surprise, for that matter.

High overhead, the morning jet to Tel Aviv made a bright contrail in the perfectly clear blue sky, and

McGarvey turned and headed back to walk the three miles to the decommissioned lighthouse he'd used as his refuge from time to time. He'd worked practically all his adult life first for air force intelligence, then the CIA had picked him up, trained him as a field officer, and he'd gone to work doing black ops for the national clandestine service. He'd become a killer for his country—an assassin, a soldier who didn't march in a platoon but one who worked alone. His kills were face-to-face and very personal.

But then they'd promoted him to run the clandestine service, and by happenstance—the right president at the right time—he'd been appointed and confirmed by Congress as the director of the CIA. But that job hadn't lasted long; he wasn't an administrator. He'd respected most of the people, but he'd hated the job, so he had retired.

After that it seemed like every few months someone came to him to do something about a situation that the Company simply could not handle on its own. Something extrajudicial. Something strictly forbidden in the U.S. and almost everywhere else by international law. But something that needed to be done. In Russia, in Japan, in Israel and Mexico and Cuba, and even one job in North Korea, possibly the strangest of his career. He had stopped a missile attack on Israel's nuclear weapons storage depot; had stopped an outright invasion of Texas and New Mexico by drug cartels; and even came face-to-face on two occasions with Osama bin Laden before 9/11.

Before each of those assignments, he had gotten

the feeling as if a target had been painted on his back and someone was taking a bead on him.

He stopped on the crest of a hill that looked down at the lighthouse. No one was around. Sometimes tourists hiked up here, and he usually treated them nicely, though he'd always turned down their requests for a tour.

Someone from the Company had come to him twice before—last time it was Marty Bambridge, the deputy director of operations. And then as now he'd been emotionally banged up. He'd come here to recuperate, get his brain rewired, so that he could rejoin the civilized world without finding the need to constantly look over his shoulder.

This time he'd run here for two reasons. The first was his last assignment, in which he'd battled a team of terrorists from Germany hired to kill all the SEAL Team Six guys who had gone to Abbottabad to take out bin Laden. And the second was Pete Boylan, a former CIA interrogator who'd moved up to clandestine services, where she'd helped with two of his assignments.

A couple of years ago his wife and daughter had been assassinated right in front of his eyes, and he'd never fully recovered from the trauma. He'd been rubbed totally raw, his emotions naked on the surface. And then Pete had come along—vivacious, talented, no nonsense whatsoever, and dedicated to the same ideals he'd been dedicated to all his life: defending the U.S. and, in fact, defending anyone or any idea from the bullies of the world. From the bin Ladens and the extremists of any stripe.

The fact was that he'd become emotionally attached

to her. He'd begun to fall in love, so he had run here. Every woman in his life—including his wife—had lost their lives because of him. Because of what he did, who he was.

He didn't want it to happen to Pete.

If the two who'd gotten off the chopper had come to see him, it would take them at least a half hour to get up here. Only a narrow dirt path rose up from the town, much too narrow and rocky for a jeep or just about anything else to make it up, unless it was a motorcycle. Most people who came up here made their way on foot.

At the lighthouse he went up to the second level that had been fitted out as a small bedroom suite, and took a shower, changing into a pair of jeans, a light T-shirt, and moccasins. He checked the load on his Walther PPK, in the 9-mm version, stuck it in the waistband of the slacks at the small of his back, and went downstairs.

He opened a bottle of ice-cold Retsina wine, then brought it and three glasses out to the patio. There he could watch the path from town. He settled down to wait.

A long time ago, when he was an air force second lieutenant in the OSI, a colonel told him he would burn out before he was thirty, because he was too angry. He had a chip on his shoulder. Years later, after the Cold War was pretty much over with, a DDO had called him an anachronism. His kind of dedication to what he'd called McGarvey's Superman complex—truth, justice, and the American way—was sadly out-of-date.

"Fact of the matter is, McGarvey, there's no room for you any longer. We don't need you."

But that was long before 9/11, and as it turned out, the DDO was the one who was no longer needed.

A figure appeared over the crest of the hill about two hundred yards away, stopped for a few moments, and then started down the path.

McGarvey shaded his eyes, but he could not make out who it was—even if it was a man or a woman—though from the way the person moved, he figured she was a woman. And even before she got close enough for him to recognize who it was, he knew it was Pete, and that the other person who'd gotten off the helicopter was probably Otto, and that something serious was going down, or about to happen.

Although he hadn't brought a laptop or iPad with him, nor had he activated his cell phone, he did walk down to Livadi for lunch at least once a week, if for no other reason than to watch an hour or so of CNN. Over the past several weeks nothing much had been going on in the world he figured he should get involved with. The Euro troubles in Athens and Madrid had not filtered down here; the Snowden case was back in the news, linked with another NSA whistle-blower, and the CIA had come under congressional scrutiny for its domestic operations contrary to law. Egypt was still on fire, as were Iraq, Afghanistan, and North Korea, with the deaths of several top generals—supposedly at the hands of South Korean assassins. And Paris and Brussels.

Floods, droughts, wildfires, hurricanes, a very active tornado season, and three strong earthquakes along the San Andreas fault dominated U.S. news. But none of it rose to the level of sending Pete and Otto all this way to talk to him.

He found that not only was he curious, but he was looking forward to seeing them. Except for a few people in town and the occasional tourist, he'd spoken to no one in three months.

Pete Boylan, in her late thirties, about five-five, wearing a light shirt with sleeves rolled up above her elbows, and baggy khaki trousers that did nothing much to hide her figure, stopped a few feet out. Her pretty, round face was dominated by her vivid blue eyes that were wide and expressive, framed by short dark hair cut almost boyishly, and rich lips that were formed into a dazzling smile.

"Hi, Kirk," she said, smiling. Her voice was soft, her accent slightly Southern, though she was a California girl.

"Why didn't Otto come up with you?"

"I asked him to give me twenty minutes before we got to business," she said. "How are you?"

"Good. You?"

"Wanting to see you, but giving you space. No one likes to be crowded."

McGarvey got up and she came to him, almost hesitantly at first, not sure of her reception until her took her into his arms and held her close for a long time.

"How are you really?" he asked.

"Lonely as hell, but we have a problem Otto hopes you can help with."

SEVEN

Otto gave them less than ten minutes before he topped the rise and started down the other side to the lighthouse. "He's got the bit in his teeth, and nothing's going to stop him from talking to you," Pete said.

They'd not had the chance to cover what had been happening over the past few months since McGarvey had left Washington, nor had she brought up the reason she and Otto had made the trip.

She'd been doing mostly office work, catching up on the reports dealing with the SEAL Team Six assignment. The only bright light had been a two-week stint at Camp Peary. She'd engaged in learning urban infiltration tactics, and had given a few lessons in hand-to-hand combat.

"Bruised a few tender male egos, I think," she said. "Some of the kids took me for granted."

McGarvey had to laugh, which was a first for him in a long time. It felt good to be with her, even like this, like now.

Otto took his time getting down to them, even though he was in good enough shape these days to have sprinted from town. "Hiya, Mac," he said, sitting down.

McGarvey poured a glass of wine, which Otto downed in a couple of swallows. He held out his glass for more.

"How you doing out here? Getting bored yet?"

"I was thinking about coming back to Florida to

open the house, maybe take a trip on the boat," McGarvey said.

He had a place on Casey Key south of Tampa on the Gulf Coast, and a forty-two-foot Island Packet ketch, which he and Katy had used to sail to the Keys and twice out to the Bahamas. When he was in for the season, he taught Voltaire at the University of South Florida's New College in Sarasota, but last semester the dean had suggested he might take a year or two sabbatical. There'd been some trouble connected to him, trouble in which a car had exploded in a campus parking lot, killing not only the driver but two innocent students who'd happened to be in the wrong place at the wrong time.

After that, teaching Voltaire had lost some of its charm for him.

"We have a problem," Otto said. "Walt sent me out to fill you in, and Pete asked if she could tag along."

"I had a feeling I was going to get involved," she said. In her job as an interrogator, she'd been one of the CIA's all-time best. Her good looks, slight build, and the fact that she was a female who also had a kind, understanding manner made her subjects *want* to talk to her. Sometimes she even brought them to the point where they begged to tell her their story. And she was never judgmental, which was even more effective.

"There's been something in the news over the past couple of weeks that Walt could be stepping down. They've mentioned Daniel Voight to replace him. This have anything to do with why you're here?"

Voight was the former Democratic senator from California who'd first made a name for himself as a defense attorney for a very large Washington law firm before he'd gone home to enter politics. A lion's share of his career had been designing and pushing for reform in the intelligence community. He'd been dead set against creating the office of national intelligence, calling it little more than another layer of government bureaucracy. He was called the Architect at Langley and the other fourteen military and civilian intelligence agencies.

"Walt doesn't want to leave on this kind of a note. It's why he agreed to let me ask you for help."

"Voight is a good choice."

"Probably, but it's better the devil you know than the one you don't. Morale is a little low on campus. And it's going to get lower once our problem gets out."

"Marty sign on for you coming out there?"

"No. He wants to do this himself. Everyone thinks he's angling for Fred Atwell's job."

Atwell was the deputy director of the CIA, and since it wasn't likely he would take the top spot when Page left, it was assumed he would resign. He was a professional intelligence officer, and the biggest problem in the CIA for a very long time was that its directors were almost always politicians, not professionals, while the DDCIs were. Bambridge, as much as McGarvey didn't like him, would be the logical choice.

McGarvey sipped his wine. Otto and Pete were skirting the issue, which was highly unusual for both of them. Whatever it was had to be big.

"What is it?" he asked. "Why's Walt asked for my help?"

"We have a serial killer on campus," Otto said. "Two bodies so far, but there could be more. Everyone involved thinks it's likely."

"No one is allowed to go anywhere on campus alone," Pete said. "Everyone's in pairs. Marty's taken the blame for it, telling everyone that part of the Agency's new strategic plan is to expect a possible terrorist incursion and get ready for it."

"That would take someone from the inside," McGarvey said.

"Right. Everyone is a suspect, so no one works alone."

"Even for bathroom breaks," Pete said. "People have started calling the OHB Gestapo Headquarters."

"That's not the real issue," Otto said. "It's how they were killed that has Blankenship and his people freaked out. Me too, because it makes no sense unless the killer is a total psycho. But nothing like that shows up on anyone's psych evals."

"I'm listening," McGarvey said, and glanced at Pete. She was a little pale.

"Both of them bled to death. Their carotid arteries were ripped out of their necks."

"Ripped or cut?"

"The killer ripped them out with his teeth, like a wild animal. And then while they were bleeding out, he chewed off their noses and lips—even their eyebrows. We found saliva, and we're running DNA matches as fast as the lab can get the work done. Be a couple more days."

McGarvey had heard of things like this happening in the early days of the Vietnam War. And he said as much to them. "It was a tactic of the Degar. The French called them the Montagnard, the 'mountain people,' and they were fierce. We used them as guerrillas against the VC, who were frightened of them, and rightly so. These guys left their calling cards wherever they went. *Go back to Hanoi and leave us alone, or no one will be safe.* They cut off heads, genitals, put men headfirst in cages of starving rats. Shoved poisonous snakes down their throats. Made their prisoners swallow the shoots of live bamboo plants that would grow right through their stomachs and intestines, and then let them make it back to their own units."

"This guy was a Vietnamese soldier?" Pete asked skeptically. "He'd have to be seventy."

"No, but someone who studied the tactics, because they worked. If we'd given the Montagnards more support and then gotten out of their way, the VC just might have gone back to Hanoi and stayed out of it. He'll be a NOC," McGarvey said.

"Eighteen of them on the night shift," Otto said. "Three of them women, and Wager and Fabry leave thirteen. Soon as we get the DNA results back, we'll nail the bastard."

"He's already thought of that, which means it won't matter to him what DNA he left behind. It won't be in his records. He'll have gotten around that. It's the whole point: their asses are out in the field, and they sure as hell don't want anything pointing to their connections with the CIA."

"Then we'll take cheek swabs of everyone on the shift," Pete suggested.

"He may not have worked that shift. Getting on campus through security isn't all that difficult to do."

Otto sat back. "Are you in?"

"Of course," McGarvey said. From the moment Pete had shown up, there'd been no doubt in his mind. "I'm going to need a list of any field assignments Wager and Fabry were ever on together."

"We already have that," Otto said. He opened a file on his iPad and passed it across. "Called Alpha Seven. April oh three, little over a month before we started the second Iraq war."

Wager and Fabry were part of a ground team spread out in the mountains above Kirkuk. They were looking for WMDs. Of the five others, Joseph Carnes was dead, killed in a car crash in Athens last year, and none of the others were currently on the Company's payroll.

"You have current addresses on three of them, but the fourth is off the grid," McGarvey said. It was how he would have played it.

Pete was surprised, but Otto wasn't. "Larry Coffin," he said. "He and Carnes were pals. Could be our guy?"

"Probably not, but I'm betting he knows something we can use."

"He could be anywhere," Pete said. "And he's certainly demonstrated he doesn't want to be found."

"I'll find him," McGarvey said.

"Where?"

"Athens."

"I'm coming with you."

"No," McGarvey said. "You're going back with Otto to help set up a public funeral for Wager and

Fabry. Their families are going to insist, and only a very brief mention of their participation in the war will be released to the media."

"Marty will never go for it."

"Let him think it was his idea. We just want to know if any of their Alpha Seven buddies show up."

"Then what?"

"Let Marty figure it out, because I have a feeling none of those guys is the killer."

"Then why the ruse?" Pete asked.

"To keep the killer distracted."

EIGHT

Lawrence Thaddeus Coffin sat alone at a sidewalk café in the Plaka district of Athens, very near the Acropolis and on top of the ancient city. It was a historical district and almost always busy with tourists, which made it anonymous. It was one of his favorite people-watching spots in a city he'd come to love, because of its international flavor.

Greece from ancient times had been at the crossroads of trade not only in goods but in ideas, among them the arts, the sciences, and government itself.

He was a slender man, a bit under six feet, with thinning light brown hair and pale blue eyes that had always made him seem like a dreamer to those who didn't know him. Someone whose thoughts and concerns were far away from the everyday.

The waiter brought him another ouzo and a

demitasse of very strong coffee, his third for the late afternoon, along with his bill on a tiny slip of paper.

He'd had no idea anything had started to go bad until he'd read the brief squib in the *International New York Times* this morning about the funerals for two CIA officers who'd openly been identified as Wager and Fabry. It was a fact he found extraordinary. NOCs were never given public recognition. When they were killed in the line of duty, they were given a star on the granite wall in the lobby of the OHB. And that was that.

After Carnes and now these two, it left only him and three others who he expected would eventually make their way here to him. But it was all for nothing, especially after Snowden and the others had taken the fall. Nothing was left, except for *Kryptos,* which was the key if anyone took the time to understand the message—the entire message, which was scattered all over the campus.

A game, actually, he told himself. *Deadly, but a game nevertheless.*

When he was finished, he paid his bill, then got up and made his way down the block and across the street, traffic horrible at this hour. He was safe from retaliation to this point because of the measures he'd put into place more than a year ago. Necessary, he'd thought then, and still did. With Wager's and Fabry's deaths, the issue would soon be coming to a head. He could finally make his move.

A half dozen blocks from the taverna, he stopped across the narrow cobblestone lane to light a cigarette while he studied the two-story house he'd paid nearly a million euros for three years ago. The front was stuccoed in a pale pink, two iron balconies on the second floor—one for the sitting room and the other for the master bedroom, which jutted out over the street.

On March 25—that was the Greek independence holiday from Ottoman rule—each of those three years, he'd hung the Greek flag and bunting on the balconies as most of his neighbors did and went out into the streets for the festival and dancing.

He'd fit in very well, because that was what he was trained to do by the CIA. Blend in with the surroundings, mingle with the people as one of them. And the entire key to success, he'd learned very early on, was lying to yourself and believing it to such an extent that even under torture you would never reveal anything except your legend, the lies.

In the field, he'd played the part of an oil exploration engineer—studying enough textbooks and technical manuals to convince even another oil engineer. A UN aid worker, even issuing aid checks, and helping drill freshwater wells while spying on a military installation. Working as an independent arms dealer, a financier from London, a chef from San Francisco in Saudi Arabia to understand Arab cooking, and to introduce California fusion dishes to royalty while spying on them.

But his latest role, that of an independently wealthy dealer in rare books, artwork, and pieces of antiquity, had come about when all but the last panel on the *Kryptos* sculpture at CIA headquarters had been decrypted, and the talk on the Internet hinted that the fourth was soon to fall.

He'd allowed himself to be caught red-handed

with three tiny Greek sculptures: one of Aphrodite, the goddess of love, beauty, desire, and pleasure; Hera, the queen of the heavens and goddess of marriage, women, childbirth, heirs, kings, and empires; and of Athena herself, the goddess of intelligence, skill, warfare, battle strategy, handicrafts, and wisdom.

After a brief hearing before a judge five months ago, during which he'd pleaded guilty, he'd been fined one hundred thousand euros or one year in prison. He refused to pay the fine.

The house was quiet, the same blinds in two of the upstairs windows half drawn, as he'd left them. No suspicious car with its left wheels up on the sidewalk, no telltale glitter from the lenses of binoculars, no radio antenna, no small satellite dish of the kind often used as a television receiver but could also be used for burst transmissions to and from a satellite—the same sort he and the others on Alpha Seven had used.

A taxi rattled past. Tossing his cigarette aside, he crossed the street and let himself inside using the code on the keypad. He was dressed in tight jeans and a plain red muscle T-shirt rather than the sport coats or suits he'd worn as an arts dealer.

In the past he'd hinted he was gay, and his neighbors—most of them married couples—left him alone. Coming here like this, as he had for the past four months, raised no suspicions. It was just one of his gay friends stopping by from time to time to check on things. He sometimes stayed for several hours, but he always left before eight in the evening.

The downstairs hall was deathly silent. He took

the SIG Sauer pistol from the hall table, held his breath, and cocked an ear to listen for a sound. Any sound that would indicate someone was here.

No out-of-place scents were on the air; the slight layer of dust on the table and on the cap of the newel post and the stair rail had not been disturbed since the last time he'd been here. Nevertheless, he methodically checked the hall closet, reception area, guest bathroom, dining room, kitchen, and pantry, as well as the breakfast nook, which looked out over a pretty courtyard with a small fountain at the rear of the house.

Upstairs he checked the three bedrooms and attached bathrooms and closets before he went into the sitting room he had used as his office. Before he'd left for prison, he'd destroyed anything that tied him in any way to the CIA, but left everything else. Since the police raid and investigation, nothing else had been disturbed.

He checked the street from a window, but no one had shown up since he'd come inside, and he breathed a small sigh of relief.

Downstairs, he opened a good bottle of Valpolicella and took it out to the small iron table in the courtyard, where he sat listening not only to the sounds of the neighborhood but to his inner voices— the ones he'd very often had trouble understanding.

He'd been a man alone for most of his life. Growing up as a child in Detroit, mostly on the streets and later at the community college in Lansing, where he'd studied psychology, running out of money six months before graduation. Afterward he'd learned to count cards, and he went to Atlantic City, where he made twenty thousand before he had to run to avoid getting arrested or, at the very least, beaten up.

For the next years, he'd taught himself disguises—simple hair dyes, glasses, fake mustaches, clothing—and most of all: attitudes, mostly meek to blend in, or sometimes as an expert on some subject. He'd supported himself primarily by gambling, and a few con games involving illegal guns or drugs. And he'd never been caught, because he was good.

For two years he studied psychiatry, learning enough to understand even more about the manifestations of personalities, which made his job of blending in easier. And finally he'd applied to the CIA, using a fake degree in psychology and a line of bullshit that went right over the heads of interviewers and didn't come to light until his deep background investigation.

They'd actually admired him. Told him he was perfect for what they had in mind. After all, they'd explained, the best man for the job as a NOC was a con artist.

"You talked your way through the door without any help; you'll go a long way with ours," the final recruiter told him.

All that time from the streets of Detroit, to Lansing and to casinos around the country, he'd been alone. But in the CIA he'd finally found a place where he could be respected and even liked for who and what he was.

A few minutes before eight, Coffin went back into the house, rinsed out and dried his wineglass, and, checking out the window, let himself out of the house.

At the corner he took a bus to the metro station. From there he boarded a train for Piraeus—Athens's port town twelve kilometers to the southwest.

He was due back in his cell at the Korydallos Prison Complex no later than ten. He was scheduled to interview a female prisoner first thing in the morning at the psych ward where he worked. She had delusions she was someone else, though she couldn't say exactly who it was. It was a condition he knew very well.

NINE

McGarvey packed a few things, then flew up to Athens with Otto and Pete in the Aegean Airlines charters helicopter. The noise over the eighty-mile flight was too great to talk out loud without shouting, and he didn't want to use the intercom and headphones. What he had to say wasn't for the pilot's ears. In any event, Otto had brought up the dossiers on all seven of the Alpha team, and he'd read them.

Nor was it for the ears of their taxi driver on the way to the Athens Hilton near the U.S. embassy. And it wasn't until they'd checked in, three separate suites on the eighth floor that looked down across the city toward Syntagma Square, and agreed to meet at the Galaxy, the hotel's rooftop bar, that he shared his plan.

"I'm betting Larry Coffin has a setup here in Athens. If we can find him and prove he went to the

U.S. in the past few days or week, then he'll become a likely suspect."

"We need a motive," Pete said, but Otto held her off.

"What if he's here and never left?"

"The connection between Wager, Fabry, Carnes, and Coffin was Alpha Seven. And I'm guessing something happened in the mountains above Kirkuk that not only bound those guys together but is the reason three of them were killed."

"You're saying Carnes didn't die in a traffic accident?" Pete asked.

"He died, but it probably wasn't an accident. The question in my mind is why now? Why go through the trouble and risk of penetrating campus security to kill two of the team?"

"Doesn't have to be a reason that'd make sense to us," Pete said. "The killer is obviously a psychopath."

"That's too easy," McGarvey said. "We need a trigger. Something recent."

"What's going on in the region that has a bearing?" Pete asked. "Iran's nuclear program for one. Their ballistic missile tests. ISIS."

"I don't think it's going to be that pat. I mean, I don't think we're looking for a threat to the U.S. It has to be something that benefited the team."

"Not another treasure hunt."

"No."

"What then?" Pete asked. "You're not making any sense, Mac. Anyway, we're back to a motive, because if we can't come up with that, then the killings, and the way they happened, make no sense."

"First we need to find Larry Coffin," McGarvey said.

"Maybe not so easy," Otto said. "If this guy was as good a NOC as his reputation had him, he won't be found if he doesn't want to be found."

"He's either the killer or if he isn't, he's heard about the funerals, and he'll want to know what's happening."

"You're betting the latter."

"Because it's going to be the easiest," McGarvey said.

"If you're right, he'll have to guess someone has made the Alpha Seven connection and will be coming after him," Pete said. "Either the killer or someone from the Company."

On the way up from Serifos, McGarvey had thought about the easiest, most direct approach. Something to dig the guy out of hiding. Coffin had been a NOC, which meant in order to survive as long as he had, not only in the field but in hiding from his own people, he had to maintain at least minimal contact with the Company. It didn't have to be a personal contact. Someone on the inside but maybe an electronic contact.

"The CIA retirees' newsletter is online these days, right?"

Otto nodded. He was grinning. "Why sneak in the back way when you can ring the front doorbell?" he said. "How do you want it to read?"

"Alpha Seven reunion. Give him your e-mail address."

Pete got it. "He'd be a fool to answer."

"Either that, or he thinks he's smarter than we are," Otto said.

"Or desperate," Pete said.

"Smarter," McGarvey said. "But curious."

Otto posted the announcement online and took the CIA's Gulfstream home. But Pete had refused to go with him. "At the very least, Coffin is a psycho himself—a very smart and successful psycho. I'm going to stick around to watch your back."

"You'd better move in here with me so I can watch yours," McGarvey said reluctantly. He didn't want any sort of entanglement, especially not just now. Whoever this guy was who'd killed Wager and Fabry and then had chewed off their faces was crazy, but he was also a professional field officer, which made him doubly dangerous.

Pete moved her things over, then went downstairs and checked out of her room and into his. She was back for just a minute when someone knocked at the door, and McGarvey went to answer it.

An older man with a very thick shock of white hair who was dressed in a ratty old sports coat and slacks that hadn't seen an iron in a month held out his Athens metro police badge. "Spiros Moshonas," he said. "Mr. McGarvey, I presume?"

McGarvey let him in. "What can I do for you?"

Pete came to the bedroom door, and the detective smiled and nodded. "I followed you up," he apologized. "The hotel won't reveal anything about their guests, not even to the police."

They had checked in under their real names—no

reason at this point for them to have used work names and false papers.

"Actually, the NIS asked my department to send someone over to have a little chat," Moshonas said. The NIS was the Greek intelligence service headquartered here in Athens.

"Good," McGarvey said. "Maybe you can help us." He got the tablet Otto had left with them and pulled up Coffin's dossier, which included a half dozen photos, and showed them to the cop.

"You're looking for this man?"

"Yes."

"May I ask why?" Moshonas smiled. "What I mean to say is that it's highly unusual for a former director of the CIA to come here so openly, and then apparently in pursuit of someone. Is this business for you?"

"We want to have a little chat with him," McGarvey said.

"May I know what you wish to discuss with him?"

"He used to work for us, and something has come up we'd like to ask him about."

"The service would want a more detailed answer."

Pete came the rest of the way into the sitting room. "Do you know where this man is?"

"Of course. I was the one responsible for putting him there," Moshonas said. "If you'll give me something I can report, any little thing, I'll take you to him."

"He's wanted for questioning in the murders of two CIA employees a few days ago."

"That would be impossible," Moshonas said. "Mr. Cooke was convicted of trafficking in stolen artifacts last year. At the moment he's serving time at Kory-dallos prison in Piraeus."

For just a moment McGarvey allowed himself to be surprised, until he realized what was wrong. Coffin would never have allowed himself to be caught doing something so simple. "Did he plead guilty?"

Moshonas's eyes narrowed. "In fact, he did."

"Was he offered a plea bargain, maybe if he named his sources?"

"He turned it down."

"Maybe a fine instead of a prison sentence?"

"He turned that down as well, though he was living in a very expensive home, without a mortgage. He wanted to go to prison, which none of us understood."

"Let's go talk to him, and I'll tell you what I can on the way down."

"Would you like to see his house?"

"No," McGarvey said. "There'd be nothing there of any interest to us."

Moshonas nodded. "I'll bring you to him, but I want to sit in on the interview, and there are a few questions I'll have to ask you afterward."

TEN

Coffin, wearing gray scrubs of the sort used by doctors in hospitals, walked down the corridor of the maximum-security section for men, his eyes lowered, a slight scowl on his face. No guard accompanied him; he was treated more or less as a special guest because of his generous contributions to the warden's pension fund, and funds for the families of guards who were out of work because of injuries or illness. He was well liked here and practically had the run of the place.

He'd been convicted and sentenced as an antiquities thief, but he'd presented himself, complete with diplomas, as a clinical psychiatrist specializing in the mental disorders of habitual offenders— especially females, of which there were still a few in Korydallos.

The prison, which was infamous with Amnesty International for its horrible conditions, maintained a vastly out-of-date and underequipped hospital and mental clinic. Always short of money and personnel, the medical director was initially overjoyed to have Coffin's help. And no one ever bothered to question his credentials, even though some of the staff had their suspicions.

At the end of the long corridor, he was admitted through a steel door into the medical section that divided the women's cellblock from the rest of the complex.

"Good morning, Doc," the guard said in Greek, a language Coffin had managed to become reasonably proficient in over the past couple of years.

"How is your child?"

"It was very close. Without your help, his appendix would have burst and he would have died."

"Is he out of hospital?"

"Two days ago, and he'll start back to school on Monday."

"Glad to hear it," Coffin said, patting the man on the arm.

Dr. Vasilis Lampros, the prison's medical director, was waiting at Coffin's office door when he came into the clinic. He was a stern, rough-looking old man who'd worked in Greek prisons all his medical career. He looked more like a rock cutter in a marble quarry than a doctor, and he trusted no one.

"Good afternoon, Doctor," Coffin said pleasantly. He'd been expecting bad news for the past several days, but he wasn't going to let his mood show here and now. The old bastard would jump on it and suspect the worst—whatever that might be in his mind.

"Your examination with Ms. Pappas will not be necessary," Lampros said.

"Is she being transferred?"

"She hung herself last night. Told everyone at dinner you tried to rape her at your most recent session."

Coffin laughed. "That's ridiculous, and you know it. The woman was delusional, lived in a fantasy world her entire adult life. It's a fact that in the three months I treated her, she was completely unable to distinguish truth from lies."

"It's a common condition here, as you well know." Something in the tone of the man's voice was bothersome. "Is there a problem, Doctor?"

"You're a prisoner."

"Indeed I am. And you're understaffed. Perhaps I could underwrite the salaries of a couple of nurses. They would help lighten your load."

"Go back to your cell, Cooke," Lampros said. "You're no longer needed here."

"As you wish," Coffin said. He shrugged indifferently and turned to walk away.

"No one at Harvard has heard of you. There are no records."

Coffin turned back. "That's not surprising. May we go into your office so I can explain?"

"Nothing I want to hear."

"But I think you will want to hear this," Coffin said, smiling.

No one else was in the clinic evaluation room at the moment. Coffin took the doctor's arm, and they went into the office and closed the door.

"You're a fraud," Lampros said.

"Of course I am," Coffin said. He shoved the doctor back against the desk and clamped his fingers around the older man's neck with enough pressure to the carotid artery to cut off blood flow to the man's brain but not enough to cause a bruise.

Lampros tried to pull away, but Coffin was much stronger and trained in hand-to-hand combat. In a surprisingly short time, Lampros went unconscious and slumped to the floor.

Coffin followed him down, keeping pressure on the man's neck until the heartbeat became thready and finally stopped.

He threw open the door. "Someone get me the crash cart!" he shouted. He went back to the doctor's body, ripped open Lampros's shirt, and pulled up his T-shirt. "Let's go, let's go!" he shouted, and started CPR.

One of the nurses came in with the defibrillator at the same time Coffin felt a very slight pulse, and he stopped the chest compressions until the machine came to full power.

One of the orderlies came in as Coffin applied the

paddles to the doctor's chest. "Clear!" he shouted. But nothing happened. The machine was broken and had been for some months.

He listened at the doctor's chest and then felt the artery in the man's neck. But the pulse had stopped. He sat back on his heels and shook his head. "It's no use. Dr. Lampros is dead."

One of the nurses said something Coffin didn't catch.

He looked up.

"Dr. Lampros turned down a request for a new defibrillator," the other nurse said. "He didn't think the prisoners were worth it."

Coffin got up. "Perhaps it's best if I went back to my cell. But call the warden and let him know you tried to save his life, but his heart gave out."

"Yes, sir," the one nurse said.

Coffin walked out, though what he wanted was to kick everyone out of the office and look at the good doctor's computer to erase whatever e-mails he'd received from Harvard. But he'd already come to the conclusion several days ago, especially since learning about the deaths of Wager and Fabry, that he would have to go very deep and very soon.

The wolves were gathering, and it was time to remove the scent from the pack.

Back in his cell, he powered up his tablet and launched a search program he'd designed with the CIA's clandestine services as a major target. It was the program that had picked up the two deaths. This time a starred story keyed on the CIA retirees' newsletter. A reunion of the Alpha Seven operators from

Iraq was announced. But there were only five others, including him, plus one now.

He sat back in his chair. A call to arms, since two of their own had been murdered? A call to safety? Or a dragnet for the suspected killer?

Shutting down, he stuffed the tablet into his shoulder bag and phoned his substitute.

"I need you again for this evening."

"I can be there by eight," the American expat he'd paid more than one hundred thousand euros over the past several months promised.

"I need you now. How soon can you be here?"

"As it turns out, I'm in Piraeus. I can get to you in fifteen minutes. Another overnight?"

"Might be several days."

"That place is a shit hole. It'll cost extra."

"Twenty-five thousand."

"Thirty?"

"Fifteen minutes," Coffin said, and he hung up. In addition to what he'd paid the warden, he'd also paid more than one hundred thousand euros to the prison's administrator of the guard force, depositing the money into a personal bank account Coffin had arranged.

He changed into a pair of khaki slacks, a white shirt with the sleeves rolled up, loafers, a baseball cap, and sunglasses, and, shouldering his small bag, looked around his cell for the last time.

This place had been a safe house for him. The last place anyone would think to look for him. But as was almost always the case, good things came to an end. He was on the run now until he figured out who was coming after him and how serious the threat was.

If the last piece of the *Kryptos* puzzle—the one sculpture still unknown—had been solved, he would have to fight back if for no other reason than to save his life.

ELEVEN

A slightly built man in khaki slacks and white shirt was getting into a cab in front of the prison's main gate, another similarly built man getting out, when McGarvey, riding shotgun, and Pete, sitting in the backseat, arrived in Detective Moshonas's battered old Volvo station wagon.

They were met at the gate by a man introducing himself as Hristos Apostoulos, who was a representative of Nikos Hondros, the chief of prison security, who apologized that neither his boss nor Warden Kostas could have met them in person.

"We've had something of a tragic afternoon," Apostoulos said. "Our chief medical officer had a heart attack in his office less than an hour ago, and his wife and sons are here already. Tragic."

"In English please," Moshonas said. "We're here to interview one of your prisoners."

"Yes, Livermore Cooke, a British citizen. We've set up a room where lawyers usually meet their clients."

They headed on foot through the gate and then across to the main administration building, where they were searched, and Moshonas had to give up his weapon. McGarvey and Pete had left theirs at the hotel.

"It's doubly difficult for us," the aide said on the way down a long corridor.

"How's that?" Moshonas asked.

"With Dr. Lampros gone, it leaves us very short-handed. Except for Dr. Cooke, who's been a real help, we'd have to send our serious cases up to Athens."

"I didn't know he was a medical doctor," McGarvey said.

The aide gave him a sharp look. "A psychiatrist, but he's had medical training. A great man. We'll miss him when he's served his time."

"Because of his medical help?"

"Yes, and he's a generous man."

The prison was noisy, someone was shouting in one of the cellblocks, and the place stank badly of human waste and of diesel fumes. But they encountered no one. Except for the noise and odors, the prison could have been deserted.

Moshonas asked about it.

"We're in temporary lockdown."

"Because of your doctor?"

"No, one of our inmates hung herself last night, but there may be some evidence that she was murdered." They came to the interview room, and the aide gave them a hard look. "This is a placed filled with very bad people. And until now, Dr. Cooke's presence has had an almost calming effect. Don't ask me how, but the past five months have been easy for us."

He opened the door for them. The room was small and contained only a table and two chairs.

"Unless you need my presence, I have other duties to attend to. I'll have Dr. Cooke sent over."

"Dr. Cooke and a guard?" Moshonas asked.

The aide smiled slightly. "He has respect here. There's no need for him to walk through the prison with protection."

Moshonas started to say something, but McGarvey interrupted.

"That's good to know. Thanks."

The aide turned to leave.

"Who was with your medical director when he had his heart attack?"

"Dr. Cooke. In fact, he performed CPR, but it was too late."

"They were friends?"

"Of course. As I said, Dr. Cooke is very well respected."

"What was that all about?" Pete asked when the aide was gone.

"We're going to find out when Coffin, or whoever is here serving time for him, walks through the door," McGarvey told them. He'd had a feeling when Moshonas explained about Coffin's sentencing that the man would never have let himself be sent to a place like this unless he needed to disappear for some reason. Nor could a man of Coffin's training be kept under lock and key.

"You think he has escaped?" Moshonas asked.

"I have a feeling he comes and goes anywhere he pleases, including out the front door."

"Then why hasn't he just disappeared?"

"I don't think he's needed to do it until just now."

"He killed the medical director," Pete said.

"I think it's a good bet," McGarvey said. "Probably because they found out he wasn't a psychiatrist."

"Who is this guy?" Moshonas asked.

"He was a deep-cover spy for the CIA. Part of a team in Iraq several years ago. Seven operators, two of whom were murdered recently. I have a feeling he knew it was going to happen, and maybe even who would do it, so he committed a crime and got himself sent here, where he figured he'd be safe for at least a year."

"But his story started to unravel," Pete said.

"If his real identity got out, this place wouldn't be safe for him. It'd be like shooting fish in a barrel."

"You think he's gone?" Moshonas asked. "Then what are we doing here?"

"I want to see who comes through that door."

"The security officer to admit that Cooke has somehow escaped?"

"Maybe not," McGarvey said.

"You're not making sense."

"I think Cooke walked out the door from time to time to test the waters, or maybe just to have a nice dinner and a couple of drinks somewhere. I don't know if I could stay here very long without a break."

"He would have been reported missing."

"Not if he hired a substitute."

"Mother of God," Moshonas said. "The guards would have to be in on it."

"Apostoulos said Cooke was generous."

A slender man dressed in gray scrubs came to the door. "You wanted to speak to me?"

"Dr. Cooke?" McGarvey asked.

The substitute nodded. "Yes?"

"Come in and sit down. I'd like to ask you a couple of things."

The substitute did as he was told, but Pete took the chair across from him.

She smiled. "Are you being treated well here?"

"As well as can be expected in a place like this."

"How did he first contact you?" she asked.

"I don't understand."

"I think you do. Your name is not Cooke, but then neither is it the real name of the man who paid you to stand in for him from time to time. But none of that is of any real interest to me. I merely want to know how he first contracted you? How much he paid? What were the arrangements? And how was it that the guards allowed this to go on?"

The substitute said nothing.

"Detective, since this guy is a stand-in, could he be charged as an accessory to the murder of the medical director here?"

"Yes," Moshonas said.

She smiled again. "In that case, you would come here for real, and most likely for a very long time."

"Wait a minute," the substitute blurted. "I don't know anything about a murder. You can't pin something like that on me."

"The man who hired you probably killed the medical director this afternoon, and is gone, leaving you holding the bag. He won't be coming back. And now we need your help to find him. It's the only fair deal you're going to get today."

"Shit."

"Help us find him, and you'll walk out of here a free man. And even get to keep the money he's already paid you."

"I have something to say about that," Moshonas said.

"No," McGarvey told him. "Trust me: if we can get to Coffin, you'll have your murderer."

"You're an American?" the substitute asked.

"We're CIA, and so was the man who hired you," Pete said. "Help us, and we'll help you."

The substitute had no way out, and it was obvious he knew it.

Pete took a notebook and pen out of her purse and laid them on the table. "Dates and places you met. Money he's already paid you, and the bank and account number it was paid into, unless it was cash."

"In an account he set up for me."

"We're not interested in the money—only the account number. We have someone who can trace it back to him."

"Christ, he said he'd kill me if something went wrong."

"We'll see that it doesn't," Pete said. "The bank?"

"Piraeus Bank."

"Do you live in Piraeus?"

The substitute nodded. "I think it's why he picked me, because I was so close to the prison."

"The account number," Pete said, "and then we'll see about getting you out of here."

"It's electronic," the substitute said. He told her the bank's e-mail address, then his online account name and password. "I don't want to spend another night here," he said.

"You're coming with us," McGarvey said. "But if you've lied to us, we'll turn you over to the Greek cops, and you'll end up back here " He turned to Moshonas. "Can you get him out of here?"

"Guaranteed."

TWELVE

Coffin sat in the rooftop garden of the Alkistis Hotel in Athens's market section, nursing a beer and considering his options, which had narrowed considerably. It was early evening, and this section of the city, bustling during the day, was all but deserted now. The hotel was one of the cheapest in the entire metro and reasonably safe for the moment. It was off-season, and no one else was on the roof with him. Nor had he seen anyone except for the clerk in the lobby when he'd checked in.

It had been Kirk McGarvey at the prison. He'd caught a glimpse of the bastard as the taxi was pulling away, and it was one of the biggest shocks of his life. He'd been with some old guy and a broad, but the point was, he'd been looking at the taxi. The son of a bitch knew where to show up, as impossible as it seemed.

Coffin had actually met the man once, a number of years ago in Afghanistan, when a meeting had been arranged with bin Laden. It was impossible for McGarvey to have remembered him, because he was just one of a group in the middle of a deployment into the Kandahar region, and they didn't speak.

Yet McGarvey was here.

He'd had the cabby drop him off a few blocks from his house, and went the rest of the way on foot, very careful with his tradecraft. McGarvey knew about the prison; he almost certainly knew about the house.

But no one had been there. No cars, no one lingering at the corner, no one on the roofs across the street or in any of the windows. At least nothing he could see was out of the ordinary. But there could have been a drone circling overhead, quiet and completely out of sight. Or perhaps McGarvey had contacted the NIS and they had set up an electronic surveillance operation.

McGarvey himself wasn't a threat to his life, but by coming this far, the former DCI could very well have led the only man Coffin feared to him. And the woman with him was a mystery, as was the older man. McGarvey's rep was as a loner.

Coffin had gone around the back and gotten into his house through a rear door. He wasn't armed, but that really didn't matter. If it came to a fight, he could take care of himself with his bare hands. Everyone in Alpha Seven, plus their control man who'd shown up only at the last moment with surprising new orders, had the background and training to do so. It was one of the mission's requirements.

No one had been there, and he was in and out in less than ten minutes with a small bag, a few items of clothing and toiletries, and a 9-mm SIG, a suppressor, two magazines, and a box of twenty-five bullets he had hung in a satchel on a hook in the basement wine cellar. The cops hadn't been very thorough in their search. He'd been an art thief not a killer, and they had the evidence he'd led them to. Show them what they wanted to see, and hide everything else right under their noses.

He'd walked a few blocks away before he'd taken a cab out to the airport, and from there, twenty minutes later, a cab into the city, and a third to this hotel.

The question now was what to do with the situation that had landed in his lap. Run, or stay and fight back? He didn't want to go up against McGarvey, but he had to consider it as one of his options. The other would be going to him for help.

For the first time in his professional life, Coffin didn't know what to do. He had plenty of money stashed under different names in a half dozen banks around the world, so he could run and live in reasonable comfort just about anywhere. Plastic surgery, new papers. The trouble was, he'd eventually be tracked down. Either by McGarvey or the other one. A man whose real name none of them had ever known.

Assuming Wager and Fabry had been murdered, the others would probably be next, and the only reason he could think why was because one of them had cracked the last puzzle. It was the one thing he'd feared from the beginning. The main reason he had run.

He finished his beer, got his iPad from his room, and walked up toward the Acropolis. The Parthenon, the museum, and all the grounds were closed at this hour, the gates locked, guards and closed-circuit television cameras everywhere. But tourists still flocked to the place, because even from outside the fence, they could get great photographs.

A table at a sidewalk café was open, and he sat down and ordered an espresso. When it came, he powered up his tablet and went online. For just a moment he hesitated, but then went to the Alpha Seven reunion address in the newsletter and logged on with one of his old Internet names: G. Washington.

His only real option, he decided, was finesse.

When the site came up he wrote: *When? Where? Why?*

It took nearly two minutes for the reply to come. *You're a difficult man to find, Mr. C.*

Who wants to find me?

The man getting out of the taxi behind you this afternoon.

I'm a fugitive. Is that why he came?

You were a suspect until this afternoon.

Then what does he want?

Answers.

Coffin looked up as a police car cruised slowly past. The cop behind the wheel glanced over indifferently for just an instant, but he didn't linger.

What's the question?

Why the murders? Why the two from Alpha Seven?

This is a hackable connection, Coffin wrote back, and he was about to power down and get away when the reply came.

No, it's not.

Still Coffin hesitated, his finger on the power off button.

Backscatter encryption in both directions.

Who are you?

Otto Rencke. I'm in my third-floor office at the OHB. You may have heard of me, Mr. Coffin; we've heard of you. We know you are probably still in Athens, and we know that for the past five months, you have been in hiding. We would like to know why.

The same police car cruised past, and Coffin was about to get up and find the back door, but the cop never looked over.

Will the police be looking for me?

Do you think the killer will come after you?

It's possible, but it depends on a set of circumstances.

What circumstances?

The translation of the last Kryptos *tablet,* Coffin wrote.

Could be something new. It needs to be found and recognized for what it is. Evidently, it hasn't been yet.

Someone must think so.

Yes.

An attractive woman came around the corner and stopped at his table. "May I join you, Mr. Coffin?" she said.

Her name is Pete Boylan, the message appeared on his screen. *She is a CIA case officer and came with Kirk McGarvey to find you. Help us, and we'll help you.*

Coffin's iPad powered down by itself, and he managed a smile. Like McGarvey, Otto Rencke was a legend in the CIA. A wizard. "Would you like a coffee?"

She sat down. "Actually, Mr. McGarvey would like to talk to you."

"Where?"

"We have a safe house not far from here."

"An NIS safe house?"

"Yes, they're cooperating."

"I'm armed."

"Yes, we know this."

"Am I wanted by the police?"

Pete laughed softly. "On a number of counts, the least of which is escaping from prison."

"The doctor had a heart attack. I was trying to save his life. Let's just get that off the table before I agree to anything."

"Most likely you killed him, but the police aren't all that concerned. Dr. Lampros was not a doctor; in fact, he himself was a murderer. Killed a female prisoner last night and made it look like she hung herself. Apparently, she wasn't his first."

THIRTEEN

Coffin followed Pete around the corner, where the same old man who'd been with her and McGarvey outside the prison this afternoon was waiting by a battered Volvo station wagon that was painted green.

"You took a pistol from your house, and when we searched your hotel room a few minutes ago, it wasn't there," Moshonas said. "Give it to me, Mr. Coffin."

"I think he'll feel safer for the moment with it, Detective," Pete said.

"Actually, it's Special Agent Moshonas. I work for the NIS."

"Yes, we know. But I don't think Mr. Coffin will shoot us."

"He murdered Dr. Lampros."

"Almost certainly, but we've come here to save Mr. Coffin's life. And I think he understands that in order for us to do our job, he needs to do his. One hand washes the other."

Moshonas muttered something but then got in behind the wheel, Pete in front and Coffin in the back, and they headed away from the Acropolis and southwest for the short drive out of the city to the commercial waterfront at Piraeus.

McGarvey had sent Pete to soften the blow, and Moshonas for his authority, rather than approach Coffin himself. "He'll be on a hair trigger. If I show up, he might want to shoot first and listen later."

And it had worked, along with allowing him to keep his weapon. But Pete realized she resented Mac's attitude just a little, even though he was right. If Coffin had pulled his weapon, she was sure she would have been able to handle herself.

She turned and looked back at him. "You could have shot me and simply walked away. Why not?"

"Wouldn't have been very sporting. In any event, I'm sure you would have responded in kind, and both of us would be on our way to the hospital or the morgue."

"So, what's the point? Why'd you set yourself up for the fall? Who'd you think was coming after you?

Not us. Your record was clean when you walked away from the Company."

"It's more complicated than that, as Walt and Istvan found out."

Pete understood. "Almost everything usually is."

"What about the other Alpha Seven operators? Are they okay? Have you managed to make contact?"

"You were our first. We're still working on the others."

"Rencke is?"

"Yes. Wager and Fabry were the only ones left still working for us."

"They're dead now. So might the others be."

"We found you," Pete said, and faced forward as the lights around the harbor came into view. Her skin crawled, having an armed man—especially one of Coffin's character—sitting behind her.

She'd only ever met a few NOCs in her career, and all of them had been singularly egotistical liars, cheats, and con men—she'd not met a woman NOC field officer. But those traits were the prime requirements for the job of going into badland to spy and not get caught. They had to screw over people on a regular basis in order to fulfill their assignments.

Mac had told her about the one couple who'd moved in next door to an Egyptian major who worked in logistics and supply for the air force. The man was married and had four children, and as a major he was barely making ends meet.

The U.S. wanted to know what aircraft spare parts were most in demand, so Boeing and Northrop and other U.S. suppliers would not only have a leg up in their business dealings with the Egyptians, but so Washington would have a better handle on the actual workload the air force was under.

It started easy. The NOC and his wife, who had two children of their own, invited the major and his family over for an old-fashioned American backyard barbecue, complete with beer and tapes of a couple of Packers football games.

A couple of weeks later the NOC's oldest son, who was ten, taught the major's son, who was eight years old, how to ride his bike. The lessons went on for a week, until the major's son demanded a bike like their neighbor's boy had.

It was an impossible demand on a major's pay, so the NOC bought a bike from the BX at Ramstein Air Base in Germany, had it shipped to Cairo. And within two days the major's son was riding around the neighborhood.

The major had been unable to resist the pressure from his son and his wife to allow the boy to keep the bike, and that had been the beginning of his conversion to a spy for the U.S. against his own government.

The NOC had targeted the major, figured out his weakness, and had homed in on it. Mission accomplished. Two years later, after the NOC and his family transferred out, the major came under suspicion so he killed his wife and children and then put the pistol into his own mouth and pulled the trigger. It was an easier way out for him than military prison.

"Thing is," McGarvey had told Pete, "we never really needed the information. The parts were all made in the U.S. and the suppliers had all those records."

The NIS safe house was aboard a passenger ferry that had blown its engine three months ago and was on chocks on dry land, waiting for a replacement. From the outside, the 110-foot boat was a rusting wreck; on the inside, it wasn't a lot better, though everything aboard worked, including the galley. No crew was assigned at the moment, so it was just Moshonas, Pete, and Coffin who came aboard.

McGarvey was waiting for them in what had been the crew's mess belowdecks, just forward of the engine room. Both portholes were open, but still the room was stuffy and smelled of diesel oil.

Eight people could sit around the table, and when Coffin came in, he pulled up short when he spotted the Walther PPK in front of where Mac was sitting.

"I'm glad you could join us without trouble," McGarvey said. "Give your weapon to Ms. Boylan, please."

Coffin stepped back a pace, but Pete and Moshonas were right there. Pete reached inside Coffin's jacket and took the SIG.

"Just so there're no mistakes," McGarvey said. "Sit down."

Coffin did as he was told. Pete sat astraddle a chair across the room, her arms draped over the back of it, while Moshonas leaned up against the door.

The mess was functional, but little more than that. Pete had no idea what was coming next, except that Coffin seemed to be in an agreeable mood. But she couldn't tell if he was for real, or if he was simply working the situation like any good NOC was trained to do. And by all accounts he was one of the best.

FOURTEEN

"The Alpha Seven operation was a long time ago," McGarvey said. "Where's the bridge to Wager's and Fabry's deaths and you running to ground?"

"It's been a long day, and I would like something to drink," Coffin said. He sat back and crossed his legs. "A glass of wine?"

"I'll get it," Pete said, and started to get up, but McGarvey waved her back.

"Maybe later, but for now I want Mr. Coffin to take us through the scenario. I want to know what the hell is happening."

"How were they killed?" Coffin asked.

"Their carotid arteries were severed, and they bled to death."

"Any DNA evidence at the crime scenes?"

"None that match any CIA employee," McGarvey said.

"I thought not," Coffin said. "What weapon did the killer use? A knife? A gunshot to the side of the neck? A piece of broken glass?"

"Teeth."

"Animal or human?"

"Human."

Coffin looked away for a moment. "Were their faces destroyed? Lips chewed off, noses, eyebrows?"

"You know who it is?" McGarvey asked.

"I think so. But you'll need to hear the entire story, or you wouldn't understand the motive."

"I want his name."

"I don't know it. None of us ever did. In addition to the seven of us on the team in Iraq, our control officer showed up out of the blue, and I mean, literally out of the blue. He parachuted down on our position above Kirkuk in the middle of the night. None of us heard the aircraft that brought him across the border either from Turkey or maybe Syria, which means he had to have made a HALO jump—high altitude, above twenty-five thousand feet, and free-falling down to a thousand feet or so to make the low opening."

The team had been assembled in Saudi Arabia for their initial briefing before being staged at Frankfurt and then moved to their training site in the mountains above Munich. That was in the winter of 1999, and when the mission had been fully explained, they'd all gotten a laugh out of the logic—send a team to be trained in midwinter for a mission that might not develop until the summer in a hostile country where temperatures could soar to well above 110.

But the point of learning the op in Germany was to do so in complete secrecy, right under the noses of the BND—Germany's intelligence service, whose headquarters at the time were still at Pullach, just outside of Munich.

"If you get caught up here, if even a hint of our

presence becomes known, the mission is a wash," their chief instructor had told them.

Which was the entire point. They were hidden in the Bavarian Alps, with orders to spy on the BND's headquarters. They were to slip into town at night, carry out their surveillance operations, and then disappear back into the mountains before daybreak.

"Thing is, they picked the seven of us because no one spoke even a smattering of German," Coffin said.

"You needed to complete an op without being able to talk yourself out of a difficult spot?" Pete asked.

Coffin looked at her. "Being able to blend in was why we were hired in the first place. I was a chameleon. Give me a few days with a couple of textbooks or instruction manuals, and I could play the part of just about anybody. Airline pilot, surgeon, plumber."

"But you had to be able to speak the language," Pete said. "The mission was Iraq. Why didn't the Company send someone who spoke Arabic or Kurdish?"

"Not many of them around in those days," Coffin said.

"The German mission evidently was a success."

"Yes. The BND never knew we were there. Some of us even used to go into town for a couple of beers and some wurst. Played the part of tourists."

"Your instructors didn't jump you over it?"

Coffin laughed. "They were sending us to Iraq. If we were expected to get past the BND guys, which we did, and then the Mukhabarat operators, slipping past our own people was easy."

"Anyway, it was fun," Pete suggested.

"None of it was ever fun—interesting and all that, but not fun. We were going into badland, and there're never any guarantees."

"You think the killer was your control officer?" McGarvey asked.

"I never said that. The killer could be anyone of the team still alive."

"Including you?"

"You can't believe how easy it was to walk out of Korydallos. Greece is in financial meltdown. A few euros here and there do wonders."

"Then why did you walk for good today?"

"Dr. Lampros found out I wasn't a real shrink. I'm next on the list, and whoever is killing Alpha Seven had me in their sights."

Pete picked up on it. "Their sights?" she asked.

"One of Alpha Seven was a woman, if you want to call her that."

McGarvey brought up the list on his iPad. Otto had come up with it from some old paper file buried in archives. Almost nothing had been written down except names, DOBs, and what evidently were faked medical data, including blood types.

"No woman on the list."

"Alex Unroth, from Philly or someplace out east. None of us were ever sure about one another. She was a good-looking girl, five years younger than the rest of us. She'd obviously been picked for the team because of her looks, though she turned out to be seriously tough. The rag heads totally lose their cool when a Western woman bats her eyelashes at them. She was one of our secret weapons."

"What else?" McGarvey asked.

Coffin hesitated. "I think she was the daughter of someone important. The way she acted, as if she were privileged, as if she were owed something. The way she talked. What she expected from us. She wasn't our control officer, but half the time she moved as if she were. And even our actual control officer deferred to her as if she were some VIP."

"Was she sleeping with him?"

Coffin laughed. "No, but she was having sex with him. All of us did at one point or another."

"Could she be the killer?" Pete asked. "Is she capable of something like that? Wager and Fabry were trained field officers. They couldn't have been all that easy to take down."

"She could have taken them down on one of their good days."

"Where is she?"

"I don't know. I didn't even know where Walt and Istvan had gotten themselves to until I read about their deaths. All I did know was someone would be coming for me sooner or later."

"Why?" McGarvey asked. He wanted not to believe Coffin, and yet the man's story had the ring of desperation—which was often one of truth.

"The cache in the mountains."

"Containing what?" McGarvey asked.

Coffin took a long time to say nothing, and McGarvey got the distinct impression that the man was truly afraid. Not of some killer coming for him, but of something else. Something even more important than a threat to his life.

FIFTEEN

"The Second Gulf War started on the twentieth of March oh three," Coffin said. "By then we'd been inside Iraq for three months, looking for WMDs, which we never really found. At least not the ones we'd been told to look for."

"What did you find?" McGarvey asked.

"Not what we were supposed to find."

Moshonas pushed away from the wall. "That's enough. This piece of shit will tell you only what he thinks you want to hear. He murdered a man in prison, and combined with his art theft conviction, he's going back."

"This is a matter for the CIA," Pete said. "We have the murders of two innocent men we have to figure out."

"The CIA has no jurisdiction in Greece."

"Take care, Special Agent," Coffin said, his voice quiet, but with conviction. "The NIS might not want to get involved."

Moshonas started to object, but McGarvey held him off. "What did you people find in the mountains? What was in the cache?"

"I need to tell you the circumstances about the other operators, because you're going to need that information if you're going to do something about the situation."

"That still exists after ten plus years?" Moshonas asked.

"Yes," Coffin said, and the way in which he said it, quietly, confidently, struck McGarvey as ominous.

"Let's start with Joseph Carnes right here in Athens," McGarvey suggested. "He was the first to die."

A light came into Coffin's eyes. "You think I killed him. It's why you came here. That's the connection you were looking for. Well, you're wrong. I never even knew he was here until I saw the squib in the paper about him being killed. They even had his real name, which meant he wasn't undercover."

"Was there a reason for you—and not him—to be hiding under an assumed identity?"

"You're damn right I was after Iraq. Check the Company's records. Every one of Alpha Seven quit the Company."

"Except for Wager and Fabry," Pete said.

"Yeah, and even hiding out in a place they figured was secure didn't help them in the end."

"Nor did it help you hiding in Korydallos," McGarvey said. "Are you sure it was Carnes? Did you go to the morgue and identify the body?"

"Are you kidding? Soon as he was killed, I came up with my little bit of fiction. I figured if I dropped out of circulation for a year, whoever it was might try somewhere else. Which they did. Joseph just made a dumb mistake, staying out in the open like that. He must have figured the threat was over and done with. But he was wrong."

"But now you're out. Maybe we should just cut you loose and see what happens."

"Carnes was the weakest link, and the oldest. We celebrated his thirtieth birthday in Munich a few days before we shipped out to our staging spot in Turkey, a place called Van, which was a hundred and fifty klicks from the Iraqi border. There was an airport there. Anyway, we all had too much to drink at the party, Joseph the most. He passed out, and we had to carry him back to our position. The instructors were pissed, but by that time it would have been impossible to replace anyone. We'd become a pretty good team."

"Letting off some steam isn't such a terrible thing before going into badland," Pete said. "Was there more?"

"He got drunk just about every night. We never found out where he got the stuff, but he was a damned good operator. One minute he was standing right next to you, and if you happened to turn away for just a second, he was gone. Never gave an explanation. Alex started calling him the Magician, and it stuck."

"You were the Chameleon, and Carnes was the Magician. What about the others? How about the woman?"

"We called her the Working Lady."

"She didn't mind?"

"None of us did. Walter was MP—Mister Ponderous. Istvan was the Refugee. Roy Schermerhorn was the Kraut, of course, and Tom Knight was the last to get his handle."

"Which was?"

"Don Quixote, because the day after we settled down in country, he wanted to go work, blowing up shit. There were big oil fields nearby, and he figured we could go down there and raise some hell."

"You were supposed to be looking for WMDs."

"Everybody knew they weren't there, just like

everybody knew the war was coming. Tom wanted to pave the way. Saddam's military wouldn't be very effective if they ran out of gas."

"But you didn't let him go."

"Of course not. Alex said he was just trying to tilt at windmills, which was how we came up with his handle. And he liked his more than the rest of us liked ours."

"What did you do?"

"Tracked the movements of military convoys, mostly. There was a lot of activity around Kirkuk."

"We were putting up Keyhole satellites as early as seventy-six," Pete said. "I expect they could have done a better job monitoring the military's goings-on up there."

"The Iraqis were smarter than that. They hid their shit right out in the open—up next to where waste gas was burning day and night. Infrared equipment was useless from overhead, but from ground level we didn't have that problem."

"So you did go down to the oil fields."

"Yes, but not to blow up anything, just to look," Coffin said.

"They must have had security patrols," McGarvey said.

"They were mostly easy to avoid."

"Mostly?"

"There were a couple of close calls."

"What'd you do with the bodies?"

"Buried them in the foothills," Coffin said. "Anyway, we were just going through the motions out there. Like I said, there were no WMDs, and everyone with half a brain at Langley knew it."

McGarvey suddenly got it, or at least part of what Coffin was leading up to. "You had to report by radio every day?"

"Every twenty-four-hour period on a rotating schedule. Never the same time of day or night. Encrypted burst transmissions to one of our spy birds in geosync orbit about thirty degrees above the horizon."

"Alpha Seven never found anything, but you didn't report it that way."

"Of course not," Coffin said. "When the war wound down, where do you think the coalition force inspectors went looking?"

"The caches Alpha Seven found and marked," McGarvey said. "All of it fiction."

Coffin looked over his shoulder at Pete, almost as if he were appealing to her for an understanding he wasn't getting from McGarvey. "Pretty much," he said. "May I have that glass of wine now?"

Pete went to the galley in the adjacent compartment and came back a minute later with a glass of red wine for Coffin, who sipped at it delicately and then smiled. "We should have stopped at my place first. I have a decent cellar."

"Pretty much . . . ?" McGarvey prompted.

"We got out shortly after the shooting began, but they wanted to hold us, possibly for our testimony in camera on the Hill. We got out the same way we came in: airlifted across the border into Turkey and from there Incirlik, then Ramstein and home, straight to Camp Peary, where we were debriefed."

"No weapons of mass destruction were ever found," Pete said.

"We were just another mission that had gotten things wrong."

"Not all your reports to headquarters were fiction. You said pretty much. Take me back to Iraq before the war began," McGarvey said.

SIXTEEN

It had begun to rain. They could hear the heavy drops hitting the decks, and the light from the partially open hatches had darkened, casting a pall over the mess. Pete got up to switch on a light, but McGarvey gestured her off. The gloom fit his mood just now, because he expected a line of bullshit from the former NOC, who was, after all, probably fighting for his life in the only way he knew how—the big lie, the big scam, the legerdemain, misdirection.

"The one and only report we transmitted that was an actual fact, they ignored," Coffin said. "Worse than that, I learned later they'd buried it. And all things considered, I suppose it was the right thing to do at the time."

"How'd you find out?" McGarvey asked. "I thought you and the others walked away?"

"We did, except for Walt and Istvan. Walt told me about it, and Istvan confirmed it. They were worried out of their wits. It was the last lifeline they were going to throw me. From that point I was on my own. Just like the others."

"Lifeline?" Pete asked.

"A bit of solid information I could use if the need ever arose. But *only* if it was important."

"Important enough to die for?" McGarvey asked. "Like now?"

Coffin nodded.

"Did the others also know this dark secret had been buried?"

"I think so."

"Is it why Wager and Fabry were murdered? And why you went deep?"

"Almost certainly."

"Did you ever get the feeling someone was coming after you?"

"Not until a couple of days ago," Coffin said. "Could I get a little more wine?"

Pete got up and took his glass. "What I don't get is why didn't you go public."

"You have to be kidding. My life was on the line as it was—still is—and if I'd blown the whistle, someone from the Company would have come after me."

"We don't assassinate our own people," Pete said, a very hard edge to her voice.

"Not unless there's a valid reason for it."

She looked at him for a moment then went to fetch more wine.

"Do you think your control officer—the guy who parachuted in—is the killer?" McGarvey asked.

"I've had a lot of time to think about it," Coffin said.

"It's only been a couple of days since the murders in the CIA."

"I knew someone would be coming for us."

"Who?"

"Either our control officer or Alex. They were a thing the moment he dropped into our camp. It's like they'd known each other all their lives."

"His name?"

Coffin smiled. "We came to think of him as the Avenging Angel. The first time he came down to the oil fields with us, he took out two roustabouts—I don't even think they were Iraqis. It didn't matter to him. The next time, Alex came with us—it was a first for her—and she was just as good and ruthless as he was. They made a hell of a pair."

"Avenging Angel—why that name?" Pete asked, coming back with the wine.

"The war was close, he told us, so it didn't matter how many bodies were stacked up in plain sight. He *wanted* the Mukhabarat to know someone was looking down on them and taking revenge for all their sins."

"They didn't send someone up to search for your guys?"

"They did for a couple of days, but when all hell began to break loose, they took off—some of them to the front but a lot of them across the border into the already big refugee camps in Turkey and Syria."

"You didn't call this guy by name?"

"George."

"American?" Pete asked.

Coffin shrugged. "Brooklyn maybe. An East Coast Jew. At least that's what I thought at the time."

"But you know better now," McGarvey said, careful to keep his voice neutral. He'd heard stories from Otto and others inside the Company, especially when he'd served briefly as the DCI, about hidden caches of money or heroin—besides the WMDs—in Iraq. But they were rumors. Popular myths. Internet "truths" that the conspiracy nuts loved to hash out.

"Damned right. It didn't make sense to me then. But I saw it with my own eyes, and gradually began to realize what had happened and why. I just didn't think they'd kill to keep it a secret. And especially not the way Walt and Istvan were done. But I understand now."

"We're listening," McGarvey said.

"The thing is, I don't think there's a damned thing you can do about it. You get involved, and you're a dead man walking."

"We're already involved," Pete said. "So tell us this big secret of yours."

"Shit," Coffin said. He was in distress. It had come to him slowly during the interview, and now he had a crazy look in his eyes, almost as if he were a wild animal that had been cornered. But the odds were so overwhelming, he didn't know how to fight back.

"Quit the bullshit," Moshonas said. "If you have something to say, get on with it, or I'll take you in this minute. And I won't give a damn if I have to shoot when you try to escape."

"You have to understand that it's more than what's buried in the hills above Kirkuk."

"An area where the inspectors never searched," Pete said.

Coffin nodded.

"So it's still there—whatever the *it* is."

Again Coffin nodded. "And it'll never be found unless you have the coordinates."

"Which you have."

"All of us did."

"Now it's only Knight, Schermerhorn, and the woman."

"Plus our control officer."

"What'd he say at your debriefing when you got back to the States?"

"He never came back with us. He got as far as Ramstein, but when we boarded the plane to come home, he wasn't aboard."

"Nobody ever mentioned him?" Pete asked.

"No."

"Not you or the others?" McGarvey asked.

"No."

"Why?"

"Because of what he told us about *Kryptos*. The solution to number four, he told us, would lead to what he called the 'empirical necessity.'"

Everyone in the mess knew about the encrypted sculpture in the courtyard outside the New Headquarters Building. Every day employees eating in the cafeteria looked at it, though most never really saw it.

"Only the first three panels have been decrypted so far," Pete said. "They're mostly nonsense."

"Except two talks about something buried in an unknown location," McGarvey said. "Otto mentioned it to me once."

"Did he solve four?" Coffin asked.

"Two has the latitude and longitude of the burial site, which, as I remember, was a couple of hundred feet or less southwest of the sculpture."

"That's wrong," Coffin said.

"And three is just a paraphrase of what the archeologist Howard Carter supposedly said when he looked inside the tomb of King Tut for the first time."

"Which leaves four. Maybe you should have Mr. Rencke try his hand at translating it before someone else is killed."

"You're saying whatever's on panel four makes sense of what's buried in the hills above Kirkuk."

"That's what George told us in the end, when he swore us to secrecy. 'The truth will come out sooner or later,' he said. 'When it does you'll understand. The entire world will understand the empirical necessity.'"

"So what's buried up there?" Pete asked.

Coffin got up and handed his empty glass to her. "Another one, please," he said. He moved around the table to one of the open portholes.

"Sit down," McGarvey said.

"I need some air," Coffin said, looking back. "The rain smells good."

"Sit down, God damn it."

Coffin was suddenly flung forward off his feet, a small red hole in the back of his head and his entire face exploding in a spray of blood, bones, and brain matter.

SEVENTEEN

Thomas Knight arrived at the CIA's ground-maintenance building just after six thirty in the morning. He was short, something under five ten, with a stocky build that had turned a little soft over the years. His eyes were wide and deep blue—his best feature, his wife, Stephanie, told him. The worst, the back of his head, where a bald spot was growing bigger every year.

This was his favorite time of the day, just before dawn, when everything was cool and peaceful. The campus always looked the prettiest to him at this hour. The lights of the OHB in the distance—American's bastion against the real world—safe and secure, reassuring.

He parked around the side, unlocked the service door, and powered up the three garage doors, behind which were the riding mowers, tree-trimmer buckets, and other grounds equipment.

He lit a cigarette and then brought the Starbucks he'd picked up on the way in from Garrett Park, across the river, to the open door, where he breathed deeply of the woodland scents.

He was wearing his usual white coveralls, the CIA's logo on the breast pocket, totally spotless. How his wife got the grass and mud stains out was the big mystery to the crew.

"She's a magician," one of the guys had said.

Knight had to smile, thinking about it. No, that had been Joseph, but he was dead now, like Walt and Istvan. And maybe the others, because none of them had stayed in contact once the op was finished and they'd been debriefed.

Larry Coffin had suggested they go deep and never make contact with one another.

They'd met at a McDonald's in Williamsburg just a few miles from the front gate at Camp Peary—the Farm. Even Alex had shown up, and she'd told them she'd never eaten at a McDonald's in her life.

"Yeah, right," Fabry said. "Even in Paris, on the Champs-Élysées, there is a McDonald's where you may have *le hamburger* and a glass of wine. And you have been to Paris."

"*Oui*, but lunch at Le Jules Verne," she'd said. It was the restaurant on the third level of the Eiffel Tower.

They'd all laughed, but the tension had run high that day, because once they left the restaurant, they would be on the run. And there was no telling how long it would be, if ever, before they could resurface.

"Hide the thimble," Carnes had said. It was the children's game in which a thimble used for sewing something by hand was placed out in the open when all the contestants were out of the room. When they came in, they were supposed to find it. But it was a frustrating game, because even though the tiny thimble—it was small enough to fit over the tip of someone's thumb—was in plain sight, almost everyone had a hard time seeing it.

Carnes was going to hide somewhere in plain sight, under the theory that if George were looking for them, he'd look deep, not on the surface.

But that hadn't worked.

Someone was coming, as he'd known they would

ever since they'd gotten back from Iraq and George wasn't with them. The fact that no one ever mentioned the man's name or his absence had been the clincher.

"Let sleeping dogs lie," the Magician had cautioned. "But go deep, at least for the time being."

The others had disappeared, except for Walter and Istvan, who, like him, had come back to the CIA, but under new identities. Nothing whatsoever connected them to their careers as NOCs, and especially not to Alpha Seven. Even their fingerprints, blood types, and DNA on record with the Company were false.

They'd learned to blend in—or at least they'd learned to enhance the skills of something they'd been doing most of their lives. The one thing they had in common was the ability to lie so convincingly that most of the time they believed it themselves.

Knight was a kid from Des Moines who'd been a dreamer all his life. He lived in books, and at times he played the roles of his heroes. Don Quixote had been his hands-down all-time favorite, for reasons even he couldn't say. But one of the guys—or maybe it was Alex, on one of their soul-searching evenings after they'd had sex—had found out about his near obsession and then came up with his operational handle. He'd never objected.

When he finished his cigarette, he went inside and started the wide-swath riding mower he was to use for this morning's assignment. He was working the fringe on both sides of the driveway up from the main gate to the OHB, and after lunch he and Karl Foreman would be working the slope from the rear of the OHB down to the woods, past and around the dome.

Mindless work, but satisfying for all of that, because until two days ago he'd begun to relax, begun to actually take a deep breath from time to time.

Before he got up on the seat, he pulled out his 9-mm Beretta 92F pistol and checked the load. No crazy son of a bitch—whether it was George, their control officer, or Alex, who Coffin never trusted—was going to get the better of him. Rumor was that Walt and Istvan had not only been murdered, but their bodies had been mutilated.

Crazy things had been done to the Kirkuk roustabouts, some of them not even Iraqis.

"We're here to send them a message," George had told them from day one.

And such a message they had sent that, when they got back, even their debriefers handled them with respect—and maybe a little fear. Alpha Seven consisted of the most out-of-control operators in the entire national clandestine service.

Knight put the pistol back in the holster strapped to his chest under his coveralls, and headed out the door and down the gravel path to the driveway a quarter of a mile away.

The morning shift hadn't started coming in yet, and the sun was just peeking over the horizon, the day still cool, the sky perfectly clear. Saturday he and Stephanie were thinking about driving down to Williamsburg for the day and maybe a night.

She was from St. Paul. "F. Scott Fitzgerald's town," as she liked to boast. As a kid, and still as a grown-up, she lived in her own literary fantasy world. It was one of the many reasons she and Knight had connected.

He'd chugged past the lower end of the parking lot and was turning onto the fringe beside the driveway when Foreman drove up in his Ford F-150, driver's window down, and pulled over.

"What the hell in sweet Jesus are you doing out here already?" he demanded. He was from Oklahoma, and at fifty-five had done his twenty and was retiring in a year or so. He liked Knight, but then again he liked everybody.

"Mowing the grass. What the hell does it look like I'm doing, you dumb Okie?"

Foreman tilted his head back and laughed from the bottom of his boots. "Dumb Okie—I gotta remember that one."

Knight had been calling him a dumb Okie since shortly after Knight had come to work here ten years ago.

"We're supposed work in pairs," Foreman said.

The order had come down two days ago after the murders.

"Whoever's doing it wants the spooks, not us," Knight said. "But if you're so goddamned worried, get your ass in gear and come on down."

Foreman laughed again. "Be down in a hog's fart," he said, and took off up the hill.

Whatever the hell that meant. Knight engaged the drive and started down the gently sloping hill, still a half hour or so before the early birds began showing up.

Barely one hundred yards down the hill, the engine began acting up, running rough, sputtering nearly to a stop, and then revving up as if the carburetor float were sticking.

Knight shut down the mowing blades, put the engine in neutral, locked the brakes, and dismounted, but before he could check the problem, the mower suddenly steadied out.

The equipment wasn't exactly new, but it was in good shape. Their two mechanics made sure of it.

All of a sudden the engine revved up to its maximum rpm, the mower blades suddenly engaged, and the machine lurched backward.

Knight tried to step away, but his left foot caught under the traction wheel and he was pulled off balance, falling backward.

The base of the machine climbed up over his lower legs and then knees, the pain impossible. He pulled out his walkie-talkie and keyed the push-to-talk switch. "Karl, you copy?" he shouted.

But then the edge of the mower blades bit into his feet, and he screamed.

He tried to push the heavy mower away, but the machine kept coming, the incredible, impossible pain climbing up his thighs.

When the three-feet-in-diameter blades reached his abdomen, he passed out, and when they reached his face, mangling it, he was already dead. Still the mower continued up the hill, blood and gore splashing down the slope and across the trunks of the trees.

EIGHTEEN

The NIS cleanup crew had come at once to remove the body and sanitize the boat. Searching for the shell casing would have to wait until first light, but it was obvious to McGarvey that Coffin had been shot with a high-power rifle and probably from a distance of a thousand yards or more. Something like the American-made .50 caliber Barrett sniper rifle could have done the job from as far as a mile out.

He and Pete rode with Moshonas back into the city and to their hotel at two in the morning.

"If the killer was sloppy, which I don't think he was, he would have left a shell casing lying around," McGarvey told the Greek intelligence officer.

"You're probably right, but it'll give our people something to do. Something to put in their report."

"What about us?" Pete asked. She was shook up, but she held her feelings close.

"I don't know," Moshonas said after a thoughtful hesitation. "What are we supposed to do with you? You'll have to at least come in for questioning."

"Tell me about Joseph Carnes's death," McGarvey said.

Moshonas gave McGarvey an odd look. "I don't know. He was killed in a car crash."

"His body crushed? Maybe burned in a fire?"

Moshonas shrugged. "What's your point?"

"How was the body identified? Was there a match with his passport photo?"

"As I recall, his face had been totally destroyed."

They were sitting in the car in the hotel's driveway, one piece of the puzzle dropping into place for McGarvey. Carnes, Wager, Fabry, and now Coffin had all been killed by the same person, who had left them some bizarre message by wiping out their faces, erasing their identities.

Moshonas got the connection. "Whoever shot Coffin waited until he turned around so they could hit him in the back of his head, destroying his face."

"It was the same with the two men killed at CIA headquarters," McGarvey said.

"Two here in Athens and two in Washington. Leaves three on the original team plus the mysterious control officer. One of them is the killer?"

"It's possible."

"Find them before someone else dies," Moshonas said.

"That's why we came here."

"Too late," Moshonas said. "And now you're returning to Washington, or wherever the others are. Do you know where?"

"No," McGarvey had to admit, but he had a bad feeling they were going to find out and very soon.

Moshonas nodded. "Then I wish you good hunting. No one will interfere with your leaving in the morning. But when it's over, I'd like to sit down with you two over a couple of beers and hear the whole story. Whatever is buried out there is important enough to kill for. I'd like to know what it is."

"Any ideas?" Pete asked.

"Many of them. But none that make sense."

* * *

When they got upstairs, Pete jumped into the shower, and McGarvey opened a Heineken and went out to the eighth-floor balcony. Syntagma Square was lit up as it always was, and a few people wandered around, despite the hour.

To him, the city had always smelled like what he thought olive oil and fresh fish should, clean with a sense of something good, something promising. But this morning the city smelled like death. Like old mothballs, an old lady's sachet, scents to cover something disagreeable.

The CIA's old acronym for why people spied was MICE: money, ideology, conscience, or ego. Except for Alpha Seven's control officer telling them that the solution to the puzzle would show that what was buried above Kirkuk was an empirical necessity, he would have bet anything that the motivation was either money or ego, or a combination of both. But he wasn't so sure now.

He called the CIA's travel agency in Paris and, using his coded phrase, booked first-class seats for him and Pete on the British Airways flight out of Athens leaving in the early afternoon and getting to Dulles at eight thirty in the evening. Otto had set up the account for him a few days ago, and though finance would bitch about first class versus economy or even business, he didn't give a damn.

Nor thinking about it did he wonder if he gave a damn about a group of NOCs taking some grudge out on one another. It happened once in a while. These people, living out in the cold very often for years at a time, developed deep-seated paranoid fantasies that sometimes tipped them over the edge into insanity. Sometimes they put a pistol into their mouth and pulled the trigger. More often they got divorces or went from one affair to another, looking for something they couldn't even define.

They were more likely than the average person to explode in road rage, or become drunks or drug addicts. Half of them walked around feeling superior to the rest of the world, while the other half slunk into dark alleys, their eyes downcast, convinced they were no better than pond scum.

A few became thieves. And a few became murderers.

Yet without them, we would lose the same war we had been fighting for two-plus centuries. No one was beating down the walls to immigrate to China. No one was crossing some ocean to illegally reach Angola or Vietnam or Yemen or Iran or Iraq. But they sure as hell were stowing away on ships, crossing rivers, even taking leaky old rust buckets from Cuba or Haiti to reach the U.S. And for the most part even the poor people getting out of Syria because of the conflict loved their home country, and wanted to go home as soon as it was safe to return.

The real problem wasn't illegal immigrants; it was the kind of people who were so seriously pissed off that everyone wanted to come here, they were willing to kill to stop it, knock it down, make the point that whatever ideology floated their boat was the *only* ideology—the U.S. was the land of the Satans that had to be destroyed.

"A penny," Pete said, coming out to the balcony. She wore only a bath towel, and her hair was still damp.

"I have no idea what the hell they want, and it's driving me crazy."

"Money?" she suggested. "I was thinking a stash of heroin, a cash cow on the open market. Or maybe someone grabbed a bunch of Saddam's gold at the end and hid it up there until things settled down and they could go back for it."

McGarvey shrugged.

"But it isn't that easy, is it?"

"Never is."

She took the beer from him, and drank some. "There's nothing left here for us," she said.

"We're going back to DC, but the flight doesn't leave till after one."

"Good, I'm tired."

McGarvey's cell phone rang on the bed, and he went inside to answer it. Otto was on the line, and he sounded breathless.

"We've had another one, about two hours ago," he said.

He motioned for Pete. "I'm putting this on speakerphone. What happened?"

"Marty's sent a Gulfstream from Ramstein for you guys. The whole place is in an uproar. No one knows what the hell to do."

"Tell me," McGarvey said, not at all surprised.

"He was a goddamned groundskeeper, name of Bob Maddox. Worked for the subcontractors about ten years. Happened before seven this morning our time. Looked like an accident. He was run over by his own moving machine and ripped all to hell. I found out about it twenty minutes ago, and what struck me right off the bat was that his face had been destroyed. I told security to look for a remote-control device, which they found. FM band, line of sight. They screwed with the engine, and when he got off to check it out, the machine backed over him, the mower blades running. Makes three."

"Five," McGarvey said, and he told Otto about Carnes and Coffin.

"Two to go," Otto said.

"There was a control officer Coffin only knew as George. Maybe Brooklyn, a Jew."

"Only seven show on the op file."

"This guy along with the woman—Alex Unroth—supposedly were quite the pair. If anyone would know the control officer, it would be her."

ΠΙΠΣΤΣΣΠ

Security at the CIA's main gate was tighter than it had ever been, and Marty Bambridge himself had to drive down to personally vouch for McGarvey and Pete, even though they had been picked up at Andrews by a pair of CIA security officers in a Company Cadillac SUV. And even though Mac had once been the DCI.

They followed the deputy director back up to the VIP parking garage in the OHB.

"What about your bags, sir?" one of the security officers asked.

"Have someone take them up to the impound area. They can pick them up on the way out," Bambridge said. The impound area was actually a locker where items people weren't allowed to bring past security in the lobby were kept while they were inside.

McGarvey and Pete surrendered their weapons, which included a couple of extra magazines of ammunition and, in Mac's case, a silencer.

"Did you find Larry Coffin?" Bambridge asked in the elevator on the way up to the seventh floor.

"Yeah, but someone shot him to death while Pete and I and an NIS officer were interviewing him," McGarvey said.

"Good Lord. Any notion who the shooter was?"

"A couple of ideas, and no one will be happy about what we found out."

Bambridge scowled. "No one usually is when you get back from one of these things," he said. "But it's not over, is it?"

"Not by a long shot."

Walt Page was waiting for them in his office, along with Carleton Patterson, the CIA's general counsel. Otto breezed in right after them, a flushed look on his round face. It looked as if he hadn't slept or changed clothes since Serifos.

"I can't lie to you and say we're making much progress here, and that the campus isn't in nearly complete shambles," Page said. "So I hope you two have brought something useful back from Athens."

"How'd you know Maddox was one of the Alpha Seven operators? Larry Coffin told us none of their real fingerprints or DNA samples were on record."

"Otto gave us the heads-up when he told us to

look for a remote-control device, which we found," Bambridge said. "Soon as it was confirmed it wasn't an accident, we went looking in the old files."

"I found photographs of all of them," Otto said. "Knight's was the closest match. He was one of two cryptographers on the team, and one of the guys he works with on the maintenance crew said he was always messing around with puzzles, like Sudoku, the Rubik's Cube, stuff like that."

"You weren't authorized to conduct interviews," Bambridge snapped. "Stick to your computers." He was totally on edge.

"Just a phone call. I needed to make sure of the match. At this point it looks as if Wager and Fabry were hiding in the open, but Knight was here under a work name."

"He was the most frightened," Pete suggested.

"Of what, my dear girl?" Patterson asked. He was an old man, nearly eighty, and long past his retirement age. But he loved the business and, he'd confided to McGarvey a few years back, most of the people.

"Me excluded?" McGarvey had pulled his leg, one of their rare lighter moments.

"You especially. Because you're just about the last of a dying breed I most admire. A true conservative without any left-wing biases or right-wing allegiances."

The insiders, the few people in the Agency who had known McGarvey almost from the beginning, had slapped the moniker of Superman on him—behind his back, of course—when he served as DCI. Superman's motto from the beginning had been: "Truth, justice, and the American way." Those few words pretty well summed up who and what he was.

"Afraid of exactly what happened to him," she replied.

"And why," McGarvey added.

Everyone looked at him, the moment frozen in glass. Bambridge especially wanted to know; he was clearly the most agitated.

"What happened in Athens?" Page asked, breaking the silence. "What did you two find?"

"We found Larry Coffin, the fourth member of Alpha Seven, serving time in Korydallos prison for art theft."

"He's okay," Bambridge said.

"He was shot to death while we were interviewing him in an NIS safe house. A high-power rifle, possibly a Barrett. They took a shot through an open porthole to the back of his head."

"Destroying his face," Bambridge said softly. "A pattern. Someone is targeting the Alpha Seven operators. But why, for heaven's sake? That war's been over for a long time; it's not like Iran or Syria. And why the mutilations?"

"We don't know yet, but it means something to the killer or killers, and there's more."

"There always is," Bambridge said.

McGarvey took his time going over everything he and Pete had done and learned, including their connection with Spiros Moshonas, the NIS officer, and the manner in which Carnes had died, his face completely destroyed.

"That is a great deal to take in," Patterson said, making the understatement. "But aside from whatever supposedly has been hidden in some mountain cache in Iraq, Alpha Seven wasn't the only team looking for weapons of mass destruction over there. All of them consistently reported that they'd found nothing. Only the one team was sending glowing reports."

Bambridge shot him a look, and Patterson smiled.

"I have access to operational records. I can read and draw conclusions," Patterson said. He turned back to McGarvey. "But there were none, of course, and you're saying the team sent false reports to steer the inspectors away from the cache—whatever it contained."

"And suddenly, after all these years, someone is running around killing all the Alpha Seven people, to keep the secret, maybe because someone is getting too close to finding it or knowing about it? What?"

"The manner in which they were murdered has significance," Page said. "We're being sent a message."

"Or it's simply the work of someone truly deranged," Bambridge said. "Which is something I think is more likely. Even if there is this something— whatever—buried in the hills, it'd be damned near impossible to go back, dig it up, and get it out without some al-Qaeda nut case or some trigger-happy Taliban hill people finding out."

"A brilliant someone," McGarvey said. "Among perhaps two or three people—the two left from the old Alpha Seven team and their control officer, whose identity we don't have yet."

"Whoever it is, they're still out there, and they have money and intelligence resources," Otto said.

"Mac gave me the bank account number and password for the guy Larry Coffin was using as a substitute prisoner in Korydallos. He wanted to confirm that Coffin was the paymaster. Well, he might not have been. I've found most of his money in Athens and a few other places, but the money to pay the substitute came from Bank Yahav, a password account, of course, and a pretty sophisticated one. Has to be more than eight characters. One of my darlings has been working the problem for six hours and hasn't come up with the solution yet. But it'll happen."

"Israel?" Pete asked.

"Yeah, Jerusalem," Otto said. "But you guys won't like the next part. The full name translated from Hebrew, is 'Bank Yahav for Government Employees Limited.'"

All the air left the room.

Page sat back, a stunned look on his face, his mouth set. "I don't know if I very much want to go in that direction," he said.

"It's not a government bank," Otto said. "Just a government employees' bank. Like one of our government employees' credit unions."

"Does it mean Coffin was working for the Israelis?" Bambridge asked. "I don't get it."

"Either that, or someone knew about Coffin's situation and paid the substitute fee," McGarvey said.

"Why?" Page asked.

A dozen threads were running through McGarvey's head, the first of which was panel four of the *Kryptos* sculpture. "I don't know," he said absently. "But I'm going to ask them just that."

TWENTY

Otto's safe house in Georgetown was a three-story brownstone with a parking area and a garden in the rear. From the outside, it looked ordinary, like just about every other brownstone in the neighborhood. But inside it was comfortable and completely impervious to mechanical or electronic surveillance of any sort.

He and Louise had another safe house, off the grid so far as the CIA was concerned, in McLean—a traditional colonial where they lived when their daughter, Audrey, was in residence. But whenever there was trouble, like now, Audie, who was going on four, was sent to Camp Peary, and he and Louise came here.

Otto called ahead, and when he got home with McGarvey and Pete in tow, Louise had cold beers laid out, baked potatoes keeping warm in the oven, and steaks on the barbie.

She and Pete hugged. "How about putting together a salad? Everything's in the fridge."

"Glad to," Pete agreed.

Louise and McGarvey hugged. "So, Otto tells me you've got another bone in your teeth. This one not so nice or tidy as some of the others." She was a tall woman, well over six feet and slender. She was almost as bright as her husband, and for a long time worked as chief photo analyst for the National Security Agency. Now she was Otto's partner in every meaning of the term.

"Five people are dead already, and it's likely at

least one more will be murdered soon," McGarvey said.

She sat him down at the kitchen counter and gave him a Dos Equis with a lime in the neck of the bottle, but no glass. She gave Otto a bottle of lemon-flavored carbonated water.

"I need to tend to the steaks," she said, and went out to the rear patio.

Otto set up his tablet, which had once been an iPad until he and a couple of friends in the science and technology directorate had modified it, and brought up the *Kryptos* file, with detailed photographs of the main sculpture itself, along with the translations of the first three panels.

"Coffin said it was an empirical necessity," Otto said.

Pete was across from them, pulling the salad fixings out of the fridge. "Not logical, but empirical," she said. "What do you make of it? Was their control officer just blowing smoke rings?"

"Logical wouldn't work—nothing mathematical about something buried in the hills, except for the fact itself. A latitude and longitude. There'd be no consequences. But an empirical necessity? Whatever's up there could change things their control officer thought should be necessary."

"Coffin guessed him to be from Brooklyn, maybe a Jew. And the bank you came up with is for Israeli government employees."

"Mossad?" Pete suggested.

Otto looked up from his tablet. "It's a thought. Iraq's certainly in the neighborhood, a possible staging point for an attack through Syria's back door. Maybe a staging point for an attack against Iran. Or at least it was when we had serious boots on the ground there."

"Something the Israelis knew couldn't last," Mc-Garvey said. "We were going to leave sooner or later."

"Doesn't explain why they want the Alpha Seven operators dead," Pete said.

"They know what's in the cache, and for some reason the Israelis want them to keep quiet about it," Otto said.

"Okay, but despite the timing, why the brutality? The way those guys were murdered is not the methodology of an intelligence service. It's more like that of total insanity."

"Pete's right," Louise said, coming in with a platter of steaks. "Who fits that sort of a profile?"

"And what's their agenda? What do they want?"

Otto brought up the translations of the first three panels. "Okay, here it goes. You know that the sculptor, Jim Sanborn, worked with Ed Scheidt, who headed up our Cryptographic Center, to come up with the codes. And Jim said there was a riddle within a riddle that could only be solved after all four panels were decrypted. So far only the first three have been cracked."

"Why haven't you played around with it?" Pete asked. "It's right up your alley, isn't it?"

"It's a toy, and I've always been busy with real shit, ya know? Bill Webster, when he was DCI, is supposedly the only one Sanborn gave the plaintext to, but wasn't much after that when Sanborn reneged and said he'd not given the entire decryption. Show business."

"But not now," Pete said.

"Panel one," he said, bringing up a printout of the letters chiseled into the copper plate. "It's a periodic polyalphabetic substitution cipher using ten alphabets, and was actually quite simple. I checked it, and the decryption seems valid. They used the old Vigenère tableau, just about the same one they used on two. Anyway, the key words were *Kryptos*—Greek for "hidden"—and *Palimpsest*—also Greek, for a manuscript page on which the writing has been erased so some new text can be set down."

He brought up the decrypted text and turned the iPad around so everyone could read it.

BETWEEN SUBTLE SHADING AND THE ABSENCE OF
LIGHT LIES THE NUANCE OF IQLUSION.

"Doesn't make a lot of sense," Louise said. "And there's a misspelling."

"Sanborn supposedly put the *q* in to keep the code breakers on their toes," Otto said. He brought up the much longer decryption for panel two. "Same substitution cipher, except this time he used only eight alphabets, and the key words were *Kryptos* and *Abcissa*—which is a high-school math term for the 'horizontal position on a two-dimensional graph.'"

IT WAS TOTALLY INVISIBLE. HOW'S THAT POSSIBLE?
THEY USED THE EARTH'S MAGNETIC FIELD X THE
INFORMATION WAS GATHERED AND TRANSMITTED

UNDERGROUND TO AN UNKNOWN LOCATION X DOES
LANGLEY KNOW ABOUT THIS ? THEY SHOULD IT'S
BURIED OUT THERE SOMEWHERE X WHO KNOWS
THE EXACT LOCATION ? ONLY WW THIS WAS HIS LAST
MESSAGE X THIRTY-EIGHT DEGREES FIFTY-SEVEN
MINUTES SIX-POINT-FIVE SECONDS NORTH SEVENTY-
SEVEN DEGREES EIGHT MINUTES FORTY-FOUR
SECONDS WEST X LAYER TWO

"It mentions something buried," Louise said. "But
that latitude and longitude isn't in Iraq; it's right
here."

"Actually, about one hundred fifty feet southeast
of the sculpture," Otto said. "So far as I know, nothing's been found there. But that could have been a
ruse to throw everyone off. Maybe the key was 'it's
buried out there somewhere.'"

"WW, William Webster?"

"That's the current thinking, but he's never been
willing to answer any questions about it. Like I said,
I always thought the thing was nothing more than a
toy."

He brought up the decryption for the third panel.
"This one is a transposition cipher. A regular mathematical system that shifts the letters on the sculpture
to the plaintext ones."

SLOWLY DESPERATELY SLOWLY THE REMAINS OF
PASSAGE DEBRIS THAT ENCUMBERED THE LOWER
PART OF THE DOORWAY WAS REMOVED WITH
TREMBLING HANDS I MADE A TINY BREACH IN THE
UPPER LEFT-HAND CORNER AND THEN WIDENING THE
HOLE A LITTLE I INSERTED THE CANDLE AND PEERED

IN THE HOT AIR ESCAPING FROM THE CHAMBER
CAUSED THE FLAME TO FLICKER BUT PRESENTLY
DETAILS OF THE ROOM WITHIN EMERGED FROM THE
MIST X CAN YOU SEE ANYTHING Q

"It's Howard Carter talking when he opened King
Tut's tomb in 1922. And the question at the end was
asked by Lord Carnarvon, who was standing right
there. To which Carter supposedly said something
like: 'Yes, wonderful things.' "

"The big problem is the dates," Pete said. "The
sculpture was dedicated in ninety, which means Sanborn must have been working on the thing in the
late eighties. But Alpha Seven didn't get to Iraq until
the spring of oh three. So unless the guy could see
into the future, the coded message has nothing to do
with what's hidden outside of Kirkuk."

"Coffin didn't mention anything about them
burying whatever was out there—just that they saw
it," McGarvey said. "Could have been buried before *Kryptos* was devised. Webster was the DCI
from eighty-seven to ninety-one. Maybe it was buried
then."

"Maybe he knew about it," Pete said.

"Or maybe it was buried five thousand years ago,"
Otto said. "But I'm betting in the last five or ten
years."

"Why?" McGarvey asked.

Otto brought up the fourth panel. "This one hasn't
been solved yet, even though a lot of seriously bright
cryptographers have been working on it since ninety.
A few years ago Sanborn published a clue. He said

letters sixty-four through sixty-nine—*NYPVTT*—en clair read BERLIN."

He turned the iPad so everyone could see the screen. It was split in two columns of fourteen lines each.

```
NGHIJLMNQUVWXZKRYPTOS     TMQSRSYUZMRYDKRYPTOS
ABCDEFGHIJOHIJMNQUVWX     ABCDEFGHIJDPYSHJQMLKUC
```

"They're different," Pete said.

"Yes," Otto said dreamily. "The column on the left is the one that's been published since 1990. The one that's in all the books and on every Internet site. The one the code breakers have been working on since then."

"The one on the right?" Pete asked.

Otto looked up at her and then Louise and finally McGarvey. "I took that picture this morning."

"Jesus," McGarvey said. "Someone changed the panel."

"Probably not long ago. Otherwise, someone might have noticed it," Otto said. He brought up a photograph of a husky-looking man with a broad Teutonic face and square jaw. "Until last year this guy worked for us as a maintenance man. Name was Ludwig Mann. Part of his job was cleaning the outsides of all the buildings on campus, including the New Headquarters Building."

"In the courtyard of which is *Kryptos*."

Otto brought up another photograph, this one of a man who could have been a very close relative of Mann. Hair a little thicker, a face bit thinner, but with the same jaw and eyes. "Roy Schermerhorn," Otto said. "Alpha Seven."

"Let's put something up on an encrypted site the CIA normally uses to contact its officers, that Carnes and Coffin were murdered in Athens," McGarvey said. "We want the rest of Alpha Seven to contact us immediately because their lives are in danger."

"The killer will see it too," Pete said.

"Right. In the meantime, Otto can work on cracking the new code on four."

"My darlings are working on it right now."

"What about us?"

"We're going to see if we can find Mr. Schermerhorn. He somehow changed the message on four, which means he knows something and maybe has posted a warning."

"Where do we start?"

"His social security number when he worked here. It'll be a fake, of course, but it'll list an address."

"And?" Pete said.

"I'm betting that once the message goes up on the bulletin board, someone will be calling in," McGarvey said.

"Or one of the other team members will get themselves killed," Louise said.

"If they're as good as they're supposed to be, they'll know that the killer has also seen the message and they'll be on their guard. But for now Roy Schermerhorn is our best bet."

TWENTY-ONE

On the way home from the Milwaukee Public Library, Roy Schermerhorn took a great deal of care with his tradecraft, switching buses twice, backtracking his way for several blocks downtown. Stopping to light a cigarette while he watched the reflections in a store window of people and cars. Watching the roof lines for snipers. Even a passing police cruiser gave him pause.

He turned suddenly and walked into a tavern already busy mostly with people in suits and ties stopping in for a drink or two before going home. This was beer town USA; stopping in for a beer and a shot after work was the norm.

Sitting at the end of the bar from where he could watch the front door and the short hall back to the restrooms, he ordered a Mich Ultra draught.

Ever since he'd moved here, his normal weekday routine was to stop at the library after work to use one of its computers to cruise the Internet, especially the CIA bulletin boards, and the numerous *Kryptos* sites. Until this afternoon nothing concrete had been happening, though the campus apparently was conducting some sort of a lockdown drill. One day of which would have been understandable, but it had been going on for three days now.

Then this afternoon he'd used an old password to get into one of the encrypted sites the Company used as a bulletin board, and the Alpha Seven message popped up.

His beer came, and he forced himself to raise the

glass with a steady hand, though he was truly more frightened than he'd ever been since '03, after they'd gotten out and George had disappeared.

Carnes had left first, and a couple of months later Coffin had come over to where Schermerhorn had been living at the time, in Chevy Chase, and said he was going to disappear for a while.

"Just to be on the safe side," he said. "You know how it's probably going to work out."

"No, I don't," Schermerhorn had told him, though he did know what he expected everyone else had figured out. But he had wanted to hear it from Coffin's mouth.

"Alex has disappeared."

"Probably went with George."

"That's right, and you know damned well where that is. And why she left."

"I know where. Why don't you tell me why?"

"Don't be so goddamned dense, you dumb Kraut. The shit's probably about to hit the fan. My guess is that someone has either found the cache, or is about to, and all of us are going to be in the crosshairs."

"You think one of us will be blamed for blowing the whistle?"

"Of course I do. I'm going deep, and I suggest you do too. Right now. And I do mean *right* now."

They'd been sitting on the balcony of Schermerhorn's third-floor apartment. He lived alone, except for Henry, his cat, and after his brief but superintense fling with Alex, he preferred things that way. "Where are you going?"

Coffin got to his feet. "Take care of yourself," he'd said, and walked out the door.

Schermerhorn had thought about going away too, but he could not leave things just like that, or else the Georges and Alexes of the world would win. He spent the next two weeks altering his appearance, thinning his hair, aging his face, and building himself a new legend, complete with social security number, driver's license, military records, and even photos of a family he didn't have. Bulletproof enough that when he applied for a job as a maintenance man at the CIA, he would pass the background investigation.

It took nearly six weeks before he was hired and had started on the job, and nearly another year before he got into the position he'd wanted. When he was finished, he walked away, changed his appearance and legend again, and disappeared to Milwaukee, where he got a job managing a Hess station and convenience store.

Mindless work, not satisfying but bearable because of Janet, his live-in girlfriend. They wouldn't last for the long haul, of course, nor would Milwaukee. All of it here was designed to be disposable, like just about every previous day of his life had been.

And it had worked until now.

Someone in a sports coat and tan slacks, his tie loose, came in, and Schermerhorn stiffened, until the bartender pulled out a Bud and set it on the bar for the man. He was a regular, and he didn't look like George.

Schermerhorn finished his beer, paid for it, and left the bar. Two blocks later he caught a cab and gave the driver an address a couple of blocks away from the small house he and Janet rented. She worked as a nurse at Columbia St. Mary's Hospital on North Lake Drive and would be getting home about now.

He called her cell phone, but she didn't answer, and the call flipped over to voice mail. A little thrill niggled at the nape of his neck. She always answered her phone when she was on break or away from the hospital. She had a lot of friends she texted on what seemed like an around-the-clock schedule.

"What do you guys talk about?" he'd asked once.

She'd just smiled at him. "Stuff."

He didn't normally carry a weapon with him, though his 9-mm Beretta was stashed behind some paint cans in the one-car garage. But since the bulletin board announcement and Janet's not answering her phone, he wished he had it now.

The tree-lined street where the cabby dropped him off was a typical Milwaukee neighborhood—mostly small houses, some of them bungalows, many with brick fronts and almost all with fireplace chimneys. For now it was very neat and orderly, but once the leaves turned and started to drop, the place would be a mess. As fast as you raked them up and bundled them in big lawn and leaf bags, the more would fall.

Used to be you could burn them, and fall in the upper Midwest had always smelled of smoke. Pleasant.

He phoned her again, but she didn't answer. He shut the phone off and then removed the back and pulled the battery. He tossed the pieces behind some bushes spread over a full block.

At the corner half a block from their house, he

didn't slow down, but almost instantly he cataloged everything going on. No strange cars or trucks or vans. The Wilson boys shooting hoops across the street two doors down from his house. Douglas driving up in his old Saturn SUV. He waved when he got out, and Schermerhorn waved back.

No cops, no sirens, no fire trucks or ambulances.

Their car was in the driveway. Janet usually put it in the garage.

Everything else was normal, but Schermerhorn's instincts were screaming in high gear. He remembered an instructor from the Farm telling them one of the Murphy's laws the SEAL Team Six operators swore by: *if everything is going good, you're probably running into an ambush.*

It felt like that now.

He crossed the street in front of his house and let himself into the garage by the side door, got his Beretta, checked the load and the action, and stepped across the paved path to the kitchen door.

Janet was on her back in the doorway to the dining room. One leg was crossed over the other. She was still wearing her sneakers, but she usually took them off as soon as she came in the house. The shirt of her blue scrubs was completely drenched with blood. The left side of her neck had been ripped away, and most of her face had been destroyed.

He only knew it was her because of her clothes, her size, and the fact that this was their house. She belonged here.

Her blood was already well coagulated, so what happened here had happened an hour or more ago. Someone had to have called her at the hospital and told her there was an emergency and she needed to come home immediately.

Holding the pistol in the two-handed shooter's grip, he checked the house, but the killer was long gone. They'd left a message: *Not only aren't you safe, but anyone close to you is a valid target.*

Back in the kitchen, he looked at Janet's body for a long ten seconds, not able to keep himself from imagining what it had been like for her.

But then he stuffed the pistol into his belt, got her keys from the counter, went back out to the garage— where from an old paint can he retrieved a plastic baggie that held an ID kit including a passport that identified him as Howard Tucker—then got in the car and drove away.

TWENTY—TWO

Pete shared a cab into the city with McGarvey. She had an apartment just off Dupont Circle, and the afternoon work traffic was terrible, as it usually was on a workday, so it took forever to get from Langley, the fare almost sixty dollars.

They didn't say much to each other on the way in, McGarvey's thoughts drifting between the new message on panel four, the Alpha Seven mission in Iraq in '03, and the nature in which the operators were being killed one by one. Only two were left now— Schermerhorn and Alex Unroth—plus the control officer, which narrowed the list of possible killers.

But the real clue, Otto had told them derer's intel sources.

He or she knew not only the security and routines inside the campus, which al them to make the three strikes, but they'd also known how to find Carnes and somehow manage to kill him and track down Coffin to the NIS safe house.

Only someone very well connected could have possibly known all of that. And in such a timely fashion.

"Come up for a minute. We need to talk," Pete said, breaking him out of his thoughts.

The cabby had pulled up to the curb, and Pete was paying with a credit card.

"It'll be a while before Otto comes up with anything, and I need to take a shower and get some sleep."

"Five minutes, God damn it," she said, her tone brittle.

"Do you want me to wait?" the driver asked.

"No," McGarvey said. He got his bag out of the trunk and followed Pete up to her second-floor apartment. He had a fair idea what she wanted to say to him, and he didn't want to hear it. He wasn't ready, and they were in the middle of something he couldn't quite grasp. It was just at the edges, but he wasn't there yet.

"May I fix you a drink?" Pete asked. "Something to eat? You must be starved."

They hadn't eaten since the flight from Greece.

"I'm cutting you loose," McGarvey said.

"Loose? What are you talking about?"

his is getting too dangerous. It could have been you in Piraeus instead of Coffin. I'm taking this the rest of the way alone."

"I don't want to hear it. Don't forget it was me and Otto who came to you in Serifos in the first place."

"You'll be safer staying here."

"Yeah, like Wager and Fabry and Knight. The story has gotten out, and it's only a matter of time before the media gets ahold of it, and when that happens, just about anyone on campus will be out of the loop. Everyone will become a suspect. Just getting in and out will mean running the gauntlet. And if there're any shooters out there, we'll all be sitting ducks."

"It can't be helped."

Pete was stricken. "Can you at least tell me where the hell you're going?"

"That depends on Schermerhorn and Alex Unroth, whoever contacts us first. But I suspect I'll end up in Jerusalem at the government employees bank and then Tel Aviv."

"You think the Mossad is somehow involved?"

"I think their control officer is or was a Mossad operative."

"You'll need someone to cover your back. It's something I've done before."

"I'm not going to risk it," McGarvey said. "You're staying here."

"What?" Pete shrieked. She put a hand to her mouth and turned away for a moment. "I'm not going to do this, God damn it." She turned back. "I'm not your dead wife, Kirk. She wasn't a professional, and from what I read in the case file, she wasn't even the target—you were."

All that horrible time came blasting back at him in one ugly piece. He'd been in the car behind the limo in which Katy and their daughter were riding from the funeral of their daughter's husband when the limo drove over an IED. Right in the middle of Arlington National Cemetery. They'd been killed instantly, with absolutely zero chance for survival. Nothing of their bodies had been identifiable, except by their DNA.

Every woman he'd ever allowed to get close to him had died, had been murdered because of him. It was a never-ending nightmare from which he couldn't escape, not even hiding on Serifos.

"The Company has trained me well. I can take care of myself and you know it, so whatever reason you're cutting me loose has nothing to do with protecting a helpless female. If I were a man, it would be different."

"It's not that," McGarvey said, knowing damn well what was coming.

"What about Otto, then? He's still on campus. Don't you think it's possible someone will come after him? Or what about Louise, at their safe house? How about her life?"

"They were never Alpha Seven."

"Neither was I."

McGarvey picked up his bag from where he had dropped it by the door. "Take care of yourself," he said.

"I've fallen in love with you," Pete said.

"Don't."

"Don't what? Do you think I need this, or want it?"

"I work alone."

"Don't make me beg, Kirk," Pete cried. "I will, if I have to. I don't have a shred of self-respect left when it comes to you. I'll do anything you say. Just don't tell me to turn my back and let you walk away."

McGarvey dropped the bag. "I don't want you to get hurt," he said. "It's as simple as that. People around me tend to become targets."

"And I don't want you to get hurt."

McGarvey was at a loss for words. The situation was surreal, and yet he'd been here, done that before. Too many times before.

She laughed. It was strained. "How many interrogators do you know who're also good shots?"

It had been wrong for him to come up here, knowing what she was probably going to say to him. And he felt bad for her that she was pleading this way. And yet he wanted to take her into his arms and make love to her. And that was the problem. Once that happened between them, he would never take her into the field with him. Out there, he watched his own back. If he got shot, it was *his* fault, *his* problem, no one else's. And he wanted to keep it that way. Clean and simple.

On the other hand, if he did bring her with him, if he did allow her into his inner circle and they worked together on this thing, and something happened to her, he didn't know how he would be able to live with himself.

He didn't know if he could handle such a loss

again, because he felt very deep down, in some secret compartment, that he, too, was beginning to fall in love with her. He felt guilty for betraying Katy and yet . . . and yet . . .

His cell phone chirped. It was Otto.

"Where are you?"

"I'm at Pete's apartment. What's happened?"

"Roy Schermerhorn made contact through the bulletin board. He wants to meet in the next twelve hours."

"Where?" McGarvey asked. He switched the phone to speaker mode so Pete could hear.

"Anywhere except the campus."

"How about the Farm?"

"No. Somewhere neutral. He wants an escape route, if from no one else than us."

"Union Station," Pete said. "Below the Attic block on the main floor."

Otto heard her. "Good. Exactly where and when?"

"*Prometheus*—the statue. Ten tonight."

"Stand by, he's online," Otto said.

Pete looked at McGarvey. "It's a break," she said.

"Eight in the morning," Otto said. "And there's a potential problem. His live-in was murdered—and he's the main suspect."

"Where?" McGarvey asked.

"Milwaukee."

"Can you confirm it?"

"An APB for Dana Peterson," Otto said. "I've aged the one photo of him we have—I'll send it. But he could have altered his appearance as well as his name."

TWENTY-THREE

McGarvey and Pete showed up at the south entrance of Union Station by seven in the morning, and they had a clear sight line on the huge statue of fire above the main floor. The place was chockablock with commuters, mostly those coming into the city, and just about everyone was in a hurry.

Otto had sent them an old file photo of Schermerhorn that was useless except in a very general sort of way—mostly the man's build and the shape of his head and face. But Otto had sent back decent photos of Mac and Pete.

"Makes us sitting ducks," she'd said last night.

They'd agreed that once they'd made initial contact with the former Alpha Seven operator, they would move the meeting to her apartment. She'd not lived there very long, so it had only taken them a couple of hours to sanitize the place and move her things over to McGarvey's apartment in Georgetown, a few blocks from the Renckes'.

He'd taken the couch and had pretended to be asleep the two times she'd gone to the bedroom door to look at him. She been wearing only a sleep shirt that didn't reach her knees, and she had looked wonderful to him.

But he wasn't ready. Especially not now in the middle of an op.

In the morning he was up first, and after she got dressed, she came out and had coffee with him.

"If the killer reads the same bulletin boards, he

could show up at Union Station," she'd suggested, and he'd agreed.

"As long as we can get to Schermerhorn first, he should be able to ID Alex or their control officer."

Security was loose on the main concourse, only a few uniformed cops patrolling on foot, looking for needles in a very large haystack. They'd been trained to look for signs, even small signs, of developing trouble. Spot the face of the nervous man, or a woman wearing too many clothes for the weather. But someone reasonably well dressed walking up behind a person and firing one silenced shot into the small of their back and walking away, this would not be noticed until it was too late.

"There," Pete said. She was looking across the concourse at a man standing directly below the statue of Prometheus.

"No," Schermerhorn said behind them.

Pete turned and reached into her shoulder bag for her pistol, but McGarvey stayed her hand.

Schermerhorn appeared much older than in the photograph Otto had come up with, though his general build was the same, as was the shape of his face. He wore jeans and a long-sleeved white shirt, untucked, the sleeves rolled up above his elbows. It was impossible to tell if he was armed.

"I understand you're wanted in Milwaukee for murder," McGarvey said. "Might be a good idea if we got out of here and went somewhere more secure."

"It was my girlfriend, and I think whoever murdered her murdered the others—and in just about the same fashion," Schermerhorn said. His voice held the very slight British accent of a Londoner, and he could have been discussing the weather. It was an act.

"Whoever did it wanted you and has probably read the same bulletin board message and even hacked your contact with us. It's possible they're here."

"Rencke's better than that," Schermerhorn said. "But they managed to penetrate the campus. Not so hard—all of us did it at one time or another as an exercise. A lot of NOCs have. Where do you have in mind?"

"I have an apartment not far from here," Pete said.

"And who the hell might you be?"

"Could be one of your newest best friends."

They drove over to Pete's apartment in McGarvey's Porsche Cayenne. He circled the block a couple of times before parking around the corner. The morning was starting to cloud over, and already it was sticky.

"You'll be safe here," Pete said.

"Yeah, right," Schermerhorn said, laughing.

"Just until we can figure out what the hell to do with you," McGarvey said.

"You wanted to talk to one of us—well, here I am. And when we're done—which won't take long, I guarantee it—I'm gone. So don't be handing me any crap about protective custody or safe houses."

"No, it didn't work for you in Milwaukee. The

question on my mind is if they wanted you, why didn't they stick around after killing your girl-friend?"

Schermerhorn looked away. "I don't know."

"Maybe they were sending you a message," Mc-Garvey said. "Not to talk to us."

"But here I am," he repeated, "so let's get on with it."

McGarvey had made sure they hadn't been followed; nevertheless, Pete went ahead to make sure the apartment was clean before she phoned the all clear. Upstairs, she was waiting at the end of the short corridor, her pistol in hand. The door to her apartment was open.

"What about the other people in the building?" Schermerhorn asked.

"This is a singles' place; everyone is at work," Pete said.

"Did you check all the apartments in the building?"

"No."

"Sloppiness like that might get you—maybe the both of you—killed one of these days. I suggest you tighten up your act. You have no idea who you're up against this time."

"This time?" McGarvey asked, once they were inside.

"I read your file, Mr. Director, or at least some of it—I suspect there's more. You've been around, and you've survived. It's the only reason I'm here for now and not long gone. But if you don't watch your step with these people, you'll be dead." He glanced at Pete. "Both of you will be."

He went to the window and looked down at the street and across to the apartment buildings.

"Do you want a beer?" Pete asked.

"No," he said. He went to sit on the arm of the couch. "Not such a hot idea to drink when you're on the run. Impairs the judgment."

"Who's after you?" McGarvey asked. "Let's start there."

"I don't know. Could be Alex. She was capable of doing something like this. My girlfriend's face was destroyed. Was it the same with the others?"

"Yes."

"Then it could be her, or George. They were the hot item at the end. I was—we all were at one point or the other. But it didn't take very long for me to figure out that being with her was a guaranteed one-way street straight to hell."

"Do you have any idea where she is?"

"In the States somewhere. Probably back here in Washington by now, if it was her in Milwaukee."

"Who else could have done this?" McGarvey asked.

"George? It could have been him, too—or the both of them together. They were certifiable. George would do something a little outrageous, and Alex would jump in and top him. Then he would try to top her, and it just kept going. Crazy shit, you know."

"No, I don't know. But they're the last two."

Schermerhorn laughed. "Don't count on it. If it was the Israelis, then they have the entire Mossad or even Aman to draw from. And some of those people are seriously disturbed. Just like a lot of our people."

"Israeli military intelligence?" Pete said.

"Yeah."

"Why? What are they protecting after all this time? Was it something they buried in Iraq? We were told there was a cache you guys discovered in the hills above Kirkuk."

"I don't know for sure. Could have been them, could have been Saddam. Hell, it could even have been us or the Russians, or the North Koreans."

"But you do know," McGarvey said. "It was you who changed the fourth panel on *Kryptos*."

"Insurance," Schermerhorn said. "But you contacted me, and that means you haven't decrypted it yet."

TWO

The light x the confusion
x the salvation . . .

TWENTY-FOUR

When Alex Unroth was sixteen and a freshman at Pine View School for the Gifted just outside Sarasota, Florida, she was a slender attractive girl, short with beautiful dark eyes and silken black hair. The girls didn't like her because she looked like an athlete—all lean muscle—though she never went out for sports. And the boys didn't care for her because her breasts were too small and she was smarter than just about everyone in school.

Her stepfather, Leonard Unroth, was a drunk, and her mother laid around most days, reading movie magazines, eating candy and other sweets, and bitching about everything.

She remembered one night in particular, the start of her real education, when her stepfather came into her bedroom around two in the morning, pulled down the covers, pulled down her pajama bottoms, and began fondling her. She was a virgin, though she had begun masturbating and reading books like *Lady Chatterley's Lover* two years earlier, so she understood all about sex. Especially its uses for control.

She touched his hand. "If Mom wakes up, she'll hear us," she whispered.

Leonard stopped for just an instant. "Fuck her," he said, his breath from booze, cigarettes, and bad teeth nearly unendurable.

"Tomorrow's Saturday. You'll take the fishing boat out, and I'll come with you. I'll tell Mom I'm going shopping with my friends."

In the dim light filtering in from outside, she could see the confusion on his face. And suspicion.

"Some of the boys in school want to fuck me. But I don't know how to do it, and I don't want to make a fool of myself. You'll teach me. But you'll use a rubber."

"Fuck you," he said.

"Go ahead. And when you're done, I'll call the cops and you'll end up doing jail time. It'll have been the most expensive piece of ass you've ever had."

He was stopped, directly over her.

"Either that, or we have a deal. Wait until tomorrow, and we'll anchor someplace and you'll teach me. It'll be a deal we can both walk away from happy."

Leonard backed off. "You're a fucking whore," he said.

"Not yet," she'd replied.

The day was blazing hot and humid. Leonard found a relatively isolated spot to tuck in just north of the Holiday Inn near the airport. The boat was a battered old twenty-four-foot Chris Craft cabin cruiser, and belowdecks, with the hatch closed, the interior was like an oven.

Alex took off her clothes and lay down on the settee, spreading her legs for him.

It was only ten in the morning, but he was drunk on beer already. He pulled off his shorts and underwear, and spread her legs farther, pawing her with his calloused fingers.

She pulled a razor-sharp skinning knife from where she'd hidden it in the crack of the cushions and buried it to the hilt in his chest, directly into his heart. He gasped once and fell back on the cabin sole, dead almost immediately.

She checked the ports, but no one was around. For the next fifteen minutes she mutilated his body. Starting by cutting off his penis, she worked her way up to his neck, which she sliced from ear to ear, and then his face, which she skinned—cutting off his nose, his lips, his eyebrows, and his ears, leaving them lying in the incredible mess where she'd dropped them.

She drew water from the sink and washed her body, checking the long mirror on the back of the door into the tiny head to make sure she hadn't cut herself. At that time she didn't know all the details of forensic police work, but she didn't want to leave any of her own blood behind in case she could be identified.

She'd brought a bikini, which she put on, and stuffed her clothes into a watertight plastic bag. Before she went out on deck and jumped overboard to swim ashore, she checked the portholes on both sides of the boat again to make sure no one was nearby to see her leave.

Onshore, she made her way across the rear property of the Holiday Inn, where behind a Dumpster she changed into a pair of shorts, a T-shirt, and sandals. Then, stuffing the plastic bag into her purse, she walked around the long end of the hotel's parking lot, unnoticed, and out onto Tamiami Trail and to the first bus stop.

Her mother didn't report her husband missing until the next morning, and it wasn't until late that afternoon that his body was found. His time of death couldn't be fixed to anything closer than a six-hour window, and when Alex's mother had been questioned, she had no alibi. It was Alex who produced the time-and-date–stamped receipts from a couple of department stores that fell within the six hours, and she told police she had come home immediately after shopping, and then she and her mother had watched television together.

The brutal murder of Leonard Unroth was never solved and eventually went into the cold-case files. But for a time the people of Sarasota had been traumatized that a seriously disturbed nut-case killer was running around loose among them.

Alex graduated at the top of her high school class and then did three years at Northwestern, earning her degree with honors in foreign affairs with a double minor in Russian and Chinese. She had only a handful of boyfriends, but in Sarasota she sometimes worked the North Trail as a prostitute, and the kinkier the sex, the better she liked it.

At college, during the short breaks between the

spring semester and summer semester, and then until the fall semester started, she went out to Las Vegas, where she worked first as an ordinary prostitute. Then one night a high roller picked her up—because he liked young stuff—and her second real education began.

She got a taste for the seriously bizarre, including role-playing, S&M, and a few other tricks, including orgasm at the moment of suffocation. Timing was everything in that game. At exactly the right instant during sex, her on top and her John on the verge, she would place a plastic bag over his head. At the instant he was about to pass out, he would come.

A certain type of man and a few women she had sex with liked it that way, and were willing to pay top dollar. Until the one night it went too far. Her John, paying her one thousand dollars, begged her to put the bag over his head, but he was too early. He had a heart problem, and he died while she was astraddle him.

She was honest with the hotel security people, who she'd always tipped very well, and they let her go.

"You just can't come back here, sweetheart," the chief of security told her with regret. He liked the money, but he also liked his sex with her straight.

Two weeks later she was in Washington, applying for a job with the CIA. And two weeks after that, her initial background check completed, she was called to an office in a federal building on the Beltway for her second interview with a case officer who wasn't much older than she was and who sported an actual military-style crew cut. He said his name was Dominick.

"Northwestern's a good school, and you picked the right studies," Dominick told her. He looked up from her file. "What do you want to do for the CIA?"

She had smiled. The office was plain, only a table and two chairs, with a lousy view of the parking lot four stories down. The walls were bare, the floor a bland off-white tile, and there was nothing else.

"Truth, justice, and the American way—isn't that what I'm supposed to say?"

Dominick showed no reaction.

"Seriously, I want to be a field officer. A NOC."

"Why's that?"

"I want to kill bad guys. I think this country has some serious shit coming its way. I want to be one of the guys on the front line, but I definitely don't want to join the Marines."

"Says you were questioned in the murder of your father when you were sixteen. Did you kill him?"

"Stepfather," she said automatically. "No, but I should have. The son of a bitch tried to rape me. Someone else just beat me to it."

"You don't think you'd have any trouble killing a human being?"

"It would depend on who it was."

Dominick gave her a long, appraising look. "You're staying at the Hay-Adams. Expensive hotel."

"I have a little money set aside," she'd said.

"An inheritance?"

"No, I earned it the old-fashioned way."

Dominick closed her file and got up. "We'll get back to you, Ms. Unroth."

"Don't take too long. I was thinking about going to work for Microsoft."

"You know computers?"

"I get by. But they're going global, and they need someone who understands Russian and Chinese."

Dominick showed her out, and she took a cab back to the Hay-Adams, where, before she went inside for an early lunch, she stopped a moment to look across Lafayette Park toward the back of the White House. Troubling times were coming for the country, and she wanted to be part of it. Soon.

Two weeks seemed to be the magic number for the CIA, because it wasn't until then that they called her again, and in the same office she spent the better part of the day with a couple of clerks, filling out forms and questionnaires about her work preferences, her previously unreported skills, her work history, her next of kin—which was no one. Her mother had drunk herself to death last year.

The next day she was driven in a panel van with three men about her age to Camp Peary where her third real education began.

Marty Bambridge came into the director of Central Intelligence's Office, and Alex looked up and smiled. The nameplate on her desk said: DOROTHY GIVENS.

"Good morning, sir. Go right in. The director is expecting you."

"How was your vacation?"

"More like a long weekend," Alex answered. "But it was good to get away from all the hullabaloo around here."

"Amen."

TWENTY-FIVE

It was coming up on noon, and McGarvey had left the bulk of the interrogation to Pete, content to let her lead because she was damned good. Schermerhorn, even as cynical as he was—as most NOCs tended to be out of necessity—had warmed to her, and a couple of times in the past half hour he had actually anticipated a question and answered it before she could ask.

"Would you like to stop for lunch?" she asked. "We can eat here, or there's an Olive Garden not too far away."

"We're almost done. When I walk out the door, I'm going deep and I won't be back."

"We're up to late oh two, just before the Second Iraq War, when you met Alex for the first time in Munich," Pete said. "Tell us about it."

"I'd never met the others till then," Schermerhorn said. "I hadn't even heard of them. And actually, it was in Frankfurt, at what had been an old Nazi Kaserne."

This last bit came as a surprise to McGarvey. "The Drake Kaserne?" he asked.

"Yes, you know it?"

"I spent a couple of days there a while back. As a guest of the BND. If you were there, they knew about your op."

Schermerhorn glanced at Pete and grinned. "Actually, we were thumbing our noses at them."

"That makes no sense."

"It was Bertie Russell's idea. He was our chief mission-training officer. Been with us from the beginning. He was sort of like a father figure, except to Alex, who didn't trust him. And the feeling was mutual.

"Our first task was to get to the Kaserne without being detected by the Germans, and simply knock on their door. We had passes that were worthless anyplace else. They scrambled, but they let us in. It was a fallback, you see, in case something went wrong in Munich. Bertie wanted us on record as being in country, so if it came to it, we wouldn't get shot. And that was a possibility."

"What was your cover story in Frankfurt?"

"Extrajudicial rendition. It was supposedly the real start to the hunt for bin Laden. The Germans were content to go along with us as long as we didn't cause trouble for any German citizens. They were just happy we had let them in on what we were doing."

"Did they ever catch on?"

"No. When we were done in Munich, we just packed up and left. In the mountains one day, and up at Ramstein on the big bird for Saudi Arabia the next."

"This Bertie Russell, would he confirm any of your story?" Pete wanted to know.

"Ran over an IED in oh four, after all the bloody fighting was supposedly done and gone."

"Convenient," McGarvey said.

Schermerhorn flared. "Look, I came out of the woodwork to help you guys."

"Help save your own life."

"That's bullshit, and you know it. Walt, Isty, and Tom didn't do so well on campus. What makes you think it'd be any different if I let you take me into protective custody? So just let's get that shit out of the way. I'm here to help."

"With what?' Pete asked, and the sharp question from her stung Roy.

Schermerhorn took his time answering that one. He got up again and went to the window, this time with a lot more caution. "Who else knows I'm here?"

"Otto Rencke."

"Who else?"

"By now our deputy director of operations and the DCI," McGarvey said. Otto had texted a query earlier, and McGarvey's cell phone was on vibrate-only mode. He had excused himself and gone into the bathroom to answer.

"Bloody hell."

"If you can't trust people at that level, then what are you doing here with us?" Pete asked. She sounded as if she were gentling a skittish horse.

"Preventing world war three," Schermerhorn said, coming back to the couch. "It's there, the warning on panel four."

"Save us the trouble and give us the message."

"It's not going to be that easy. You, Otto, whoever, needs to come up with the decryption if you're going to believe it. *Kryptos* is the Holy Grail in a lot of people's minds. My telling you won't wash. Especially not on the Hill or at the White House."

"You're playing games with us now," McGarvey said. "Your life is at stake here."

"Here, yes, it is. Once I walk away and as long as I stay on my own and on the move, I'll be fine while you do your job."

"Okay, Roy," Pete said. "Tell us how you did it. Changed the carvings on four. To this point we've stayed totally away from it. We didn't want to call any attention to the thing. Everyone knows what's carved into the copper plate, so no one really looks at it."

"I suggested that the sculpture looked like shit, weathered and green. My supervisor didn't agree, said copper out in the weather was supposed to look like that. It was the effect Sanborn was looking for. I couldn't push it, of course, so I bided my time, until I pointed out that all the steel and burnished aluminum on the outside of the New Headquarters Building looked shiny and new. *Kryptos* didn't match. It'd be my job to take off the crud and make it look new. And maintain it that way. If someone complained, we could also let it go back to natural."

"And they went along with it?"

"Lots of really smart people work on campus. Lots of PhD's, but if you ever look real close at them, you'll find out just how naive and gullible they are outside their own narrow little specialties. They were easy."

"You polished the sculpture. Then what?"

"Actually, it was a big job, because I not only had to do the plates themselves, but I had to polish the insides of each carving by hand, one by one. When I got to four, instead of polish, I used liquid metal to which I had added a copper tint."

McGarvey saw the possible flaw. "In order to

make something like that work, you couldn't have changed, let's say an *A* to an *I*, or vice versa. You would have needed to work out whatever message you wanted to put on panel four, and then figure out the code that would work as an overlay on the original letters."

Schermerhorn shrugged. "I had a little help with my laptop, but my specialty was cryptography, and I just needed to come up with a modified one-time cipher. It's completely random like the original, which is why no one was able to break the thing in the first place."

"But you did."

"You have to learn to think in random."

"What's on panel four?" Pete asked. "What did you try to tell us?"

"Something you wouldn't believe if I just sat here and mapped it out for you. Plus, I don't have all the answers—none of us ever did—except for maybe George. Listen, I'm just one guy on the run, a liar, con man, thief, killer by trade. And there's only me and Alex left from Alpha Seven."

"Plus George."

"Yeah, but my guess is he's never been on campus. Most NOCs never go near the place."

"Except for Wager, Fabry, and Knight."

"But someone on the inside, someone with access to real-time intelligence information has to be," said Schermerhorn. "Surely, you guys have figured that out by now."

"Security has turned the entire campus upside down," Pete said. She was clearly frustrated.

"Tell Otto what I said about four, and he'll decrypt it in no time at all if he's as smart as everyone says he is."

"The only one left from your team is Alex Unroth," McGarvey said.

"The Working Girl."

"So you're saying it's she who killed the three on campus? What about Carnes and Coffin in Athens?"

"She moved around a lot. One day here, the next day somewhere else. Did it during our training at the Farm—sometimes she'd bug out for a day or two, and no one could get anything out of her. She did it in Germany, and of course in Iraq with George. We should have called her the Ghost, because she was damned good at disappearing right while you were looking directly at her."

"She's on campus in plain sight?" Pete said.

"Ever play Hide the Thimble?" Schermerhorn asked. "She's there."

"And you're going to help us find her," McGarvey said.

TWENTY-SIX

Otto showed up at Page's office twenty minutes behind Bambridge, and fifteen minutes behind Carleton Patterson. He was distracted and didn't wait for the DCI's secretary to announce him; instead he just barged in.

"You're late," Bambridge said.

Page was behind his desk, Marty and Carleton

seated across from him. The office was large, book-cases on the west wall, big—surveillance-proof—windows looking out over the Virginia countryside on the south, and a couple of good Wyeth paintings on the east.

Otto went to Page's desk and wrote a note on a memo pad: *When's the last time this office has been security scanned?*

Five days ago, Page wrote.

Otto motioned him to silence, and he used his cell phone to call a friend of his in the directorate of science and technology's office of electronics. "Come up here now, would you?"

He hung up and again motioned for Page and the others to remain silent as he went to the director's desk, picked up the phone console, and turned it over to look for any obvious signs of tampering.

"I just talked to Mac, and he and Pete are at a dead end," he said. He got on his hands and knees and followed the phone cord to the jack in the floor.

"I didn't think this was going to be all that easy," Carleton said, picking up on Otto's ruse.

"This kinda stuff never is," Otto said, getting to his feet. "Toni Borman is on her way up with the old tapes of the preliminary interviews we did with Wager, Fabry, and Knight. Might be something we missed. Mac suggested it."

He removed the battery and SIM card from his cell phone and laid them on Page's desk, and then motioned for the others to give him their phones, which he dismantled as he talked.

"Thing is, we think whoever whacked our guys is long gone. I don't know how the hell they got off campus, but there's no way in hell they're still here. Not with all the extra security we've put in place in the last thirty-six hours."

Bambridge was frustrated, but Page had gotten it, and he motioned for his DDO to stand down. "So, what's Mac suggesting?"

"If we can find something linking the three of them to someone else, a fourth party, it'd be our best lead. But it's a long shot."

"Nothing else we can do at this point, I suppose," Patterson said.

Toni Borman, lanky, pleasant smile, and almost as tall as Louise was announced by Alex, and she went to work following Otto's lead.

"Did you bring the interview tapes with you?" he asked.

"Actually, a thumb drive, encrypted of course," Borman said. She took an electronic device about the size of a smartphone out of her pocket and methodically started on the room. High across the ceiling first.

"Did you listen to the interviews?" Otto asked.

"Some," Borman said. "Mostly boring." She worked her way across the walls, top to bottom, especially the light fixtures and electrical sockets, and the wall-mounted flat-screen television.

"Anything stand out in your mind?"

Borman shrugged and Otto shook his head.

"No, not really," she said. She lingered at Page's desk and his computer, and when she was done, she looked up. "You have the thumb drive—you listen. Maybe you'll hear something I didn't. But I didn't pick up anything."

"Thanks for your help," Otto said, and went with her to the door.

"The director asks, we're not to be disturbed for just a bit," he told Page's secretary.

"Of course," Alex said.

Otto closed the door and sat down with the others.

"What the hell was that all about?" Bambridge fumed. "Security sweeps every key office on the entire campus every week."

"On a schedule I know and we think someone else probably knows. We need to randomize the sweeps and notify no one of the time or office. The security people will just show up, and everyone will have to accommodate them."

"Obviously, you believe there's leak somewhere that whoever the killer is has access to," Page said.

"Mac thinks there might be two of them, one still on campus and another free to travel around. Whoever the second one is was in Athens last year to do Joe Carnes, then again a few days ago to kill Coffin, and yesterday in Milwaukee to try for Schermerhorn. But they missed and killed his girlfriend instead."

"Has he surfaced yet?" Bambridge asked.

"He showed up this morning, and he's with Mac and Pete, plus with something else we'd already guessed. Or at least partially guessed."

"How do we know he's not the second killer?" Patterson said. "He kills his girlfriend, and his informant here on campus tells him we're closing in on them, so he comes to us to ask for what? Protection?"

"He said he came to help find the killers. He doesn't want to be next."

"Does he know who they are?"

"Could be Alex Unroth, who's the only other Alpha Seven operator still alive, or their supposed control officer, who they only ever knew as George. Trouble is, the team's actual control officer was Bertie Russell—I checked—but he was killed in Iraq in oh four. There's no record anywhere of a control officer with the work name of George who joined them on their mission three months before the war started."

"What about when they came home?" Bambridge asked. "They must have been debriefed."

"He didn't come back with them, and apparently, the man was never missed."

"None of them said anything? They didn't ask their debriefers what happened to George?"

"No."

"Why?" Patterson asked.

"Because of what George showed them was buried in the foothills above Kirkuk," Otto said, and hesitated just as Kirk had told him to do.

"Well, come on, dear boy. Don't keep us in suspense," Patterson prompted. "What was buried?"

"He refuses to say."

"This is bullshit, Walt," Bambridge said. "Let's get the guy in here right now. We have people who'll find out whether he's lying."

"He's already given us the answer," Otto said. "He worked here for a couple of years as a maintenance man, and one of his jobs was to take care of the grounds, especially the statues and sculptures."

"Including *Kryptos*," Page said. "He has the solution to panel four."

"Yes, but it's not the original cipher, and he won't give us the solution to the new one. But my darlings are already chewing on it, and I suspect it'll only be a matter of a few days before they come up with the solution."

"And?" Page asked.

"He changed the cipher on four," Otto said, and before Bambridge could object again, he told them how Schermerhorn said he had done it. "I took a photo of panel four yesterday and compared it with the original. They're different, all right."

"Then he knows the answer," Page said.

"Yes, he does. But Mac says he won't tell us, because no one on the Hill or in the White House would believe him. They'll have to see it with their own eyes when four has been decrypted."

"This has gone from stupid to ridiculous," Bambridge appealed to Page. "I say we bring him in immediately and end this right now."

"They are bringing him in," Otto said. "As soon as I finish my homework. It's either Alex or George. I have their general descriptions, from which we can probably eliminate ninety percent of the personnel on campus. My darlings are working on that, too."

"That's something," Patterson said. "But explain to me why he came to us either for our help, or to help us, and yet he refuses to tell Mac the message he put on the panel for everyone to see. What does he want? What's his game?"

"He says he wants to help prevent world war three."

TWENTY-SEVEN

Schermerhorn had told his story, and he was agitating to leave. No way in hell was he sticking around to see how things turned out, and he sure in hell wasn't going out to Langley to look at faces.

"I don't care what Alex or George did to change their identities; it's the eyes. I never forget the shape, and especially not the expression," he'd told them.

McGarvey phoned Louise at two in the afternoon, after Schermerhorn had promised to at least give them until dark.

"I want to bring our guy over to your place, just for the night," he said.

"We have the third bedroom upstairs. Anyway, Audie's safe."

"I didn't ask Otto yet, because he'd say yes no matter what."

"Will Pete be with you?"

"Yes."

"Then if he gets out of line, there'll be three of us to shoot him. See you in a half hour."

McGarvey had phoned from the bedroom of Pete's apartment, and when he came back to the living room, Schermerhorn was again staring out the window at the parking lot and street that led up to Dupont Circle. He was looking for someone to show up, and he turned around with a start.

"Who'd you call, some minders?" he asked. Minders were security officers. Like babysitters with guns.

"A friend at another safe house. We're moving you there immediately."

Schermerhorn was alarmed. "I said I'd give you until dark, but then I'm out of here. If you want to ask me some more questions, go ahead. But then that's it."

"We've already told your story to the DCI and the director of clandestine services, plus the Company's general counsel. They know about the fourth panel, and they know you're here."

"Shit," Schermerhorn said, and made for the door.

Pete pulled out her gun and pointed it at him. "I will shoot you, Roy," she said.

Schermerhorn pulled up short and turned to her. "And then what?" he asked. Suddenly he didn't seem so concerned.

"There'll be a good chance you'll be dead before we can get an ambulance over here."

"I meant, I'm going with you to another safe house. But then what?"

McGarvey motioned for Pete to put down her gun. "We're getting out of here just in case the leak at Langley also knows where you are. Could be we're saving your life."

"Noble of you."

"Just protecting our investment. And when we're done, you'll be free to walk."

"Providing I give you what you want."

"The killer."

Schermerhorn had brought nothing with him. He'd stashed what he'd taken from Milwaukee somewhere safe nearby, and when it was time to leave, he'd get out of Washington clean.

"To go where?" Pete asked on the way over to the Renckes' safe house in Georgetown.

"Someplace safe."

"That's what Carnes and Coffin thought," McGarvey said.

Schermerhorn fell silent, but he glanced over his shoulder out the rear window every ten seconds or so.

Pete was driving. "We haven't picked up a tail," she said.

"What about the gray Caddy Escalade? Been with us since we crossed Rock Creek."

"It's not one of ours," Pete said. She turned left on Twenty-Seventh Street NW, and one block later right on O Street. The Escalade was no longer behind them. "Okay?"

"Yeah," Schermerhorn said.

McGarvey called ahead, and Louise opened the iron gate to the parking area behind the brownstone. She was waiting at the door for them as the gate swung shut.

"So who's the mystery guest? One of the Alpha Seven crowd?"

Schermerhorn introduced himself and held out his hand, but Louise just looked at him for a moment then stepped aside so they could come in.

"Otto should be back any minute," she said, leading them through the rear hall to the kitchen. "Said he'd finished with the meeting."

"How'd it go?" McGarvey asked.

"Just about the way you said it would," Louise said. "Anyone want a beer?"

Schermerhorn shook his head. "You're Otto Rencke's wife," he said.

"So they tell me," she said. "Someone killed your girlfriend."

Schermerhorn nodded.

"Chewed her up just like the others."

"It was meant for me."

Louise got a couple of beers from the fridge for Pete and Mac, and one for herself. "Doesn't seem as if you're shook up about it."

"Should I be?"

Louise gave McGarvey a look, as if to say, *Scumbag*, and Schermerhorn caught it.

"It's the nature of the job," he said. "You folks trained me."

"Don't get me started. I've known plenty of NOCs," Louise said. She looked up at the monitor unit on the wall next to the back hall. "Otto's home."

"Does he know I'm here?" Schermerhorn asked.

"He does now," Louise said.

Otto breezed in, gave his wife a kiss, and put his iPad on the counter. "Roy Schermerhorn, the Kraut," he said.

"Did you come in clean?"

Otto laughed. "I don't know. I never did check my rearview mirror," he said. "You guys up for pizza tonight? We can order in."

"Did you narrow down the range of possibles?" McGarvey asked.

"Thirty-seven of them, nine women, all of them about the right age, or close, though I wouldn't trust the personnel files with my life. Nothing obvious jumped out at me, but these guys were professionals."

"I'm not going to be able to tell you anything from looking at a bunch of files," Schermerhorn said. "You're wasting my time."

Otto turned on his iPad and shoved it in front of Schermerhorn. The photograph of Walter Wager came up on the screen.

"Jesus," Schermerhorn said, sitting down. "It's Walt."

"Mr. Ponderous," Otto said. He brought up Fabry's and then Knight's photos from their personnel files. "They were hiding out in the open, hoping being inside they'd be safe."

"Isty and Tom," Schermerhorn said softly. He looked up. "Could I have that beer after all?"

Louise got him one.

Otto brought up Coffin's prison photo. "Do you recognize this one?"

Schermerhorn stared at the image for a long time.

"The eyes ring any bells?" McGarvey asked.

"It's Larry, all right. I'd recognize him anywhere. But he looks different. Worn-out, maybe sad. I don't know. Not himself."

"He was running for his life, just like you are," McGarvey said. "Only he wasn't quick enough. Neither were Carnes or the others."

"Or your girlfriend," Louise said into the sudden silence.

"You can see it in his eyes," Schermerhorn said.

"He didn't look like that the last time we saw him," McGarvey said. "He took a sniper rifle round to the back of his head. Completely destroyed his face."

"That's what Alex and George did to the rag heads in the end," Schermerhorn said, his voice soft.

"Are you ready to look at the rest of the pictures?" McGarvey said.

Schermerhorn took a deep drink of his beer then nodded. "Sure," he said.

TWENTY-EIGHT

Alex sat at her desk, trying to keep her heart rate normal, the expression on her face pleasantly neutral, as staffers came and went into the DCI's inner office. The Speaker of the House had called for an update on the goings-on across the river. The president's chief of staff asked Page to come in at nine in the morning to help with Norman Hearney's briefing—Hearney was the new director of national intelligence. And Stanford Swift, an old friend from IBM, had called for lunch tomorrow, but Page had declined. "Full plate just now, Stan."

The problem was trust, something Alex didn't know if she could count on for much longer. In the four years since she'd started here first as a substitute for Page's secretary, and then the full-time position when the woman was killed in a car accident, the DCI had come to trust her.

The most immediate problem was the Kraut showing up here in DC. By all rights, after the Milwaukee incident with his live-in, Alex had expected

Schermerhorn to run for the hills. One less operator to have to worry about in the short term.

But sometimes, like right now, she felt like a juggler with too many balls in the air while standing barefoot on a slippery slope that kept moving. The center was starting to fall apart; it wouldn't hold for much longer, and then God only knew what would happen next. Except the fallout would be lethal.

Her desk console chirped. It was the director.

"Dotty, could you come in for a minute?" he said.

"Yes, sir," Alex said.

She'd heard what Rencke had said inside. In the last three years she'd heard *everything* that had been said in Page's office. Was privy to all his phone calls, all his e-mails, even his private ones, and especially the encrypted ones. She'd recorded everything against the day—which might never come—when she needed some insurance. Though what she knew of the recordings wouldn't be of much help now.

Getting up, she considered taking her subcompact Glock 29 from its hiding place in her desk, but decided against it. If she had to kill the DCI, she would do it only if she had a decent chance of escaping. She took her iPad and stylus instead. Sometimes he liked to dictate letters or notes the old-fashioned way.

Page was staring out the window, his back to the door when Alex walked in.

"Have a seat, please," he said, his back still to her.

She sat down across the desk from him.

"Hell of a way to go out," he said.

"Sir?"

Page turned around. "I'm going to resign. I'm sure you've already guessed. A lot of people have. Means you'll be handed your walking papers. New DCIs seldom keep their predecessor's private secretaries."

"It's all right, Mr. Director. I've been thinking about retiring myself."

"But you're too young."

"Thanks for that, sir, but so are you."

Page let that hang on the air for several beats. He smiled. "I have a problem. This agency has a problem, and I don't know what the hell to do about it, except I don't want to leave without some sort of a solution."

For once, Alex didn't know what to say.

"I don't mean to put any burden on you, but the fact of the matter is, I've read your personnel file."

Alex stiffened. "Sir?"

"Harvard. International law. Impressive then and impressive now, according to your résumé."

Alex had built a top-shelf résumé for herself mostly out of whole cloth, in which under various identities she had worked in a number of highly sensitive government positions—all of them as a private secretary to men who were dead. She'd fabricated pay records and all the paperwork to support her work history. And everyone vaguely remembered her, though no one could exactly remember what she looked like.

Again Alex held her silence, not knowing where he was going.

"Fact is, I need your advice. Not to be a sexist pig, but I need a woman's point of view."

Alex couldn't help but laugh. "Not to be a sexist pig myself, sir, but sometimes a man does need a woman's point of view."

George had called her a man's woman. It was something she'd resented at first, but operating side by side with him in the field, and in the evenings in bed, she'd come to respect him and had come to understand what he'd meant. Most men were total idiots, but George had been special. And Walt Page, in his old-fashioned gentlemanly way, was special as well.

"You're aware of the terrible business of the past few days. Three of our people murdered. What you're not aware of is two other murders, both of them in Athens. Both of them were NOCs, on the same surveillance team in Iraq before the second war."

"Alpha Seven."

"Yes. All that's left of them now is a man and a woman, plus some mysterious man who supposedly was their control officer. But he doesn't show up in any of our records."

"Do you think one of them is the killer?"

"We thought so, but one of the operators who was living in Milwaukee showed up, and Mr. McGarvey has him at a safe house."

"Maybe he's the killer."

"Mac doesn't think so. Leaves the control officer, who for all we know might work right here on campus. It would explain how he could have gotten to Wager and the others."

"And the woman," Alex said, fighting to keep her voice and manner perfectly normal.

"Otto's come up with a list of people who fit the general descriptions and who are about the right age. They're showing the man photographs from personnel records. Thirty-seven people, nine of them women, you included."

Alex forced a smile. "Me?"

Page nodded. "I had Otto pull your picture from his list. It would have been a waste of time."

The photo in her personnel file was four years old, and she didn't look anything like she had before the war. She had put on about thirty pounds, mostly around her hips and ass—which wasn't all that terrible. During the war she had been mostly skin and bones. Too skinny, George had told her a couple of times. Her hair then had been thick and dark, but she had thinned it with chemicals, lightened it and highlighted it with blond streaks. Her face was fuller, and she even dyed her eyebrows and lightened her skin tone. The biggest change, and the one she liked most, was the Botox injections into her lips. And she smiled now, something she'd hardly ever done before. These days almost everyone warmed up to her the first time they met.

But the Kraut knew her just about as well as anyone else on the team, except for George, who she thought had truly loved her.

"Wasn't a very flattering picture, as I remember."

"I saw it, and everyone else who did wondered why you were smiling. Most of the personnel pictures look like mug shots, but not yours."

"I guess I'm just a happy person," Alex said.

Page nodded. "You don't fit the profile of a killer, and Otto agreed."

Alex laughed. "That's a relief to know. But you said you need my advice."

"I want this mess cleared away before I step down,

and the president agrees. It's where you come in. I want to lean on your woman's intuition. If one of those eight women on Otto's list is the killer, I think you could spot her before any of us could."

"You want me to interview them?"

"Not until tomorrow. I'll give you the list of names, and I'd like you to spend a couple of hours this afternoon going through their personnel files, see if anything jumps out at you. Look at their photographs, study their eyes. Toby Berenson thinks sometimes whatever's going wrong shows itself in the eyes."

Berenson was the Agency's psychologist. The suicide rate among CIA field officers was much higher than the general population. And so were the rates of drug addiction, alcoholism, and suicide. He claimed to be able to detect the early signs by looking into the officer's eyes.

"I'll give it a try, Mr. Director," Alex said. Her eyes were the same as they'd always been: neutral. But she was happy Page had pulled her file from Rencke's list.

"Let me know by morning."

TWENTY-NINE

It was past eight when Schermerhorn got up from where he'd been seated in front of Otto's computer in an upstairs bedroom and went to the window to look outside. A car passed, but the streets in this part of Georgetown were almost always quiet, according to Otto.

"Makes it easier to spot someone trying to sneak up on you," he'd said.

"But not impossible for the right man," Schermerhorn had replied.

None of the photos Otto had brought back on his iPad rang any bells, nor did they even when displayed on the much larger screen upstairs. After dinner, Otto had retrieved the Agency's complete dossiers on each of the thirty-seven possibles, and Schermerhorn had spent a couple of hours going over them.

"Nothing?" McGarvey asked at the door.

"No. It's quiet out there."

"I meant in the files. Did you recognize any of them?"

"There were two or three guys who looked possible. But unless their files were faked, none of them ever had the field experience the rest of us had."

"How about the eyes?"

"No. But there's a problem with the files."

"What's that?"

"There were supposed to be nine women, but I only count eight. One's missing."

Otto appeared on the monitor. "She's Dorothy Givens, Walt Page's secretary," he said. He was seated at the kitchen counter, eating a piece of leftover pizza.

"That'd be just like Alex. She could be anyone anywhere."

"I'll be right up," Otto said.

"It'd explain how your killer got their intel. If it is Alex, she would have bugged the director's office."

"It's clean," Otto said, pushing past McGarvey. "We checked."

"Physically checked?" Schermerhorn asked. He'd heard this sort of crap before. It was part of one of their training evolutions. Look for the unexpected. Think out of the box.

"Old-fashioned," one instructor had told them. "Like opening someone's mail—paper mail. Peeping through keyholes, looking through bedroom windows."

"His office was swept."

"Maybe she put a water glass to her ear and listened through the wall," Schermerhorn said. He was frustrated. Otto was supposed to be the best—but that was electronically. And now his worry that he wasn't safe even here spiked.

Otto grinned. "You're right, but she checks out. You can't believe the hoops someone wanting that job has to jump through. She came out clean."

"You picked her in the first place. Where's her file?"

"Page vouched for her."

"Her file, or don't you guys give a shit?"

McGarvey nodded, and Otto shrugged and went to the computer. With a few keystrokes, he pulled up the secretary's file. Schermerhorn got the feeling he'd been had.

The photograph of a woman with a broad smile filled the screen, and Schermerhorn's first instinct was to step back. But he didn't know why. The face was more or less the same shape, a little heavier than Alex had been. And the lips were filled out. In

Germany and later in Iraq when they'd made love—
more accurately when they'd had sex—she had
complained that her worst features were her small
boobs and skinny lips.

"But I know how to use them, don't I?"

"No complaints from me," he'd said.

As he looked at her image on the screen, he was
pulled in from the get-go; yet staring at it, he also
wasn't sure.

"Well?" Otto asked.

"She's squinting."

"It's called smiling. Dotty does a lot of it."

Alex almost never smiled in the old days. And when
she did, it was as if she were laughing at you. Nothing
about her rare smiles had any warmth in them. She
measured people by what they were worth—to her
personally.

But she'd also been an expert at disappearing right
in front of your eyes. Usually she didn't have to
move; instead, somehow, she instantly became a
stranger. Someone you'd never seen before.

The last time they had made love, he had rolled
over onto his back, still inside her, and when he
looked up into her face, he didn't know who he was
making love to. The woman above him was someone
he'd never met. And the effect had been so extraordinary, instantly his mood had drained completely
away and he couldn't wait to get free.

She'd laughed. "What's the matter, Kraut? The cat
got your ardor?"

And an instant later she was the Alex he'd been
making love to, but the cat or something *had* gotten
his ardor.

It was in Iraq the week before she and George had started on their rampage, as they'd called it. "Teach 'em a little respect," George had said, and Alex had agreed wholeheartedly.

Nothing was ever the same for any of them after that, though Alex and George were the one subject all of them avoided, at all costs. The two of them were taboo. They were afraid to even approach them, the same as if the two of them were dangerous IEDs ready to explode and kill them all at the slightest touch.

In fact, thinking about them now, Schermerhorn remembered that when they got to Ramstein and George wasn't with them, they were relieved. No one wanted to bring up his name. Not even Alex had mentioned him.

They were debriefed individually, but so far as he knew, no one was asked about George. He became the forgotten man in everyone's minds. Left behind somewhere in Saudi Arabia.

All that came back to him in a rush as he stared at the image of the DCI's secretary.

"The DCI was in California, Thursday, two days before Coffin was killed," Otto said. "His secretary took Friday off and wasn't back at her desk until Monday morning when the director was back. Common practice."

"As his secretary, she potentially had access to everything he knew," McGarvey said.

"That included personnel records for everyone," Otto said. "She is in a perfect position to know what the killer knew."

Schermerhorn couldn't tear his eyes from the

image on the screen. "Did you know that when Alex was sixteen, she murdered her stepfather? She told Tom about it one night in Munich. The two of them were drunk, and he'd asked her something stupid, like, if it came to it, could she actually pull the trigger to kill someone? 'In a heartbeat,' she said. 'Been there, done that already.'"

"It was in her initial interview," Otto said. "But no charges were ever filed."

"Of course not. Even at that age, she was too good to get caught. But she told Tom that when her stepfather tried to rape her, she stabbed him in the heart, then cut off his dick and peeled his face with a fish-filleting knife."

"I pulled up the newspaper accounts," Otto said. "The murder was never solved, though the wife was a prime suspect."

"But that's Alex Unroth," McGarvey said. "What about the DCI's secretary? Can you at least make a guess? You said you would recognize the eyes."

"She's squinting," Schermerhorn said again, staring at the image. Yet his gut reactions were bouncing all over the place.

He turned to look at Rencke and McGarvey. He wanted to run and hide deep more urgently than he'd ever wanted to in his entire life. Larry Coffin and Joe Carnes had evidently tried without success in Athens. And Walt, Isty, and Tom had tried right there on campus, supposedly the safest place in the world for a NOC who'd come in out of the cold. And that hadn't worked either.

"I don't know," he said. He looked again at the

image, absolutely hating what he was going to say next. "I'll have to see her in person."

"I'll find out if she's still on campus," Otto said, and started to leave, but Schermerhorn stopped him.

"We need to go in cold; otherwise, she'll figure out what's coming her way and run."

"She knows by now," McGarvey said. "If she's not on campus, we'll go to her house—wherever she lives."

"You'd better bring the militia, and you better expect there'll be some serious collateral damage."

"She might kill again?' Otto said.

Schermerhorn laughed. "Who's left? Just me and George."

THIRTY

McGarvey sat behind the wheel of his Porsche SUV, parked in a lot adjacent to a small apartment building in a pleasant neighborhood north of Washington in Chevy Chase—coincidentally not far from the house he and Katy had lived in before they moved to Florida. It felt odd to him, being back like this.

Pete rode shotgun next to him, and Schermerhorn sat in the backseat, nervously checking out the neighborhood. Traffic was light at this hour, but except for the streetlights, it was very dark under an overcast sky.

"We'll go in first," McGarvey told Pete. He phoned her, and when they were connected, he put his cell phone in the lapel pocket of his jacket without turning it off. Whatever happened, she would hear it.

Otto had checked with Agency security, who told him the DCI had left around six thirty, and his secretary fifteen minutes later. Neither of them were still on campus. He pulled up Dotty's address from the file.

Schermerhorn had asked for a pistol before they left the house. "If it turns out to be Alex, I don't want to go up against her unarmed. You can't believe how fast she is."

Pete took a standard U.S. military–issue Beretta 92F out of the glove compartment and handed it back to him. "She won't be much help to us if she's dead."

"Neither will I," Schermerhorn said. He ejected the magazine to check its load, seated it home in the handle, and cycled a round into the firing chamber. He stuffed the pistol under his belt and beneath his shirt. "Let's get it over with. I want to be long gone an hour from now."

"We'll see," McGarvey said. He didn't feel particularly comfortable, having a man such as Schermerhorn armed, but he wouldn't hesitate for a second to shoot the man center mass if he became a threat. Or even looked like he was about to cause trouble. "You're out here tonight just to make a positive ID."

"You'd better be prepared for some serious shit to go down. Because if it is Alex, she'll recognize me the minute we come face-to-face."

It was exactly what McGarvey hoped would happen.

"I can have a SWAT team out here by chopper in fifteen minutes," Pete said.

They'd discussed it before they'd left the safe house, and McGarvey had vetoed the idea. "There'll be other people living in the building. I don't want this to become a hostage situation."

"Not her style," Schermerhorn said. "If it's Alex, she'll have a plan for getting free no matter what the odds are against her. She might shoot someone, but she wouldn't want to be slowed down with a hostage in tow."

"Let's go," McGarvey said, and he and Schermerhorn got out of the car and headed across to the apartment building.

Pete got behind the wheel and turned the car around so it faced the street.

McGarvey's main worry had always been collateral damage. Innocent people getting in the way of a gunfight. He'd been in the middle of such things far too many times in his career, and he didn't want another repeat. He'd come to the opinion that he would rather let the bad guy walk away free than corner him—or her—where other people could get hurt.

Voltaire had the same philosophy a couple of hundred years ago: he reasoned it would be better to let a guilty man go free than to convict one innocent man.

They approached the building from the front and buzzed apartment 301 at the front on the top floor. Dorothy Givens lived in 104, at the rear on the bottom floor.

A man answered the intercom. "Who is it?"

McGarvey held up his open wallet. "Metro police."

"What's this about?"

"Open the door, Mr. Reading," McGarvey said,

reading the name off the tag beside 301. "We're not here for you, but we could be."

The door lock buzzed and they went inside. Down a corridor was the elevator, to the right a row of built-in mailboxes, below which were two larger lockboxes for packages. The doors to the two front apartments were left and right of the main entrance, and the doors to the rear two down a corridor past the elevator.

McGarvey went first.

Schermerhorn hung back a little, drawing his pistol and concealing it behind his right leg.

"Don't shoot unless there's no other way out," McGarvey warned.

"I want this to be over with as much as you do. I'm tired of always looking over my shoulder. And if anybody has some answers, it'll be Alex."

"And your message on *Kryptos*."

"But they moved it, and none of us knew where. Only Alex and George."

McGarvey's anger spiked, and he turned. "Moved what?"

"The package."

"You'll fucking well tell me what it is right now. No bullshit about Alex or the message on four."

"One thing at a time. I want Alex neutralized, and I'm going to want a whole shitload of assurances first."

"We'll decrypt the thing."

"By then I'll be long gone, and it'll be your problem. The biggest problem you've ever faced."

McGarvey had considered the possibility that Schermerhorn was the killer. But he knew that was wrong five minutes after the guy had shown up at Union Station. The former NOC was determined, but he wasn't certifiable. The killer had some sort of deep-seated psychosis that required him—or her—to destroy the faces, and therefore the identities, of their victims.

If Alex had been telling them the truth in Iraq about killing her father and slicing off his face, she was the obvious fit to the profile.

The problem he was having was coming up with the reason. In his way of thinking, it had to be more than just insanity. Crazy people had purpose, though almost always their motivations were obscure and often senseless.

They came to 104. "You're here to identify her, nothing else," McGarvey said.

"And?"

"The next move will be hers."

"Christ. You have no idea who you're dealing with, do you?"

McGarvey knocked on the door. The building was quiet, and the corridor smelled faintly of cleaning fluid, even furniture polish on the shiny chair rails and oak wainscoting. Solid upper middle-class, no trouble here.

A shadow blocked the peephole.

"Who the hell are you?" a woman demanded.

"Ms. Givens? We're from Mr. Page's office."

"Shit," the woman said, and opened the door. She was tall, with a long thin neck and narrow features, high cheekbones, and blue eyes. Her hair was wet, and she was wrapped in a bath towel. "Has something happened to Dotty?"

"No," Schermerhorn said.

"She's fine so far as we know," McGarvey said. "The director has been trying to contact her, but she doesn't answer her cell phone. We were sent out to tell her there's trouble with the White House meeting first thing in the morning."

"I can't help you guys. She's not here."

"This is really important."

"She called about an hour ago, said she was spending the night with her boyfriend. She does that sometimes."

"How do we contact him?"

"I don't know. I think he's got a place somewhere in Georgetown, but I don't have the address or phone number."

"You're Ms. Givens's roommate?"

"No, just a friend from New York. We used to work together at the UN, and I come down here from time to time. She comes up to stay with me every now and then."

"Do you at least have a name for her boyfriend?"

The woman shrugged. "No last name—just George."

THIRTY-ONE

Alex had the cabby drop her off near the end of Dumbarton Avenue NW, just a block from the edge of Rock Creek Park, and less than two blocks from Otto Rencke's safe house, which itself wasn't far from Kirk McGarvey's apartment.

The evening was dark and quiet, the only real traffic and activity in Georgetown at this hour was down in the tourist section along M Street, with its bars, restaurants, and chichi shops. After work, she'd driven to her second apartment in Tysons Corner, just across the Dulles Access Road and not far from the CIA's back gate, where she'd packed a few overnight things in a bag.

She called her sometimes roommate, Phyllis Dawson, using an untraceable pay-as-you-go cell phone. "I'll be with George tonight, maybe tomorrow. I think he might propose to me."

"What trouble are you in now?"

"Nothing serious, but someone from the Company might pay you a visit."

"What do you want me to tell them?"

"The truth."

"Yeah, right," Phyllis had said, and laughed.

They'd worked together at the UN, spying on delegates for an international lobbying firm that worked for a consortium of international businesses. But they'd been too effective, both of them posing as high-priced call girls. When the WikiLeaks were made public, a couple of Brazilian diplomats had been burned, and Alex and Phyllis, who'd worked under assumed names, were forced out. Their control officer and his boss were more than satisfied when the girls simply disappeared without a fuss, happy to sweep the entire incident under the rug.

Phyllis, working under a new identity, had landed a job gathering intel for another international lobbying firm, this one dealing in the secrets of big banks.

They kept in touch from time to time to share gossip, the only people in the world with whom they could be totally open. Or nearly so, in Alex's case.

Around the corner, Alex used a universal electronic key to open the door of a Ford Fusion, started it, and drove the two blocks to the Renckes' safe house, where she parked across the street and a few doors down from the electric gate.

A few lights were on in the house. While driving past, she had spotted two old cars parked in back— one a Mercedes, the other a Volvo station wagon. One belonged to Otto, the other to his wife, who still used her maiden name of Horn.

It actually meant nothing that both cars were there. Nor did it make much sense to her to stay here very long, in case the car was reported missing and the police sent out a stolen vehicle notice on the net.

She thought there might be some obvious sign that Schermerhorn was here, but then she knew she was being foolish to hope for such luck. After twenty minutes she turned around and returned the car to where it had been parked.

After wiping down the steering wheel and door handle, she walked a few blocks to M Street, where she had a drink at Clyde's in the Shops at Georgetown Park, which backed up on the old C&O Canal. The place was busy with the late after-work crowd.

The problem was timing her disappearance. If she went back to work in the morning, and McGarvey brought Roy over to look at the thirty-six suspects, it was possible they would end up on the seventh floor. She had altered her appearance enough that she was pretty sure she would never be picked out of a police lineup. But she and Roy had been a thing in bed for a short while and had lived in close quarters in Germany and again in Iraq. He might pick up on something if he saw her. Escaping at that point would be problematic.

On the other hand, she wanted to know how close they were to solving the mystery. The only way she could get that information was by sitting in her office and listening in on what was said in the director's office via the direct wire link between her phone console and his.

She'd removed the light in the director's console that showed when she was connected. Simple but effective.

The key was if someone had shown up at the Chevy Chase apartment, looking for her. But if they'd come that far, it meant they'd put her file back on the list despite Page's removing it. It meant she was a suspect. But only Schermerhorn could possibly make that determination, and then only if he could meet her face-to-face.

Another possibility she'd considered, and the reason she'd packed an overnight bag, was her Tysons Corner apartment. There was a possibility, no matter how slight, that they had found the place. That in turn would mean they had discovered her Monica Wrigley persona. All her background preparations would unravel from that point.

But she couldn't take the risk of phoning Phyllis again in case they'd requested an NSA look and listen. Nor could she avoid the risk of going to the office in the morning as normal to find out what was coming her way, if anything.

A reasonably well-put-together man in a business suit, tie loose, collar open, came over to her. He looked to be in his late thirties, maybe forty, and he had a wedding ring. He smiled.

"No line, but you're an attractive woman," he said. "My name is Jeff. May I buy you a drink?"

"Why not?" she said, and motioned for the bartender. "Your wife out of town?"

"She works for a senator who likes to go on junkets. They're probably sleeping together."

The bartender came and refilled her glass with a Pinot Grigio.

"Kids?"

"No time."

"Never too late. Leave Washington, get a new life," Alex said, her problem of staying away from her Tysons Corner apartment for the night solved. But she almost felt sorry for the guy, and she guessed she wanted to give him a chance. "Call her right now, wherever she is, tell her you love her, and ask her to come home."

"She's an ambitious girl. It's one of the reasons we got married. But she won't leave the senator."

"When will she be back?"

"Not till Wednesday."

"Five days," she said. She took a drink of her wine and then smiled up at him. "Okay, Jeff, your place, or would you rather go to a hotel?"

He returned her smile, only the slight hint of guilt at the corners of his eyes. "I have a small place just up Potomac Street. It's walking distance."

"You've done this before."

"Like I said, she's gone all the time. And we have snoopy neighbors where we live."

It was nearly ten by the time they'd finished at the bar and walked across the street and up Potomac, to a corner building on N Street NW. His tiny apartment was up on the fourth floor, in what had once been an attic. The ceilings, especially in the tiny bedroom and kitchen, were sloped, and the place was sparsely furnished. It didn't look lived-in.

Alex dropped her bag beside the couch in the living room and went into the kitchen, where she found a half bottle of Jack Daniels on the counter.

He carried a briefcase, which he dropped on a chair in the living room, along with his jacket. He slipped out of his shoes and took off his tie as he came to her.

Alex opened the Jack and took a deep draught before she handed it to him. "Do you have to go into the office in the morning?"

"I'm giving myself a long weekend," he said, taking a pull on the bottle. He handed it back to her, and she took another drink.

"Sounds good," she said. "We have the weekend. So why not get drunk and screw? If you're up to it."

He laughed and then took the bottle back. "I've been told I'm not half bad."

They went into the bedroom, where she took off all her clothes first and then turned the covers down on the small double as he pulled off his.

"You like it a little rough?" she asked, facing him.

"I don't know."

She shoved him down on the bed and straddled him. "I'll show you how we did it in Vegas."

She bent down and kissed him at the same time she caressed both sides of his neck with her long delicate fingers. He slipped inside her, and after that it was easy.

Lightly at first, as she was fucking him, she applied pressure to his carotid arteries, and within ninety seconds he was passing in and out of consciousness, until he stopped breathing.

She held on for another three minutes, then reached down and felt for a pulse. But his heart had stopped. He was dead.

In the shower she vigorously washed her body, and after she had dried off, she rolled Jeff's body onto the floor, then lay down on the bed and pulled the covers up. She was bone-tired. It had been a long, trying day for her. And the next few could very well be worse.

THIRTY-TWO

Schermerhorn stood at one of the bedroom windows on the second floor of the Renckes' safe house, staring down at the quiet residential street. It was something he'd done a lot of since they'd picked him up. It was midnight, and nothing moved.

Otto was down the hall at his computer, trying to get some background on Dorothy Givens's friend at the Chevy Chase apartment and trying without any luck to find the George needle in the Georgetown haystack.

Dotty or Alex—whoever the hell she was—had been lying, of course.

"The woman has a sense of humor," Louise said.

"And she thinks we're on to her," Otto said. "The point is, will she show up at the office in the morning?"

"Absolutely," Schermerhorn had said with conviction. "She wants to know who's coming after her."

"If she knows we're breathing down her back, she'd be a fool not to run," Louise said.

"Not Alex. Never been her style. She figures she can win with whatever hand she's dealt."

"Beer?" McGarvey asked.

Startled, Schermerhorn turned from the window. "Why not?"

McGarvey had brought up two bottles of Heineken. He gave one to Schermerhorn. "Why do you suppose she let us know it was her, with the George joke?"

"It's always been her way. Whenever she walks into a room, she thinks she's the smartest person there, and she needs to prove it."

"Louise thinks we should just arrest her at the gate if she shows up in the morning."

"On what charge? Thumbing her nose at us?"

"Suspicion of murder."

"Look, McGarvey, there's something you guys don't understand. Even if Dorothy Givens is really Alex Unroth—and I couldn't even tell you if that's her real name—you have no proof she murdered Walt or the others."

"She was gone from the office on the same weekend Joe Carnes was murdered in Athens last year, and again when Coffin was hit."

"Check all the records, and I have a hunch you'll find she was gone other times. Whenever the DCI was out of town and she had no work on her desk, she was free to go. Wasn't it the same for your secretary when you were DCI?"

"Yes."

"So that part is coincidental."

"What about the killing of her stepfather? You said she admitted to doing it, and that she was perfectly capable of doing the same thing to Walt and the others. She and George did the same thing in Iraq."

"Just because she was capable, doesn't mean she killed our guys."

"Why the sudden change of heart?" McGarvey asked. "This morning you were convinced she was the killer, but now you're not so sure."

"I've had time to think about it," Schermerhorn said. He looked out the window again, half expecting to see her walking by or sitting in a car across the street. She was privy to everything the DCI knew, and probably a lot more than that. She would have made friends all over the place. The kind of people who fill in the blanks, the guys who tend to the details—the bits and pieces the bosses never have to deal with.

"You were in love with her."

"We all were."

"Still are?"

Schermerhorn focused on his reflection in the window glass, and he shrugged. "Yes. No. Hell, I don't know." He turned back. "But I can tell you I admire her, even if it turns out she did kill those guys."

"Christ," McGarvey said.

"You were out in the field. You know how it was."

"Never as a NOC. I wasn't that good of a liar."

"Maybe not, but you were a damned good assassin."

"Point?"

"The point is, if Dorothy Givens is Alex and we can prove she killed our guys, she won't allow herself to be taken in. Could be you who'd have to track her down and kill her."

"If need be."

"But you'd need the proof first."

"Yes."

"Hold her down long enough to maybe take a cheek swab or maybe grab a glass or a cup she drank out of. Toss her apartment—toothbrushes, hairbrushes, lipstick, makeup. Lots of places to come up with a sample of her DNA, because I can guarantee the one that's in her Company file won't be the real one."

"Again, what's your point?"

"Have you seen the autopsy reports on Walt and Isty?"

"No."

"But you know how they were killed. Their throats were sliced, their faces removed."

"There were human teeth marks. The killer chewed open the arteries and then bit off their lips and nose and eyebrows," McGarvey said.

"Right. But did you check the autopsies for DNA?"

"There was none. Apparently scrubbed away with alcohol."

Schermerhorn nodded. "And it's driving your forensics people nuts. You have a psycho killer running around loose inside the campus. But they're smart enough to leave absolutely no physical evidence tying them to the crimes. So prove it's Alex."

"First we have to find her."

"That'll be the relatively easy part. If it is she who is doing the killing, then I'm next. She'll come to me. But unless you catch her in the act, how will you prove it's her?"

"I'll ask her," McGarvey said.

Schermerhorn was at a loss for words. Looking at McGarvey, he suddenly had a very clear understanding that everything ever said of the former DCI and more was true. And for a moment he was just as frightened for Alex that she was the killer after all, as he was frightened she wasn't—and that the killer was George and they were all playing with fire.

Just the message he'd carved into the fourth *Kryptos* panel, and now he didn't know why he had done it. What was the point? He had the urge to tell McGarvey what he had written, but it wouldn't make any difference. Alex was front and center for now.

THIRTY-THREE

Alex walked back down to M Street before six in the morning, where she got a cab over to Reagan National. She rented a Chevy Impala from Hertz, using the work name documents for Alice Walker and paying for the car with a clean Capital One Platinum credit card.

Traffic was beginning to pick up, and she was careful with her tradecraft to make sure she wasn't being followed. She took I-395 up past the Pentagon—where she'd thought George had been some sort of a liaison officer, but she had never been able to prove it—and then past Arlington National Cemetery and finally I-66.

Her primary instinct was to run, go deep, because there was no way in hell she was going to spend the remainder of her life in some jail cell. At the very least, sooner or later Jeff's body would be found in his love nest, and someone at Clyde's would remember her leaving with him.

It'd all be circumstantial, of course—she'd always made sure that any evidence tying her to any crime was weak. But if the Company's investigators caught a break or two, there'd be enough to convict her.

And the thing of it was that she didn't know why she had killed the poor bastard who'd just wanted a one-night stand while his wife was probably fucking her senator. Ever since she was a child, before she murdered her stepfather, she would blank out from time to time; she'd do things that later she couldn't understand.

None of this was in any of her Company profiles, of course. She instinctively knew how to lie to shrinks, even good ones, and she never failed a question on a polygraph test, unless it was a lie she wanted to be caught at in order to prove she was human after all.

She checked her rearview mirrors at intervals, but nothing other than the Harley that had been on her tail for a mile before it passed her and sped off, and the old Lexus that had followed her all the way to where she'd turned north but had continued on I-66, no one else had been of any interest.

Driving past her apartment in Tysons Corner, she watched for signs that anyone had shown up or that a drone was circling overhead before she parked the Chevy around the corner at another apartment building a block away and went back on foot.

The car would be noticed sometime today, or perhaps tonight, but by then she figured her situation would be resolved one way or another. In any event, it would never be traced back to her real identity.

No one had tampered with the fail-safes on her front door, nor had the security panel just inside been touched. Had someone been here, the panel would have sounded a silent alarm and then gone into a default mode that was impossible to reverse.

She changed into a khaki pants suit, white cotton blouse, and sneakers. She kept a decent pair of black pumps in a desk drawer at work, which she changed into for important meetings, but like just about every other woman on campus, she preferred to be comfortable whenever possible.

Her real go-to-hell escape kit of several passports and other forms of identification, plus several credit cards and five thousand in cash—mostly U.S. and Canadian dollars, but a few hundred in euros and an equal amount in pesos—she kept in a storage unit nearby, filled mostly with boxes of old clothes she had bought at Goodwill and other thrift stores in the area. If the place were searched, half the boxes would have to be pulled out and emptied before her kit would be found.

As she stood at the door, she looked at the apartment that had been her secret home for the better part of four years. It was small, only one bedroom, and very neat and modern, with good furniture, top-shelf appliances, a big flat-screen TV and sound system, and some nicely framed art reproductions on the walls. But it meant nothing to her. In her entire life she'd never had a home that meant anything.

She tossed her big leather purse onto the passenger seat of her deep-green BMW 330ci convertible and headed to work as normal, expecting she would get a few answers she needed, but that she would be on the run again by noon.

The line of cars at the main gate was shorter than it had been for the past several days. When it was Alex's turn, she handed the officer her ID and gave him a smile.

"Good morning, Don. Looks like you guys have got this down pat," she said.

"Everybody's finally cooperating," he said, handing her ID back. "Have a good day, now."

"You too."

Driving up through the woods to the OHB, she

decided today was routine unless the security officer was a damned good actor. Which she didn't think
he was. Evidently, no one had been put on alert
about her.

She parked in the basement lot, the only secretary
on campus who was assigned a space inside. As she
swiped her card through the reader at the elevator
door, a security officer's image came up on the screen.

"Good morning, Ms. Givens," he said, and the
elevator door opened.

She smiled. Everything to this point seemed normal, but her instincts were starting to ramp up. Their
instructors at the Farm loved to quote the Navy
SEAL litany of Murphy's laws. Number one was: *If
everything is going good, you're probably running
into an ambush.*

The seventh-floor corridor was empty this morning, but she was early; it would be another twenty
minutes before most of the VIPs and their assistants
and secretaries started arriving. Except for the five
people in the Watch down the hall from the DCI's
suite, most of the offices were still empty.

The door to Page's inner office was open when she
walked in and set her bag behind her desk then
looked in. Page was already there. He seemed to be
in good spirits.

"Good morning, sir. You're early," she said.

"I think we're going to hit pay dirt this morning.
I don't have to be at the White House until two, so
maybe I'll have some good news for the president by
then."

"Sir?"

"We think we have our killer narrowed down to

thirty-six people. McGarvey is bringing someone in who might recognize them."

"That's wonderful news. But I thought your White House meeting was at nine."

"It's been moved. Sprague came on board when I explained what was going on."

Peter Sprague was the president's new chief of staff. He ran the White House with an iron fist. So far the media hadn't caught on to the killings on campus, and the president had made certain there would be no leaks from anyone on his staff. Sprague made sure of it; just as the security team on campus made sure there were none from here.

"That's good news," Alex said. "I'll update your agenda. I'm sure there'll be a few additions."

"Check with Ken, see if he has anything from the overnights I need to know about."

Kenneth Whiteside was the midnight-to-noon chief of the Watch this morning.

"I'll do that first," Alex said.

She powered up her computer and, while it was booting, walked down the hall to the Watch and entered the director's code on the keypad. Since the campus had been locked down after the first murder, the door did not automatically open. Whiteside had to make a personal identification of whoever wanted in.

When he saw it was her, he buzzed open the door.

"I'll be glad when we can get back to normal," he said. He was a short, slightly built man with sandy hair, already turning gray at the sides even though he was only in his late thirties.

Five days of twelve-hour shifts, with only the next

four off, had taken its toll on him, as it had on the other four analysts in the long narrow room. They had the pallor of people who worked under fluorescent lighting and never got out in the sun much. They either worked here or they were at home, catching up on their sleep.

"You and me both," Alex said. "The boss's White House briefing has been pushed back to two, but he'd like to know if anything interesting showed up in the overnights."

"I expected he would," Whiteside said. He handed Alex a gray folder marked TOP SECRET. "The Pakis walked out on their talks in New Delhi six hours ago."

A delegation from Pakistan had been in New Delhi for the past four days, trying to hammer out a nuclear disarmament treaty with their Indian counterparts. It was something President Langdon wanted very badly. He had been working with both governments for the past nine months to bring it about.

"They've run back to their embassy before."

"They should be landing in Rawalpindi anytime now."

"It's serious, then."

"The White House won't be happy."

Alex patted him on the arm. "They don't shoot the messenger any longer."

"Let's hope not."

Whiteside was one of the people on campus who Alex liked. He was a dedicated man who was happy with what he did because he loved his country. He was anything but cynical.

"I'll let myself out," she said, and opened the door

in time to see McGarvey and a woman get out of the elevator with a man she would have recognized from across a football field.

She closed the door.

Whiteside had gone back to his desk. He looked up. "Forget something?"

"If we get anything new from our Islamabad and New Delhi stations, Mr. Page will want to know before he goes over to the White House. He'll be leaving around one thirty, so anything at all until then."

"I figured as much. I'll give O'Connor the heads-up when he comes in." Dale O'Connor was the incoming shift supervisor.

"Let's hope it's good news for a change."

THIRTY-FOUR

McGarvey had to go through a major rigmarole to get Schermerhorn past the main gate and then badged so he could be taken upstairs to the seventh floor.

"So this is our Alpha Seven operator," Page said when they walked in.

"What time are you expecting your secretary?" McGarvey asked.

"Why?"

"She might be the one."

"I don't think so. She's been with me for my entire tenure. Damned fine worker, bright, loyal."

"Sounds like Alex," Schermerhorn said. "I just

want to take a look at her, and then we'll check the others."

Page looked at him as if he were a disagreeable insect. "I sent her to the Watch for an update on the overnights."

"I'll check to see if she left her purse behind," Pete said.

"If it's her, she wouldn't carry anything incriminating," McGarvey said. "Just close the door, please."

"I don't like this, Mac," Page said. "I've built a damned fine staff loyal to me because I trust them."

"We're not going to ask her any questions," McGarvey said. "When she gets back from the Watch, ask her to bring you the overnights. Schermerhorn will take a look at her, and when she leaves, it'll be up to him for the identification, and you for the next move. But you did ask for my help."

Page had been standing behind his desk. He nodded and sat down. "Nothing like this has ever happened here. The few people who have any idea what's been going on are frightened out of their minds, and the rest on campus don't know what to make of the tightened security. They know something's up. But not what, and it's got them on edge."

They all sat down across from him.

"How's the situation between Pakistan and India coming along?" Schermerhorn asked unexpectedly.

Page was taken by surprise. "What?"

"Nuclear disarmament. It's important out there. Christ, we don't need a nuclear war, because no matter how local it is, once the genie's out of the jar, it'll spread."

"What the hell are you talking about?" Page asked.

Pete gave McGarvey a questioning look, but he motioned no. He suspected Schermerhorn was trying to tell them something in his oblique way. NOCs, even when they were telling the truth, never told it straight on. They tested the waters first. Always.

"I read the newspapers and the blogs—between the lines. Every now and then even al-Qaeda hits it on the head. Bin Laden kicked the Russians out of Afghanistan. Didn't make him stupid afterward, just rabid."

"I still have no idea what you're talking about."

Schermerhorn shook his head. "Goddamn bureaucrats. Linear thinkers."

"Enough of this."

"Be careful where you tread, Mr. Director. One of these days something just may rise up out of the dust and bite you squarely on the ass."

Page's intercom buzzed. It was his secretary.

"Mr. Whiteside has an update on the situation in New Delhi. May I bring it in?"

Page hesitated, but McGarvey motioned yes.

"Please do," the DCI said.

Alex walked in, nodded to the others, her expression neutral, and handed the file folder to Page. "Mr. Whiteside said if anything new comes up before one thirty, they'll let you know."

"Thanks, Dotty."

Alex walked out, closing the door softly behind her.

* * *

She reached her desk, picked up her phone, and hit 70# in time to hear Page say: "Well?"

Schermerhorn was there; she'd recognized him the moment their eyes had met.

"I don't know," he said. "I mean, I'm not sure."

"Be sure," McGarvey said. "Otherwise, we're talking about an innocent woman."

It was a fabrication. She'd heard it in Roy's voice. He was lying for her benefit because somehow they knew she was listening in.

She pulled her Glock 29 pistol and silencer from its elastic holster attached to the underside of the bottom drawer, stuffed it into her purse, and slipped out the door.

A few people had started to show up, and she smiled and nodded as she made her way down the corridor and around the corner, stopping only long enough to make sure no one was coming after her.

Taking the stairs down two at a time, she reached the second floor before an alarm sounded.

"Attention, Security, OHB is currently under lockdown. This is just a drill. Repeat, the OHB is currently under lockdown. This is just a drill."

She sprinted the rest of the way down to the parking garage. The stairwell doors were only locked from the outside. No security procedures were required to exit; nevertheless, she pulled out her pistol, shifted her bag to her left shoulder, and held the gun at her side.

A lot would depend on the next sixty seconds. If the lockdown included the garage, the security barriers would be raised from the floor at the driveway out and she would be stuck here.

She pulled open the door and stepped out just as a security officer she only vaguely recognized came around the corner at the elevator door, twenty feet away. His sidearm was holstered.

He turned to her. "Sorry, ma'am, we're under lockdown. You'll have to go back up."

Alex walked directly toward him, her eyes on his.

"Didn't you hear?" the officer asked. His name tag read: SOLDIER.

Alex raised her pistol and pointed it at him. "Lay your weapon and your radio on the floor along with your security badge, and then step back."

The man reached for his gun.

She changed aim to his head. "I don't want to kill you, but I will. Do as I told you, immediately."

The officer unholstered his pistol and laid it on the concrete floor, then took his radio from its holster on the opposite hip, unclipped the shoulder mic, and laid them on the floor.

"Your security badge."

He took it off and laid it down.

"Turn around and walk away. If you shout for help, I will shoot you, and trust me, Soldier, I'm an expert marksman."

"No way in hell are you getting out of here."

"You're probably right, and you can take credit for slowing me down. Go, and don't look back."

The officer hesitated for just a moment, but then turned around and headed toward the opposite side of the long garage.

Alex picked up his radio and badge, and then followed him just to where her car was parked. Making sure he wasn't turning around, she got behind the wheel, started the car, and headed for the up ramp.

At that moment a klaxon blared.

She raced the rest of the way up to the exit just as the security barriers began rising from the floor.

A security officer stepped into view in the middle of the driveway.

Without slowing down, she aimed directly for him.

At the last moment he leaped aside, and she passed over the barriers, one of them ripping out her catalytic converter and muffler, and she was outside and free.

She had worked out this scenario before, and in fact, three years ago she had taken a drive around the campus, figuring out ways to get to the rear of the campus, via Colonial Farm Road, which connected through to an automatic gate that then led to Highway 193.

The gate would be locked down for her badge, of course, but she had Soldier's.

THIRTY-FIVE

Page was on the phone with Bob Blankenship, the CIA's chief of security. He put a hand over the mouthpiece. "She just made it out of the garage," he told McGarvey. "We'll have her at the main gate."

"Give those guys the heads-up that she's armed," Pete said, coming in from the outer office.

"Stand by."

"She had a pistol of some kind attached to the bottom of one of the drawers in her desk. She must have heard what we were saying, because she was in a big hurry. She got her gun but didn't close the drawer."

"No," Schermerhorn said. "She *wants* us to know she's carrying. She's thumbing her nose at us because she has a plan."

"Excuse me," McGarvey said, and took the phone from Page. "Bob, Kirk McGarvey. She's armed, but she won't try for the main gate. Did any of your officers have a one-on-one encounter with her?"

"Tom Soldier in the parking garage just a minute or so ago. She disarmed him, but she didn't shoot him."

"Did she take his security badge?"

"Yeah, and his radio, but she left his sidearm on the floor."

"No one got hurt?"

"No."

"Stay off the radio. She's going to try for the back gate, using your security officer's badge, which I assume hasn't been locked out."

"Shit," Blankenship said. "I have two people back there."

"Tell them not to approach her, or she will shoot."

"Can't use the radio, so what do you want me to do? Write them a letter?"

"Radio them. But have the Virginia state police a block off one ninety-three and one twenty-three a couple of miles either side of the gate. If she gets out, she'll try to commandeer a car or truck."

"I'm on it," Blankenship said. "But she's just the DCI's secretary, for Christ's sake."

"She was a NOC and a damned good one, from what I'm told. How soon can we get a couple of choppers in the air in case she abandons her car and tries to make it through the fence on foot?"

"At least fifteen minutes."

"Too late. Tell your people to watch themselves."

"This is unbelievable," Page said. "Are you sure she's the right one?"

"No. But she did take off with a gun she'd hidden in her desk, and she disarmed a security officer."

"She didn't kill him, did she?"

"No."

"Why not?" Page asked.

"I'm going to ask her when I pick her up," McGarvey said. "Roy's coming with me."

"Do I get a gun again?"

"Not this time."

"What about me?" Pete asked.

"I want you to organize someplace secure here on campus for an interrogation. And I do mean secure. At least four people for muscle, and I want it done within the next half hour or less."

"If she's as tough as Roy thinks she is, it may take a while to get through to her."

"Stock the cupboard," McGarvey said.

Out in the corridor, he and Schermerhorn raced down to the stairwell. Several people out in the hallway moved aside as they passed. None of them knew exactly what was going on, but several of them recognized McGarvey and figured that if the former

DCI was in such a hurry, whatever was happening to cause the lockdown had to be big.

"Unit two, copy?"

The radio on the passenger seat next to Alex had fallen silent—until now.

"Two, copy."

"It's possible she's going to try to talk her way through the main gate. I want you to get over there ASAP. Take up position down on the Parkway in case she does manage to get through."

"We'll have to take the long way."

"Hustle."

Alex pulled off the road a hundred yards from the back gate, just as two men got into a Company SUV and drove off. It didn't smell right to her. First there'd been a lot of radio chatter, then nothing, and finally the last exchange. It was a setup, of course. By now they would have notified the Virginia state police to block off 193 and 123 on either side of the gate. And it was also possible, though she wasn't sure of the technical requirements, that the rear gate had been locked down even for security personnel.

"If you start to get sentimental, you might just as well write your will," Bertie Russell had told them before they'd headed to Iraq. "Let it take over, and you'll end up dead meat."

Alex could not remember ever hearing any remark of his that could have been the least positive. But he'd always been right. And he'd been the only man in her life she hadn't been able to seduce.

Just before Germany she'd gone to his quarters on the Farm, carrying two glasses and a bottle of Veuve Clicquot, an inexpensive but decent champagne. It was after midnight, but he had been awake, and he answered almost as if he had been expecting her.

"Couldn't sleep," she said.

He was in a pair of gym shorts and a T-shirt. She was in sweats, nothing on underneath, and it was obvious.

He laughed a little. "I prefer Dom Pérignon, actually."

"Not on my salary," she said. And remembering the incident now, even in the middle of everything from last night and this morning, she'd been embarrassed at that moment. She'd felt shabby. Even cheap.

He'd shrugged. "Go back to your quarters, Alex. Get some sleep. We're shipping out in the morning right after our final briefing."

"I can sleep just as easily in your bed as in mine."

"Go home."

"What? Are you a eunuch?"

"No, just discriminating," he'd said.

He was the only man who'd ever turned her down who she hadn't wanted to kill. And she'd thought about him almost every day, wanting to try again, except he was dead. Only bits and pieces of him—nothing much identifiable as human—had ever been brought back for burial or cremation or whatever had happened in the end.

She powered the window down and searched the sky. They would have choppers up before long, looking for her on foot. Blankenship would know by now that she would try to make her way out the back gate. It was the obvious reason he'd broken radio silence.

She put the BMW in gear and slowly made her way down the shallow drainage ditch and into the woods. This part of the campus bordered on Langley Fork Park, which was for the most part heavily wooded. There were hiking trails through the northern portion of the sprawling park, but nearer the highway were baseball, soccer, football, and other sports fields. On weekends and throughout the summer, the place was busy. But this morning she figured it would be empty or practically so.

She pulled up about thirty yards from the tall razor-wire–topped chain-link fence that marked the edge of the CIA's property. On the other side, no trespassing notices had been posted, marking it a restricted government area. Federal parks and roads property, a fiction no one had believed for a long time.

Stomping down on the gas, she headed straight for the fence, smashing halfway through but destroying the front end of the car. The engine bucked and heaved, then stopped.

She got out, stood beside the ruined car for a moment or two, but then retrieved her bag, her pistol, and the radio. She headed back the way she had come, but staying in the woods and out of sight of anyone passing on the road.

THIRTY-SIX

McGarvey pulled up just off Colonial Farm Road, where tire tracks led off into the woods to the west, took out his pistol, and got out of the car. The morning was bright and sunny.

In the distance to the south he could hear at least two sirens, possibly more, probably the Virginia state police setting up roadblocks.

"God damn it, I want a gun," Schermerhorn said.

"In the glove compartment," McGarvey told him. "But if you shoot at her for anything other than self-defense, I'll shoot you myself."

McGarvey started along the tire tracks, not believing for one minute she would try to kill him. She had had the chance, once she was armed, to walk back into Page's office and kill them all, because she knew they hadn't been allowed to pass through security while carrying their firearms.

She'd also had the chance, and the cause, to kill the security officer who'd confronted her in the parking garage. But she had merely disarmed him and let him walk away, knowing he would report the contact once he reached a phone.

Schermerhorn came after him, the Beretta 92F in his left hand.

McGarvey looked at him. "Are you ambidextrous?"

"No, always been a lefty."

"What about Alex and George?"

"George is right-handed. Alex is a lefty just like me," Schermerhorn said. "We were the only two." He suddenly caught on. "The killer is right-handed?"

"The autopsies on the three killed here on campus showed they were murdered by someone right-handed. The CSI people confirmed it."

"Lets me off the hook," Schermerhorn said. "And Alex."

"Leaves only George," McGarvey said.

Schermerhorn stopped and scanned the woods ahead and to the left and right. "Then why the hell did she run?"

"Maybe she doesn't trust you."

"Great," Schermerhorn said. "I will defend myself."

They followed the tire marks another fifty yards or so through the woods until they came to the clearing, across which the green BMW convertible was crashed halfway through the fence. On the other side was a matching clearing that bordered the thick woods. Highway 193 was a mile or so off to the left, on the other side of the playing fields.

McGarvey walked to the car and looked inside. No blood, no purse.

In order to make it past the car to the other side of the fence, Alex would have needed to have gotten up on the hood and slid across. The car didn't look as if it had been washed in the past week or so, and was a little dusty. But there were no marks on the hood.

He looked in the car again, but the radio was not there. She hadn't left it on the passenger seat, or tossed it onto the floor or in the back. But once off campus, it would be out of range, so there was no reason for her to have taken it.

"She's on foot. Shouldn't be hard for the cops to round her up," Schermerhorn said. "But they should be given the heads-up that she's armed and she knows how to use a gun."

McGarvey holstered his pistol and headed back to where he'd left his car. He phoned Pete.

"Did you get her?" she asked.

"We found where she crashed her car through the fence and then abandoned it. But she didn't try for the highway. She's still somewhere on campus."

"That doesn't make any sense."

"She's not the killer, neither is Roy, so it has to be George. It's why she came back to work for Page, and why she changed her mind this morning. She wants to find him to save her own life."

"So what do you want to do?"

"Set up a place where we can talk to her."

"I'm on it now. The maintenance people are on their way over to the Scattergood-Thorne house, and I'm just leaving Bob Blankenship's office. He's sending four of his top people. But if she's not the killer, this is mostly meaningless."

"She knows who it is, but I think she also knows why."

"What about you and Schermerhorn?"

"We'll be there in ten minutes. In the meantime, tell Blankenship to cancel the lockdown and have all his people except the four stand down. And bring one of their radios with you. I want to talk to her."

Alex was about to cross the road to the maintenance garage when McGarvey's Porsche SUV passed, and she quickly ducked back into the woods. She'd only gotten a brief glimpse, but it was enough for her to recognize Roy in the passenger seat.

When the way was clear, she went across. Several pickup trucks with the CIA logo were parked in back, but no one was out and about. After ducking into the big six-bay garage, she held up in the shadows behind a stack of boxes marked MOTOR OIL in various weights.

Someone was talking inside what appeared from her vantage point to be a break room to her left. She could see a fridge and cabinets, and a coffee maker on the counter. Whoever it was sounded agitated, though she couldn't make out the words.

To the right was a locker room with low benches and a dozen lockers adjacent to the showers and toilets.

She slipped inside then stopped again to listen, but the showers weren't running. Everyone on duty was apparently either out on the job, mowing lawns, or in the break room. She opened six lockers in quick succession, finally finding a pair of coveralls and a ball cap that weren't vastly too big for her, and put them on.

Whoever was in the break room was still arguing about something, and no one came out to see her slip through the rear door and get into one of the pickup trucks, start it with her universal electronic key, and drive off.

The questions in her head at this moment were the same as they had been from the day she had come back to the Company for a job inside: What the hell happened in Iraq, and what she should do about it, if anything?

Last year, when Carnes was killed in Athens, she'd

damned well known it had been no accident. Joseph and no one else on the team, would have been so sloppy to allow something like that to happen.

She'd become ultracautious with her movements. It was when she had rented the second apartment in Tysons Corner and put the pistol in her desk.

And when Walt and Isty and then Tom had bought the farm—one, two, three—she knew she was somewhere near the top of the list, and her radar had risen. Someone was coming for her; it was just a matter of time, and just a matter of being prepared.

Coffin's assassination in Piraeus had not come as a surprise, though he had danced all the proper steps to stay safe, ingeniously hiding himself in prison. But when McGarvey got involved, she'd known it was a foregone conclusion the rest of them would be killed. They had to be silenced.

The trouble was, she didn't really know the entire why of it.

She drove past the large cluster of buildings on the main campus and headed the rest of the way up to the Scattergood-Thorne house, where she figured she would make her stand. She would see to it McGarvey came to her.

He was the one man other than Page who she felt she could trust her life with. But Page was an administrator on his way out the door, while McGarvey was a force within the intelligence community. A tough man, but she'd always heard, a fair one.

THIRTY-SEVEN

The lockdown was over, and people were beginning to move around the campus as business slowly returned to normal. McGarvey and Schermerhorn showed up at the Scattergood-Thorne house just as the caterers were stocking the larder in the pantry, and the four men from Blankenship's flying squad were activating the electronic security system for the house and grounds.

McGarvey had been here once during his brief tenure as the DCI, hosting a strategic planning briefing for the heads of the US's four major intel trading partners from Great Britain, Canada, Australia, and New Zealand. Along with the U.S., they were called the Five Eyes.

Pete met them in the front entry hall. "We should have everything squared away here within the next few minutes. With her still on the loose, I figured you'd be in a hurry."

"Get rid of the muscle," McGarvey said. "She came back because she wants to tell us something."

"Bob thought you'd say something like that. He wants to keep at least two of them here at any given time. They can rotate on twelve-hour shifts."

"Only one at a time, and as long as he stays out of the way."

Otto came in, a big grin on his face. "That whole situation could have gone south in a New York minute. No one got hurt. She wants to talk."

"That's what I figured," McGarvey said. "What about panel four? Are you making any progress?"

"My darlings are still chewing on it. But if Roy would help out, it would speed things up."

"It's a transposition code; I've already told you that much," Schermerhorn said. "And you already have the six-letter solution Sanborn gave us. *NYPVVT* spelled out *BERLIN* in 2010."

"You changed the code."

"Yeah. But *BERLIN* is still there, still in the same position, just a different set of letters."

"Damn it," Otto said. He never swore unless he was frustrated, and he almost never got frustrated. "More lives are at stake here."

"Including mine," Schermerhorn said. "But the solution has to come from you; otherwise, no one will believe it."

"No one meaning who?" McGarvey asked.

Schermerhorn shook his head. "You'll see."

One of Blankenship's men came in from the back door. "We found a pickup truck parked behind the garage. It was taken from the maintenance unit about ten minutes ago."

McGarvey took the radio from Pete, switched it on, and hit the push-to-talk button. "Alex, this is Kirk McGarvey. I'm here with some people who would like to talk to you. Why don't you come in and join us?"

"If you've given Roy a gun, take it from him," Alex replied. "And tell whoever Blankenship sent over to wait outside."

"Pete Boylan is with me."

"She's okay."

"Leave your pistol behind."

"Not until I'm sure I'll be secure," she said. But not over the radio.

They turned around in time to see her coming down the stairs, the silenced Glock in her left hand.

The security officer reached for his pistol, but McGarvey motioned him back.

Roy had the Beretta out and was pointing it up at her.

"I asked you to take Roy's gun," she said tightly.

"No firing pin," McGarvey said.

"Shit," Roy muttered. He handed the gun butt first to McGarvey. "Thanks. If she had come out shooting, I would have been shit out of luck."

"I lied," McGarvey said, stuffing the pistol in his belt. "Nothing's wrong with the firing pin."

Alex laughed. She lowered her pistol and came down the stairs to them.

"You've come as something of a surprise," McGarvey said. "But we know you're not the killer and neither is Roy."

"We're left-handed," Alex said. She handed the pistol to McGarvey, who gave it to the security officer.

"Leave us now," he said.

"Yes, sir, I'll be just outside."

"Tell maintenance I'm sorry I screwed up their fence and then stole one of their trucks," Alex said. "I also lifted a set of coveralls and a ball cap from someone's locker. They're upstairs in one of the front bedrooms, along with Soldier's radio."

Otto was staring at her with open admiration. "You were damned good," he said.

"I still am."

"I'm going back to my darlings to tweak the decryption program. I'll let you know when I come up with something."

"Even a partial something," McGarvey said.

The room set up for them was the same one the conference had been held in. The windows were double glazed, white noise pumped between the panes to block out any laser surveillance. The walls were covered with sound-absorbing material that gave the appearance of an expensive damask treatment. And the entire space, top to bottom, was inside a Faraday cage to block electronic signals from coming in or going out.

McGarvey and Pete sat across the long table from Alex while Schermerhorn took up position at the end nearest the door, as if he wanted to bolt if necessary or even stop Alex if she tried to run.

"What made you think to come here of all places on campus?" Pete started.

"You wanted to ask me some questions, and had the tables been reversed, this is where I would have set up. Away from the OHB and out of the fray, so to speak."

"But this is where Fabry was murdered."

"I know. Almost a symmetry to it, my being here to help you catch George." Alex pursed her lips. "It's why we're here like this, isn't it?"

"Do you really give a rat's ass about any of them, or me?" Schermerhorn asked.

She thought about it for a moment. "At first you

guys were fun. We were a team. But then George dropped in on us, and everything changed."

"For the better?"

"Just changed," Alex said.

"Would you recognize George if you saw him, the same way you recognized Alex?" McGarvey asked Schermerhorn.

"Damn right."

"He's not here," Alex said. "When Wager was hit, I started looking to see if anyone from the old team was here, besides him, Isty, and Tom."

"But you didn't try to warn them after Wager was murdered," Pete said.

Alex shook her head. "It all happened so fast. There was nothing I could do that wouldn't reveal my true identity. I found out about Joe Carnes and Larry Coffin, which left only Roy and George. Neither one of them were on campus, so far as I was able to tell."

"But you knew the killer was right-handed, and that both of us are lefties," Schermerhorn said angrily. "So then there was only George."

This time Alex smiled. "Remember the story you told me a few days after we got to Iraq? About when you were a kid in Catholic school in Milwaukee?"

"What are you talking about?"

"We'd just had sex, so your memory might be a little fuzzy. But I know what you said."

"I'm listening."

"The nuns thought being left-handed was deviant, so they beat you for two years straight, making you use your right hand for everything. They put your left in a thick mitten. Put your arm in a sling. Even tied it to your side."

"It didn't take," Schermerhorn said. "Soon as I got into public school, I went back to being a lefty."

"Yes," Alex said. "But you'd learned to use your right hand just as good as a natural."

THIRTY-EIGHT

"That's a refreshing bit of news," Pete said. "Puts us back to two possibilities." She made a point of laying her pistol on the table. "George and Roy. Sounds like a comedy act."

"Not Roy. He was never capable of anything like that. Only I and George were."

"You told us you looked, but George was not on campus."

"I told you I looked. Doesn't mean he isn't—or wasn't—here."

"Then you think he's gone?"

"I wish it were true. But as long as Roy and I are here, he'll stick around or, at the very least, come back. He wants us both in order to finish his cover-up."

"We could move you somewhere else, somewhere safer," Pete said.

Schermerhorn laughed. "You said he found Larry Coffin in some Greek prison. He'll find us unless we find him first."

"For once Roy is right," Alex said. "Why do think I turned around and came back inside? Maybe between the four of us, we can stop him."

McGarvey noticed that a small bead of perspiration had formed on her upper lip, and her nostrils flared as if she were trying to catch her breath. She was frightened, and from what he'd learned about her background, and from her performance over the past four years and especially this morning, he was impressed.

"Stop him from doing what?" Schermerhorn asked.

"From killing us, for starts," she shot back.

"And?"

"What the hell are you talking about? And we're dead. That's it. All of Alpha Seven gone."

"So what? Why should we care? By your own admission, it was only you and George who were capable of chewing people's necks away so they would bleed to death. Then destroying their faces so they would be unrecognizable even to their wives and children. Do you know Fanni Fabry is still in the hospital? She had a serious heart attack, and on the way in she kept telling the paramedic that she knew something like this would happen someday."

Alex looked away. She was shivering.

"What wife *knows* her husband will die in that way?" McGarvey demanded. Katy had been afraid for him from the day she'd learned what he really did for a living. But she once confessed she couldn't imagine the shock and pain of getting shot. It was beyond her ken. Beyond what normal people experienced or even thought about.

But knowing your husband would have his neck ripped open, his blood drained, and his face mutilated?

"I don't know what he told her. He was a sweet guy—a good operator—but naive. Never was anything cynical about him. He believed in the best in people."

"Including you?" McGarvey asked.

She nodded. "Even me until near the end."

"That was when you and George went on your rampage in the oil fields."

She'd become a little pale, much of the color gone from her face. She held her hands together in front of her on the table, her eyes downcast, and McGarvey had the feeling she was putting on an act for them. Maybe even for herself.

"George," he prompted.

"He came swooping down on us early one evening, just around dusk. When he landed, he said he was the avenging angel. And I guess all of us believed him in one way or the other."

"I didn't," Schermerhorn said.

Alex flared. "Bullshit, you all but put him on an altar and kissed his ass, just like the rest of us—"

"Why?" McGarvey interrupted. "This guy swooped down on you—exactly how, and what, did he say to make you not open fire first and check credentials afterward? Your team was in badland. He could have been anyone. Mukhabarat. Spetsnaz, GRU—the Russians had interests over there, still do."

"He made a HALO jump, but it wasn't until Carnes spotted his chute about a thousand feet up and maybe a klick or so out that we realized someone was dropping in for a visit. If it had been the Iraqi or Russian Special Forces or intel people, they would have sent in more than one man."

This was her story and no one interrupted her, not even Schermerhorn, who looked as if he had been transported back to that time. His face was filled with a lot of emotion. Nothing hidden, unless it was another act.

"Besides, by the time he walked into our position, we had him covered. If he had so much as given any of us a bad look, we would have shot him. He just came up the hill and said 'Hi, I'm your new control officer. You may call me George.'

"Chameleon challenged him, but he just said something to the effect that he knew where we were hiding and what our mission was. Said it was stupid at best and everyone at headquarters knew it, so he had come out to save our asses."

"Those were his only credentials?" McGarvey prompted after she fell silent for several moments.

"That and he knew all our handles, something only Bertie knew. It was enough for us."

"Why didn't Bertie come with you?"

"I don't know."

"Who was your team lead before George showed up?"

"Larry was."

"The Chameleon," McGarvey said.

She nodded. "Anyway, our new orders were to harass the enemy. We weren't going to confront them in a shootout. 'This won't be another O.K. Corral,' he said. 'We're the insurgents. We'll sneak down at night, take out a handful of soldiers, officers if possible, and then scoot back up into the hills.' "

"The Iraqis must have reacted."

"At first they sent out patrols on foot, but we just

avoided them. It was easy to do in that terrain. When they started sending up helicopters, it got a little tougher, but we managed."

"Was that when you and George stepped up your attacks?" McGarvey asked. "Picked up the level of savagery?"

Alex glanced at Schermerhorn but then looked away. "He said they deserved whatever we could give them. It wasn't just about the coming war; it was about a millennium plus of senseless murders in the name of a supposed prophet."

"Muhammad."

"He was rabid on the subject. We all thought he was probably a Jew, with his New York Brooklyn accent, or maybe even Upper East Side. Maybe had relatives who'd died in the Holocaust, maybe even people he knew in Israel."

"Could he have been Mossad?" McGarvey asked. "It would explain his dedicated hatred."

"Some of the guys thought so, but his English didn't have the British accent Israelis learn in school."

"I thought he was Mossad," Schermerhorn said. "Born in New York but emigrated to Israel."

"Then why in heaven's name did you cooperate with him?" Pete asked gently but in genuine amazement. She wanted to hear his side of the story. "Maybe it was the fog of war?"

"I don't know. But by then I think all of us, including Larry, were willing to follow Alex's lead. And she seemed to think this guy was something special."

"He was," Alex said.

"How soon after he showed up were you sleeping with him?" Pete asked.

"A couple of microseconds. He said he had come bearing a gift—a secret that was going to change everything. And I wanted to find out what it was."

"And did you?" McGarvey prompted.

"We all did, and believe me, it was nothing we expected."

THIRTY-NINE

The sun had come around so that it shined directly into the conference room windows, which darkened automatically, giving the bright day the look of an overcast one. It seemed to fit Alex's and Schermerhorn's moods.

"Could I have something to drink?" she asked. "Coffee, water, I don't care. It's been a long morning."

"You were telling us about a gift George brought you," McGarvey said.

"He didn't exactly put it that way. But he said he'd come to help."

"And it did change everything." Schermerhorn said.

"First something to drink."

McGarvey nodded, and Pete went out of the room to get something. She left her pistol lying on the table, directly across from where Alex was sitting.

After a beat Alex stood up and went to the windows. "A white van is just leaving," she said. "Blankenship's minders?"

"I suspect it's the caterers. They came to stock up for us."

"You're thinking about keeping me here, along with Roy, till this thing is figured out? It won't be that easy, though. Not without George. So I suppose we'll be the hand-carved ducks floating in the pond, the hunter hiding in the weeds."

She went back to the table and looked at the pistol before she sat down.

"Will he show up?" McGarvey asked.

"It depends on his orders, I suppose, but he's already demonstrated what he's capable of. Five down, only the two of us left."

"You looked for him here, but you said you couldn't find him. Maybe he's not the killer."

Alex laughed, but it was without humor. "You still can't imagine how easy it is to get in and out of this place. Especially if you're willing to kill someone for it."

"Are you?"

Alex looked straight at McGarvey. "Under the right circumstances, you bet. But so far no one has held a gun to my head."

"What about the security officer in the parking garage?"

She laughed again. "Come on, McGarvey. You know as well as I do that most of your rent-a-cops are outclassed. As long as everyone plays by the rules, the system works. But step outside the playbook, and Blankenship only has a few good men who know what the hell they're doing."

Pete came back with a couple of liter-and-a-half bottles of Evian and several paper cups.

Alex opened one of the bottles, poured half a

glass, and handed it to Pete. "You have to be just as thirsty as I am by now."

"Yeah, listening to bullshit always makes me thirsty," Pete said, and drank the water. She shrugged. "Sorry to disappoint you, Ms. Unroth, but I'm not suddenly going to go all glassy-eyed and start telling the truth because something's been put in the water. Though it'd be good if you and Roy did. Maybe we could get somewhere and actually save your lives."

"Give Roy and me guns and a lot of ammunition and put us in a safe room here. Then send us a video feed of every single male and female on campus— George was a pretty boy. Narrow face, nice eyes, great lips. That would include all employees, including the guys in the Watch, the janitors and other maintenance people, the caterers who just came and went. Bus drivers and taxi drivers who drop people off at the OHB. Tour guides, along with all the VIP congressmen, Pentagon staffers. FBI people and any other LE person who've ever come on campus. The people who come in to fix the leaks in the roof, or the plugged-up toilets, or the electrical outlets that spark. The crews that blacktopped the road six months ago. The cable people—we just upgraded our fiber-optic network. How about pilots and passengers flying across our airspace? Anyone notice the hang gliders down in Langley Fork Park? Or hikers or campers not far from where I crashed through the fence? How about tunnels, storm water drainage pipes? You guys have all that covered?"

"I expect we have most of it," McGarvey said, getting her point.

"Most of it's not good enough. And who watches the watchers? Who minds the minders? This place leaks like a sieve."

Pete sat down. "Wager and the others thought they were safer in here than outside," she said.

"They were wrong, weren't they?" Alex flared. "Like shooting fish in a barrel. You people still don't get it."

"Then why didn't you run when you had the chance?" McGarvey asked. "Why'd you come back into the barrel, knowing all that?"

"Because of you."

"Thanks for that, but I didn't do such a hot job in Athens."

"But you did. You were the lightning rod. George has an inside source here. You were hiding out in Serifos when Pete and Otto came to talk to you about the murders here on campus. Mr. Page knew about it, and so did I. But Marty Bambridge knew, and I expect there were people on his staff who also knew. And excuse me, Mr. Director, but when's the last time you had your lighthouse swept for bugs? Or debugged your phones or computer? When Otto talks to you, he uses his backscatter encryption system no one has been able to break. But that in itself is a dead giveaway. He makes an encrypted call to Serifos, and voilà, someone like George could know he's talking to his old friend Kirk McGarvey."

"Nice speech," Pete said.

"I'll stay here as long as I think it's safe for me to

stay. But give me something to protect myself with when George does show up."

"You'd just walk out the door?"

"Christ. Haven't you people heard a thing I just said? Yeah, if the time comes, I'll just walk out the door."

"Let's make sure he's coming, and then help us to catch him," McGarvey said.

"He's on his way, Mr. Director, if he's not already here," Alex said.

"We'll do what you've asked, except arm you. Otto can set up the video feeds, starting with personnel records of everyone on campus, along with the surveillance records for the past week. No need to get beyond when Walt Wager was murdered. Pete will take care of nailing down every opening in the physical plant, and I'll stick it out here with you two."

"Send Blankenship's minders away."

"I didn't sign up for this shit," Schermerhorn said.

"Fine," McGarvey said. "We'll ship your ass back to Milwaukee and let the cops straighten things out."

"I want a pistol."

"The surveillance system is pretty good here."

"Didn't help Walt."

"It wasn't armed when he was killed. You want to do this, I'm it."

A look passed between Alex and Schermerhorn. "Set up the video feed for us, and if George is on campus, we'll spot him," Alex said.

"Something's buried in the hills above Kirkuk," Pete said.

"That's what George came to tell us. And that's the whole point, even though it still makes absolutely no sense."

"Well, what is it, for goodness sake?" Pete asked.

Alex hesitated. "It isn't so much what it is—or was, because I think it may have been moved after we left—but why it was, and its pedigree, if you will."

"You're making no sense," Pete said.

"I know. But first decrypt Roy's redo of *Kryptos* four, and let's try to take George alive to give us some answers. Because without them, all our lives in this room—even yours, Mr. Director—will be forfeit."

"Nothing's that big," Pete said.

"This is," Alex and Schermerhorn replied almost simultaneously.

FORTY

Alex knew George was coming for her. They'd all known it to one degree or another. But she thought she was special, not so much for the sexual relationship she'd had with him, or for the rampages they'd gone on down in the oil fields, but because of her position of influence with the DCI. So she figured she would be the last.

It was very late, and while standing in front of the window in the back bedroom, she began to rethink her options. Perhaps coming back hadn't been such a good idea, except that after looking at all the photos Otto had sent over—several hundred of them and many more to go—she was convinced George had left the campus.

And she had a pretty fair idea where he'd gone and why. Killing her and Roy wouldn't be so easy for him now that McGarvey had become involved, and he had to know it. Maybe in the end he was becoming the duck decoy, and they the hunters.

Getting out of here and going to him seemed to her to be the only sensible thing to do now.

As luck would have it, Pete had checked her bag before they brought her back upstairs. She'd taken the radio, of course, and the Glock, but had left her spare underwear and wallet with her Givens's things. But none of them had thought to search the room for her cell phone, universal car key, or the papers she'd used to rent the car at the airport.

McGarvey showed up at the open door. "Don't you guys ever sleep?" he asked.

The house had settled down a couple of hours ago after he'd declared it a night. There'd be more videos and photos to see in the morning, but Blankenship had been given her list of the campus's security defects, and his people were busy attending to them. Or at least starting.

"Only when it's safe."

"None of us understand why you don't just tell us what George showed you up in the hills."

"I suppose you don't," Alex said, turning to face him. Her room was dark, only the light from the hall spilling in. Schermerhorn's door was closed. "Is Roy asleep?"

"He's looking at some of the photographs again. Says he might have found a couple of possibilities."

"Maybe I'll help him."

McGarvey looked at her for a long time. "Get some sleep. Tomorrow will be a long day, and you guys need to be ready for it in case George does show up."

"He could come tonight."

"Daylight attacks so far."

"What about security?"

"One of Blankenship's guys is outside."

"What's his name? Maybe I know him."

"Maybe you do," McGarvey said. "Get some sleep."

"Yeah," Alex said.

McGarvey went back downstairs. She could hear his footfalls, and then low voices, his and Pete's. She wondered if they were sleeping together.

She retrieved her universal key and the Alice Walker IDs, credit card, and cash, and stuffed them into her pockets. Slipping on the maintenance man's coveralls and ball cap, she went across the hall and tapped lightly on Schermerhorn's door, keeping her eye on the head of the stairs in case McGarvey came back.

Schermerhorn didn't answer, so she went in.

At first she thought he was gone. The computer was on, a man's face on the screen. But then she realized he was standing in the deeper shadows in the corner.

"I'm getting out of here, but I need you to buy me a little time," she told him.

"What the hell are you talking about?" he demanded. He was bright enough to keep his voice barely above a whisper.

"They're bound to check in the next hour or so. And when they find I'm not in my room, they'll come here. Stuff some pillows under the covers next to you and tell them we're sleeping together."

"McGarvey won't buy it."

"He might if you're loud enough."

"Christ, how the fuck are you going to get out of here? And where are you going?"

"The how has always been my business, and I think you know the where. But just keep looking for George's picture and keep your mouth shut. They're not going to shoot you for helping me."

"You're crazy, do you know that?"

"Just like all of us were for keeping our mouths shut when we had the chance to blow the whistle."

"Would have been our death warrants."

"Still could be."

"Just don't kill any of the good guys," Schermerhorn said.

"Might already be too late for that, Roy. Just watch your back, okay?"

She slipped out of his room and went to the end of the hall, where she crept down the narrow servants' stairs that led to the kitchen pantry and the room with the dish cabinets and sinks for washing up.

Early in their careers, NOCs were trained to work on the other guy's expectations. Do what they thought you would do, only in a different fashion. McGarvey and the minders expected her to stay and help them find George. And that was exactly what she was going to do—help them find George. Only in the way they hadn't thought of.

She would leave them a trail of cookie crumbs so they could get the story from the horse's mouth—in such a way no one in the White House or on the Hill could possibly deny it.

The door to the kitchen was open. A dim light illuminated the stair hall at the front of the house. The only sounds were the motors on the fridge and the deep freeze.

At the back door, which would have been the servants' entrance and the place for deliveries, she hesitated for just a moment before she went out into the night.

The officer who'd been in the front stair hall had to have been relieved by now. So whoever was out here was on his own, and he hadn't seen her.

A Cadillac Escalade, the semiofficial car of the CIA, was parked down by the garage next to the pickup truck, which hadn't been returned to maintenance yet. A man was seated in the Caddy's driver's seat, which was sloppy as hell. Considering what had happened on campus over the past several days and what was possible to happen here at any moment, the officer's disregard for security bordered on criminal.

She angled away from the house and approached the Caddy from the driver's side, and it wasn't until she got to within a couple of feet that the officer realized someone was coming up on him. He did a double take when he saw the maintenance department coveralls and ball cap.

"Who the hell are you?" he demanded, his door coming open.

"I came for our pickup truck," Alex said, keeping her voice low. "They told me you would be back here somewhere."

"How the fuck did you get here? No one told me anything."

"They dropped me off," she said.

All of a sudden he realized he'd made a very bad mistake, and reached for his pistol holstered at his side.

Alex waited until he had it out then suddenly stepped inside his reach and snatched it out of his hand, twisting his wrist sharply to the left. It was a big Glock 20. She turned the pistol on him.

"If you cooperate for the next twenty minutes or so, I wiil not kill you," she said. "And you can start by making no noise and by keeping your hand away from your radio. Nod if you understand."

The officer hesitated only a moment, embarrassment all over his face, but he nodded.

"This is the plan. You're going to drive me through the main gate and down to Turkey Run Park on the river. I'll take your radio and the Caddy, and you'll have to hoof it up to the Parkway to hitch a ride back."

"I can't let you do this; it'd mean my job," the officer said.

"Don't, and it'll mean your life. When you get back, you can tell them you were doing a foot patrol around the house when I came up behind you with my own weapon, and you had absolutely no choice."

"Did you kill those people?"

"No. But I have a pretty good idea who did, and I'm going to find him. You can tell them that, too. Give me your radio and get in the car."

He did as he was told.

"VIPs get the armored version of this car, but I'm betting you guys don't. So don't do anything stupid. A ten-millimeter round will go through the windshield with no problem."

Keeping the gun on him, she hurried around the front of the car and got in on the passenger side.

"No lights until we're away from the house," Alex told him. "Now go."

FORTY-ONE

McGarvey and Pete stood together at an upstairs window facing the back. He had his cell phone out, and as soon as the security officer's Caddy disappeared down the hill and around the sweeping curve through a copse of trees, he phoned the main gate and got the duty officer.

"This is Kirk McGarvey. Do you recognize my voice, or do I need to have Mr. Page phone you to verify?"

"No, sir, I was here when you were DCI," the man said.

"A CIA Escalade will be coming through the gate within the next few minutes. A man driving, a woman in the passenger seat. Don't interfere with them."

"No, sir. The lockdown has been canceled."

"I know. But I want you to call me as soon as the Caddy passes your position, and then confirm that both of those people are in the car."

"Yes, sir," the duty officer said with some hesitation. "Has this anything to do with our trouble?"

"Yes," McGarvey said. "Call me." He hung up.

"You're taking a big chance she won't shoot the guy soon as they get clear," Pete said.

"She's not the killer," McGarvey told her on the way downstairs. "Call Blankenship and have him send over another one of his people."

Pete glanced up. "What about Schermerhorn?"

"He's not our killer either. It's George—whoever the hell he is. And Alex has gone to find him."

"Or join him."

"I'm going to follow her and find out just that," McGarvey said. "Call Blankenship now, and watch yourself. This is far from over."

"You too," she said at the door. She gave him a peck on the cheek, which stopped him in his tracks. It was unexpected.

He looked at her for a beat. "Take care of yourself, Pete. I don't want to lose you."

"And I don't want to lose you."

Outside, he got into his Porsche SUV and headed down the narrow blacktopped road that led around the OHB and main cluster of administrative buildings.

His cell phone chirped; it was the OD at the main gate.

"They just passed."

"Thanks," McGarvey said. He called Pete. "They're out."

"Blankenship isn't happy, but he's sending two of his people up here. He wants to know why we can't go after his man."

"Tell him I'm on it," McGarvey said. He phoned Otto and told him the situation.

"We caught a break. We're at the extreme end of a pass. I can task the satellite, but it'll take a minute or so, and the angle will be very low."

"How's the decryption going?"

"Close," Otto said. "Hang on."

A couple of minutes later McGarvey drove past the main gate and down the hill toward the interchange with the George Washington Parkway, which to the right headed downriver toward Washington and, to the left, upriver, where it ended in a couple of miles at I-495.

Traffic was all but nonexistent at this time of the night, and when McGarvey got within a hundred yards or so from the interchange, he slowed to a crawl.

"They turned left," Otto came back. "But that's all I can give you for another eighteen minutes until a new bird comes up over the horizon."

"How far behind am I?" McGarvey said, speeding up.

"About three minutes, but if she spots you, it's game over unless all you want to do is get her back. And that could end up in a hostage situation gone bad, though I don't think she'd take it that far."

"Get back to the decryption. I want it as fast as possible," McGarvey said, and hung up.

He swung left along the long curving entrance that merged with the Parkway, and tucked in behind a Safeway eighteen-wheeler that, the way it was driving, looked as if it were heading unloaded back to a distribution center somewhere just outside of the city.

The truck was speeding, about fifteen miles per hour over the limit, and he figured Alex wouldn't be doing anything to attract any attention, so she would probably have the security officer drive only five or ten miles per hour over the speed limit.

Before long he would catch up with her.

At the last moment he caught a glimpse of the Escalade turning off the highway and disappearing into the woods toward the river. The brown National Park Service sign announced it was the entrance to Turkey Run Park.

Standing on the brakes, McGarvey managed to pull over about fifty yards past the entrance, the Escalade well out of sight. A car coming up in the distance seemed to take forever before it reached him and passed.

He slammed the Porsche in reverse and headed back to the park entrance, worried he'd read her wrong and she was capable of killing an agency security officer in cold blood. She could leave his body somewhere in the park, and by the time it was discovered in the morning, she would be long gone.

As he pulled into the park, he saw that the entry road paralleled the highway for a little ways before it passed the upriver exit road. He switched off his headlights and slowed down. In the distance a narrow blacktopped road turned right, while the main entry road continued to parallel the Parkway before crossing over to connect with the downriver-bound highway.

The park's gate would be closed, but most of the area was heavily wooded, with hundreds of places to pull off and hide a body.

McGarvey took the road right into the park, slowing to a crawl. Less than one hundred yards in, he caught a glimpse of the Caddy ahead, and he got off the road. He jumped out of his car and ran through the woods, pistol in hand.

It was more than possible he had underestimated the woman and would be in time to see her gun down the security officer.

The road here was very narrow, trees close in, making it next to impossible for her to turn around. When McGarvey got to where the Caddy was stopped, the security officer was standing next to the car, his hands above his head, Alex ten feet away from him. McGarvey couldn't hear what they were saying, but the officer shook his head, lowered his hands, and walked away down the road, deeper into the park toward the river.

Alex watched him until he was just about out of sight, and then she stuffed the pistol she'd been holding into the pocket of her coveralls.

McGarvey turned and raced as fast as he could to where he'd parked his Porsche, managed to get it turned around, and headed back to the access road, where he got lucky with a spot to pull through some brush and into a stand of trees.

Less than a minute later, Alex at the wheel, the

Escalade passed and sped off to the upriver access to the Parkway, toward I-495, where she would either turn north up to I-270 into the Maryland countryside of small quaint towns, or south on I-495 and on to Dulles.

He got his car back up on the highway, headlights still out, and stayed well behind until he merged with the Parkway and spotted her taillights three-quarters of a mile away.

The highway crested a hill, and he lost her for a half a minute. He switched on his headlights and paced her, turning with her south onto I-495, where, within a couple of miles, traffic started to pick up and tailing her became much easier.

He called Otto. "She's heading south on four ninety-five. Call Blankenship and tell him his officer is in Turkey Run Park, unharmed."

"If she's going to Dulles, we'll have to get a team out there to look for her. I don't know what ID she'd be traveling under."

"How soon will you have a satellite in position?"

"Seven minutes. Do you want me to alert Dulles security?"

"If she knows we're on her tail, she'll break off and go deep. I want to know where she's heading."

FORTY-TWO

Alex took the battery out of the security officer's radio and tossed it out the window just before she reached the Dulles Access Road and continued straight. It was possible that the unit had a built-in GPS, though she hadn't heard of that being the case, but she wanted to minimize her risks while it was still possible to do so.

She'd taken a lot of care with her tradecraft. Slowing down, speeding up, switching lanes so suddenly, the drivers she cut off blew their horns, all the while checking her rearview mirrors. But nothing stood out.

It was possible they thought she might still be on campus, though the officers on the main gate had to have seen the Caddy passing by. But unless they suspected trouble, there would have been no reason to report it. The only issue she could see was that McGarvey or someone had by now discovered that the officer and his car were missing. She'd left the radio on to make sure he wasn't supposed to make regular radio checks, but there'd been no queries.

In fact, she was just slightly disappointed McGarvey wasn't on her tail. She'd figured it was a strong possibility he'd come after her. But then Pete Boylan was in love with him, and maybe she was making it obvious to him this morning.

She got off at Tysons Corner a few minutes after four and drove in a very roundabout way to the self-storage unit, using the keypad to gain entry. Her small locker was at the rear of the big facility, well out of sight of Leesburg Pike.

The only noise back here was from the light traffic on the highway. Washington was like New York City in that it almost never completely shut down. And there always seemed to be traffic on the Beltway.

Her unit was filled with cardboard boxes, mostly of old clothes, dishes, pots and pans, curtains, sheets, blankets, and pillows.

Making certain no one was coming, she crawled up on top of the pile and, near the back, moved several cartons, finding a large one that contained several layers of old shoes. Near the bottom she pulled out an attaché case, under the leather cover and linings of which were hidden several passports—two of them Canadian, one British, and two American—plus credit cards, driver's licenses, international permits, and other forms of ID to match each identity. All the passports were well used and well within their expiration dates.

The cover and linings were formed into patterns that allowed X-ray machines to see through to the inside, but because of the patterns, the existence of the passports and other documents did not show up; instead they blended in.

One separate envelope contained a thousand dollars in cash, most of it American. In addition, a half dozen contracts for travel magazine pieces were contained in a file folder. Several travel guides for Europe and the Middle East, along with a compact Nikon digital camera and several copies of the magazines *Travel + Leisure* and *Condé Nast Traveler* filled the case.

From another carton she took out a small roll-about

suitcase that contained enough clothes and personal toiletries to last her for at least two weeks of travel. They were a little musty, though she changed the items every month or so.

She took the attaché case and roll-about to the Caddy, then came back and put the cartons in place in the pile so it would take someone searching the locker hours to discover something might be missing.

All that had taken less than twenty minutes before she was driving out the gate and back onto the Pike.

Traffic had picked up a little, a lot of it garbage trucks, delivery vans from bakeries, and fresh produce suppliers for restaurant prep chefs. By six or six thirty every road from the Beltway into the city would be jam-packed. White noise.

Again taking care with her tradecraft, she drove back to her apartment in an erratic route, again pretty sure she hadn't picked up a tail, though every hour that passed, the likelihood that the security officer had managed to call in to report his situation grew exponentially.

No suspicious cars or vans were parked anywhere near, nor had the Impala she'd parked next door been disturbed so far as she could tell by merely driving by.

She made two more passes before she parked the Caddy on a side street a block away, and walked back to the Chevy, where she put the attaché case and roll-about into the trunk. Before she drove off, she quickly checked the trunk, under the seats, in the glove compartment, and under the dash for any bugs or homing devices. So far as she could tell, the car was clean.

Three blocks later she pulled into a service station and filled up the tank. The sign in front advertised that a mechanic was on duty twenty-four hours every day. One of the service doors was open, the bay empty.

She walked in and the mechanic came over. "Good morning. You have a problem?"

"Might be leaking a little oil. Wonder if you could put it on the lift and check it out."

"That's a Hertz rental. Have them come out and switch cars."

"I don't have time to screw around with them this morning unless there's problem. I'm driving up to New York."

"Sure, bring it in," the mechanic said.

She drove slowly into the bay, and the mechanic raised it on the lift. She started her own inspection of the undercarriage and wheel wells from the rear as he checked under the engine for leaks.

"Technically, you're not supposed to be in here. Insurance."

"How does it look?" Alex asked, moving forward.

"I don't see anything wrong. What makes you think there's an oil leak?"

"Just a feeling. My dad was a wrench, and he checked our cars every time we took a trip. Guess it just rubbed off."

The mechanic stepped aside as she checked under the engine and in the front wheel wells, again finding nothing suspicious.

She gave him a smile. "The brakes look good too. What do I owe you?"

"Make it a twenty and we're even."

When the car was down, she paid him and drove off. The inspection only proved that the Company wasn't using obvious bugs. The ones the size of a book of matches. But with the right satellite overhead, something as small as the end of a pencil would work, and no casual inspection would have found it.

Still, she didn't think the car had been traced to her.

Instead of driving back to I-495, she took the Leesburg Pike a couple of miles north, where it connected with the Dulles Access Road, traffic definitely picking up as people headed to the airport for their early morning flights.

She continued to watch her tradecraft, but with the increased traffic she had no need for such drastic action as before. But each time she changed lanes to pass, she watched behind her to make sure the same car behind her wasn't doing the same thing.

If someone was following her, she decided they were a lot better than she was.

It was just six when she pulled into the Hertz return lanes, and a man with a clipboard came out, checked the car over, entered the odometer and date and time into a handheld unit, and printed the receipt for her.

She got her bags from the trunk as another car drove up, and the attendant went to check it in. While no one was paying attention to her, she opened the attaché case and pulled out a passport, Gold Amex card, a few hundred in American dollars, and other items of identification under the name Lois Wheeler, and stashed her Unroth and Alice Walker papers inside.

The airport was the weakest link in her flight plan. Once they knew she was gone, they would expect her to run. But Dulles and Reagan National were obvious, especially since very few flights to Europe took off until later in the afternoon—most of them between four thirty and seven. It would leave her exposed her at the airport for nearly twelve hours, during which an even casual sweep would pick her up.

Except for Air France flight 9039 if she could book a last-minute seat.

She went into the main terminal, where she found a seat by a window and connected on her cell phone with the Air France website. Picking up reservations, she went to 9039 for this morning's 11:45 A.M. flight to Paris. All but four seats were filled, one of them in tourist and the other three in first class. She booked a first-class flight, paying for it with her American Express card.

Next she called the Hotel InterContinental and booked a suite for five days, beginning this evening, so that when she arrived, she would have a room.

It was a bit of irony. The InterContinental was the hotel McGarvey often stayed at.

FORTY-THREE

At Dulles, McGarvey watched as Alex passed through security into the international terminal and disappeared down the long walkway into the concourse. So far as he had been able to determine, she had not spotted him behind her from Turkey Run Park down to the Tysons Corner storage facility, over to the apartment building where she'd left the Caddy and had picked up the Impala, or out here to the airport.

But a couple of times it had been close. She was a damned good field operator, and paranoid as hell now. Rightly so.

A forensics team had been dispatched to the storage facility and to the Caddy, but those moves were only a moot point designed to appease Blankenship, who was beside himself with anger.

"I'm sorry, Mr. Director, but if you had allowed me to leave four of my people there in the first place, none of this would have happened. As it was, Lloyd could have been shot to death. There's no telling what this woman is capable of."

"She is not the serial killer," McGarvey had said, trying to calm him down.

"You bet the life of one of my people on that opinion, you know."

"Yes."

He phoned Pete next and brought her up to speed. "She made a couple of phone calls in the main terminal here at Dulles, and ten minutes later went to the Air France ticketing counter, where she got her boarding pass. She just now went across to the international terminal."

"She's getting out of Dodge. Paris?"

"Possibly, but most of those flights don't leave until later in the afternoon or even early evening."

"She won't want to hang around there that long," Pete said. "Maybe she's leading you on a merry chase and plans on going out the back door."

"I don't think so."

"Just a hunch?"

"Something like that."

"Then my question stands: What about Schermerhorn? Do we cut him loose, let him walk away?"

"Hold him until I find out where Alex is off to. We still might need his help."

"Are you going after her?"

"Don't have any choice," McGarvey said.

He phoned Otto, who sounded excited. "Oh wow, Mac, the decryption is really close. I got Berlin, but it's just a key, not the real part of Schermerhorn's message."

McGarvey explained where he was and what Alex had done.

"Give me a sec," Otto said. He was back in less than fifteen seconds. "Air France flight 9039 leaves for de Gaulle at quarter to twelve this morning. Gets to Paris at noon."

"It'd be a last-minute booking, within the past fifteen minutes."

Otto was back again in under fifteen seconds. "Lois Wheeler, first-class, five A. Hang on." Ten seconds later he came back. "I ran the passport number she used—it's valid—and her Gold Amex just came up also as valid."

"Arrange a jet for me at Andrews. I want to be waiting for her."

"What about clothes, your passport?"

"I'll stop at my apartment on the way."

"That'll take too long with traffic on the Beltway. I'll send someone over to pack your things and meet you at the plane."

"You'll want to know my fail-safes."

Otto chuckled. "This is me you're talking to, kemo sabe."

"Right," McGarvey said, and started back to where he'd parked his car a few rows from the Hertz return lanes.

"I know it's redundant to say, but watch yourself, Mac. If she joins up with George, there's no telling what they'd be capable of doing. To you or anyone who gets in their way."

Morning rush-hour traffic was in full swing when McGarvey got back on the Beltway. Joint Base Andrews was just over forty miles away, skirting to the south of Alexandria and across the river. Near Annandale an eighteen-wheeler had jackknifed and crashed on its side, blocking all but one of the eastbound lanes. Traffic slowed to a crawl for nearly forty-five minutes.

Otto called him. "Are you caught in that mess?"

"Right in the middle of it."

"I have a Gulfstream standing by with its crew, and your things are already on board. Do you want to get off the highway somewhere? I can send a chopper for you."

"How soon do we need to be airborne to beat the Air France flight?"

"We have all morning, but you might run into some trouble with the DGSE. It's possible they won't let you off the plane." It was France's primary intelligence agency.

McGarvey and Otto—but especially McGarvey— had a sometimes bloody history in France. The French intelligence people had long memories. Although he had been of some service to them at one point or another, trouble always seemed to develop around him.

"That's something I'll have to deal with when I get there."

"Do you want me to call Walt, see if he can pull a few strings?"

McGarvey thought about it. "No," he said.

"Okay, are you trying to tell me something?"

"I don't know. But she and Schermerhorn said that whatever is going on—*has* been going on since oh two—is bigger than we can imagine, and they're both frightened out of their wits. Five people have already lost their lives over this thing. Alex has gone runner, and Schermerhorn took the huge risk to change the inscription on panel four. And yet they won't come out and say what the hell they saw buried in Iraq."

"I can think of a lot of possibilities," Otto said after a beat. "None of them pretty and at least one so political, the fallout would be more than bad."

"Bad enough to kill for to keep it quiet?" McGarvey

asked. He knew exactly what Otto was talking about. He had thought about it since he and Pete had gone to Athens to talk to Larry Coffin.

His biggest problem was reconciling what he thought with what he thought he should do about it.

Traffic finally began to move, and a half hour later he was at the Andrews main gate, where he was expected and waved through.

He drove across the field to where the Navy's C-20H Gulfstream, which the CIA borrowed from time to time, was waiting in its hangar, the forward hatch open, the boarding stairs down.

A chief petty officer directed him to park his Porsche off to the side, at the back of the hangar, and the jet's engines spooled up.

"Your partner is aboard with your things, Mr. Director!" the chief had to shout.

"Thanks!" McGarvey said, knowing exactly who it was and why.

The pilot turned in his seat when he came aboard. "Soon as you're strapped in, we'll get out of here. We have immediate clearance."

"Give me a minute," McGarvey said, and went back to where Pete was seated, sipping from a bottle of mineral water.

"Before you start bitching at me, Blankenship assured me Schermerhorn was secure," she said.

He supposed he was happy to see her, but he was vexed. He worked alone; it's the way he liked it. But Otto had helped him almost from the start. And so had Louise, and his daughter and his son-in-law. And Pete had helped him a while ago in an operation that had gotten her shot. And here she was again, in love with him.

The flight attendant, a young petty officer, first-class, came back. "Sir?" she asked.

"Button up and let's get out of here. And as soon as possible I want a very large cognac."

FORTY-FOUR

Over the past few hours the images on Otto's main monitor had begun to change in a way that was significant to him, and he was unable to stay seated now that he knew he was coming close. He bounced from one foot to the other, something he did when he was excited.

The 120-inch extremely high-def OLED flat-screen mounted on the wall above one of his desks was visible from anywhere in his primary office, but he had to look away from time to time or he knew he would explode.

He was always the odd duck. And when he was a kid in Catholic school, his classmates teased him unmercifully. And sometimes, after school and on the weekends, a few of the class bullies who'd singled him out would beat him. One time they'd broken a couple of ribs, another his nose and even his arm, and one winter his left leg—which still ached on rainy days.

It was impossible for him to go to the nuns about it, because they didn't like him either. By the age of six or seven he was already smarter than they were in just about every subject—especially in math and science. But instead of treating him like a prodigy, they called him a liar. He was already solving college-level mathematical equations in his head, and they accused him of simply parroting the words and symbols he'd seen on paper. They'd never bothered to call someone who knew the math to check him out, because they were afraid of him. Instead of being proud of the genius they had in their classrooms, they were scared silly, mostly because he was already questioning the basic tenets of the faith, and they knew if he learned too much too soon, he would become an atheist and they would have failed as teachers.

It was just about the same for him in high school and even in college, because he'd developed the unfortunate habit—which he later managed to break—of laughing at people who couldn't just "get it." He had the tendency to solve problems they were grappling with and telling anyone who'd listen how stupidly easy they were.

He'd finally dropped out in his third year, and he spent several years of intense reading—not studying because he could "get it" just by reading—supporting himself by cooking in restaurants and any number of other jobs where he didn't have to use his brain. But each time, he was fired because whatever he was doing, he did it better than the boss.

At one point he went to work for a Catholic diocese, running its books and doing some teaching, but by then he had discovered sex in a big way, and he was fired because he had not only seduced the dean's twenty-year-old daughter but the dean's nineteen-year-old son as well.

And then he came to the attention of the CIA.

Some letters and even scraps of words were beginning to emerge when his phone chimed softly. But it wasn't Mac. The call was internal, ID blocked. He answered anyway, though the interruption just now was irritating.

"What?"

"Good morning. Marty asked that I check in to see what progress you were making." It was Tom Calder, the assistant director of the national clandestine service. Bambridge had no idea how to deal with Otto, so he had taken to sending Calder to talk to him.

"I'm slammed down here, Tom. Tell him I'm being a bastard." In Otto's opinion, he was one of the smarter guys on campus.

Calder chuckled, his voice, like his manner, soft, even gentle, but refined. "I know, and I apologize, but I'd like come down for a chat. I'll make it brief; we don't want him going ballistic on us now."

"Okay," Otto said. He hung up and sat down at his desk, facing the big monitor.

Just about everyone in the CIA was ambitious. Everyone worked hard at their jobs; there was no doubt about it. But a lot of them worked just as hard at securing their career paths. Everyone wanted promotions, not only for the money, but for the prestige, for the increased power. The flavor of the intelligence business had always been the thrill of knowing something the general public hadn't an inkling of.

Calder was no different than most of them. He wanted to take over and run the directorate the way he thought it should be run. He was doing that by making the clandestine service look so good,

Marty would be promoted. Calder would be the logical choice to fill the vacancy.

In that much, at least, Otto agreed. Although Calder was in his late fifties, and starting to get a little old to run a directorate—by now he should have been the assistant director of the entire CIA—he would have done a much better job running the spies overseas than Marty had ever dreamed of doing.

It meant Calder was a spy for Marty. Part of his job.

Otto's fingers flew over the keyboard, and the image on the screen changed, the train of characters slowed down, and the background went from a pale blue to a medium violet.

He didn't disturb the ongoing decryption program—just hid it—and instead brought up on the monitor a version of the search that was six hours old, just before the word *BERLIN* had popped up en clair.

The state of his search was no one's business except his and Mac's. Everyone else—and that was everyone with a capital *E*—was an outsider as far as he was concerned. When the decryption was a done deal and he had shared it with Mac and they had produced the results they were after, then it might be time to spread the wealth. Until then, nada.

One of his monitors chimed. "Excuse me, dear, but Mr. Calder is at the door." The computer voice was Louise's.

"Let him in, sweetheart."

The door lock popped, and Calder walked into the outer of the two rooms that were Otto's domains. The first meant for a secretary or assistant he used for generally unclassified searches: the weather at some specific place and time, tides, moon phases (most operators liked to go out in the field during a dark night), airline, train and ship schedules, social security, passport, and driver's license information—the easy stuff.

"In here, Tom," Otto called.

Calder came into the inner sanctum and looked up at the main monitor. He was a slender man, thinning hair—a prematurely old man's malady, one of many, he liked to say—and a shuffling gait. His expressions were always pleasant, and his eyes, pale blue, were kind and intelligent. Otto thought that he was a pleasant man, someone people immediately thought could be a friend.

BERLIN came up on the monitor.

"Ah, progress," Calder said.

Otto glanced up at the monitor. "Just a key word. It's come up several times."

"What's your best guess? Twenty-four hours maybe?"

"Twenty-four hours, twenty-four days, twenty-four years. Maybe never."

Calder laughed softly. "I might believe that coming from anybody but you," he said. "Marty's keen on this, you know."

Otto shrugged. "I'll let you guys know soon as."

Calder held his gaze for a beat then nodded. "Do that, please. We'd like to get this mess behind us."

"Sure."

Calder started to leave. "Have you heard from Mac or Ms. Boylan? Bob Blankenship wants to know what's going on. Quite an embarrassment with his guy being taken and all."

"He got back in one piece?"

"Thankfully."

"They're off campus, is all I know at the moment," Otto said.

"Right," Calder said, and left.

"Lou, is he gone?" Otto asked.

"Down the hall to the elevators," his computer replied. "You have an interesting development on your *Kryptos* search engine."

Otto brought up the decryption program in real time. After the briefest of pauses, he sat back and laughed, suddenly knowing with certainty what was buried in the hills above Kirkuk, and the why, but not who had buried it, though he had his strong suspicions.

AND GOD SAID, LWET TRHER BE LIGHT: AND THERE WAS LIGHT X AND THE LIGHT WAS VISIBLE FROM HORIZONQ TO HORIZON X BERLIN X AND ALL WAS CHANGED X ALL WAS NEVER THE SDAME X AND GOD SAID LET THERE BE PROGRESS X AND THERE WAS X PEACEF

FORTY-FIVE

Once McGarvey and then Pete Boylan had left, the entire atmosphere of the house had changed. It was late afternoon, and Schermerhorn stood at the head of the stairs, nervously listening to the clomping around on the ground floor.

Pete Boylan was an unknown, Mac had been the

Rock of Gibraltar, but Bob Blankenship's guys downstairs were amateurs. They were pretty good at what they did, providing muscle for security details. But so far as he'd ever been able to determine, they'd never make it in the field. Even the odd lot NOC would chew them up for breakfast without raising a sweat.

And right now he wasn't feeling a lot of comfort.

He went back to his bedroom, which was at the front of the house, and looked out the window. Two Caddy SUVs were parked in the driveway, and he spotted at least three guys in dark nylon Windbreakers down there; one was behind a tree at the end of the driveway, another was off to the left at the edge of the woods to the west, and the third was leaning against the fender of one of the vehicles. He was actually smoking a fucking cigarette.

McGarvey had apparently suspected that Alex was going to slip away, and the fact that she had believed George was no longer on campus. He and Pete were following her; at least he figured that was their plan, though following Alex wouldn't be so easy. She was damned good at spotting a tail and then evading it. Even double or triple teams were no match for her.

But it left two major concerns in Schermerhorn's mind: Alex only suspected George was gone, and even if he had left, maybe he would double back to finish the job.

They'd all fallen in love with him almost from the moment he'd dropped in on them, with his urbane self-assurance, his ready smile, and his intellect and talent. All of them were smart, and well trained by some of the best instructors in any secret intelligence or military special forces organization in the world. But George outclassed them all from every angle.

The first was how he had come to them, with absolutely no fuss or bother. One day they were on mission, and the next he was in their midst and the mission had changed.

"You and I know no WMDs have ever been found here," he'd told them.

"Not yet," someone—it could have been Alex—had shot back.

George had laughed, that soft upper-crust British chuckle that said so much about his sophistication versus theirs and exactly what he thought about the difference. "No, not yet."

"So what are you doing here?" Schermerhorn had asked.

"To put the fear of God into the rag heads down there," George had said, waving an arm in the general direction of the oil fields a few thousand feet below.

He hadn't meant the ordinary roustabouts, the drillers, the guys who worked the rigs; he'd meant the Iraqi military clumped around the waste gas fires, in hiding from infrared spy satellites.

At the time none of them knew exactly how he was going to accomplish the new mission, and if they had known, Schermerhorn wasn't so sure they wouldn't have gone along with him.

Isty had suggested they use their satellite burst transmitter to get a clarification of their orders. He had meant to keep his conversation private with a few of them, but George had been right there, in the darkness, like an apparition, and had heard everything.

"Excellent idea, Mr. Refugee," he'd said.

And it hadn't dawned on any of them until later that George had known their handles along with their nicknames—like Isty instead of Istvan.

"But you might want to consider a couple of things before you actually phone home. Not everyone has approved the new mission orders, so you're likely to get some foot-dragging until a decision is made. In the meantime, the clock ticks, and when the troops come pouring across the border, a lot of the enthusiasm for battle we would have drained from the Iraqis will be in full strength. A lot more troops will lose their lives."

As he thought about it now, it struck Schermerhorn that George had never once said *our* troops. He'd used the term *the* troops. But none of them had caught it at the time.

"What else?" someone had asked.

"We're not going to fight a conventional war. I want you to understand that from the beginning. What I propose has nothing to do with the Geneva Conventions, because we will be taking no prisoners. No quarter for the wounded. What I do propose is terrorism, raw, up close, and bloody. I'm here to ram it home to the bastards, with or without your help."

They'd gone along with him at first, but when a few of them had balked because of the savagery of their attacks—Schermerhorn among them—George had taken them to the cache, which was a couple of miles away and a thousand feet lower.

Schermerhorn had remembered his exact feeling the moment he'd understood what was buried there. It was slick. The entire thing was uptown. And he and Alex and maybe Larry had started to laugh, until it dawned on all of them that from that moment, their lives were all but forfeit unless the thing stayed where it was buried for all time, or unless it was found in just the right way, by just the right people. Any other circumstances would have been a disaster.

Still could be a disaster for them.

And it was exactly that, only in a way none of them had foreseen.

A bright flash followed by a small explosion went off somewhere a hundred yards or so into the woods. It was a flash bang grenade.

A diversion. It came into Schermerhorn's head at the same moment: someone was right there behind him, and before he could move or even call out, a terrible pain ripped at his neck, and blood poured into his trachea, drowning him even as he began to bleed to death.

George had come back, or had never left in the first place. That thought crystallized in his head as he managed to half turn so he could face his attacker.

"I'm not who you expected, Roy?" the man asked.

His voice was vaguely familiar, but Schermerhorn wasn't sure who it was, though in the back of his dying brain, he thought he should know.

"It was clever of Alex to get out while she could. But then she always was the cleverest of the lot."

He sounded a lot like the Cynic to Schermerhorn's ear.

Schermerhorn reared back and tried to put his shoulder through the window to alert the security guys outside, but the pane was Lexan, not glass, and he was rapidly losing his strength as he fought to clear his throat so he could take a breath of air.

"It's too late for that," the Cynic said. "Anyway, they're all running after the first of the flash bangs I planted. They'll be kept busy for a bit. Long enough."

Schermerhorn heard music. Organ music, but more complicated than the hymns in church. And he thought he'd heard it somewhere before, though in his befuddled state, he couldn't quite place where or when.

"None of you ever had any culture. Too bad for you. But then you were bred and trained to be liars, charlatans, and thieves. Killers without conscience if the need arose."

Schermerhorn's knees began to buckle, and the Cynic held him up, blood soaking the front of his white pullover.

"You want to know why. They all did. Even Joe when he lay dying on the pavement in Athens. I could feel that at the moment of impact, when he knew in a flash he was a dead man, that he wanted to know why."

The music was Bach's Toccata and Fugue. It came to Schermerhorn all of a sudden, and he knew who the Cynic was. But like the others, he didn't know why. And he couldn't understand how this was happening in broad daylight.

"Despite your faults, all of you were so lovely. Maybe not so young, some of you, but naive."

The day they'd all feared had finally come.

"In the end you guys were extra clever: you illuminated the new cache, and I wanted to know the GPS coordinates and the password, but that will have to wait for Alex."

Schermerhorn was weak. He couldn't exactly make out what the Cynic was saying to him, but he could still hear the music, maybe coming from a small player in the man's breast pocket.

And then the Cynic began to eat his face, starting with his lips, and though Schermerhorn could still feel pain, he couldn't cry out, nor could he even try to push back away from the horror of it.

PART
THREE

And God said,
lwet trher be light. . . .

FORTY-SIX

It was early evening, Washington time, and Maggie Jones, their flight attendant, came back and touched McGarvey on the shoulder. His eyes were closed, but he wasn't asleep.

He looked up. "Yes?"

Pete was curled up in one of the wide leather seats near the back of the cabin, wrapped in a blanket, a pillow under her head.

"There is a call for you. The captain says you may use the aircraft's phone system; it's in your console."

"Thanks."

"May I get you something, Mr. Director?"

"How far are we from landing?"

"One hour."

"You might wake Ms. Boylan and see if you can come up with something to eat—I suppose breakfast would be best."

"Yes, sir."

It was Otto on the phone, and as soon as McGarvey picked up, he switched on his backscatter encryption program.

"Schermerhorn was killed less than two hours ago. I just got off the phone with Blankenship. The entire campus is in a serious uproar this time. Somehow the White House finally got wind of what's been happening, and the president has sent for Walt."

"Tell me," McGarvey said.

Pete had been awakened by the tone of McGarvey's voice. She came forward and sat down across from him.

McGarvey put the call on speakerphone.

Otto relayed everything Blankenship had told him, including the business with the three flash bang grenades hidden in the woods, either timed to go off at three-minute intervals or remotely detonated.

"Could be the bastard set the grenades and got into the house hours ago—maybe right after Alex left and you and Pete went after her."

"She didn't double back, so it wasn't her," McGarvey said.

"George?" Pete suggested. "Could be she's led us on a wild goose chase so George would have an open field."

"Blankenship said he had four of his guys on the outside and another two in the house," Otto said. "Makes him damned good."

"And when the first grenade went off, no one thought to go upstairs to check on Schermerhorn," McGarvey said.

"They were focused outside," Otto said. "And after he made the kill—there was blood everywhere—he apparently took a shower and changed clothes."

"Find out who passed through the gate after that time; maybe something will pop out."

"Already did it. Nada. The bastard could still be on campus."

McGarvey glanced at Pete. She shrugged.

"She could have run to save her own life because she knew George would be coming after her and Schermerhorn," he said. "But why specifically Paris?"

"Good city to get lost in," Otto said. "Obviously, she wanted to draw you out. Maybe she knew your background in France and counted on the DGSE to slow you down."

"But not to meet George, unless she knew he was going to kill Schermerhorn and she was going to Paris to wait for him to join her. Drawing me and Pete off helped."

"Or unless it was someone else," Otto said. "Someone we don't know about. Another Alpha Seven member. Someone connected with the mission. Someone who is desperate enough to make sure that whatever was buried in Iraq stays hidden."

"Back where we started from," Pete said.

"We still have Alex," McGarvey said. "And if there is a third person, we also have George."

"A Frenchman?"

"At this point I'm betting Mossad."

"It would fit with what I'm thinking," Otto said. "But at this point, only Alex and George know what's buried out there and where it's buried."

"Schermerhorn knew," Pete said.

"So did everyone else on the team. It's what got them killed. Someone wants to keep it a secret at all costs."

"Who's directing it?" Pete asked. "Who's pulling the strings? Because if you guys are suggesting what I think you're suggesting, it has to be someone who was either in the White House during that time period, or someone very high in the Pentagon."

"Colin Powell," McGarvey said.

Pete was surprised. "I'm not going to buy anything like that," she said.

"Not him, but there had to have been people on his staff when he was at the UN who liaised with the White House and the Pentagon. Maybe someone on the Joint Chiefs of Staff, or on the security council."

"You're talking about a fall guy in case something went wrong," Pete said. "If that's the case, he or she has to be pretty nervous by now."

"I'll see what I can come up with," Otto said. "In the meantime, what are you going to tell the DGSE if they show up? And I'm betting they will."

"Depends on who they send," McGarvey said.

"But not the truth."

"Some of it, but not all."

Charles de Gaulle ground control directed them to a hangar well away from the commercial gates, near an Air France maintenance facility not occupied.

As soon as they were parked and the jet's engines spooled down, Maggie opened the hatch and lowered the stairs. She stepped aside and ducked into the cockpit as an older man with thick gray hair came aboard.

McGarvey recognized him at once. "Captain Bete," he said, rising.

"Actually, its colonel now, and no one calls me *bête noire* any longer." *Bete* was French for a "beast" or an "animal," and a *bête noire* was a bugbear. Twenty years ago he'd resented the play on his name.

McGarvey introduced him to Pete, and they shook hands and sat down across from each other.

"I will come directly to the point, *Monsieur le Directeur.* Why have you come back to France? Your presence is making a number of people nervous, as you can well imagine."

"Your service might be aware of a disturbance at the CIA."

"There have been rumors."

"We have a serial killer on the campus who has already murdered four people at Langley and another two in Athens. We've followed a woman we think may know something about it."

Colonel Bete sat back in his seat. "You are a dangerous man, and violence seems to find you. But you have never been a liar. Is yours an official service-to-service request for assistance?"

"No."

"I thought not," Bete said. "Who is this woman?"

"Her actual name is Alex Unroth, though she's traveling under the name Lois Wheeler, coming in on an Air France flight from Dulles in an hour or so."

"Who is she, exactly? Dangerous?"

"Extremely. She was a NOC, and very good at killing."

"Do you want us to arrest her?"

"No. She's come here to meet someone. I want to know who it is. And when the meeting actually takes place, I'll make the decision either to take her into custody or continue to follow her."

"An action she will resist."

"Yes."

"With force."

"Yes," McGarvey said.

FORTY-SEVEN

Air France 9039 pulled up to the gate ten minutes early, and Alex was among the first off. She'd been exhausted, and had slept in the wide first-class seat that converted into a flat bed, not staying awake for the afternoon meal or complimentary champagne.

At this point she was awake if not refreshed, and she took care with her tradecraft after she was passed through immigration and had picked up her overnight bag and attaché case. Making her way through the main concourse, which was busy, she kept within groups of passengers so far as it was possible.

Twice she darted into a ladies' room, the first time lingering in one of the stalls to see if anyone suspicious came in—but no one did. And the second time, walking in, turning around immediately, and heading back to the gate she had landed at.

A number of the passengers seemed somewhat suspicious to her, but then they either passed by or went to the ticket agent at a gate.

Airport cops were everywhere, mostly traveling in pairs, but in this day and age their presence wasn't unusual, and not one of them paid her the slightest attention.

As she headed down the escalator to the ground transportation exits, she paused for a moment to wonder if no one paying her any attention was in itself significant. She was still an attractive woman, and just about everywhere she went she turned male heads. But then this was Paris—the city of well-put-together women.

The only things she could not gauge were the overhead cameras, but she kept her head lowered as much as possible.

Outside, she got a cab and asked the driver, in French, to take her to the InterContinental. "The one on Avenue Marceau."

By the time they left the airport and got on the ring road traffic was heavy and until she got to the hotel, it would be impossible for her to make sure she wasn't being followed. She'd considered taking the cab to the vicinity of a train station, and from there another cab to a metro entrance, and from there eventually back to the hotel. But she had decided against it. It wasn't likely she had been followed this far this soon.

She had picked the InterContinental as a sort of a message to McGarvey: *Here I am. Do you want to talk on neutral ground?*

Of course he would not, and in fact, he would probably try to take her into custody. But she had read enough about him in his Agency files that although he was a dangerous man, he was principled. He was a man of high morals for whom collateral damage of any sort was completely out of the question.

If it came to a stand-up fight in the hotel, or on a crowed street—the Champs-Élysées was just around the corner—he would hesitate. It would be enough for her to escape.

The only dark cloud was the poor bastard she'd

killed in Georgetown. She had no idea why she had done it, except that it had been a release for all the tension she had been under since Walt and the others had been murdered on campus. She knew George was coming after all of them, her included, to keep them quiet. It had only been their superinflated egos concerning their abilities that had stopped them from coming forward with what they knew. That, and the likelihood that if they were to blow the whistle, they could very well be signing their own death warrants.

Either George was going to kill them, or someone else would—so it was up to them to go deep.

But it had not worked for Walt and the others on campus. Or for Joseph or even Larry in Athens. Nor for her in the DCI's office.

All that was left was coming face-to-face one last time with George and hopefully leading McGarvey to him. If George told what he knew, she figured she would have a shot at guaranteeing her own life and maybe her freedom.

Except for the guy in Georgetown.

The cabby dropped her off at the hotel, and a liveried doorman in a blue morning coat came out to help her with her bags.

"*Bonjour, Madame,*" he said, and followed her to the front desk, where the night manager stood.

"Madame Wheeler?"

"*Mademoiselle,*" Alex said, graciously smiling. She handed over her credit card and passport.

The manager was a younger man with a short haircut. He was impeccably dressed in a tasteful blue blazer and vest, white shirt, correctly knotted tie.

The InterContinental under new management had transformed from the iconic former mansion of the Comte de Breteuil, used as a stuffy hotel, into a hip boutique hotel. She had to wonder if McGarvey had been back since the change.

She signed the card. "Have my things brought up, and in two hours have my bed turned down and draw me a very hot bath. First I'm going to take a walk."

"Of course."

Alex smiled again. "Thank you."

"May I suggest that if you walk, stay away from the Jardin. It is sometimes dangerous at this hour of the morning."

Alex walked out of the hotel and headed down to the Jardin des Tuileries, the morning pleasantly cool after Washington's humidity. She didn't bother with her tradecraft for the moment. If McGarvey had traced her this far already, she wanted to see if he could be induced to approach her. Away from people, away from any danger of collateral damage.

She was betting, however, that if he had followed her to Paris and had not tried to stop her from leaving the campus or getting on the flight, it was because he figured she was on her way to meet George.

Two possibilities, she thought. Either he would try to arrest her, in which case her best immediate defense was to always surround herself with innocent civilians. Or he wanted her to lead him to George, in which case he might show himself but would leave her alone.

Coming here to the deserted park at this hour of the morning would test the second possibility. That, and she was feeling irascible again, and she wanted someone to try something with her.

The Jardin was one of the more highly structured parks in the city, with rows of flowers and trees and a couple of ponds. From just about anywhere inside the park, Paris was highly visible, unlike much of Central Park, which in many places hid from the city. And yet Alex felt a sense of isolation here, as she had even in times past when the place was busy with old couples resting on benches, or young fathers pushing baby carriages, or children running and playing—almost too quiet, as French children often were.

Maybe if her life had been different as a child, if she'd had a normal upbringing, a normal father, she might have turned out differently. Maybe she would have gotten married—a lot of NOCs did. They had their careers *and* their partners.

A half dozen kids—two of them girls, all of them in their early teens—suddenly appeared on the path to her left. They had wild haircuts, Mohawks and the like, tattoos, piercings in their ears and noses and lips and eyebrows, and they were either drunk or high.

One of the boys pulled out a knife and, holding it low, swooped in toward her, swinging the blade at her midsection.

At the last moment she stepped aside, took his wrist and, using his momentum, yanked his arm up and sharply backward, dislocating his shoulder and tearing his rotator cuff.

He skipped out of the way, howling in pain.

The others, all of them with knives in hand, circled her. No one except the kid with the screwed-up arm said a word, and he only muttered something dark Alex couldn't quite catch.

Coming to the Jardin against the advice of the night manager and getting into the middle of something like this was exactly what she had wanted in some perverse way. Maybe to prove that after too many years of sitting behind a desk, she still had some moves left.

One of the girls came in from the right, while at the same moment a tall-drink-of-water boy who might have been sixteen or seventeen ran at her from her left.

Alex turned, grabbed the boy's wrist and elbow, and spun him around so his knife rammed into the shoulder of the girl, directly above her right breast.

The others moved in at the same time.

FORTY-EIGHT

McGarvey and Pete sat in the back of a Police Nationale Citroën parked on the Rue de Rivoli, watching images on a laptop computer. A nearly silent camera-equipped drone had been circling overhead ever since Alex had left the InterContinental and strolled into the Jardin as if she were a woman without a care in the world.

Bete, who was sitting in the front passenger seat,

watched the images from the drone on another laptop. "She is an impressive woman, *hein*?"

"That she is," McGarvey agreed.

"Shall we send someone to help her?"

"Not unless you want to save the kids from themselves. She knows I've followed her, and she's staged this thing, figuring I would get involved."

"To save the children."

"Something like that. But she won't kill them."

All of it, the stealth helicopter that had followed her cab from de Gaulle, the use of Sûreté officers and the air force drone, had been put into play within minutes after the colonel had signed on. But only after McGarvey had explained what he thought was going on.

"Your government might not be so pleased if you uncover their little secret," Bete had said on the Gulfstream.

"The reaction of my government is not my concern right now. I'm trying to solve a murder mystery. I know the likely why of it now, but not the who."

"Not her?" Bete asked.

"No. She's here to try to avoid being the next victim."

Two more kids went down with dislocated kneecaps, and the last two boys stood in front of her, panting because of their exertions, and pissed off but obviously wary. Alex was a slightly built woman. An ancient in their minds. An obviously easy mark for a little fun—a rape for sure, and maybe even a few euros if she had any on her, or jewelry. Maybe a watch. But all of it for fun plus a little drug money.

The angle of the camera was wrong, so the expression on her face wasn't clear on the monitors, but the way she held herself, nonchalant, just about hip-shot, arms at her sides, waiting for the boys to come in at her, was of a woman without concern for her safety.

After what seemed like a very long time, she turned and walked away, not bothering to look over her shoulder.

The boys stood there for a while but then pocketed their knives and helped the others. Within a few minutes they were gone, in the opposite direction of Alex.

"Formidable," Bete said.

"If you want to arrest her, you'll have to give your people plenty of room," McGarvey said.

"What now, Colonel?" asked the young Sûreté officer behind the wheel.

"We're finished here. You may recall the drone, and give my thanks to Major Lucien."

"Where may I drop you, sir?"

"That's up to Monsieur McGarvey," Bete said.

Alex was heading up toward the Champs-Élysées.

"Looks like she's going for a walk," McGarvey said. "Get back to the InterContinental and toss her room. I doubt if she'll have left anything important behind, maybe a passport or two and some cash and credit cards."

"How delicate shall I be?"

"Use a soft touch, but let her know someone was snooping around."

"What about me?" Pete asked.

"Check us in, and try for the same floor," McGarvey said. "I won't be long."

"She's looking for trouble," Pete warned.

"She knows I'm here, and she's sent me a message."

"Which is?" Bete asked.

"That she can handle herself, but that unless she's seriously provoked, she won't kill anyone. She's here to meet someone, or at least get word to him."

"George," Pete said, but not as a question.

McGarvey took a last glance at the monitor, then got out of the car and started walking fast back toward the Pont de la Concorde, figuring that if Alex were intending for the Champs-Élysées, he would be in time to tuck in behind her.

The Place de la Concorde, with its slender obelisk, was at the foot of the Champs-Élysées, and it was alive with traffic, including pedestrians on their way to sidewalk cafés on the avenue or even the McDonald's for their morning coffees and croissants.

McGarvey crossed the Rue Boissy d'Anglas, dodging traffic and heading along the upper side of the avenue, paying attention to who was coming up behind him or shadowing him from the other side. Alex was the only one left from Alpha Seven, and since she hadn't killed Schermerhorn, nor almost certainly the others, it meant she was the last target.

But whoever the killer was had a very good source of intelligence inside the CIA. Not only good enough to pinpoint Wager, Fabry, Knight, and Schermerhorn, and Alex, but to get on and off campus without raising any alarms.

He and Otto had suspected it might be someone

working for Blankenship—or possibly even the director of security himself. But Blankenship had been in his office when Schermerhorn was murdered, and had been driving through the main gate when Knight had been attacked. Nor had he been absent from his desk when Coffin had been shot and killed on the boat in Piraeus.

Alex's alibis weren't as tight—she was on a long weekend when Coffin was shot, and as a NOC in Iraq she had been an excellent marksman with the Barrett sniper rifle—and she was definitely off campus when Schermerhorn had been murdered.

But if she thought the killer was George, and that he was somewhere here in Paris, and if he was indeed the killer, she was playing with fire, because it was possible he knew she had come to Paris.

Two-thirds of the way to the Arc de Triomphe, he spotted her sitting at a sidewalk table at the Café George V. The waiter had just set two coffees down and was walking away.

She was obviously expecting someone. McGarvey waited for a couple of minutes, watching her, waiting for whoever it was to show up, but when no one came, he walked over.

"Your coffee is getting cold," she said, looking up.

"I thought you might be waiting for George," McGarvey said, sitting across from her.

She smiled. "He's the last person I wanted to see. Tell me about Roy. Do you think he'll survive the night?"

"That why you ran?"

She looked at something across the broad avenue. "That's obvious, isn't it?"

"Then why the little display in the Tuileries?"

"Just kids out to have a little fun."

"They'll think twice before they attack another woman."

She smiled again. "That's the whole point, Mr. McGarvey. I can take care of myself, and I mean to do so."

"I found you."

"I let you find me. But unless you or Pete or Otto have told anyone about my movements, I figure I'll be reasonably safe here for a few days or so."

"Then where?"

"That'll be up to you, won't it?" she said. "If you find George, I'm home free. Relatively speaking."

"Otto's decrypted the fourth panel."

"What'd it say?"

"'Let there be light.'"

Alex laughed, the sound low from the back of her throat. "Sounds like Roy. Anything else?"

"And there was peace."

She nodded wistfully. "Then you know what's still buried over there."

"Schermerhorn's dead."

For a long moment Alex didn't react, but then her face fell by degrees, and she looked down. "I thought by leaving it would draw him away. I thought he'd come after me, just like I knew you would. And if my luck held, the two of you would come face-to-face."

She'd laid a copy of *The International New York Times* on the table, and a chance breeze ruffled it. She suddenly moved to the left to reach for it, when a rifle shot struck a nearby male patron in the chest, and he was slammed violently backward. He had been seated at the table just behind them.

McGarvey rolled to the right and dropped to the sidewalk, searching the roof line across the broad boulevard in time to see a figure in a second-floor window disappear.

A woman passing by screamed, and people in the café began to react, some of them scrambling out of their seats, trying to escape what to them had to look like the start of another terrorist attack.

When he looked over his shoulder, Alex was gone.

FORTY-NINE

Alex raced through the restaurant, into the busy kitchen, and out the back door and onto a narrow lane across from the rear of the U.S. Embassy, which fronted on the Avenue Gabriel. She turned left and, walking fast, made it to the Rue de Miromesnil before she looked over her shoulder to see if McGarvey was behind her. He wasn't.

The shot had been fired from a high-power rifle, which to her had sounded like a Barrett, and it was only by happenstance that she'd suddenly moved to keep her newspaper from blowing away. But she'd been in time to glance up and get a quick glimpse of the shooter, who'd been in the second-floor window of the building across the avenue.

It had been a man, she was certain of it. But she got the impression he was tall and very ruggedly built—the opposite from George. And that only made sense if George wasn't the one doing the killings—or if he wasn't working alone.

At the corner, she turned around and walked back to the Champs-Élysées, half a block up from the George V. A crowd had gathered in front of the café, and two police cars had already arrived. A cop was in the middle of the street, directing traffic, as an ambulance, its siren blaring, came around the corner two blocks away.

If McGarvey was somewhere down there, he was lost in the crowd.

She headed up the avenue toward the Arc de Triomphe, and in the next block she entered the VIP World Travel Agency, housed in a small storefront.

A young woman seated behind the desk looked up and smiled. "*Bonjour, Madame,*" she said pleasantly.

"Good morning," Alex said in English, and the young woman switched languages.

Alex put her real passport on the desk. "I would like to make a trip to Tel Aviv, but first I need to get a message to your director."

The agent glanced at the passport but did not reach for it.

George had told them all that if ever they got in over their heads over the business in Iraq, they were to get word to him through the travel agency either in Washington, London, Berlin, or here, in Paris. The procedure was to lay their real passport—no matter what other name they might be using—on the agent's desk, and ask to get a message to the agency's director before making a trip to Tel Aviv.

The company had been set up by the Israeli Mossad in the late fifties as an elaborate front so that its agents could travel to Argentina to capture Adolf Eichmann and bring him back to Israel. The thinking was that if they used their own travel section, the operation might not be discovered and Eichmann would not disappear again.

The company had remained in existence all this time because it was successful as an ordinary travel agency, and it was even expanded to Berlin, London, and Washington from its original office here in Paris. It wasn't a very closely guarded secret—at least not from the CIA—that the occasional Mossad operator still used the company.

"Do you have the name of our current director?" the woman asked.

"It's been some years."

"What name do you know?"

"George."

The agent took Alex's passport to a machine in one corner, made a copy of the bearer's pages, and brought it back.

"And when would you like to travel to Tel Aviv?"

"As soon as George responds to my query."

"Are you staying in the city?"

"Yes, but I'll call you at noon," Alex said.

"What is the message?"

"'I'm the last. Shall I come?'"

"Very well. It will go out within the hour. But I cannot guarantee there will be a response, or if there is one, when it will arrive."

"Will there be a fee?"

"No, but I will take an impression of your credit card to make the travel arrangements," the agent said.

Alex handed her the Lois Wheeler credit card. The agent made a copy of it, but she said nothing that the name was different from the passport.

"I won't wait long," Alex said.

"I understand," the agent said.

Alex caught a cab a half block away and ordered the driver to take her back to the InterContinental.

McGarvey had followed her to Paris, which had been no real feat of tradecraft, not with Otto Rencke's wizardry. And she'd known he would be right behind her, so she'd put on the little show for him in the Tuileries, and then had gone to the sidewalk café, figuring he would want to talk.

What she hadn't counted on was the shooter also tracing her to Paris and to the specific restaurant. Whoever it was, they had information from inside the CIA.

It came back to George. If he was the killer, he had help this morning from the shooter across from the sidewalk café. And if it was him, he also had help inside the CIA. Someone on campus, doing his dirty work. But whoever it was had to be insane not only to kill the Alpha Seven team one by one but to mutilate those who'd been on campus.

That last bit was the sticking point for her. George had done horrible things in Iraq—and so had she—but those had been done as acts of war. Acts to demoralize the enemy, which in fact had happened.

This now, over the past few days, made no sense from her perspective.

And the last bit that gave her some pause was the hotel. She'd been traced here by McGarvey and by the shooter. The hotel was no longer her safe haven. Yet she decided it was the only place for her to be. If the shooter came after her again, she would be on familiar ground, McGarvey as her backup.

FIFTY

McGarvey got to the river in time to see the shooter reach the bottom of the stairs from street level and head to the right, toward the Pont de l'Alma. He recognized the guy from the dark jacket and yellow shirt he wore, and the fact that his haircut was military.

The Barrett had been left where the sniper abandoned it: leaning against the wall next to the window of what was a two-room office being remodeled. Painters' drop cloths covered the wooden floors, and plasterwork around the crown moldings was drying. The walls had been stripped, in some places down to the bare laths, and even the light fixtures and wall outlets were still missing.

The shooter's intel had been spot-on. So much so that he had even picked the one empty room within shooting range of a sidewalk café where he somehow knew Alex would be. Even if he had insider information from the CIA, more was going on here than made sense.

But from Schermerhorn's and Alex's descriptions

of George, the shooter was too big and too young to be the same man. Either someone else was gunning for her, or George had help—damned good help.

Some of it pointed to the Mossad, and that made a certain kind of logic to McGarvey's thinking. But other bits didn't fit. They were still missing something, because it made no sense that Schermerhorn and Alex had both been so circumspect about who was coming after them and why, even though their lives were on the line.

McGarvey reached the bottom of the stairs at river level, and started after the shooter. A fair number of people, many of them couples, hand in hand, strolled along the river walk. A Bateaux-Mouches less than half full passed, going downriver, and McGarvey could still hear sirens in the distance, up toward the Champs-Élysées.

The man was taking his time, and McGarvey easily came up behind him before he reached the bridge. He was a head taller and perhaps in his late twenties or early thirties, with a military bearing and stride to match his haircut.

It did not appear he was carrying a pistol. His jacket was snug fitting, and there was no telltale bulge at his waist or under his arm.

"You left your rifle behind," McGarvey said.

If the man was startled, he didn't show it. He merely glanced over his shoulder. "Beg your pardon?"

"The Barrett. Though how you could miss at that range is beyond understanding for a man of your training. I'm sure George will be disappointed when you get back to Tel Aviv."

The shooter stopped and faced McGarvey. "I have no idea what you are talking about, Monsieur. Shall I call the police?"

"If you'd like, although the DGSE has taken an interest in this business."

The man's eyes were dark, a five-o'clock shadow on his broad chin. He looked dangerous. "Stay out of this, Mr. McGarvey. We have no ill will toward you."

"By we, do you mean the Mossad?"

The man glanced up as a couple pushing a baby carriage passed by. They were laughing and talking. The morning was perfect, nothing to worry about.

"Was it you in Piraeus? The Greeks found the Barrett where it was left. No fingerprints of course. And that shot was a good one. Fifteen hundred meters. But then Coffin's head was framed by the open porthole. Made a good sight pattern."

"You're not here officially," the shooter said, and the comment didn't really come as a surprise to McGarvey. "You followed Alex from Langley and actually sat down to have a cup of coffee and a friendly chat with her. Strange."

"She's looking for George. She thought he'd be here. And until you took the shot, he was our best suspect in the killings. But if he and you are Mossad, the problem becomes even more interesting."

"I suggest you stop right now and go home. Perhaps it's time you visit with your granddaughter. We understand she's a lovely child."

"I think the DGSE will be interested in having a word. You killed an innocent civilian this morning."

The shooter backed up a step, his arms loose at his

sides, his eyes narrowed, his legs slightly bent at the knees. "No way to prove it."

"I think there might be. The French don't have the same aversion to waterboarding as my people do. Who knows what information you might be willing to give up if a deal were put on the table?"

There were more sirens in the distance, but none of them were getting any closer.

"Or you can talk to me," McGarvey said.

"Get away from here while you still can, old man."

"Whatever happened to interservice cooperation, or just plain politeness?

The shooter came at him, swinging a roundhouse punch, but McGarvey sidestepped it at the last instant, grabbed the shooter's wrist and arm, and levered the man forward to his knees.

He bounded up and came back again, moving fast, swiveling to the left and taking two karate chops, which Mac easily deflected.

The shooter moved like a ballet dancer, up on the toes of his left foot as he swung his right leg in a long arc.

McGarvey caught the leg and flipped the man onto his back.

A couple of young guys had stopped to watch, and they applauded and said something McGarvey couldn't quite catch. Out of the corner of his eye he could see that several people, including the couple with the baby carriage, had turned around to watch the spectacle.

The shooter was on his feet in an instant, charging and swinging blow after blow that McGarvey batted aside as he retreated a few meters.

Suddenly the man bent down and pulled a small pistol, almost certainly a subcompact carry-and-conceal Glock, from an ankle holster under his khaki trousers.

McGarvey stepped forward and a little to the left, and snatched the pistol out of the man's hand. "You've already done enough collateral damage for the day, you stupid bastard."

The growing crowd all applauded. They thought they were watching a couple of street entertainers doing a skit. It was common on the river walk.

McGarvey ejected the magazine and tossed it into the river, levered the round out of the firing chamber and field-stripped the pistol, tossing the pieces over the edge.

"You're unarmed now—no Barrett, no Glock. You're obviously not much of a street fighter, though you've been trained somewhere—by the IDF, I suspect."

The shooter came in, head down, butting McGarvey in the chest, and knocking him backward on his ass.

Before he could turn and run away, McGarvey hooked a foot around the man's leg, bringing him down.

The man was up on his feet in a flash, and McGarvey had to roll left to avoid a kick to his head, and he sprung to his feet.

He pulled his Walther from the holster under his jacket at the small of his back. "That's enough now."

The shooter backed up warily.

More people had gathered, but they kept their distance.

Someone had apparently called the police, because a patrol car, its siren blaring, screeched to a halt on the street above.

"For now it's out of my hands," McGarvey said.

The shooter glanced up as two uniformed police officers came down the stairs on the run. He turned on his heel and in three steps was at the edge and threw himself into the river.

The cops were shouting. *"Arrêtez! Arrêtez!"*

McGarvey laid his pistol on the pavement, then backed up to the river's edge in time to see the shooter swimming very fast downstream with the current, toward the bridge.

The cops were on McGarvey just as the shooter reached the middle arch at the same time a commercial barge came upriver, its horn blaring five warning blasts.

The shooter was swept aside by the bow of the boat, and for several seconds it seemed as if he would get clear, but then he was sucked underwater just forward of the stern. Almost immediately the river turned red, his body caught in the screw and chopped up.

FIFTY-ONE

Alex got out of the cab, but instead of immediately going into the hotel, she walked a few doors down to a Godiva chocolate shop, where she dawdled over buying a small box of truffles and having a pleasant chat with one of the clerks.

The place was reasonably busy, mostly with tourists—some of them Brits, and a few Germans and a Russian couple. But no one suspicious. No one was following her now.

Back at the hotel, the uniformed attendant held the door for her and she went down the short corridor directly to the elevators. Again, to her eye, nothing seemed out of the ordinary.

Presumably, McGarvey had come back here after the shooting, and it was more than likely that Pete Boylan had stayed behind, probably to search her room.

Upstairs, a maid was coming out of her room. "Mademoiselle, your room is ready," the woman said.

"*Merci,*" Alex said, and gave the woman the box of chocolates. The woman thanked her, surprised.

Someone other than the maid had been in the room. The attaché case was lying at a different angle on the luggage stand, and the zipper on her overnight bag was completely closed. She had left it unzipped by half an inch.

It was made to look like amateurs had done this. It was possible that the maid or someone else on the hotel's staff had been looking for something to steal, but it was more likely in her mind that she had been given a message. Hopefully, by McGarvey or Pete Boylan.

She tossed her purse onto the bed and searched the attaché case and the overnight bag, but nothing was missing, though some of the contents had been very slightly rearranged.

Her room looked down on a pleasant courtyard

with a small fountain, some trees, and flowering bushes. No way out from there. It left only the front door and presumably a delivery entrance and dock, and possibly a path across the roof to another building.

She had not been the least bit surprised when McGarvey had shown up; in fact, she had expected him. Her only concerns were that she had not detected him behind her, and that she had come into France unarmed.

She got undressed, and took a quick shower, mostly to refresh herself. It was the middle of the night her time, and she was beat, but her adrenaline was pumping hard enough that she was wide-awake. She had come looking for George, and she had sent him the message. She wanted to be awake to find out if he responded, not only to that but to the failed assassination attempt.

She phoned room service and asked for a pot of tea with lemon, and a croissant with butter and raspberry confit.

Paris was already coming to an end for her. If George responded, it would possibly be off to Tel Aviv or wherever he suggested. If not, she would have to go deep, and it would have to be a lot deeper than any of the others had gone.

Roy had changed the fourth panel on *Kryptos*, which she had to admit was pretty clever, and now McGarvey knew what was probably still buried above Kirkuk, though possibly not the entire reason why, nor who had put it there.

When she was dressed, she called the operator and asked to be connected to McGarvey's room.

Pete answered on the first ring. "Where are you?" She sounded stressed.

"In my room. Has Kirk returned yet?"

Pete hesitated for just a beat. "Quite a show you put on in the park."

"You saw it?"

"Yes. And when you took off, Mac followed you on foot. Did you see him?"

"Briefly at a sidewalk café on the Champs-Élysées, where someone tried to kill me. I managed to get out of there, but Mac didn't follow me. I suspect he went after the shooter."

"Did you see who it was?"

"Some guy with a rifle in a second-floor window across the avenue. I think it was a Barrett."

"Hard to miss at that short a range," Pete said.

"I got lucky."

"Was it your George?"

"I didn't get that good a look, but I don't think it was George."

"Who else wants you dead?"

Alex managed to laugh. "I can think of a few people. An Iraqi or two, among others. But George could have sent someone. I've left word for him."

"Where?"

"Doesn't matter. What does is whether or not he answers and what he says."

"What was your message?"

"Just that I was the last of the team, and did he want to meet with me?" Alex said. "What about Kirk? Have you heard from him?"

"Not yet," Pete said. "Look, I'm coming to your room. We need to talk."

"I just got out of the shower. Give me a couple of minutes."

"Okay."

Alex went to the window and called the travel agency on her cell phone. "Has there been an answer yet?"

"Yes," the agent said. "One word: *Come*."

"How soon can you get me there?"

"You're booked business class on Turkish Airlines, flight eighteen twenty-four, leaves de Gaulle this afternoon at five."

"Any other information?"

"No," the travel agent said. "Have a good flight, Ms. Wheeler."

Someone knocked at her door. "Room service," a man called.

Alex ended the call, tossed the phone onto the bed, got a couple of euros from her purse, and answered the door.

An old man with a barrel chest and thick gray hair stood there, holding up an identification wallet. "I'm Colonel Roland Bete. I'd like to ask you a few questions concerning a shooting at a sidewalk café on the Champs-Élysées."

"I don't know what you're talking about."

"Mr. McGarvey was there. At the moment he is in the custody of the Sûreté. Evidently, he was involved with an incident a few blocks away by the river in which a man was killed in a boating accident. Witnesses said there was a fight."

"What does that have to do with me?"

"It would be for the best if you allowed me to come in, unless you would rather be taken to an interrogation cell, from which point your fate would be completely out of my hands."

Pete came down the corridor. "I heard," she said. "What's the real issue?"

"He was armed," Bete said.

"Can we have him released?"

"Perhaps, if Mademoiselle cooperates," Bete said. "But it will have to be soon. Major Lucien has given me one hour to present a proper reason why." He looked at Alex, his expression completely neutral. He could have been discussing the weather. "We found the documents in your attaché case. And we know a seat has been booked on a Turkish Airlines flight to Tel Aviv for a Lois Wheeler."

Alex stepped aside to let them in. "It was you who tossed my room? Very unprofessional."

"It was suggested we let you know. And Monsieur McGarvey is a very persuasive man. He was allowed one call, and it was to me. Your life is in danger."

Alex laughed. "I got lucky in the café."

"The shooter was a professional. Perhaps Mossad? What do you hope to gain by going to Tel Aviv? Is it to meet with this person you have only identified as George?"

"Yes."

"And what would stop him from merely having you killed? Perhaps a random shooting. Incidents like that happen all the time. Israel is a violent country."

"McGarvey," Alex said, and watched for a reaction in Pete's eyes. And she saw exactly what she expected to see.

FIFTY-TWO

McGarvey looked up from where he was seated at a small metal table across from the two Sûreté officers who had been interviewing him, when a whip-thin man with a large Gallic nose and dark complexion came in.

"Monsieur McGarvey is cooperating, but we've got nothing of any use so far," one of the interrogators said.

"I've been listening," the dark man said. He was jacketless, his tie loose, the sleeves of his white shirt rolled up above the elbows. "Leave us."

The two interrogators left the room, and the dark man sat down. "I'm Major Lucien."

"Colonel Bete mentioned you. He said you were aware I came into France with a weapon. Do you know if he's made contact with the woman I was seated with at the café?"

"I just spoke to him on the telephone. She is at the hotel with him and the CIA officer you arrived with this morning."

It was the first piece of good news this morning. "Then she's corroborated my story."

"That she was the target of an assassination attempt in which an innocent bystander was killed instead. And that both of you left the scene before the police could arrive."

"She ran to save her life, and I ran to catch the killer."

"Neither of you stayed to offer assistance to the man who had been shot."

"It was a sniper rifle. Little hole in, big hole out. He never had a chance, something I told your people."

"And the man you confronted by the river—do you think he was the shooter?"

"Yes. Did you recover his body?"

"What there was left of it. But he carried no identification, nor were there any traces of blowback from the Barrett—which we found in the upstairs office across the avenue."

"Let me guess," McGarvey said. "You found a pair of rubber gloves."

"In the gutter around the corner. But we haven't been able to find any usable prints or DNA; the insides of the gloves had been coated with Vaseline or some substance like it."

The shooter hadn't learned that from the IDF. "I need to get out of here before someone else makes another attempt."

The major shook his head, and McGarvey knew what was coming next.

"I've never been an enemy of France."

"No, but each time you have been here, people have died. This time the death toll is two. So far. How many more will it be if I release you?"

"Did Colonel Bete tell you why we came to France?"

"Something about a serial killer in the CIA. It's not France's problem."

McGarvey leaned forward. "It might be, the next time the DGSE needs some help preventing another terrorist attack. France is crawling with Muslims. Mosques on just about every corner in all the poor districts of Paris and every other city. Breeding grounds for Islamic dissidents."

Lucien said nothing, but he was steaming.

"The Sûreté has a problem. You have a problem."

"My job is to deal with current problems. And at this moment you and the woman you followed here are it."

"She's committed no crime here."

"But you have, by carrying an undeclared firearm into France."

"Check with Colonel Bete."

Lucien rapped a knuckle on the table. "*Salopard.* The service is not in charge of internal affairs. That falls to the Sûreté. In Paris, to me."

McGarvey's sat phone, which was lying on the table, chimed.

"There can be no signal in this building," Lucien said, staring at it as if it were a dangerous bug.

The phone chimed again.

Lucien picked it up and answered it. Otto's voice came over the speaker.

"Major Pierre Lucien of the Sûreté, Paris homicides, if I'm not mistaken."

"There can be no telephone calls in here," the Sûreté major said.

"To your switchboard, and then through the building's wiring," Otto said. "Easy shit, actually. But we have a problem you need to solve before more bodies start to pile up in Paris. Wouldn't do much for your nearly spotless record. And with less than eight years until retirement, you wouldn't want to be dismissed. What would your wife, Pauline, say?"

"You son of a bitch," Lucien said, and reached to turn off the phone.

"Technically, you're right, but let's leave my mother out of this. The point is, we have a serial killer on the loose in Langley, and in order to find out who it is, we followed Ms. Wheeler to Paris so she could attempt to make contact with someone she thought could help with the investigation. Instead someone tried to kill her. You can't take her into custody, because she's broken no laws there. So she should be free to go."

"That'll be up to Colonel Bete."

"Yes. She has a flight to Tel Aviv this afternoon. We think she will be killed when she arrives. We want to prevent that."

"I don't care."

"But you must," Otto said. "Mr. McGarvey and his partner, Ms. Boylan, must be allowed to leave Paris this afternoon."

"Monsieur McGarvey will be brought before a magistrate this afternoon, where he will be formally charged with accessory to murder and entering France with an illegal firearm. We have strict laws."

"But that would be a mistake."

Lucien tried to switch the phone off.

"Hang in there, Mac," Otto said. "I've recorded everything from the moment you were arrested. Your aircrew has refueled the Gulfstream and is ready to leave as soon as you and Pete get to the airport."

"Is Pete okay?"

"She's with Bete right now."

Lucien tried to switch off the phone again.

"I'll spring you in about five minutes," Otto said, and was gone, but the phone would not power off.

"Who was that?" Lucien demanded.

"Otto Rencke. He's director of special projects for the Company, and he, too, lived here a number of years ago, but you probably won't find anything in your databases. He's pretty good with stuff like that."

"We're past that point," Lucien said. "The rest will come out at your trial." He got up and, not bothering with the sat phone—it was something he couldn't control—left the room

"You still there?" he asked.

"Yes, but pick up. They're recording everything," Otto replied.

The speaker function shut off when McGarvey picked up. "What do you have in mind?"

"Do you know the name Andre Tousseul?"

"He used to be the director general of the Sûreté."

"Still is. He was listening in on your interview—especially with Lucien. I had Walt explain the situation to him earlier, and he understood perfectly. Mostly because he wants all this to go away. The sooner you and Pete and Alex are out of France, the happier he'll be, though he promised Walt any assistance he could give to the CIA."

"Her flight leaves in less than three hours. She takes it, there's a good chance she'll be killed when she gets there."

"I think Pete should go in her stead. You and Alex can fly over in the Gulfstream. I'll have your clearance to land within the next thirty minutes."

One of the officers who had conducted their initial interview came in. "If you will come with me, sir, I'll have you signed out and your belongings returned to you."

"On my way. Thanks, kemo sabe," McGarvey said. He switched off the phone, and this time it stayed off.

"Sir."

"Where is Major Lucien?"

"He's been called away."

FIFTY-THREE

Room service had brought up a cheese plate with mousse and pâté de foie gras, along with a good bottle of ice-cold Pinot Grigio. Pete and Alex sat at a small marble-topped table in front of the open window. That she had a minder wasn't lost on Alex, but she made no bones about it, for which Pete was grateful.

She didn't like the woman, but she felt sorry for her. Being a NOC had been the only possible profession for her, and yet the years of service in the field, and since Iraq, the constant looking over her shoulder, had taken its toll. She could see it around the corners of her eyes, the sometimes firm set of her mouth, and the tilt of her head, as if she were listening for something gaining on her.

Bete was waiting downstairs for McGarvey to arrive, and when he got there, they would head to de Gaulle, where Pete would take Alex's place on the

Turkish Airlines flight, and Alex would go with Mac on the CIA's Gulfstream. They would leave as soon as possible in order to get to Tel Aviv before Pete's flight arrived. He wanted to be at immigration first to see who showed up to meet the flight.

"It's a dangerous game you're playing," Pete said.

"You, too, going in my place."

"I don't get it. Someone tries to kill you here, and yet you've sent a message to George and he's told you to come to Tel Aviv. Right into the hornets' nest. What do you think you'll achieve?"

Alex shrugged. "If he kills me, then I guess it'll prove he still has something to hide after all these years. But you have to know he isn't your serial killer."

"How did you send him the message that you wanted to meet? I mean, did you call some number direct? Maybe an Israel country code?"

Alex told her about the Mossad-backed travel agency, but Otto had already traced the Turkish Airlines booking to the agency on the Champs-Élysées not far from the sidewalk café.

"We were given a code phrase to use if we needed help. The travel agent made the call or sent the e-mail."

"So the call could have gone to a private cell phone at Langley. Or more likely to a blind number somewhere in the vicinity. The killer still could be George. He could have hired the hit man here in Paris, and since that failed, he's made arrangements for you to be taken out in Tel Aviv."

"We'll see when we get there," Alex said.

She seemed to Pete to be resigned. Too resigned? "Do you think you'll recognize him?"

"It's always the eyes," Alex said. "You can wear contacts and change the color, and you can even have plastic surgery. But you can't hide what's in them." She nodded. "If we come face-to-face, I'll recognize him."

"And then what?"

"I'll ask him why he did it. We kept our mouths shut; there was no reason to kill everyone. And especially not the way he did it."

"The same as you and he did in Iraq."

"For different reasons. I keep telling you the same thing. Anyway, we've grown up since then—or at least, I have."

Pete's cell phone vibrated. It was Mac. "We're on the way up. Are you ready to leave?"

"Anytime you are. I'm in her room with our things."

"You're taking a cab to the airport. Do you have her passport?"

"The pictures don't match."

"They never do," McGarvey said.

Pete hung up. "One last thing I don't get," she told Alex. "When Walt Wager was murdered, why didn't you contact the others and set up a defensive position together? You'd worked as a team before."

"When Joseph bought it in Athens, I thought it was just an accident. But when Walt was killed, I knew what was going on. The only trouble was, I didn't know where the rest of them were."

"Okay, I can buy the likelihood that you guys didn't know where the others were hiding. But after Wager went down, you didn't even try to look for the others. You were out just for yourself, just to save your own skin."

"You're damned right," Alex said. "Survival is the name of the game—the *only* game worth being good at."

She got up and went to her bag, grabbing a billed cap. She gave it to Pete. "Wear this—it'll at least cover your hair. You're flying business class, but don't get off at the front of the crowd. Stick around till most of the tourist-class passengers get off. Might buy you a little time."

Someone knocked.

Pete drew her weapon and went to the door. "Who is it?" she asked.

"Me," Mac said.

Pete let him in. Bete hadn't come with him.

"We're going first," he said. "Give us five minutes, then check out and take a cab to the airport. But listen: anything goes wrong, even if you have the slightest suspicion something is about to happen, push the panic button. Otto's programs are watching for it."

Star 111 on Pete's sat phone would set off an alarm that Otto would pick up immediately. It would give her precise GPS position anywhere on Earth and at any altitude.

"Nothing's going to happen in the air, and you'll be in Tel Aviv at the international terminal when I get there," she said, though she had a little flutter in her stomach.

She was primarily an interrogator—and a damned good one. It was a job she'd always liked. The only reason she'd become a field agent was because of

Mac. She supposed she had fallen in love with him almost from the first moment she'd laid eyes on him. But she had given him room because of the death of his wife.

"Give me your weapon," he said.

Pete handed over her pistol, and Mac stuffed it into his bag. Then, at the door with Alex and her attaché case, he turned back and went to her.

"When this is over, we're going to New York to dinner in the Village. I know an Italian restaurant, homemade pasta, a great Bolognese sauce, and Valpolicella. It'll be a Saturday, and we'll make it late and wander around until the Sunday *Times* comes out. We'll find a bakery just opening and have coffee and something sweet for dessert. Date?"

"Absolutely," Pete said.

He kissed her on the cheek, and he and Alex left.

She stood for a long moment or two before she went back to the window and looked down at the pretty courtyard. She hadn't known for sure if she had a chance with him. But now she knew, and she also knew she would move heaven and earth for him.

Traffic was heavy out to Charles de Gaulle, as it always was on just about any highway in or around Paris. The cabby dropped Pete off at the Turkish Airlines counter, where she showed her Lois Wheeler identification and picked up her boarding pass.

At the international terminal, she showed her passport and boarding pass. The male security officer looked at the photo, then at Pete. "Doesn't look like you, Madame," he said.

"It was taken a few years ago. I'm a little older now."

"Your hair is not the same."

Pete smiled. "What woman's is?" she asked. "It's our prerogative."

The officer looked again at the passport photo. "What is your birth date?"

Pete gave him the date from the passport. It was a few years older than she was.

The officer initialed her boarding pass and handed it and her passport back. "The photo does you no justice, Madame."

Her shoulder bag and the one carry-on bag were sent through the X-ray machine, and she passed through the security arch.

The man ahead of her was taken aside for a pat-down, but she was allowed to collect her things and head down the broad corridor to the gates, the first and easiest of her hurdles behind her.

Tel Aviv wouldn't be so easy, because it was possible someone would be gunning for Lois Wheeler.

FIFTY-FOUR

Colonel Bete had three Citroën C5 black sedans waiting in front of the hotel. McGarvey and Alex rode in the back of the middle car, Bete riding shot-gun in the front seat. Two men sat in the front of the lead and follow cars, in the backseats of which were a man and a woman.

"There have already been two deaths in Paris over

this business," Bete said as they pulled away. "Lucien, for all the problems he faces now, was correct in his concern over your presence here. I personally want to make sure you are gone as quickly as possible."

"Thanks for your help," McGarvey said.

Bete turned around in his seat. "You are a good and capable man, *Monsieur le Directeur*, and in many ways France owes you and the CIA a debt of gratitude. But you are like a lightning apparatus. You attract trouble. I'm not the only one who will breathe a sigh of relief when you are gone."

"Maybe I'll come back on vacation someday."

Bete laughed. "I sincerely hope not. You have not been officially designated as a persona non grata, but I think the next time you would not be allowed entry."

"Too bad for France, Colonel," Alex said. "One of these days you might need his help. But then if France asks, he'll probably come running. It's what he does, didn't you know?"

Bete didn't answer.

They took the feeder road that ran alongside the Seine to the ring road that connected to the A3 out to Charles de Gaulle, sweeping past traffic, their speeds sometimes topping 150 kilometers per hour.

At the airport they were passed through the security gates to the commercial hangar, where the Gulfstream had been trundled out to the tarmac, its engines idling, its hatch open, its stairs down.

Bete got out with them. "I understand your sentiment, Mademoiselle Unroth. Despite who you are, Monsieur McGarvey has stepped into the fray to help save your life, though it's beyond me why, except that, as you intimate, he is a good man. But he is no longer welcome in France." He glanced at McGarvey and nodded. "At least not in the near term."

He and McGarvey shook hands, and Alex went first aboard the Gulfstream, McGarvey right behind her.

Their pilot, Donald Roper, was turned in his seat as Maggie pulled up the stairs and closed and dogged the hatch. "We'll have to hustle to beat the Turkish Airlines flight by the one hour you want. She's a 747-400 and has about ten knots on us."

"Anytime you're ready, Captain," McGarvey said.

He and Alex went aft and strapped in.

Maggie came back. "We're eighth for takeoff. May I get either of you something to drink? I'll be serving steaks with baked potatoes and salads once we're at ten thousand feet."

"May I have a glass of champagne?" Alex asked.

"Of course. For you, Mr. Director?"

"A cognac, and then I'm going to get some sleep. It's been a hell of a long day."

"No dinner?"

"Not for me."

The attendant went forward.

"She's a pretty girl, but then so is Pete," Alex said. "She's in love with you."

"Stay out of it," McGarvey growled.

They started away from the hangar and onto the taxi way, toward the active runway, and joined a lineup of six much larger jets and a Boeing 777 just turning into place for takeoff.

"Once they find out Pete's an imposter, they'll figure out I came in the back door with you, and George will send someone to try to kill me."

"Then why are you doing this? Why go to him?"

"To see if someone actually tries."

"Then what?"

"I'll find him, providing you let me keep Pete's papers and CIA identification booklet. And her gun."

"The Israelis won't appreciate the CIA bringing in a ringer right under their noses. Armed."

"Only to defend myself."

"That's what the Hezbollah terrorists claim."

Alex looked away. "I'll do it on my own if I have to," she said. "But once Pete is outed, the Mossad is going to take a real interest in you. They might even bring you to someone who will claim to have been the control officer for the op in Iraq. But you won't have any possible way of knowing if he himself isn't a ringer."

"Not with you there."

Alex looked at him and nodded. "You're probably right," she said.

It was early evening, Tel Aviv time when the pilot called McGarvey and said they were one hour from landing at Ben Gurion, which would put them nearly one hour ahead of the Turkish Airlines flight.

"Who will be meeting us?"

"They didn't say, but from the tone of the guy I just got off the radio with, it'll be Mossad. They've already checked Langley to find out who we were.

Your name and Ms. Boylan's were mentioned, and they wanted to know the nature of your flight. I played dumb."

"Good job, Captain, thanks. I'm going to make a sat phone call now."

"You may use the aircraft's equipment."

"Thanks, but from this point, they'll be monitoring every transmission that comes from us."

"But not your sat phone?"

"Mr. Rencke designed it," McGarvey said.

"I see."

Otto was at his desk when Mac's call came in. "The Mossad has taken an interest in you guys," he said. "But Walt's still backing you up, over Marty's objections."

"Is anyone on the Hill or the White House asking questions?"

"Nada, except they want updates on our serial killer. But everyone's damned glad the problem seems to have gone away. I let it slip that the killer was definitely off campus, and probably out of the country. Marty sent our station chiefs the heads-up."

"No mention of Alex?"

"None. Unless someone takes a look at the Sûreté's day sheets over the past twenty-four hours. But the DGSE has promised to temporarily delay making positive IDs on you or Alex."

"I'm sure no one in France is happy about it."

"A firestorm would be more accurate. Wouldn't have been half so bad except the guy who took the hit at the café was a stockbroker. He was there meeting his mistress, who is the wife of the minister of finance. *Figaro* is speculating he was assassinated on the minister's behalf, and that his recent string of successes on the Paris Bourse were because of insider information he was getting from the wife."

"That story won't hold for long," McGarvey said.

"How much time do you need?"

"Seventy-two hours ideally, but at least forty-eight. I think we're getting close."

"Somebody else does too; otherwise, they wouldn't have taken the risk of trying to take her out in Paris," Otto said. "One other thing: the DGSE thinks it has a positive ID on the shooter they fished out of the river. The Barrett was registered to a fictitious name at an accommodations box in London, which led them to an SIS investigation of a Brit by the name of Hamid Cabbage—mom was an Israeli, dad was a Scotland Yard counterterrorist officer who sometimes did contract work for the Mossad. Thing is, the son took off on his own and did some freelance assassinations."

"Trained in Israel, but then left after a short period?" McGarvey asked.

"The French sent over blood and mouth swab samples for a DNA match. But that's going to take a few days."

"He could have been working for the Mossad, or for someone else," McGarvey said.

Otto turned his battered old Mercedes diesel over to the valet parker at the Hotel George, just down the block from Union Station, and went inside to the bistro and bar. He gave the name Tony Samson to the maître d', who had a server take him to a table upstairs, where an older woman with gray hair, sagging eyelids, and drooping jowls was just finishing a martini.

"Mrs. Fegan," Otto said.

The woman looked up and then smiled uncertainly. "Actually, it's been Ms. for the past five years. You're Mr. Samson?"

Otto nodded and sat down. The waiter came, and Otto ordered a house red. She ordered another Tanqueray martini straight up.

"I don't know how much help I can be. I don't have any proof. Only things I heard."

The woman had been on Robert Benning's staff when he was the assistant ambassador to the UN. Her job had been to expedite the briefing papers and books he used. She'd made it clear during their two Skype conversations before she agreed to meet that she had never created any positions, or even interpreted the raw data that came into the office. Her job was just a small step above a secretary's.

Louise had dressed Otto for the occasion, with new boat shoes, crisply ironed jeans, a spotless button-up white shirt, and a dark blue blazer from Brooks Brothers. His long frizzy red hair was tied in a ponytail. She assured him he looked fashionable.

"I'll work on finding the proof. I'd just like to hear your story."

"I looked up your name. You don't work for the *Post*."

"Samson's not my real name. Not at this stage of this story."

"I'll deny everything if you use my name," she said. "I just want you to know that from the beginning. You won't use a recorder or take written notes, anything like that."

Otto nodded. Last year Pete had coached him on the primary principle of being a good interrogator. "Keep your mouth shut," she had told him. "Know the answers to the questions you ask, and then let the subject do all the talking. And especially don't say a thing when it seems like they're done. Let them fret. They'll fill in the silences, because they'll either be afraid of you, or more often than not, they'll try to impress you."

The woman stared at him but then looked away as their drinks came.

"Would you like to order?" the waiter asked them.

"Not yet," she said. She took a deep draught of her martini, and Otto nearly winced, seeing her lack of reaction to the raw alcohol.

"You must have already guessed what was going on; otherwise, you wouldn't have sought me out."

Otto sipped his merlot. It wasn't bad, though when he'd lived in France, even the table wines—the *vins ordinaires*—were better.

"Everyone was so frantic to find Saddam's WMDs, they jumped on the yellow cake story. And even when it looked as if that wouldn't pan out, they couldn't just walk away. They started looking for nerve gas and biological weapons mobile factories."

Otto wanted to talk for her, lead her to cutting to the chase, but he just nodded.

She finished her second martini and held the glass up to the waiter for another. The alcohol was like water to her.

"They needed the justification so badly, they were willing to lie to make it true. But you can't imagine the pressure all of us were feeling. It even filtered down to the janitors, who weren't allowed into the offices until someone signed off that any scrap of paper with the least bit of sensitive material had been accounted for—either locked up or shredded.

"Finally people started whispering about the *it*. 'It was in place. It would convert the critics. Make believers out of them all. It showed we had been right from day one. Saddam had sold out his own people. Something Israel had been warning about from the start. After all, bin Laden was only one problem; we had much bigger fish to fry.' "

She fiddled impatiently with her empty glass. "It was about then that my husband and I began having our troubles. I was spending too much time at work, and he was traveling all the time. And not alone."

Pete did caution that if they seemed to be wandering off course, to jog them. "But lightly," she'd said.

"Any idea what the *it* might have been?" he asked.

She laughed, the sound ragged. She was a big drinker, but Otto figured she was also a heavy smoker. "No one wanted to come out and actually say something specific. Everyone was waiting for the other shoe to drop."

Otto sipped his wine.

"Someone was going to have to find the damned thing before it was too late, for Christ's sake. Don't be dense."

Otto waited for nearly a full minute, until the waiter had brought Ms. Fegan's third drink, before he pulled out folded sheet of paper and laid it on the table.

"I won't talk to you if you try to take notes," the woman said.

"No pencil, no pen," Otto said. Though he'd played around with superthin tablets that could be rolled up or folded and still record sounds and video, this was only plain paper.

"The last I heard, it had been moved, and only a handful of people on the ground knew where it was, and just about everyone was frantic to find out." She took a drink, her hand steady. "But that was more than ten years ago."

She knocked back her drink and looked for the waiter.

"Why don't we have some dinner first?" Otto said.

"Fuck you," she said, but not harshly.

Pete had warned that sometimes an interrogation would come to a dead end, and then you'd have to pull a rabbit out of the hat.

"What if there's no rabbit?" Otto had asked.

"There's usually at least one right under your nose."

"Have you ever heard of the sculpture *Kryptos*, over at the CIA?"

She nodded. "I went over one time with Bob, and we were given a tour. It's in one of the courtyards, as I remember, some sort of a coded message chiseled into the plates."

"Four plates, actually, three of which have been decrypted, but the fourth has stumped all the code breakers until a few days ago."

The woman just looked at him.

"We think it has something to do with what was hidden in the hills above Kirkuk."

"That's not possible. I remember we were told that the sculpture was dedicated in the early nineties."

"The message on the fourth panel was changed in the past five years or so," Otto said. "Would you like to know what it says?"

"This is bullshit," the woman said. But she nodded.

Otto read from the paper. "'And God said let there be light, and there was light, and the light was visible from horizon to horizon. All was changed, all was never the same. And God said let there be progress.'"

The waiter came and asked if Ms. Fegan would like another drink, but she declined and he left.

"The last line was: 'And there was peace.'" Otto looked up at her. "About what you guys were working for, wasn't it? A reason to take Saddam out, so Iraq could be rebuilt?"

"But it didn't work out that way, did it? In more ways than one. And now we're stuck with one hell of a big problem no one knows how to fix."

"What's buried out there?"

"Figure it out for yourself," the woman said as she got her purse and started to rise.

"Someone thinks they know, and is willing to kill for it. So far at least eight people are dead."

"Not my problem."

"I think I know who moved it and why, but at least tell me who buried it in the first place."

She was frightened, and she started to move away, but Otto jumped up and caught her arm.

"Why did you agree to talk to me in the first place if you weren't willing to tell me something I already didn't know?"

"Leave me alone," she said. She pulled her arm away and scurried downstairs.

Otto left a fifty-dollar bill on the table and followed her just as she was leaving through the front door.

She turned and spotted him, then darted out into traffic at the same time a black Range Rover accelerated down 15 E Street NW, hitting her full on, tossing her body in front of a taxi coming in the opposite direction.

The SUV continued up toward Union Station, its license plate light out.

FIFTY-SIX

It was seven in the evening local when their Gulfstream landed at Ben Gurion and taxied to an Israeli Air Force hangar. As soon as the engines spooled down, the wheels chocked by two ground crewmen, the hatch was opened and the stairs lowered.

"We've been instructed to remain aboard," Roper called back from the cockpit.

"As soon as possible, refuel and work out a flight plan for Ramstein," McGarvey said. "If we're not back in twenty-four hours, leave without us."

A dark-green Mercedes C-Class pulled up, and a short slightly built man wearing khaki slacks and a white shirt, the sleeves rolled up, got out from the driver's side and came aboard.

"Mr. Director, welcome to Tel Aviv. My name is Lev Sharon, and we met once a few years ago just before you moved off the seventh floor."

They shook hands. "You're Ariel's son?" McGarvey asked.

"Nephew, actually," he glanced briefly at Alex. "The fuel truck should be here in the next five or ten minutes, so we should be able to get you turned around and out of here well within the hour. But we're curious as to why you came, unannounced."

"We called ahead for permission to land, and were given it."

"Yes, of course. But this is an unscheduled visit, and you certainly didn't come as tourists. So we'd like to know why you're here."

"Are you still working for the Mossad?"

Sharon was young, but his shoulders were already sloped, his face filled with lines as if he were a man in his sixties, and not in his late thirties. "I can tell you this, of course. We're all friends here. Yes, I am."

"Then you have heard about the problems we've had at Langley."

"We heard some back-burner rumors, that there may have been a murder on your campus."

"Four."

Again Sharon glanced at Alex, who stared back. "What does this have to do with Israel?"

"We've traced a former CIA NOC to a Turkish Airlines flight from Paris scheduled to land in about an hour," Alex said. "She's traveling under the work name Lois Wheeler."

Sharon's expression of mild interest did not change. "Yes?"

"She sent a message through VIP World Travel on the Champs-Élysées to a man she only indentified as George, who she wanted to meet. He replied she should come."

"What does this have to do with us?"

"The travel agency is a tool of the Mossad—has been for years, since the Eichmann business—and there was a pro phrase she had been instructed to use if she wanted to initiate contact." A pro word or phrase was a code of the sort Alex had used.

"Does the CIA have any idea who this George might be?" Sharon asked McGarvey.

"We think he works, or may have at one time

worked, for the Mossad. We're simply following a lead to see where it takes us."

"And here you are. And what do you expect will happen?"

"We'd like to meet the flight without her knowing we're here, and find out who she meets and where she goes."

Sharon, who'd been leaning over the back of one of the seats, abruptly turned around and got off the airplane.

"That didn't go so well," Alex said, but McGarvey held up a hand for her to keep still.

From where he sat, he could see Sharon standing next to his car. The Israeli was talking to someone on a cell phone.

At one point Sharon looked up and spotted McGarvey in the window. He turned away.

"He doesn't know what to do with us," McGarvey said. "He's called for orders."

"What do you think?" Alex asked.

"He'll either let us in, or he'll order us to leave."

"If the latter?"

"We'll give Pete the heads-up, and have the chief of station here meet the plane."

"Then we lose."

"We'll have gotten their attention," McGarvey said noncommittally. He was more interested in her reaction than in Sharon's or the Mossad's. But her expression was neutral.

Sharon got off the phone and came back aboard. "We'll see if someone meets the plane and pulls your NOC aside when she presents herself at immigration."

"George?" Alex asked.

"It won't be one of us. No one knows who George is. Nor was any message received from the travel agency. We're just as mystified as you are."

"We'd like to be there," McGarvey said.

"Are you armed?"

"Yes."

"Your weapons stay here," Sharon said. "I want your word on it."

McGarvey took out his Walther PPK and laid it on the seat table.

Sharon smiled. "We wondered if you still carried the Walther."

"An old friend."

The Turkish Airlines flight arrived at the gate in Terminal 3 exactly on time, eight minutes later. McGarvey and Alex watched an overhead monitor one level up from the immigration hall as the first-class and business passengers began emerging from the arrivals gate.

Sharon and a female introduced as Sheila, in jeans and a khaki military shirt, the sleeves rolled up and buttoned above the elbows, waited with them.

When those passengers were off and the tourist class began unloading, Sheila stepped up. "Maybe she's not on the flight."

"She's a professional; she's biding her time," Sharon said.

"She got a reply from George, so she's expecting someone will be meeting her," Alex said. "Could be she thinks she'll be assassinated."

Sharon was surprised. "Here, in the airport?" he asked.

"No, wherever George is waiting for her."

"There may be no George," Sharon said.

"Then who answered her message at the travel agency?"

"I have no idea," Sharon said. He turned to McGarvey. "And neither do my signals people who monitor such traffic. Which either means she was lying, or your information is unreliable, or the reply came from Paris."

"Either that or your signals people are unreliable or you're lying," Alex shot back.

"Lev?" Sheila said.

"I thought your people were more efficient than that," Alex said.

Pete came from the gate area.

"It's her," McGarvey said.

She was tucked in behind a knot of a dozen tourist passengers, and she glanced up at the ceiling camera and winked.

"Resourceful woman," Sharon said. "She knows someone is watching her."

"George," Alex said. "How long before she's through with immigration and your people grab her?"

"Maybe twenty minutes. Depending on how fast her luggage is delivered."

"She only has a purse and a carry-on."

"Ten minutes," Sharon said.

"Good, because I need to take a pee," Alex said. "Would you like to come and watch?" she asked Sheila.

"I'd be delighted," the Mossad operative said.

"Not such a good idea," McGarvey said.

"Go with her," Sharon told the woman. "I'm not having anyone wander around the airport unescorted this morning. Especially no one from the CIA."

FIFTY-SEVEN

Cameras were everywhere in the terminal, and as Pete approached the passport lane, she was certain Mac and Alex were watching a monitor somewhere near. The issue was who else was here, waiting for her.

She got in line, and when it was her turn, the uniformed officer merely glanced at her passport, stamped it, and handed it back. He hadn't paid any attention to her photograph, nor did he ask her the purpose of her trip.

On the other side, she joined the line for one of the customs agents to check her bag and purse. An older man in civilian clothes emerged from an office to the left and came to her.

"Ms. Lois Wheeler?" he asked politely.

"Yes, are you George?" Pete asked. He was about the right age, but he didn't seem to have the kind of fire in his eyes she figured George would. Especially if he were the killer, or the man who had directed the killer—or killers.

"No," the man said. "If you would just come with me, I have some questions for you."

A few of the other people in line were curious, but

most of the passengers looked away. What was happening was none of their business.

"May I see some identification?"

The man pulled out an identification wallet and showed his badge. He was airport security, but she didn't quite catch his name before he pocketed the wallet. "Ms. Wheeler?"

Pete glanced up at one of the cameras in the ceiling and followed the man across the hall to the windowless office that was furnished only with a plain metal desk and a couple of chairs.

The security officer took her bag and purse and quickly searched them before he motioned to one of the chairs and sat down across from her. "May I see your passport, please?"

Pete handed it to him, and he studied it, comparing the photograph to her face.

"This is not yours."

"No, it was last-minute in Paris, and the amateur who'd come highly recommended did a botched job."

"What is your real name?"

"That doesn't matter. I assume you're here representing George, which of course isn't his real name."

"Give me a name that will be of some use."

"Alex. George and I knew each other some years ago."

"Yet you thought I was George."

"No, I was merely testing the waters. I wanted to see what your reaction might be."

The security officer stared at her. "Why did you come here?"

"I sent a message to George and he replied: *Come*."

"Yes, but why do you want to see him? What is so urgent to you now, after all these years?"

Pete suppressed a smile. There was a George after all, and he was somewhere here in Israel. Alex had been right. "There have been a series of incidents at Langley, and in Athens and yesterday in Paris. I need some answers."

Again, the man playing the role of an airport security officer hesitated. "Give me your work name."

"Alex Unroth. What do I call you?"

"Mr. Smith will do for now."

He took a small tablet from his jacket pocket, brought up an e-mail address, and entered the Unroth name. A minute later he glanced up. "You were a member of the CIA's Alpha Seven team in Iraq."

"That's right. I'm the last one."

"Last one?"

"The others are dead. Murdered. It's something George knows about."

"And you think he is somehow responsible?"

"I do."

Smith nodded, a little sadness in the gesture. "That said, you came here, which means you are a very brave woman or a stupid one. And I only say that because if you truly understood the importance of what happened in Iraq, you would have disappeared. With your skills, you could have gone very deep. But then you're not really Alex Unroth. In fact, your real name is Pete Boylan, and I expect Alex directed you in what to say and how to act. Perhaps it was even you who sent the message from Paris."

"Will you take me to him?"

"Of course, if that's what you really want. But I think you will be disappointed, because you will not find the answers you came looking for. But you might find some you don't want to hear."

As Smith got to his feet, the door opened.

Pete looked over her shoulder. A man in civilian clothes who she had never seen before was there, McGarvey right behind him. Mac winked and she grinned, but the man in the doorway did not seem happy.

Smith said something in Hebrew. He, too, was angry.

The man in the doorway stepped aside, and Smith followed him out of the office. Mac came in and closed the door.

"We don't have much time," he said. "Are you okay?"

"So far so good, but I'm glad to see you. Where's Alex?"

"She took off. Mossad's looking for her. What'd you tell this guy?"

"That I was looking for George. He checked with someone online, and he knew my real name. But he said he would take me to George if that's what I really wanted. Said I would be disappointed. But how'd Alex give you the slip?"

"We worked it out ahead of time. Soon as we saw you wink at the camera, you had to know we were watching. She went to the bathroom with her female minder, and got away."

"She didn't hurt the woman?"

"Not seriously except for her pride. She left her half-unconscious in one of the stalls."

"But why?"

"I think this guy who pulled you out of the line might take you to George, or someone claiming to be George, but they're going to want more out of you, and us, than they're willing to give. Alex will try to make her own contact."

"You trust her?"

"No other game in town," McGarvey said. "She's the only one who can ID George." He glanced over his shoulder at the door, then bent down and kissed Pete on her cheek just beside her right ear.

She looked up, surprised.

"These guys are scared shitless; it's the only reason I let Alex go. Whatever song and dance they give us, we're going along with it. I think our lives could depend on it."

Lev Sharon came back with Smith.

"I think we have it straight now," Sharon said. "You'll be taken to see General Yarviv. He played the role as an adviser for Aman during the Iraq war." Aman was the Israeli military intelligence directorate.

"Be careful with what questions you ask, Mr. Director," Smith said. "If you step over the line, you could be subject to immediate arrest and prosecution under the Israel Secrets Act."

"Don't threaten me and my people," McGarvey shot back. "We're dealing with a serial killer on campus. Some kind of a psychopath, and at this point everything has led us here to George—if indeed

General Yarviv is the guy who came to Alpha Seven in the hills above Kirkuk."

"This isn't the United States, you son of a bitch," Smith said, his temper at the edge.

"Do you want to know how the four guys at Langley were killed?"

"I don't care—"

"The same way George killed his victims on the oil installations outside of Kirkuk. He ripped out their carotid arteries, and as they were bleeding to death, he chewed off their faces like some animal."

"You have no proof linking the general to those acts."

"If I find it, and the reasons, you won't dare bring this to a court of law. The Iraqis were soldiers, but it was before any declaration of war had been given. And there was no reason to kill the Alpha Seven team just to keep them quiet. They'd kept their part of the bargain. They were simply trying to forget and to survive."

"So let's go talk to General Yarviv," Pete said, and Smith glared at her.

FIFTY-EIGHT

Alex got up from where she had been sitting for the past fifteen minutes with the people waiting for the early morning British Airways flight to London. First- and business-class passengers, along with the frequent flyer members, were already shuffling past the gate agent and into the Jetway.

A lot of airport security uniformed officers and a number of guys she spotted as plainclothes cops had streamed by, but not one of them had thought to check out the passengers waiting to board a flight at a gate that was just steps away from the women's room she'd used.

She moved forward in line as the zone one passengers were invited to board. When it was her turn to present her boarding pass, she pushed past the man ahead of her and raced down the Jetway.

The female boarding agent shouted something, and when Alex reached the aircraft's open hatch, one of the male flight attendants stepped off the plane and got in front of her. He tried to grab the strap of her shoulder bag, but she strong-armed him, shoving him backward, and slammed open the Jetway's exit door and clambered down the steps to the tarmac.

A siren sounded from behind her as she ducked under the fuselage and ran inside the baggage processing area. Around the corner she slowed down and strode normally across the big open space as if she belonged there.

A tractor hauling three carts filled with baggage for the London flight trundled past, momentarily blocking the view of a cop who appeared at the open service door at the foot of the Jetway's stairs, giving her time to slip behind a pile of luggage coming down a conveyor belt. Two men in white coveralls were loading suitcases, boxes, and other things on the carts of a second tractor.

Glancing over her shoulder to make sure the cop wasn't coming around the corner, she waited until both ground crewmen were looking the other way, then took a wheeled suitcase from the pile and walked in the opposite direction, keeping in the shadows as much as possible.

Someone was making a commotion behind her, and she sped up, coming to the entrance of a luggage carousel that wasn't in use.

After climbing up on the slideway, she parted the rubber curtains and looked out to the baggage hall, where checked luggage that had already passed security was being routed to the proper flights. Two men were loading luggage three slideways to the left, intent on their work, their backs turned to her.

She ducked out on the slideway, hurried to the right, and continued to the far end of the hall, where she opened a door a crack and looked out. The conveyor belts coming from the ticketing area two levels up, the ones used to send checked luggage down to the preliminary sorting area, were idle.

Stepping out, she crossed the large room and slipped out a door on the other side, where she found herself in the arrivals hall, busy at this hour of the evening.

She was on the outside of the secured area now, and she pulled the suitcase behind her as she went outside and then climbed into a taxi. The driver put her suitcase in the trunk and got behind the wheel.

"The Hilton, please," she told him.

"You're an American?" the driver asked, pulling away.

"Canadian, actually," she said. She took out her phone and called Otto.

He answered on the first ring. "You're not at the airport," he said.

"I'm in a cab heading to the Hilton. Is Pete okay?"

"Yes. An Aman officer met her at customs, but Mac and Sharon are with her. All hell has broken loose at the airport. Sharon is convinced it was Mac who engineered your escape."

"They can't prove it," Alex said. "But right now I need you to do a couple of things for me."

"I thought you were going to stick with Mac so you could identify George, who, as it turns out, now might be an Aman general?"

"I'm going to do exactly that, but my own way. I value my hide more than to simply walk into wherever this guy wants to meet."

"I'll have to let Mac know."

"Naturally."

"You didn't have time to make a reservation at the Hilton, so I'll take care of that right now. What else?"

A bright flash lit up the early morning sky far to the southeast, behind them.

"Hezbollah," the driver said. "And right on time."

"A Hezbollah rocket just landed," Alex said.

"It's been happening just about every night for the past week," Otto said.

"Are Mac and the others still at the airport?"

"Yes. They're still trying to figure out what to do about you. They know Pete's real identity, and Mossad wants to throw her in jail for traveling under a false passport."

"What about Aman?"

"The general has been told, but he still wants the meeting."

"Has Walt Page been informed?"

"The chief of station in Tel Aviv sent a flash message to Marty, so I'm sure he's called Page."

The situation was unfolding exactly the way she wanted it to. She needed the delay. "I want to know the moment they leave the airport, and I'll want to know exactly where they're going—that's if they haven't taken Mac's sat phone."

"He still has it. I've booked you a suite for three days, under Pete's name, with a Congolese Faith Ministries Gold Amex card." It was a sometimes-used CIA front.

Alex had to laugh. "I didn't think we still used that one."

"They're saying now that you injured one of the Mossad officers. They're going to issue a warrant for your arrest."

"I just put her down. She couldn't have been out for more than ten or fifteen seconds."

"If the warrant is issued, and the cops try to pick you up, you'll surrender peacefully. No one gets hurt."

"Sure, if it goes down that way. But if George sends some of his muscle like he tried in Paris, I will defend myself. I just want to get a look at his eyes, and then I'll back off. You have my word on it, because the next thing I need from you is a piece of equipment I couldn't bring into the country."

"A gun."

"Yes. And I'll need a car."

"The car is easy," Otto said. "I'll have to think about the other."

"Don't think too long about it," Alex said. "We're coming to the end game."

"We could cut to the chase right now, if you'd confirm what's buried out there and what became of it."

"You've figured it out. Christ, Roy practically drew you guys a picture."

"I want to hear it from you," Otto insisted.

"I want Mac to hear it from George."

When they reached the Hilton, a bellman took the suitcase from the trunk. Alex paid the cabby, and once inside, she showed Pete's passport and checked in. The morning desk clerk didn't bother looking at the photo. He just had her sign, and then gave her the key card.

Her suite was on the twelfth floor, overlooking the Mediterranean. She gave the bellman a good tip, then ordered a pot of coffee and a plate of sweet rolls.

She figured that whatever was going down would happen within the next hour or two. She didn't think that George, or the Israeli authorities, would let it drag out any longer than that.

Her coffee and rolls came, and she'd sat down to eat when someone else knocked lightly at her door.

No one was visible in the peephole, but when she opened the door, a man was rounding the corner to the elevators halfway down the corridor. He'd left a small leather valise.

Otto had arranged for her to have a standard U.S.-issue 9-mm Beretta with a decent suppressor but with only one fifteen-round magazine. She field-stripped the weapon to make sure it was in working order, and then reloaded it.

She sat by the half-open slider, smelling the Med and drinking her coffee, nothing else to do but wait until Otto called.

FIFTY-NINE

The Aman officer identified only as Mr. Smith rode shotgun in an eight-passenger Mercedes van, a taciturn young man in jeans and a T-shirt driving. McGarvey and Pete sat in the second row while Sharon sat in back. Sheila had remained behind to help airport security with the search for Alex.

"Leave her alone, and she'll show up on her own," McGarvey had told Sharon. "No one will get hurt."

"That's not acceptable," Sharon had said, and Smith had agreed.

They headed into downtown Tel Aviv directly from the airport, the early morning traffic beginning to pick up, mostly with trucks making deliveries to hotels and restaurants or collecting garbage. It was the same in every city.

An explosion had come from somewhere in the southeast, lighting up the morning sky for just a few moments, but Sharon or Smith didn't seem to be affected by it. What was common in a place became the norm, and most people ignored it.

The driver was very good, turning down narrow streets and then doubling back, pulling into hotel driveways, including the Hilton's to see if anyone could be outed behind them, then speeding off in a completely different direction.

"Is someone following us?" Pete asked.

No one answered her. She looked at McGarvey, who shrugged.

"We've passed Mossad headquarters twice, but I don't suspect he'd want to meet with us there," McGarvey said. "Not unless Mossad and Aman are on better terms than they were when I was DCI."

"Where is Alex?" Sharon asked. "Do you know?"

"She could be anywhere."

"That doesn't help," the Mossad officer said, vexed. "We're on the same page here, Mr. Director. We want to help you solve your mystery and we want to stop the killings."

"Did you know General Yarviv and Alex were lovers during the war?"

Smith laughed. "That's the woman's story. I know better."

"Do you?" McGarvey asked. "Did the general tell you what he and Alex did?"

"You've already made your accusations."

"Yes, but did you ever discuss Iraq with him—if he turns out to be Alex's George after all?"

McGarvey kept his tone neutral, though he could see he was getting to them, especially to Smith, who was probably Yarviv's chief of staff or personal friend.

"Was Mossad briefed on the Iraq operation above

Kirkuk?" McGarvey asked Sharon. "Or has all this come as a surprise?"

"Mr. Director, you have come here looking for answers I don't know we can give you," Sharon said. "But I would caution you to take great care with the questions you do ask, because you might not like the answers."

"Good advice," Smith said, his voice soft.

They left the city on Highway 1 toward Beit Dagan, the terrain rising from the narrow coastal plains within less than ten miles to the beginning of hill country, where they turned south on Highway 6, which more or less paralleled the border with the West Bank.

Just before the town of Modi'in, they turned east on Highway 443, and within a couple of miles of the border, the driver turned off the main road and took a stony dirt track up a steep hill through an olive grove to a sprawling stuccoed house nestled in a slight dip just below the crest.

Several ancient outbuildings dotted the west side of the property, and as they drove up, two young men were leading a small flock of sheep away. The scene in that direction was almost biblical.

But the roof of the main house bristled with several antennas, including one used for microwave burst traffic. An American-made Hummer with Israeli-army markings was parked around back, and a fairly new Mercedes S-Class sedan was parked directly in front.

It didn't look like an ordinary safe house to Mc-
Garvey; it was too ostentatious, and nothing was
anonymous about the place.

McGarvey and Pete and the two Israeli intelligence officers went up a white river-rock path to the
front door that opened as they approached. Their
driver had gotten out of the van, but he lit a cigarette and stayed there.

A middle-aged woman in khaki slacks and a short-
sleeved white blouse, a smile on her round face, stood
there. "Good evening," she said in English. "My
husband has been expecting you."

She showed them back to a large study, its sliders
open to a patio and pool beyond which was a garden with a riot of fruit trees and bright flowers in
full bloom.

"Lovely," Pete said.

The woman's smile broadened. "This is our favorite place of anywhere we've lived," she said. "If
you'll have a seat, the general will join you momentarily. Would anyone like coffee or tea?"

"No, ma'am," Smith said. "We'll only be staying
for a short time."

The general's wife nodded and then left the room.

The study was large, with floor-to-ceiling book-
cases on two walls, an ancient oak desk with ornate
carvings on the front and sides, and an arrangement
of a leather couch, a pair of wingback chairs, and a
coffee table. One space to the left, which could have
used a chair, was empty. Old oriental rugs covered
the multicolored terrazzo floor. A couple of very good
paintings, one of them McGarvey thought might be

an original Renoir, hung on the textured red stone walls. Altogether it was a totally masculine room of a refined man.

"Good evening," a baritone voice said, coming in from the corridor. He was a broad-shouldered man with a thick head of mostly gray hair, and a large square face with prominent eyebrows that stuck out in all directions. He was dressed in jeans and a white shirt, and he looked like a general. He was in a wheelchair, and he came around to the empty spot.

"Good morning, sir," Smith said. "Sorry to be a bother so late."

"It's okay, Uri. We were expecting some company sooner or later," the general said. He turned to the others. "Mr. McGarvey, I presume, and Ms. Boylan, I was told. I'm Chaim Yarviv. Until I retired a few years ago, I was a deputy director of Aman, but then a stupid incident put me in this chair."

"Good morning, General," McGarvey said. "Do you know why we're here?"

"Yes, and I knew someone like you might be showing up on my doorstep to get some answers, which neither of our governments would like me to give. But Ms. Unroth isn't with you?"

"We lost her at the airport," Smith said.

"I'm told she is an inventive woman, ruthless when need be, but very bright. I expect she'll be showing up soon."

"I'm sorry, General, but we think she may still be at the airport," Sharon said.

"I doubt that," Yarviv said. "So, to the business at hand. We received the properly formatted message to George, from Alex though our travel agency in Paris. It was brought to me, and I authorized the reply for her to come."

"You're George?"

Yarviv smiled. "No. That would have been Jacob Ya'alon. An utterly charming man, one of our best field operators, but a man totally lacking in any sense of morals. He was well educated, but for whatever reason, he could never distinguish right from wrong. Because of that character trait, he was one of our best tools. Shame on us."

"We have been fighting for our lives here since 1945," Smith said.

"Yes, but shame on us for using such tools. Only those who believe the ends justify the means can do such things. Hitler's philosophy. Stalin's."

"What became of Ya'alon?" McGarvey asked.

"Major Ya'alon at the end. We took him out of the field and put him behind a desk, hoping to muzzle him. But he became a hopeless drunk, and maybe used some cocaine at the end. He murdered his live-in girlfriend, and we locked him up. That was eight years ago. He went crazy in prison, tried to kill himself a couple of times. But less than a year after he was convicted, he developed cancer—leukemia, I think it might have been—and was dead within eight months."

"All this time we've been chasing a dead man," McGarvey said, certain the general was telling the truth.

"Ah, but Alex, from what Ya'alon told me, was an utterly convincing operator. The best he'd ever seen.

I think he was captivated with her. Maybe even in love, and she with him. They did terrible things together in Iraq. It reinforced who he was, of course, but it must have changed her. Given her some warped sense of herself, some skewed view of the real world. He had that effect on people."

SIXTY

Alex pushed the Range Rover through Beit Dagan on Highway 1, turning south when she reached Highway 6. They'd been at the compound now for nearly ten minutes, according to Otto. He managed to repurpose a Keyhole satellite that was permanently looking down on the region to pinpoint the compound, even to the detail that the driver of the Mercedes van was still outside and on his second cigarette, and that two men were leading a small flock of sheep off to the west.

Traffic was picking up, but Alex had gotten used to driving on the left within the first few minutes. From day one, her instructors had given her high marks: *She's nothing if not a quick study.*

She was driven, had been since she was a small child battling the abuser her mother had married. Her psych eval people had reported she was not in touch with reality, but actually, she knew the difference between her fantasy world and the real one; hers was nothing more than a defense mechanism.

You did what you had to do to survive. The Army

Rangers knew that score: Adapt, improvise, survive! Hoorah!

"You'll turn off on Highway four forty-three," Otto said. Her cell phone was in speaker mode on the seat next to her.

"How far?"

"About five miles."

"Then what?"

"There'll be a dirt road leading up through an olive grove. The general's house is on the other side, just below the crest."

Their conversation was encrypted. Whoever was monitoring the call would not be able to decrypt it anytime soon, nor would they be able to pinpoint either phone, except that their techs would guess that both phones were probably somewhere in Japan, or perhaps coastal mainland China. Otto loved screwing with the other side's techies.

"Are you monitoring their conversation?"

"I'm getting no signal. I think they took Mac's phone and pulled the SIM card. But I don't think the general is your George."

"Why not?" Alex demanded. She wanted to get there, look him the eye, and put a bullet into the middle of his forehead. What he had done to her in Iraq was far worse than anything the guy her mother had married had done to her.

"In the first place, he's a cripple. Took a round in the spine from a sniper about eight years ago. He's been confined to a wheelchair ever since."

"I don't believe it!" Alex shouted, a black rage rising inside her. She didn't want to believe it, now that she was so close.

"He's retired Major General Chaim Yarviv, married thirty-seven years to Merriam, three children, two granddaughters. Before he got hurt, he was deputy director of Aman."

"No."

"I'm sure he knew about the operation in Iraq before the second war, and he almost certainly knew George. Means he should have the answers we're looking for."

"Not the ones I need!" Alex screamed. She'd wanted to say *the ones they wanted*, but it didn't come out that way. "George told me to come. I sent him the message, and he got it."

"Leaves two possibilities. Either the general directed the killings, or someone else we don't know about has done it."

"Christ."

"Listen, Alex. If the general is masterminding this operation—never mind the question of for what reason—he won't hesitate to kill Mac and Pete if you barge in there, gun blazing. Think it out."

"I've had more than ten years to think it out."

"There's no powder in the bullets. Just sand."

"Why? Why give me a weapon? Why lead me here?"

"I needed to give them the time to make contact with George, or whoever it was who responded to your message," Otto said. "Turn around and go back to the hotel. Once Mac and Pete are out of there, they'll pick you up and take you to the airport. With any luck, all of you will get out of Israel in one piece."

It suddenly struck her that Otto was not sure. "You don't know if it's the general."

"I'm betting it's someone else."

"Why?"

"A hunch."

"We'll see," Alex said, and tossed the phone out of the car.

The dirt road was easy to spot; it was the only one at that distance leading up a hill through a grove of olive trees. Alex stopped a few meters up and, making sure no traffic was coming, pointed the pistol out the window and pulled off a shot.

The Beretta bucked in her hand. Otto had been lying to her.

She continued slowly up the hill until just before the top, where she pulled off to the side of the track, parked the Range Rover, and headed away on foot.

Near the top of the hill, she checked over her shoulder for traffic on the highway, but at this distance, she would not be identifiable by anyone passing by.

She got down on her hands and knees and crawled the rest of the way to the top, where she rose up just enough to see the sprawling stone house and the outbuildings to the west. Nothing moved. She had a clear sight line to the Mercedes van, but the driver who Otto said had been leaning up against it, smoking a cigarette, was gone, and other than a small flock of sheep well off into the distance—maybe a mile away—nothing moved.

Backing away until she was well below the crest, she got to her feet. Her wrists and the palms of her hands were scraped from the rocky soil, but now that she was this close, she was mindless of the minor discomfort.

She brushed the dirt off the knees of her jeans and headed in a trot to the west, figuring she would approach the house by keeping the outbuildings between her and the windows on that side.

About seventy-five meters from the dirt road, she got on her hands and knees again and crawled to the crest. The house was to her left, the first of the four outbuildings directly below. Off in the distance the sheep had spread out over the hillside. There was no sign of their shepherds, or of any other person.

Pulling out the pistol, she jumped up and sprinted down the hill toward the small stone building, reaching its safety in less than fifteen seconds. There, she held up.

Peering around the corner, she could see the right side of the Mercedes van, but the driver had apparently gone inside.

Something wasn't right.

She started to turn as the muzzle of a rifle touched her on the cheek.

"Please drop your weapon to the ground," a man said.

Out of the corner of her eye, she got the impression he was one of the shepherds who'd taken the flock up the hill. He was dressed in old corduroy slacks and a bulky wool shirt. They'd been waiting for her.

"No trouble, please. You came to talk to the general, and that's exactly what will happen if you co-operate. Your friends are already inside."

"This pistol has a twitchy trigger. I'll lay it on the ground," Alex said.

As she bent down, the man stepped back, which is exactly what she expected he'd do. She batted the rifle barrel away, rose up, and jammed the pistol into the man's face, just above the bridge of his nose.

"Assuming your Uzi doesn't have a twitchy trigger, please drop it on the ground, and we'll go talk to the general," she said.

"The general is not your George," someone said from behind her.

She looked over her shoulder.

"Not worth dying when you're being offered what you want," he said. He was pointing a SIG Sauer at her.

"Makes sense," said the shepherd in front of her, still holding his Uzi.

She lowered the Beretta to the ground.

SIXTY-ONE

McGarvey and the others looked up as Alex came down the front hall, one of the shepherds behind her. Her jeans were dirty, and a little blood was oozing from a cut on her left wrist. Otherwise, she looked unharmed, except for a fierce look of hatred and anticipation mixed with what might have been a little fear.

"Here's Ms. Unroth at last," the general said.

Alex stopped just inside the study door, her eyes locked on Yarviv's.

"Are you okay?" McGarvey asked.

She didn't reply.

"Alex?" Mac prompted.

She shook her head. "It's not him. He's not George."

"Of course not," the general said. "Your George died years ago in prison. Cancer."

"Who answered my message?"

"As SOP, we keep a continuous lookout for any pro phrase messages no matter how long they've been out-of-date. Every now and then one like yours turns up."

"Then who's the killer?"

"I don't know."

"Who was the shooter in Paris?"

"Sûreté identified him as a British contract killer," McGarvey said.

The play of emotions on Alex's face was amazing, almost heartbreaking to watch. Everything she had worked for, just about everything she had feared the most, had been laid bare for her. Suddenly there was no meaning.

"Mossad did not hire him," Sharon said.

"Neither did Aman," Smith said.

"He's still at Langley," McGarvey said. He had almost all of it now. "Leaves us with finding out the why before we can identify him."

"No need to stop the bastard; he's already taken out everyone except me," Alex said. "I just have to go deep, providing they'll let me out of Israel."

Sharon started to object, but Yarviv motioned him off. "My dear girl, you and Mr. McGarvey and Ms.

Boylan are free to go at any time you wish. This moment, if that's what you want."

"She hurt one of my people," Sharon said.

"She could have killed her, Lev."

"We still need the what," Pete said. "I mean, what was all this about?"

"Would you like to tell her, Ms. Unroth?" the general asked. "From what I understand, it was you and your people who moved the thing."

Alex sat down in one of the wingback chairs, her knees drawn up. McGarvey thought she looked like a little girl at that moment. Not the trained killer she was.

"Roy all but spelled it out for you on the fourth panel," she said, her voice small.

Everyone held their silence.

"Everyone was rabid to find a WMD to justify the war when no justification was needed. Saddam was a monster. He'd used gas against his own people, just like the Syrians have done. We had plenty of provocation."

She looked at the general.

"They sent us behind the lines to soften them up, which we did, but then George came, and it was a game changer. He showed us where you guys buried the thing—"

"No," Yarviv cut her off. "We didn't bury it. Major Ya'alon—your George—got a message left at one of our letter drops in Damascus from a contact in Hussein's Mukhabarat. Gave us the GPS coordinates of something interesting buried in the hills above Kirkuk. He volunteered to go out there to find out what it was. I think it unhinged him."

"Who put it there if not your people?" Alex shouted.

"I don't know. We never found out."

"You didn't want to find out," McGarvey said.

"No."

"There were no markings on it, and I'm not enough of an engineer to tell anyone with certainty whose design it was, but the only two possibilities, I think, would be us or the Russians. And besides Israel, we had the most to gain."

Sharon had become agitated. "I'm sorry, General, but I don't know if I want to hear this. Especially not if it's what I think it is."

"There were rumors," Smith said. "I agree with Lev. Maybe we should just let sleeping dogs lie."

"It was a small nuclear weapon," Alex said. "A demolition device designed to take out dams, hit bridges, major installations, things of that nature that ordinary explosives or even nonnuclear air attacks couldn't handle."

"A suitcase bomb," Pete said.

"But it wasn't in an aluminum case; it was in a heavy canvas bag. I think the damned thing weighed seventy-five or eighty kilos. Took two of us to pull it out of the hole and move it."

"No markings?" McGarvey asked.

"None I personally took the time to look for, if you mean serial numbers or writing in English or Russian."

"How do you know it was a bomb?" Sharon asked.

Alex just looked at him. "Please," she said. "Maybe the physics package was lead instead of plutonium or U-235—we didn't have a Geiger counter to see if the thing was leaking—but there was no mistaking what it was, and the reason it had been out there. It was meant for our team to find it and blow the whistle. 'Hey, look, world! The bastard did have a WMD after all!' "

"Why didn't you guys do just that?" McGarvey asked, and he thought he knew this answer too.

"Our orders changed. Maybe someone got cold feet."

"Or came to their senses," Pete said.

"Or that," Alex agreed. "Anyway, we had a little less than a month with George before he suddenly slipped away one evening, and the next day we got the burst transmission to move the damned thing."

"You radioed that you had found it?" Pete asked.

"No, and that was the odd part. We'd agreed to keep the thing a secret. I think it was Larry's idea to begin with. We had quite a discussion about it. I was all for letting the chips fall where they may. We were in the war because Saddam Hussein had WMDs, and he could be allowed to continue. God only knew what would happen in the region, especially if the nuclear genie got out of the bottle.

"But Larry kept harping on the unintended consequences that the CIA seemed really good at engineering for itself. 'Like the Bay of Pigs,' he said. 'Look where the hell that got us. We're still dealing with that mess. Think what this would do.'

"He insisted that we rebury the thing, and when it came time for our debriefing, we wouldn't bring it up first."

"No one did," Pete asked.

"No. Not in Ramstein, and not later at the Farm."

"Who sent you the order to move it?" McGarvey asked. "Did you ever know?"

"Of course. It was our original control officer, Bertie Russell."

"I thought he was killed in Iraq."

"That was a year later," Alex said. "But when we got to Ramstein, he was there, and the thing was, he never brought up George's name, nor did he even hint at his order to move the device."

"So you kept your mouths shut, and afterward you split up and tried to go deep," McGarvey said. "Why was that?"

"Come on. You know what we were facing. If the device had been found, it would have been traced back to someone—probably us—and the political fallout would have been devastating."

"I thought the thing was supposed to be found," Pete said. "Wasn't that the whole idea?"

"It was meant to be detonated."

SIXTY-TWO

At Langley, Otto was seated at his desk, his eyes gritty, his energy all but gone. Time to go home and get some sleep. It seemed to him he had been working around the clock since this business had begun.

Louise had called a couple of hours ago to ask how he was doing and when he'd be home.

"Soon as I hear from Mac. He said he'd call after they cleared Israeli airspace."

"You have the bone in your teeth—I can hear it," Louise said. "Are we any closer to making this a done deal?"

"Depends on what they managed to find out, and whether or not Alex is in jail or has been shot to death. And right now that's too close to call."

"She's not the killer? For sure?"

"For sure," Otto said. "At least not the one we've been looking for."

"Somehow that's not very comforting."

"I'll be home soon as I can. Maybe we can get this thing settled in the next twenty-four hours and take a vacation somewhere."

Louise chuckled. "I'll believe that when it actually happens. Take care of yourself, sweetheart."

"Will do," Otto said, and hung up.

Earlier he'd driven off campus to a convenience store a few miles down the Parkway, where he'd bought a half dozen packages of Twinkies, finally back on the market, and several pints of half and half, the closest to whipping cream he could find. He sat now, eating the things and guzzling the cream— his comfort food—for which Louise would skin him alive if she found out.

All the elements were laid out in neat order on one of his big-screen monitors, all of it pointing toward their serial killer still being on campus. He had to be well connected enough to know the movements of just about everyone working for the CIA—which narrowed the list of possibilities.

One of the analysts from the Watch, someone on Walt Page's staff—which was why Alex had turned up high on the list—someone on the deputy director of the CIA's staff, or on Marty Bambridge's staff in operations.

But all their personnel files were squeaky clean— some of them like Alex's: almost too perfect.

There were also several disconnected pieces. The contract killer who'd tried to take Alex out in Paris was a former officer in the British Special Air Service by the name of Tony Butterworth. So far nothing had turned up for that hit, though in the past he'd done work for the German BND, his own government's SIS, and once for the Mossad, though that had been a number of years ago.

Otto had managed to find two of his offshore accounts, one in the Channel Islands and the other in the Caribbean, and matched several of the payments to the dates of the hits. But nothing he'd found matched the dates of the killings here on campus or the two in Athens.

At this point Butterworth was a dead end, except that Otto's darlings were chewing on at least three other places where the contractor may have hidden his payments—intriguingly enough, one of them with a small credit union in Venice, Florida, less than ten miles from Mac's house on Casey Key.

The next odd bit that had turned up was the murder of a guy in a small apartment in Georgetown, just a couple of blocks up from the tourist shops and bars along M Street, and coincidentally only a half dozen blocks from Mac's apartment.

One of the bartenders told police he vaguely remembered seeing the guy leaving with a slender, good-looking woman two nights before his body had been discovered by the landlord, who'd come over to check on a bad smell the neighbors were complaining about.

The name on the lease, and on the driver's license and other documents on his body, did not match his fingerprints, but matched a former Army Ranger's by the name of Norman Bogen. But the cops had come up with nothing else—not where he worked, not where he lived, nothing about any family, except that he had no criminal record.

But Otto's darlings had come with one fact that was as unexpected as it was intriguing. Bogen maintained an account with the Midcoast Employees Credit Union of Venice, Florida. The same bank Butterworth possibly had an account.

The date of Bogen's death matched the date Alex had been on the loose. And she more or less fit the bartender's description. But if she had killed Bogen, Otto could not see the connection—though he knew there had to be one.

And last was the murder of Jean Fegan in front of the Hotel George. It had been no accident, Otto was sure of that, and he had beaten himself up that he hadn't been able to come up with a tag number. But the cops had not been able to find an SUV with front-end damage. After the hit, it had been locked away in some private garage somewhere—either that, or ditched in the Potomac.

His phone buzzed. He thought it might be Mac, but the call was from on campus, though the ID was blocked.

"Yes."

"I thought you might still be here, though I expect Louise might be cross with you." It was Tom Calder,

Marty Bambridge's assistant deputy director, the direct opposite of his boss and, therefore, universally liked by just about everyone on campus.

"You're here too. Marty must be keeping you on a short leash."

"As a matter of fact, he just left, and I wanted to get the latest from you before I pulled the pin and went home. It's been a very long few days. May I come over?"

"I'm waiting for a call from Mac, and then I'm getting out of here myself."

"It'll only take a minute, honest injun'."

Otto had to laugh. He used the same expression himself, and he thought he was the only one. "Okay."

A couple of minutes later the door buzzed, and Otto glanced at one of his monitors. Marty's number two was there, in jeans and a white shirt, an apologetic smile on his small round mouth.

Otto pushed the unlock command, blanked his monitors, and got up and went into the outer office as Calder came in.

As usual, the assistant deputy director of operations wore prescription eyeglasses that were darkly tinted. "I thought my eyes were bad, but yours are worse," he said, taking off his glasses. His eyes were bloodshot, just like Otto's. "The hours we keep to make sure our country stays safe."

It sounded pompous, like something Marty might say.

Otto perched on the edge of a desk. "You promised to make it only one minute," he said. Calder was okay, but he didn't want to screw around with the guy right now. Once Mac called, he was going home.

"Marty got a call from upstairs that he asked me to check out with you. The director apparently got a call from the State Department about one of its former employees who was hit by a car and killed. Her name was Jean Fegan. Thing is, the police said an unidentified man, possibly an employee of the CIA, may have provided the identification. You?"

"Yeah."

"The description matched," Calder said. "Anything to do with our goings-on?"

"I don't know. It's one loose end in a basketful I'm trying to run down."

"You don't think it was an accident?"

"No."

"And your being there was no accident either. You met with her at the hotel. Care to share with me the substance of your meeting?"

"No, because I don't know what the hell to make of it, except that it could have something to do with the second Iraq war and the Alpha Seven people who were among the advance teams."

"WMDs?"

"Could be," Otto said. "What's Marty's take?"

Calder stepped closer. "Don't be coy with me, Otto, please. We're all on the same team here. And we appreciate—Marty and I do—everything you and McGarvey are doing to run this to ground. But for goodness sake, all we ask is for a little cooperation. Tell us what you've come up with, and perhaps we can put our heads together. Everyone wants this to go away."

Organ music, very faint, came from Calder's shirt pocket. It sounded to Otto like Bach.

SIXTY-THREE

Roper called back from the cockpit. "We've just cleared Israeli airspace, Mr. Director."

McGarvey looked out the window as the F-16 fighter that followed them on their port side peeled off, the one on the right doing the same. The Med was a featureless gray-blue that stretched one hundred and fifty miles south to the Egyptian coast.

"I'm going to make a call now," he said.

Pete was sitting across from him, but Alex had stretched out in the back and had fallen asleep. She'd been exhausted after the ordeal she'd survived. The situation could have gone south at any moment. If she'd seriously hurt the Mossad agent who had accompanied her to the ladies' room, or if she had fired a shot—just one even without hitting anyone—there would have been nothing McGarvey could have done. She would be in an Israeli military prison cell. Or, just as likely, she wouldn't have let herself be taken, and there would have been more deaths— hers included.

The problem was that they were no closer to solving the issue, except that the killer was probably still on campus at Langley.

He phoned Otto's rollover number, which would reach him wherever he might be. Otto answered on the first ring.

"Where are you?"

McGarvey put it on speakerphone so Pete could hear. "We're headed up to Ramstein to refuel. Just cleared Israeli airspace. You?"

"In my office. Tom Calder dropped over for an update. Hang on a sec."

McGarvey could hear the sounds of a printer in the background, and maybe some music but extremely faint, as if it were coming from another room. Otto's voice was over it.

"I'll have something on your desk before noon, but besides what Mac found out in Israel, I'm in the middle of running down a couple of other leads I think might make some sense of what's been happening."

"Any hint?" Calder asked. "Even just the tiniest?"

"Well, we think we know who the killer isn't."

"That's progress of a sort," Calder said. "I'll just let myself out. Good luck, and good morning to you, Mr. Director."

The music faded to nothing, and McGarvey could hear the door from Otto's outer office closing and gently latching.

"He's gone," Otto said.

"What was that all about?"

"Someone at State called Walt, wanted to know what we knew about the death of one of their employees last night. She was hit by an SUV. Cops said an unidentified CIA employee witnessed the hit and run. It was me."

"Did Calder make the connection?"

"Yeah, that's why he came over to talk to me. Her name was Jean Fegan. She was on Bob Benning's staff when he was an assistant ambassador to the UN. I met with her to see if she knew anything about the Alpha Seven team, and something they might have found in Iraq."

"Did she give you anything?" McGarvey asked.

"Not much. She was frightened out of her mind. She admitted she knew what was buried out there, and left it to me to figure out. I read her Schermerhorn's message on panel four, especially the last line: *And there was peace*. Said it was about what they were working for—a reason to take Saddam out so we could rebuild Iraq."

"How'd she leave it?" Pete asked.

"Oh, hi, Pete. She said things didn't work out that way, and now we were stuck with one hell of a big problem no one knows how to fix."

"And?" McGarvey prompted.

"She got up and walked out. By the time I caught up with her, she was already outside and running across the street when the SUV knocked her into the path of a taxi."

"No tag number?"

"The license plate light was out."

"Anything else?"

"Yeah, I got a firm ID on the contract killer in Paris, but not who hired him to take out Alex. She's with you on the plane? She got out okay?"

"She's here."

"He did work for his own government as well as the Germans and for Mossad. I was able to track down most of his money in a couple of offshore banks—nothing matched with Paris. But I came up with one thing that at first seemed really far-fetched. It's possible he has an account at a credit union in Venice, just ten miles from your place on Casey Key."

McGarvey sat up. "At first?"

"Yeah. A guy's body was found in an apartment

in Georgetown, not far from your place. The ID he was carrying didn't match anything the cops had, but when they ran his fingerprints, they came up with the name Norman Bogen, a former Army Ranger. No known address, or criminal record. But, kemo sabe, he has an account at the same credit union in Venice. And that's fringe. Not only that, but a bartender in a place on M Street about two blocks from the apartment said he saw the guy leaving with a slender, attractive woman. Same time Alex was on the loose."

"Don't tell us his face was chewed off," Pete said.

"No, his neck was broken. But it's my guess he was another contract killer targeting Alex. She just beat him to the punch."

"Whoever knew she would be in Georgetown on the loose had some damned good intel," Mac said.

"Narrows the field," Otto said. "What about you guys? How'd it go?"

"Alex's George was a Mossad agent. He was a nut case. Died in prison years ago. When Alex's message from Paris showed up, the general answered it."

"There's no longer any George, and Alex isn't the serial killer. Leaves someone on campus," Otto said. "What we figured all along."

"What's buried in the hills above Kirkuk is a nuclear demolitions device," McGarvey said. "In a duffel bag without the aluminum case."

"That's also just about what we figured. The suitcase doesn't matter. Did they give you a serial number?"

"No, but I don't think the Israelis buried it. I
they knew about it, which is why the

out to find it. Alex's story that George showed them where it was buried was a lie."

"Alpha Seven buried it?"

"I don't know," McGarvey said. "But it's only us and the Soviet Union that ever made the things."

"That doesn't help much. About that time, maybe a little earlier, some Russian official admitted they may have lost a hundred of the things. Could be anybody who buried it."

"I hear a *but* in there, Otto," McGarvey said.

Otto took a moment to answer. "It almost has to be us," he said. "I don't think it was the president or his cabinet who authorized it—I don't think I want to go that far. But I think we were so sure Saddam had WMDs we might never find, someone took it upon themselves to somehow get a device and somehow transport it to Iraq and somehow bury it in the hills. Alpha Seven would find it and blow the whistle—let the whole world know we were right."

"Lots of *somehow*s in there."

Again Otto hesitated. "I checked, Mac. No demolition devices missing from our inventory. At least not in the records. So if it was one of ours, whoever got it had to be very high up on the food chain. Someone with lots of pull."

"Civilian or military?" Pete asked.

"Could be either."

"Whoever it was, they're willing to kill the entire ___en team," she said.

"___ay it's been done?" McGarvey said.

"___hinking through the lens of nor-___atic to do the job. Afterward they could claim insanity. Conspiracy theory. That kind of shit."

"We'll be home by nine or ten," McGarvey said. "I want you to listen real carefully to me, my friend. I want you to go home now. Trust no one. Not Walt Page or Carleton Patterson or Marty or anyone else. Lock up tight. Don't order a pizza or Chinese delivery. Don't even ask Blankenship for help, or anyone from the Farm."

"I have a couple of things to look into—" Otto said, but McGarvey cut him off.

"Do you have a pistol in your office?"

"Yes."

"Don't bother shutting off your programs. No one can get to them anyway. Just take your gun and leave right now. Otto: I mean right this instant. Hang up, take the SIM card out of your phone so no one can track you, and go. You're the next target."

SIXTY-FOUR

Otto's pistol was a standard U.S. military–issue 9-mm Beretta 92F that McGarvey had taught him how to use years ago. He checked the magazine and then made sure a round was in the chamber.

He left his darlings running but added a self destruct code that would wipe everything out sh anyone try to tamper. Rather than take the s was out of his phone, he left the phone Somebody wanting to find him w still in his office.

He checked the monitors in the corridor outside his office to the elevator, the elevator itself, and finally the parking garage.

No one was coming or going. Security was still extremely tight; Blankenship had placed the entire campus on all but a full-scale lockdown. Everyone's comings or goings would be noticed and recorded.

He hesitated at the door. The trouble was he'd never been a field officer. He was a certifiable geek whose best friend in all the world was a gun-toting operator, a man who figured out things and killed people. The thing in Otto's mind was that Mac was a hell of a lot more than just a shooter; he was understanding.

Stupid, actually, to define a friend with only one word. Mac was kind. He was gentle when he needed to be gentle—his wife and daughter had been just about his entire life, and when they had been assassinated, he'd grieved, but he hadn't gone off the deep end, as so many men would have done.

He lifted people up, he helped those needing help, he told the truth no matter whose toes he stepped on doing it, and Otto had never known anyone who'd had more love for country than Mac.

People good or bad, countries good or bad—he understood and helped where it was needed. Like

...ing the pistol at his side, the muzzle pointed down his leg like Mac had taught him, he level, and it to the empty corridor and hurried up to three. tor. The car was on the basement eeming eternity for it to come

Otto stepped aside, out of the line of possible fire—again something Mac had taught him—as the door opened. But the car was empty.

His hand was shaking a little as he hit the P1 button.

It seemed to take another eternity for the door to close and the car to start down, and another eternity before it reached the executive parking level 1.

He flattened himself against the wall of the car and raised the pistol.

His Mercedes was parked three rows to the left, nose out from the wall.

The garage was mostly empty of cars. Nothing moved. There were no sounds.

Ducking out of the elevator, Otto swung the pistol left to right as he sprinted to his car. He switched gun hands so he could dig his car keys out of his pocket and jump in behind the wheel.

Mac had told him something else about situations like these. Something important, but his heart was beginning to race and he could think of nothing except getting the hell out and into the open air. The underground parking ramp had become claustrophobic.

As he reached the exit, the security scanner read the bar code on his windshield and raised the gate at the same moment he realized not only about how Mac's wife and daughter had been assassinated with a car bomb but how Fabry had been killed by someone hiding in the backseat of his car.

He skidded to a halt, snatched the pistol from the passenger seat, jumped out of the car, and stepped back.

But if it had been a car bomb, it would have exploded the instant he'd switched on the ignition. And so far as he could tell, no one was in the backseat.

He moved back to the car and, holding his pistol at the ready, yanked open the rear door. For just an instant he didn't know what he was seeing except for shadows cast by the streetlamp, until he realized it was his own shadow cast into the rear of the car, and he lowered the pistol at the same moment he released a pent-up breath.

The couple of times he'd been in a firefight, Mac had been at his side. And at home he would have the electronic security of the place, as well as Louise at his side. He only thanked his lucky stars they had sent Audie down to the Farm, where she would be safe.

Otto breezed through the checkpoint at the main gate, and on the long drive back to McLean, where he and Louise had moved a few days ago, he kept looking in his rearview mirror. There was other traffic on the road, none of it apparently following him. Nevertheless, he passed his normal exit off the Parkway and got off instead at Kirby Road, then took Old Dominion the back way to their main safe house.

He drove through town almost to where the road reached the Beltway, before he turned around and went home, reasonably sure no one had followed him.

Louise was at the kitchen door when Otto came

into the garage. As soon as he got out of the car and she could see his face, she hit the button to close the service door. She was holding a compact Glock pistol.

"No one followed me," he told her.

"How would you know?" she asked sharply.

"Mac taught me what to do."

As soon as the door was closed, she pulled him inside the house with her free hand and threw her arms around his neck. "Christ, I was worried sick about you."

"I know," Otto said. After a moment he reached back, took the pistol out of her hand, and laid it on the kitchen counter. "I'd rather not get shot by my own wife."

"Oh," she said, flustered. "I tried to call you, but your phone just rang. So I called Mac, and he said he told you to get the hell out of there. Did you take a gun?"

"It's on the passenger seat."

"No trouble getting out?" she asked, searching his eyes.

"It was spooky, but no," Otto said. "We have to button up this place right now."

"I took care of it as soon as I talked to Mac. When I picked you up on the east camera, I opened the center front portal to let you in. It's closed again. We're good here."

"For now," Otto said. He went back to the car and got the Beretta.

Louise had made coffee, and she poured him a cup and got a package of Twinkies from the cabinet. "I couldn't bring myself to buy whipping cream, but I thought you might need a lift."

"Shit," he said, and sat down at the counter. "I already had some at work."

"About what I figured, but none here," Louise said. "Mac didn't tell me everything that's going on, except that the killer wasn't George but he was probably still on campus. He wants us to stay put until he and Pete get here."

"And Alex," Otto said. "He's going to use her, and me, as bait."

"Peachy," Louise said without humor. It was an expression she'd picked up from Mac's wife, Katy. "So, who's the killer? What's your best guess?"

"Could be anyone from Walt Page or Fred Atwell all the way down to Marty Bambridge or someone on his staff, or Len Lawrence and his staff." Lawrence was the deputy director of intelligence.

"You're not serious?"

"I am," Otto said. Louise had poured a cup of coffee for herself, and Otto handed her one of the Twinkies, which she tried.

"Jesus, this shit tastes like fuel oil."

He laughed. "And all the time you thought I liked them."

Her pent-up tension suddenly released, and she laughed so hard, tears streamed from her eyes. She drank some coffee. "I bought another package."

"They do sorta taste artificial."

Louise put down her cup, suddenly stricken as if the worst news of her life had just come into her head. Otto got it immediately.

Her cell phone was on the counter. He phoned the duty officer at the Farm. "How's everything down there this morning?"

"Mr. Rencke, just fine. Something I can do for you?"

"Just got back home, and we were missing our daughter."

"She'll probably sleep till nine or ten. Had a busy day out on the water. We were doing exfiltration drills, and Audie was on the observer boat. Time to bring her home?"

"Soon," Otto said.

"She misses you guys like the devil, but we're going to be sad to give her up."

SIXTY-FIVE

They were refueled and airborne west over France toward the Atlantic after a two-hour delay at Ramstein, Germany. Once they were at altitude, McGarvey went forward to the cockpit. He was dead tired, his eyes gritty, but he was pumped with adrenaline.

"Thanks for getting us out of there so fast," he told Roper and the first officer. "But I have an even bigger favor."

"No need to ask," Roper said. "I got clearance at thirty-seven thousand, an Air France flight from Paris found a two-hundred-knot tail wind."

"Jet stream?"

"No, just winds aloft. Don't know how far it'll last, but we're in it right now. ETA Andrews at 0800 local."

"Good enough," McGarvey said, patting Roper on the shoulder.

He got a cognac from the galley before he went aft and took his seat. It was pitch-black outside, only the stars, no moon, and a cloud deck below them, obscuring the lights of Paris, but they were chasing the sun.

Pete was in the head and Alex was still asleep, leaving him alone with his thoughts. From near the beginning, he'd thought that the killer had to be someone on campus. But everyone connected with Alpha Seven, except for Alex, was dead, so it wasn't one of them.

The weapon was almost certainly American made and had been buried in Iraq, so when it was found, it would prove our case that Saddam did indeed have WMDs. At least the one nuke.

But Alex had told them the bomb had been meant to be detonated. Probably blamed as a last-ditch stand by the Iraqi military unit still hiding in the oil fields.

Evidently, the Mossad had somehow found out about it, and had sent George to find it and perhaps neutralize the thing. But the Alpha Seven team had come up with a better plan. They had reburied it, where it apparently was still hidden. The only one left now who knew the location was Alex.

Still, it left them with the final problem of the killer's identity. Whoever it was had known about the plot— or had even been a part of it—and was now trying to cover up their tracks by killing just about everyone who had any knowledge of the incident. The Alpha Seven team members first, because they were loose cannons.

Then Jean Fegan because she had talked to Otto—

and Otto himself because someone knew if he knew enough to seek out the woman, it meant he had to be getting close.

Pete came forward and sat down across from him. She took the glass from his hand and had a sip. "You need to get some sleep," she said.

"It's hard to shut down now that we're close."

"I know, but we have another five or six hours, and you won't do anybody any good like this."

"You're right, of course," McGarvey said. "But I was wondering what's the worst that could happen, and what could we do to prevent it?"

Pete thought about it for a second. "You sent Otto home. And their place in McLean is like a fortress, so even if someone does go after him—maybe another hit man sent by the killer—it wouldn't do much good. Louise would push the panic button, and the cops would be all over the place within minutes."

"He's the target, but as long as he stays put, he'll be okay."

"You're a target. So am I and so is Alex. And in six hours we'll be on the ground and outgun the bastard."

"We'll find him," McGarvey said. "But Alex said the device was meant to be exploded."

"Before we started the war, or shortly thereafter, to prove our case. That's if you believe we put it there."

"I think it was us. A rogue operation. But what happens to us in the region if someone sets the damned thing off?"

"No reason for it," Pete said. "Who would gain?"

"The Chinese, for one. If they could prove it was our bomb—and that's fairly easy to do from the signature radiation after a detonation—they could make a case for kicking us out of the entire region. They'd take over, and that would include oil."

"Not to mention the Iranians, who'd love to thumb their noses at us," Alex said, coming forward. She perched on the arm of the leather chair across the aisle from them. "We've been holier-than-thou over their nuclear program. It would make us look like the biggest hypocrites on the block."

Maggie came back. "Would any of you like something?"

Pete finished Mac's drink and handed her the glass. "Another one of these, please."

"Water," Alex said.

"Syria, Egypt, especially North Korea, because we've tried to keep a lid on their nuclear weapons," McGarvey said. "We need to find the weapon and get it out of there."

"That's the problem," Alex said. "Someone moved it again after we did. The guy who took out Walt and Isty and the others has been wasting his time. None of us knew where it had been reburied. It's the part that's been driving me crazy."

"We have to find the killer, and Mac thinks he's still on campus," Pete said. "But if he doesn't know where the device is buried, we're on the edge of an even steeper cliff."

Maggie brought their drinks back. "Will anyone be wanting anything to eat before we land?"

"No," McGarvey said. "But if we do, we can manage. Why'd don't you get a few hours' sleep?"

She smiled. "Thanks, Mr. Director. I think I'll do just that."

"We have to find him first," Alex said, and something occurred to her. "You say Otto went home?"

"Yeah. He's next on the list."

"Did you talk to him just now? I was half awake, and I thought I heard voices."

"A half hour ago."

"Was he alone?"

"Tom Calder was with him. Walt Page took a call from State about one of its employees who'd been hit by a car and killed. Otto was there when it happened."

"Did you record the call?"

"No reason to," McGarvey said.

"How about Otto? Would he have recorded it?" Alex pressed.

"Probably."

Alex was excited. "Call him. Tell him to play it back for us."

"His calls could be monitored. I had him take the SIM card out of the sat phone he usually uses."

"God damn it, call him at home," Alex insisted. "Do it right now."

"You need to give us a reason," Pete said.

Alex was practically jumping out of her skin. "I think I might have heard something. Maybe I was dreaming, I don't know. Christ, McGarvey, just do it!"

McGarvey brought up Otto's home phone. The call went through, and Louise answered on the first ring.

"It's Kirk. Is everything okay there?"

"Otto and I are eating Twinkies, if that gives you any indication."

"I need to talk to him for just a minute."

Otto came on. "What's up?"

"Did you record our phone call when Calder was with you?"

"I record everything."

"Send it to me. Alex thinks she might have heard something that could be significant."

"Let me get my tablet powered up."

McGarvey's phone was on speaker mode. Alex seemed as if she wanted to snatch it from where it was lying on the table between the seats, and Pete looked as if she were on the verge of slapping her down.

Otto came back. "Okay, here it is."

They heard the door lock buzz and then Calder's voice: *I thought my eyes were bad, but yours are worse. The hours we keep to make sure our country stays safe.*

You promised to make it only one minute.

Alex leaned in and cocked an ear.

Marty got a call from upstairs that he asked me to check out with you.

"Wait," Alex said. "Go back."

I thought my eyes were bad, but yours are worse.

"Go back again," Alex ordered. "But take out the voices and enhance the background."

A second later the recording started again, only this time Calder's voice was gone, leaving something that sounded like church music faintly in the background.

"Do you hear that?" Alex said.

"I think it was coming from something in his pocket," Otto said. "Maybe an MP3 player."

"Can you raise the volume?"

Otto did, and the music, though distorted, was recognizable.

"Son of a bitch," Alex said softly. "Son of a bitch!" she practically shouted. "That's Bach's Toccata and Fugue!"

"He's a classical music buff. So am I," Otto said.

"That's our control officer's music."

"George is dead," Pete said.

"I mean the guy who trained us. Tom Calder is Bertie Russell. He's the serial killer. And I know why."

SIXTY-SIX

The man who had been Bertie Russell until he faked his own death in Iraq more than ten years ago stopped at an all-night Hess station in McLean and filled the tank of his dark-blue Ford Taurus. He'd bought the car new after he'd changed his identity and come back to the States. Now it was old but serviceable. Best of all, it was anonymous.

Otto had just finished talking to McGarvey and Alex, who were in the air over France, coming west. They would be touching down in less than six hours, which didn't give him much time to finish what he'd started, and to make his exit.

He'd be expected to end the thing the way it had originally been intended to end. But the imperative was all but gone. Yet from the beginning he'd enjoyed symmetry in all things.

And the second but, perhaps the biggest of all, was the way he had changed since Iraq.

After finishing at the pump, he parked in front of the convenience store and went inside, where he bought a cup of Starbucks regular black. Back outside, he had his iPad powered up, monitoring not only the phone at Rencke's house a few blocks away, but the security channels at the CIA.

As he expected would happen, McGarvey had called Blankenship, who'd begun issuing orders even before he got to the campus from his home down in Jefferson. Not only was the campus in total lockdown, Blankenship had ordered his people to find the assistant deputy director of operations.

Bob evidently couldn't quite bring himself to believe everything McGarvey had told him, so he had stopped short of ordering his men to make an arrest, or even to mention that Calder was just a work name.

They were going at the search in a slow and very deliberate manner, for whatever reason, so they assumed he was still on campus, and no one had thought to check with the main gate. But that lapse wouldn't last much longer.

He drove over to the street where Otto's safe house was at the end of a cul-de-sac, its backyard abutting a strip of woods, and parked around the corner at the end of the block.

Rencke held the key to the castle, so far as Bertie was concerned. They'd already figured out what had been buried over there, and even much of the why it had been buried. McGarvey had been to see the general and knew about Ya'alon—George. And Alex had almost certainly told them that Alpha Seven had moved the bomb on its own initiative.

But Rencke was a computer whiz, a genius in his own right, who would sooner or later realize Bertie Russell had gone into Iraq from Syria in the first place to hide the bomb—and this was while Saddam was still in power—no mean feat in itself.

McGarvey had mentioned it was a rogue operation, which indeed it had been, conceived by an old friend of his at the Pentagon, an Army four-star general Adam Benjamin, who was convinced we would get bogged down in Iraq and lose the will to continue unless something was done to "sweeten the pot," as he'd said over lunch in town.

"And I'm just the guy to do it," Bertie had said.

"Once the device has been planted, you can put together a team and send them in, so that if things do go south despite our best efforts, they can take the blame."

"Them and the Israelis," Bertie had agreed, warming to the idea.

"The Joint Chiefs will be kept in the dark."

"And so will the president."

"Especially the president," Benjamin said. "Will you do it? Can your country depend on you?"

The question was so rah-rah, flag-waving, and over-the-top, Bertie remembered he'd almost choked on his steak. But he had nodded. "You can count on me."

But Benjamin had been deployed to Iraq, where his helicopter had been shot down and he was killed less than one week after he'd arrived in country. And then Bertie was on his own. A one-man show.

Lights were on at the Renckes'. But the place would be an electronic fortress, impossible to storm without detection.

They knew Bertie Russell's death had been faked and he had managed to get back into the CIA with bulletproof credentials and a curriculum vitae that was backed up by computer records and phone numbers of former employers—some of whom had moved on or had died—and others who were directed straight to him so he could play the role of the employer who was sorry to see Tom Calder leave.

Rencke would figure that out sooner or later. Unravel everything, and there was little doubt in his mind that Rencke would also find the device, which by now, buried as long as it had been, would be leaking radiation detectable within a short distance— maybe ten or fifteen meters. A search party would find it in no time at all, based on the assumption that its last location wasn't far from the first two. Which it wasn't.

McGarvey was by all accounts a very bright man, but he was primarily a shooter. While Rencke, though a genius, was no ops officer.

The two of them, though, made a formidable team. The problem would be to eliminate one of them as soon as possible. As in this morning. As in Otto Rencke.

Using an iPad program, he scanned the neighborhood. As expected, Rencke's house and the entire area within a sixty-or seventy-meter radius was alive in a lot of frequencies, including VHF and UHF.

It was no good for him here.

He made a U-turn and headed to the Dulles Access Road, the new plan he had in mind simple, so long as Blankenship's net was for the most part kept on campus.

He had worked with Ya'alon for eight days outside Tel Aviv, during a joint war-planning exercise one year before the invasion of Iraq. In fact, they had become reasonably close, both of them intelligence officers, and they had developed a respect for the other's abilities.

"You think out of the box," Bertie had told him. "And that's a good thing."

Ya'alon had laughed. They were drinking Russian vodka that had been liberated in Afghanistan several years earlier. "And you're the craziest, most out-of-control son of a bitch I've ever known. And trust me, Mossad is filled with them."

"The face is the gateway to a man's soul," was Bertie's argument. "Take away the lips, and they can reveal no secrets. Take away the nose, and they can't smell what's foul. Take away the ears, and they can't hear the warnings. And especially take away the eyes so they can't see what they're not supposed to see."

"Vietnam. The Montagnards," Ya'alon said.

"Exactly."

The timing would be tight, but with any luck, he'd get to the airport, where he could park the Taurus out in the open in the short-term lot, and rent a car.

From there he would make his way down to Camp Peary—another two and a half hours tops, giving him plenty of time to make a couple of phone calls and put things in place for the end game.

SIXTY-SEVEN

A half hour from landing at Andrews, McGarvey got a phone call from an agitated Otto. "Where are you?"

"Just about ready to touch down."

"It's Calder, all right. The main gate logged him out at two thirty-five. And about forty-five minutes later, my surveillance gear showed a slight dip in energy returns. Someone was sampling the spectrum."

"Calder?"

"It would be a hell of a coincidence if it weren't him," Otto said. "Blankenship wanted this to remain an internal matter, but I think Tom's too smart for him. I gave the DC metro cops and Virginia state police the heads-up with Tom's description and the car he's driving—or least the one he left the gate with."

"He knows we're on to him, so he's not going to stick around," Alex said. "Have you checked Dulles, Reagan, and BWI?"

"Yes, but there's nothing under Calder's name."

"Bertie always kept several sets of decent working papers within easy reach. Maybe something to change his appearance—a wig, different glasses. It's not difficult."

"I'll call Blankenship and have him send people to all three airports," McGarvey said. "We might get lucky. In the meantime, have the airport cops search the long-term lots for his car."

"If I were Bertie, I'd have a spare set of plates," Alex said. "Out of state, maybe even out of country, and not so easy to quickly trace."

"It would help if we knew where he was going," Pete suggested.

They were all strapped in because of some turbulence on their descent, and Alex looked out the window. "I have a wild-assed idea where he might be headed, but it'd be pretty tough, even for someone like him."

"Where?" McGarvey asked.

She looked at him. "Kirkuk."

"Why?" Pete asked, but then she got it just after McGarvey did.

"You said the idea was to explode the thing," he said. "Make it look as if the Iraqis were trying some last-ditch stand. But that was more than ten years ago. No reason for something like that now."

"Not in your mind, not even in mine, but we're talking about Bertie Russell."

"A seriously disturbed man."

Alex nodded. "But not in the way you think," she said. "He was a superpatriot—though we called him the Cynic because he thought our country was going to hell in a handbasket. He said we'd sold out to the Japanese and Germans after the Second

World War, and now we were selling out to the Chinese because we were losing the economic war."

"Sane people don't go around chewing off the faces of people they've just killed," Pete said.

"He was rabid about the Vietnam War. Said we had bungled it badly. The White House, starting with JFK, had screwed the pooch, and by the time it was Johnson's and Nixon's turns, they made things even worse. Bertie said if we had fought the war like the Montagnards had—like we had in the beginning—we wouldn't have lost."

"So he was willing to do something about Iraq," McGarvey said. "Change things. But he couldn't have done it alone. He must have help from somewhere."

"A lot of the top brass over at the Pentagon were in love with him, or at least they agreed with him. He pretty much had free access to Iraq anytime he wanted." Alex smiled a little. "But stuff like that is what makes a good NOC—the ability to make friends and set up contacts who can help you down the line when you need it."

"Like now," Pete said. She turned to McGarvey. "Would it be worth trying to find out who he's been talking with over there lately?"

"We could try, but I doubt if anyone would give us anything worthwhile."

"He liked Paris, so it could be he'll start there," Alex said. "So did George. One of the reasons I went there. That, and Mossad's travel bureau."

"I'll scan every Paris-bound flight leaving from those three airports at any time today," Otto said.

"You might want to stretch it out for a few days," Alex said. "Could be he'll go to ground somewhere close for the time being."

"He could be driving west, maybe to Chicago," McGarvey said. "Anywhere."

"That's right, but I think he'll end up in Iraq one way or another," Alex said. "One thing is certain: whatever he does will be a misdirection. He'll get us looking one way while he slips off in another."

"I'll check every airline that leaves for Paris anywhere from the continental U.S. for the next three days."

"Under what parameters?" Pete asked.

"That's easy," Otto told her. "I don't think Calder was planning on going anywhere until after he came to my office and talked to me this morning. I'll check reservations made starting then."

"He knows how to backdate them," Alex said. "Make it look as if he made the reservations last week, or last month."

"I'll find out," Otto said.

McGarvey phoned Bob Blankenship at Langley, and when the chief of security answered, he sounded out of breath and very short-tempered.

"What?"

"Any sign of Tom?"

"I don't know what the hell you and Rencke have cooked up, but I'm having a real hard time picturing Tom Calder as our serial killer. Christ, whoever is doing it has to be a nut case, and in the five years I've known Tom, no one could be more opposite. And Marty agrees with me."

"Where is he? At home?"

Blankenship hesitated. "No. Maybe he has a mistress. Could be he stopped by to see her. We've all been under a lot of tension these past few days. Hell, I don't know."

"Have your people coordinate with the TSA guys at Dulles, Reagan, and BWI. Could be he's trying to get out of the country. Maybe to Paris. Otto will be sending you a list of possible passengers. But, Bob, if he is our guy, tell your people to go with care."

"Yeah," Blankenship said, resigned.

Maggie came back. "The captain says we're coming in on final, so it would help if you cut your call short until we're on the ground."

"Got to go, Bob," McGarvey said. "Keep me in the loop."

"Where are you?"

"Just landing at Andrews," McGarvey said, and broke the connection.

The winds were gusting, but Roper was a pro and the landing was smooth. In five minutes they were taxiing to the hangar the navy used for its VIP flights.

"So, what now?" Pete asked.

"Nothing much for us until Otto or Bob comes up with something," McGarvey said.

"No one left for him to kill."

"It's not over with yet," Alex said.

"You?" McGarvey asked.

"I think he's given up on me."

"What then?"

"I don't know. Something."

They pulled into the hangar, and as the engines spooled down, Maggie opened the hatch and lowered the stairs.

At that moment Otto called.

"The son of a bitch is at the Farm," he said. "He's got Audie!"

"Get me a chopper!" McGarvey shouted to Roper.

SIXTY-EIGHT

McGarvey picked up the call on his sat phone as he got off the Gulfstream, Pete and Alex right behind him. "Switch the call over to me."

"I need to stay on the line," Otto said, just about beside himself.

Audie's little voice came on.

"It's your grampyfather. Are you okay, sweetheart?" McGarvey said, his heart aching.

"Oh yes. I'm a little tired, you know, but Uncle Tom is a nice man. He brought me some candy."

"Where are you right now?"

"Oh, we went for a walk in the woods. I like it here."

"Is Uncle Tom still with you?"

"Yes, I'm holding his hand."

"Give him the phone for just a minute."

"Okay," Audie said.

"Good morning, Mr. Director," Bertie Russell said pleasantly. "You have a lovely granddaughter. I hope you appreciate just how special she is."

"You have her. Now what?"

"Why, a face-to-face meeting between us. At your earliest possible convenience. I'm sure you can arrange for a helicopter to get you down here within the hour. I think it's time you and I got to know each other a little better. There's so much I would like for you to understand."

Roper came to the Gulfstream's door. "A Sea Ranger is being prepped for you," he said.

"Make it fast," McGarvey told him. He turned back to the phone. "Leave my granddaughter out of it. You got my attention. It'll be just you and me."

"But then I'd have no leverage. Where's the percentage for me?"

"My word, Bertie. Give Audie back to her minders, and I'll make sure you'll be allowed to leave the base. When I get there, we'll talk, and no matter what comes up, you'll be free to walk. I'll even guarantee you a two-hour head start."

"But then you will resume your pursuit."

"Yes. But you were an NOC. Two hours should be plenty of time to go to ground."

"Is Alex with you at this moment?"

"She'll be one of our topics of discussion. At the moment she's under arrest for the murder of a man in an apartment in Georgetown."

"You say you have her under arrest?"

"Yes."

"Good luck with that, Mr. Director. But I'll do as you say. There is a camping area just west of the interstate. It's called Toano. I don't think it'll be very busy at this time of the year. Your pilot can find it on the chart."

"First I'll need to verify that Audie is back with her minders and unharmed."

"As you wish," Bertie said. "Oh, and leave your weapons behind."

"Not a chance," McGarvey said. "If need be, I will defend myself, but you have my word I'll give you two hours."

Bertie rang off.

"I'll be airborne in a few minutes," he told Otto. "Let me know as soon as Audie is safe."

"Kill him," Otto said.

"Count on it," McGarvey said, and hung up.

"I'm going with you," Pete said.

"Stay here with Alex."

"I'm going back to McLean to give Otto and Louise some backup in case the bastard tries to get to them instead of waiting for you to show up," Alex said. "Camp Peary and your granddaughter could be just a diversion."

McGarvey stepped close to her. "Don't fuck with me, Alex. The people we're talking about mean a great deal to me. If you try anything, I will put a bullet between your eyes without a moment's hesitation, even if it takes me the rest of my life. And believe me, I'll enjoy it."

Alex shrugged. "You gave your word to Bertie, and he trusts you. I'm giving you my word that I won't do a thing to Otto or Louise. I want this to be done even more than you do, because I've lived with it for nearly a third of my life now. And all my friends are dead."

"You've never had friends," Pete said.

McGarvey called Otto. "Alex is coming to stay with you guys in case Tom decides to make an end run on you. Are you okay with that?"

"Wouldn't do her any good to take us out," Otto said. He was a lot calmer now. "Send her over. Anyway, Audie's safe, and Calder is already on his way off base."

A gray Chevy Equinox with navy markings came to the hangar door. McGarvey tossed Alex the keys to his Porsche, and he and Pete rode in the Chevy, he in the front and Pete in back, over to the helicopter, its engines warming up.

The pilot was a young navy lieutenant, and he found the campground on his chart. "I grew up in Norfolk, so I know the area," he said.

"How quickly can you get us down there?" McGarvey asked.

"We cruise at a hundred and twenty knots, but I can push it to one thirty if it's urgent."

"It's urgent."

"Under one hour."

"Let's go. I'll tell you what I have in mind on the way down," McGarvey said.

Bertie, driving just five miles per hour over the speed limit on I-64, passed the Toano exit at mile marker 227, and continued back to Washington, the day gorgeous, traffic light, his mood lifting.

All his life, especially since as a five-year-old kid learning chess by studying the games of the masters, he had come to appreciate most of all the end game. The opening moves were critical. And the middle game, when the majority of the strategy was concentrated on controlling the center of the board, was intense. But it was the end, when the player who reached the jugular vein first—usually the one who lured the opposition's queen into a trap, maybe from a trade, a bishop for a queen—that he'd enjoyed the most.

Nothing had changed in the intervening years. The preparations and training for an op were interesting, and even the opening moves and first contacts were intense. But it was at the end that he soared.

He phoned Admiral Matthew Koratich's private number at the Pentagon. Koratich was assistant chief of air operations for the Atlantic area, who Bertie, as Tom Calder, had befriended a number of years ago.

They'd met at an Army-Navy game a year after Bertie's wife had died of cancer, and they had hit it off immediately. Their politics were the same brand of the conservative "America first" ideal, and it wasn't long before Bertie was passing him hard intel about Russian satellite surveillance systems the CIA hadn't been sharing with the military at the time. It had to do with not compromising the US's sources in Moscow, and Koratich's star had risen based on some shrewd decisions he'd made.

His secretary put Bertie's call through.

"Tom, haven't heard from you in a while," Koratich said. "Rumors are you guys are having some trouble over there."

"We have some nut case running around, causing us a world of shit, but it's nothing we can't handle," Bertie said. "But I need to ask you for a favor."

"Anything," Koratich said without hesitation.

"I need to get to Baghdad ASAP. I mean, like, right now."

"CIA has access to a lot of aircraft."

"I know, but this has to be on the q.t. Could be the guy we're looking for over there has some serious intel linked to a couple of Saddam's people still in hiding. I'd also need a car and a driver. But someone anonymous. Civilian."

"I can work something out," Koratich said. "How soon? Like, today?"

"I'm about two hours away from Andrews."

"Stand by," Koratich said.

Bertie reached into his shirt pocket and switched on his MP3 player, the music coming from a Bluetooth earpiece also in his pocket. Bach's Toccata and Fugue. Serious music for serious business. Precise, mathematical, and therefore beautiful. It was the remastered performance by Albert Schweitzer in 1935. Always had been his favorite.

Koratich came back. "I have a Gulfstream, just landed an hour ago. She's being refueled. I can have a new crew out there by the time you show up. How long will they have to stand by?"

"No time at all, Matt. Soon as they drop me off, they can refuel and head home."

"Happy to lend a hand," Koratich said. "I hope you find what you're looking for."

SIXTY-NINE

They flew low southeast of Richmond, following a slow-moving creek that didn't start to widen out until the campground and ten miles farther, where it emptied into the James River. Their pilot, Lieutenant Billy Cox, knew his business, his touch light on the controls, sometimes just skimming the creek, the trees close in on both sides.

Otto called when they were just a few minutes from Toano. "He left his car in the short-term parking lot at Dulles. He made reservations for a flight to Paris this evening under the name Walt Wager."

"He has a sense of humor," McGarvey said.

"But I also came up with reservations for Istvan Fabry out of Baltimore, Larry Coffin from LaGuardia, and Roy Schermerhorn from O'Hare. I'm sure I'll find reservations—all of them for Paris—under the names of the other Alpha Seven operators. But security at the Farm said he was driving a Chevy Impala. I checked Dulles again, and a guy matching his description rented the car from Hertz for six days."

"Hang on," McGarvey said. He tapped Cox on the shoulder. "We're looking for a black Chevy Impala."

"The campground is just around the next bend. Sixty seconds."

"We're just about there," McGarvey told Otto. "Is Alex behaving herself?"

"She never showed up."

"Shit," McGarvey said. "Get us the hell out of here!" he shouted to the pilot.

At that same instant, Cox was already hauling the chopper in an almost impossibly tight turn to the left. "We have an incoming missile," he said calmly.

"The son of a bitch led us into a trap," McGarvey told Otto. "We're being fired on. He and Alex were working together all the time."

"Hang on. This will be close," Cox said. He could have been discussing the weather.

"Find them," he told Otto, and rang off.

Flying just off the surface of the creek, Cox jinked farther left toward the highway at the last moment, into an opening in the trees just a few feet wider than the diameter of the main rotor's blades.

A second later the man-launched missile that had been fired exploded in the trees so close to them, Cox nearly lost control of the chopper.

But then they were out and over a clearing.

"Someone down there doesn't like you, Mr. Director," Cox said. "That was a Stinger."

"Circle around. I want you to put me down at the edge of the woods," McGarvey said. "I'll go the rest of the way on foot."

"Pardon me, sir, but shouldn't we get the hell out of here, or at least call for backup?"

"Drop me off and go," McGarvey said.

Cox hauled the chopper around and into another tight turn, setting them down with a flourish at the edge of the clearing.

McGarvey popped the hatch and jumped out, but before he could close it, Pete, pistol in hand, jumped out beside him.

"They were shooting at me, too," she said before he could object.

McGarvey hesitated for just a moment before he closed the hatch. He and Pete, keeping low, headed into the woods and in the direction of the campground as the Sea Ranger lifted off and headed northwest, in the clearing and below the level of the treetops.

In a few minutes they got to a point where the woods abruptly thinned out, beyond which was what looked like a parking area, and they held up.

Behind them on the other side of the clearing was the interstate highway, and ahead, just beyond the parking area, was the creek. A plain white windowless van was parked off to the right. Nothing else was out there that McGarvey could see, but he smelled the characteristic odor of burnt solid fuel, almost like Fourth of July fireworks. The Stinger had been fired from somewhere along the edge of the creek.

"It's not Tom," Pete said, her voice barely a whisper.

"He sent someone," McGarvey told her. "Camp Peary was just a diversion to get me down here."

"Alex warned us."

"Yes, she did."

"How many?"

"At least two, a shooter and a spotter."

"They must have figured out by now that the chopper dropped us off," Pete said. She was mostly hidden behind the bole of a tree.

A piece of the thick trunk just at her chest level suddenly exploded, shoving her backward off her feet, and an instant later they heard the whipcrack of what sounded to McGarvey like an M16.

He dropped to his knees and scrambled over to where Pete lay on her side. Blood soaked the side of her polo shirt from a gash just above her left collarbone. She was in pain but conscious. No major blood vessel had been hit.

"That felt like a freight train," she said, grunting.

McGarvey felt her forehead; it was cool but not clammy. "They know you're down, but they'll want to know where I am. Pretend like you're in shock."

"That won't be so tough."

"God damn it, Pete, hang in there," McGarvey said. He wanted to pick her up and get her the hell out of harm's way.

"I'll be okay, honest injun', darling."

"I know," he said. He checked over his shoulder toward the parking area, where he figured the shot had come from, but there was no movement. "I'll be close."

Keeping very low, he hurried away, deeper into the woods. About twenty feet out he pulled up behind a tree that gave him a decent sight line to Pete.

Seconds later a stocky man, dressed in jeans and a dark jacket, came from Mac's left, stopped for a second several feet from Pete, and then, keeping his short-barreled Colt Commando pointed at her, said something McGarvey couldn't make out.

Mac rose up on one knee and, steadying his pistol hand against the tree trunk, fired two shots, one missing, the second hitting the guy in the chest, causing him to stagger to the side but not go down.

Something moved in the woods off to his right, and McGarvey turned that way when the muzzle of a rifle touched the back of his neck at the base of his skull.

"Drop your gun, and get slowly to your feet, Mr. Director," a man said.

McGarvey did as he was told, and turned to face the rough-looking man, somewhat short, square face, a serious look in his pale eyes. He had to be in his early forties, and the way he stood, it looked as if he favored his right hip. Ex-GI. Probably special forces. By the time guys like him got out, their knees and hips were usually mostly shot. Still, many of them went to work for contracting companies. They knew how to kill people and blow up stuff.

"Clear!" his captor called out.

The man standing over Pete was holding the assault rifle on her, evidently not wounded. He was likely wearing a vest under his jacket.

"What do you want?" McGarvey asked the contractor standing in front of him.

"How much you've figured out."

"You mean about Tom Calder killing just about everyone who'd worked for him in Iraq? Or how he became a raving lunatic?"

A third man also carrying a Colt Commando came through the woods from the right.

McGarvey glanced over at him. He was dressed like the other two, in jeans and a dark jacket that gave his torso some bulk. Even from fifteen feet away, McGarvey could tell he carried himself like a field operator.

"Or do you want to know about the nuclear demolitions device buried in the hills above Kirkuk?"

McGarvey asked. "Maybe your boss wants to know if we have the GPS coordinates?"

"Something like that."

"Well, you can kiss my ass, you little prick," McGarvey said.

In one deceptively slow movement, he batted the muzzle of the assault rifle to one side, the weapon firing a three-round burst, stepped in close, hooked his right arm under the shooter's left, and forced the man to turn even farther to the right, the assault rifle firing another three-round burst, this one catching the contractor coming up on them in the chest, knocking him backward.

Drawing his pistol cross-handed, he used his left to shoot his captor in the side of the head, and as the man collapsed, McGarvey turned and fired three shots at the contractor to the right, who'd been staggered, two of the rounds hitting the guy in the face.

At that instant three shots from an assault rifle came from behind him, and he swiveled in time to see Pete fire one shot into the shooter's face at nearly point-blank range, and as he went down, she fell back.

McGarvey's heart hammering, he crashed through the woods to her side. Her eyes were open but fluttering, and her breath came in ragged gasps. She was pale, white. But she hadn't lost her grip on her pistol.

"Did I do good?" she asked.

"You did good," McGarvey said. He pulled off his jacket, folded it into a bundle, put it over the wound in her chest, and brought her hands up to hold it in place. "Just don't die on me."

"Promise," she whispered.

He called Otto and told him where they were. "Pete's down. Get a medevac chopper here right now."

"Billy Cox stuck around, and when he heard the shooting, he called for one," Otto said. "It's coming from the Farm. Stand by."

"It'll be okay, Pete," McGarvey said, but he was truly afraid for her.

She smiled. "Of course it will be."

McGarvey heard the inbound helicopter at the same moment Otto came back.

"Exactly where are you?"

"Just in the woods, across from a white van in the parking lot."

"We have our docs prepping for you guys. How's Pete?"

"She took a round in the chest, but she's still awake," McGarvey said, looking into her eyes. "I'm not going to lose this one, not this way, not now."

EPILOGUE

The battered old Fiat passed the stadium around two in the morning, Alex riding shotgun beside the Executive Solutions driver who had picked her up at the airport in Baghdad. It was a 250-kilometer run, and after her hasty departure from Andrews, she was beat.

"We want to take Highway 4 to the east, just past Akhi Husayn," she said.

The driver, who'd only identified himself as Bob glanced over at her. "You've been here before."

"Years ago, before the second war."

"I imagine it's changed."

"Not that much."

They hadn't said more than a few words to each other since the airport, and now, driving through Kirkuk and heading toward the hills out of the city, she wasn't disposed to changing anything. Bertie was at least six hours ahead of her, but there was no telling how much time he'd spent with some of his old cronies down in Baghdad. He'd always been a man who loved the military—though most U.S. troops were long gone, leaving behind only a couple of thousand advisers and trainers, plus the contractors.

Highway 4, which was the Sulaimani-Kirkuk Road, passed through a plain that gradually rose to the hills. The main oil fields were to the north and south, and after twenty kilometers or so, Alex sat forward in her seat.

The countryside hadn't changed as much as her memory had. When she and the others were last here, they were the enemy, the advance scouts, and until they had become acclimatized to the place, they had been strangers. In fact, it hadn't been until after George had been with them for about a week that any of them had felt reasonably at home.

An ancient stone building, its wooden roof gone, sat just off the highway on a narrow dirt track that led northeast into the darkness. She remembered it.

"Here," she said.

Bob slowed down and pulled off the paved highway and onto the rock-strewn track, and almost immediately had to change gears as the road jogged to the right and started to climb.

Alex looked over her shoulder at the lights of the city, home to a polyglot population of nearly a half million people, most of them drawn here from a dozen other countries because of the oil in the ground. She was seeing it through different eyes now— everything was different for her since the events of the past week.

But this whole business that had excited her at first, then frightened her, and just lately had become almost comforting in an odd way was coming to an end, and she was damned glad of it.

About five kilometers up the increasingly steep

road, they came to a slight widening in the track where it was possible for a car to turn around. They were at the base of a fairly steep hill that rose another hundred meters or so. The terrain was rocky and devoid of just about any vegetation except for some low scrub brush. In the spring, though, Alex remembered, there had been small patches of violet flowers, tiny delicate things. Color in a bleak landscape.

"Turn in here," Alex said.

Bob pulled off and Alex got out.

"Where the hell are you going?" he asked, jumping out after her.

Alex spotted the goat track that meandered to the crest of the hill, on the other side of which was a series of hollows and narrow ravines, some with rocky overhangs, impossible to penetrate even by low-angle satellite passes.

"What, are you fucking nuts?"

Alex laughed. "Probably," she said. "Turn around now and go back to Baghdad."

Bob looked up toward the crest. "I'll wait for you."

"No," Alex said, and started up the goat path.

"Do you want a gun?" Bob called after her.

"Get out of here, you dumb son of a bitch!" Alex shouted without looking back.

Forty-five minutes later, following one of the narrow canyons, she came around a narrow cut. Bertie was sitting there, perched on a boulder a couple of meters above her, and she pulled up short, her heart skipping a beat.

"I saw the lights," Bertie said. "Figured it had to be you." He looked to be in high spirits, the rare Cynic grin on his simple round face.

"I think I can understand why you wanted all of us dead—you wanted to guard the secret here. But why the way you did it?"

"It's a long story, Alex, my dear."

"We have the time."

"Actually, we don't. Kirk McGarvey and Ms. Boylan—though she was wounded—have survived, and with their friend Otto Rencke, they have figured out all the pieces of the puzzle. I suspect someone will be here before too long." He looked up at the sky; the stars were the only things visible. The horizon was lost to the cliffs and hills.

"Give me the short version."

"I'm nuts. Crazy. Insane. Psychotic. Schizophrenic. But I was always able to hide my condition, even from the Company psychologists. They put me down as creative but high-strung. Perfect as a NOC, and especially as a NOC trainer. Did you suspect?"

"We respected you."

Bertie nodded and said nothing for a longish time. When he spoke, he sounded sad. "Why are you here?"

"Closure," Alex said. She had given a lot of thought to it. "I have nowhere to go. Nothing to do."

"How about survival?"

"Not as great as it's cracked up to be," she said. "How much time do we have?"

Bertie looked over his shoulder at something lying behind him, just out of Alex's sight. "I set the trigger when you came around the corner," he said. He looked down at her. "Forty seconds."

"You knew I wasn't going to turn around."

"And why?" Bertie said. "Roy had it almost right when he carved AND GOD SAID LET THERE BE LIGHT. Only it won't be God, will it? Just us."

Alex was almost glad. "What do you suppose they'll think about it?"

"The world?" Bertie asked.

"Yes."

He shrugged. "The same as they think about everything else that happens. There'll be no consensus. No one will agree on what it means. But almost everyone will blame the US, even though the radiation signature will prove that we stole the device from the Russians. The Israelis will be blamed, of course. Muslims everywhere, even the God-fearing, kind, gentle ones—the women and children and fathers trying to make their peaceful way in the world—will be blamed. The UN will be blamed for not stopping it. The New York Times will be blamed for not unearthing the story. People in Florida will be blamed because everyone there has stepped away from the real world and does nothing but play golf. New Yorkers will be blamed for chasing after the almighty buck instead of keeping their eyes on the real world. The scientists who invented the thing will take the heat. And naturally so will the military—every military on the planet—along with every insurgency, terrorist, and fundamentalist group."

Alex couldn't help but laugh. "Everyone will finally agree," she said.

She finished the sentence, but the nuclear blast was so instantaneous—less than one millionth of a second—she had no knowledge of it. She was alive, and suddenly there was nothing.

AND GOD SAID, LWET THERE BE LIGHT: AND THERE WAS LIGHTX AND THE LIGHT WAS VISIBLE FROM HORIZONQ TO HORIZON X BERLIN X AND ALL WAS CHANGED X ALL WAS NEVER THE SAME X AND GOD SAID LET THERE BE PROGRESS X AND THERE WAS X PEACEF

ABOUT THE AUTHOR

DAVID HAGBERG is a former U.S. Air Force cryptographer who has traveled extensively in Europe, the Arctic, and the Caribbean and has spoken at CIA functions. He has published more than seventy novels of suspense, including *Retribution*, *The Fourth Horseman*, and the bestselling *Allah's Scorpion*, *Dance with the Dragon*, and *The Expediter*. He makes his home in Sarasota, Florida.

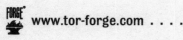